Pyrate Assassin

ISBN: 979-8-9852206-2-9 and 979-9852206-3-6

Pyrate Publishing

Cover art and images by:

Roger C. Ambrose / James R. Whirlow

Pyrate Series Novels

by

Reidr Daniels

Pyrate Rising

Pyrate Assassin

Pyrate Crossover

Pyrate: Black Flag

Dedication

For Wendy

For your guidance

For your patience

For your support

For your love

But mostly, for being you

Contents

Pyrate Assassin

I

The white fullness of its sails belied the hollow blackness of the ship's future. It emerged as a distant speck, interrupting the broad horizon separating two distinct blues—Caribbean Sea and cloudless sky. And for a brief time, *Espíritu de Los Santos* sailed calmly, unnoticed.

The young spotter at the crow's nest of the pirate ship *Red Knight* turned to scan yet another section of the white-capped waters. The warm, stiff breeze played with his unruly hair. His eyes passed and then quickly returned to the far-off image. "Sail ho," he shouted to the main deck, some thirty yards below.

"Where away?" Harker yelled back.

"Five points to starboard, Cap'n."

Given his lower angle and inferior vision, it was a few minutes before the vessel came into Harker's view. He turned to his quartermaster, Yaugaan De Graaf. "Merchant or warship—what think you?"

De Graaf squinted at the white fleck, unable to differentiate its masts. "Let it be merchant," he grinned.

As the minutes wore on, Harker noticed his prey's white sails began reflecting the descending sun differently. The unaccompanied

ship was turning—seeking to avoid contact, he surmised. Likely a merchant, then. English? French? Dutch? Spanish? Its flag wasn't yet large enough to
tell. No matter, whatever sailed these waters was fair prey.

"Full sails," Harker shouted. "Lively now." He turned to De Graaf, "Let the chase begin."

Several crew members scrambled up the rigging to unfurl the remainder of the sails. Others manned the clewlines. The soiled and tattered canvas sheets billowed in the wind before being pulled taut and secured. The tiller spun, maneuvering *Red Knight* into an intercepting direction.

With the sun virtually tasting water, the gap between the two ships finally narrowed to easy firing distance. Harker noticed the Spanish-flagged merchant sailed low in the water, heavy with cargo. That explained his closing on it so quickly.

"Bring her alongside. Ports open," he shouted. "Hoist the red."

His drapeau-de-guerre was blood-red. The color of death. It was a message to all of his prey—resist and you shall pay the ultimate price: your blood. The rough-sewn, crimson flag jerkily ascended the mizzenmast as *Red Knight* slid alongside its target's stern. The men below, hunching in the barely four-foot-high gun deck, finished priming and loading their cannons. The gunports flipped open, hammering against the ship's starboard side. Long and loaded black-iron cylinders rolled loudly into forward position, noses out. Gunners secured the carriages' rear wheels.

Espíritu de los Santos hailed from Cádiz. It was returning home from a lengthy voyage with a variety of mostly South American goods, including jewels and silver plate. It also bore eighteen chests containing gold and silver received in exchange for merchandise and supplies brought from the motherland and sold to merchants throughout the Southern Sea islands and along the Spanish Main. Captain Luis Rodriguez, the nephew of King Philip II of Spain, stood on the foredeck watching the *Red Knight* maneuver into position. Given his royal lineage, Rodriguez was a much-favored trader, sailing frequently to this treasured part of the new world. A distinguished-looking gentleman, he wore an elaborately embroidered black-velvet, V-waisted doublet, embellished with brass buttons. His well-groomed black beard came to a sharp point below his chin. "Prepare to fire," he shouted. He turned to his young aide, Julio, "I worry our attempt to outrun this pirate was unwise."

"Was there a choice, sir?"

"Perhaps not. The men are ill-prepared to repel an attack by a band of brigands in a well-armed ship. Unfortunately, our cargo constrained us like tight reins on a horse."

Harker's cannons roared, delivering four-pound iron balls chased by streaking orange flames and light-smothering smoke. A few were aimed high, targeting *Espíritu's* masts and sails; others targeted the gun deck. None were aimed below the waterline. Harker needed the cargo afloat, not sinking.

Though it returned fire bravely, *Espíritu's* mainmast took a sharp blow, spraying the main deck with knife-edged, wooden shards.

The ship's sides were peppered, opening jagged-edged holes along the gun deck and sending unlucky gunners screaming and flailing backward to the far side.

Men on both ships' main decks traded shots from pistols and crossbows. Grappling hooks flew across the gap, gripping the sides of the Spanish merchant like a hungry hawk's claws. Harker's men furiously hauled the two vessels together, ducking projectiles. A defiled *Espíritu de Los Santos* would soon yield her treasures.

————

Head down, William Tovery strode hastily along the cobblestones,
holding his wet cavalier hat tightly against the challenging wind. His long navy overcoat was drenched, flapping at his knees. The bell mounted above rang out as he flung open the door to Orion's Tavern. "Bloody Hell," he cursed loudly, stepping inside. He shook off the water and hung his hat and coat on a wall hook.

Captain Garret Connachan laughed at the sight. She'd done the very same thing herself, only minutes earlier. Seated at a table near the back, she now warmed her hands on a fresh cup of hot black koffei—a beverage Spanish Captain Bravo introduced her to during her time in the Southern Seas. She'd brought supplies of the dark, hardened beans back to London, convincing Orion's owner to purchase some. But aside from Garret and a few of her associates, he enjoyed little success in selling the hot, bitter liquid.

Garret rose to greet him. She was fashionably dressed. Naval style. Though her vest, pants and boots were masculine, she sported a playfully bright green blouse with a white ruff at the collar. The green complemented her eyes. Her auburn hair flowed longer than she'd ever worn it—evidence she now openly and fully embraced her womanhood. Presenting as male was finally behind her. She had Admiral Drake to thank for it. That and her own efforts to prove herself.

Her skin bore a reddish tint, the result of spending considerable time outdoors—practicing daily with sword and pistol, hunting foxes, and overseeing construction of her new flagship. The relaxed expression on her face was reflective of someone happy with their life.

Garret's uncommon appearance drew continual attention from the tavern's patrons, all male. She sensed their interest but chose to ignore them.

William waved to the owner and pointed to Garret's koffei. "A cup, George, if you please."

Garret watched as William strode toward her with the gait and swagger of a seasoned sailor. He was the closest thing to a brother she had. The two first met while serving as midshipmen under Drake. Through numerous voyages and naval engagements with the Admiral, each had earned their captaincy. Garret's had proven more challenging to come by, though she'd been awarded it sooner. Still bordering the age of twenty, her lengthy list of accomplishments already exceeded what most men ordinarily achieved in their lifetimes.

William pulled back a well-worn wooden chair across from her. "Give me ocean spray over this damned constant rain."

"Good day to you as well, William." Garret greeted him with a firm handshake. Though having long ago come clean with her crewmates about her gender, she still selectively maintained mannerisms that were male in nature. It helped avoid undesired awkwardness among the men. She was committed to simply being 'one of them', particularly onboard ship.

"Apologies." William sat. "I am quite ready for my next voyage. I find the firm ground underfoot most discomforting."

"Agreed." Garret sipped her koffei. "It has been far too long, William." She noticed his curly, dark-brown hair was neatly knotted in a seaman's tail, much like she herself wore at sea. He now sported a well-trimmed beard, accenting his similarly reddish-tanned face. His deep brown eyes twinkled as he smiled.

"Too long indeed. I thank you for the invitation. I imagine you have something specific you wish to discuss."

"You know me well. Better than anyone, I might say."

"Except Pantas," William winked. "God rest his soul." Pantas, the Sultan of Ternate's Ambassador to England, was her former lover.

"God rest his soul," Garret echoed. "He knew me differently, William, not necessarily better." She smiled although the pain of loss still lurked deep within. But it was okay for William to mention his name. The three had been friends. She sipped her koffei and placed the cup on the table. She returned to the matter at hand, "Well then, let me share why I have asked you here."

"Please…"

"I am in the early stages of forming a small fleet, bound for the Southern Seas. I intend to return with a portion of King Philip's purse."

"Drake's disease," grinned William. "We have both caught it."

Garret laughed. "Then join me."

George placed a cup of koffei in front of William. He warmed his hands on it. "It would be an honor to sail with you again, Garret. Besides you and Thomas, there is no one else with whom I prefer to sail." The 'Thomas' he referred to was Drake's younger brother, their former fellow midshipman. "But I am afraid I intend to serve with Her Majesty's navy."

Garret masked her disappointment. "I see. So you fancy climbing the rigging of naval command."

"I do." He sipped his koffei.

"Rather than enjoy the freedom of pursuing interests of your own choosing."

"The possibility of becoming an Admiral interests me."

"Ah, yes…societal standing, fame…pensions."

"You must admit, Garret, privateers like us are perceived by naval officers as mere second-class sailors. Besides, what freedom is there in privateering when it demands a commission from the Queen, or others, to pursue *their* interests?"

"I shall find ways to have my own freedom," Garret responded. I have a particular score to settle, as you well know." There were actually two scores she hoped to settle. One was to avenge the massacre of a dozen men under her leadership, by the villagers of Santiago del Príncipe. She alone escaped that slaughter. The other, and harder score to avenge, was the assassination of Pantas. While she suspected the Spanish, there seemed little likelihood of ever discovering the actual perpetrator.

"Might I ask how you are funding this venture of yours?"

"I have shared little of my personal affairs with anyone. Other than Pantas, of course." She grinned as she reached for her koffei. "My grandfather was counselor to numerous merchants engaged in international trade. His efforts added greatly to the significant wealth and property he had already inherited from his mother. When he died, I became sole heir and executor. The revenue generated from farming alone is substantial. I am drawing on a small portion of that to fund this voyage."

"I see."

"But I have also gained the support of several investors." She leaned in and smiled, "Their eyes gleam at the thought of Spanish treasure delivering outsized returns on their investments." She sat back. "Assisting the Admiral in securing his own funding gave me access to his sources."

"No doubt your relationship with the Queen helped as well." Garret nodded. William continued, "I envy your financial position. It must be rather freeing to pursue your own agenda."

"It is. Still, wealth must be carefully managed. I employ others for that purpose. I must admit, however…not all agree with my decision to invest in a private fleet."

"And Thomas? Have you approached him about joining you?"

"Dear Thomas. The man is so dedicated to preserving the memory and estate of his legendary brother that he has committed to staying in Devon. At least for the foreseeable future. He also serves the Queen, as an

advisor on military and diplomatic matters."

"So I understand. I see him on occasion when he journeys to London. We often reminisce about our days at sea. I always imagined he would continue in his brother's footsteps."

"That is no longer his path. He made it quite clear to me."

"So, without Thomas, or me, you shall be in need of new

leadership."

Garret smiled, wryly, "I have not given up on you yet, William."

II

A maniacal mob poured over the sides of *Espíritu de los Santos*. Knowing that fear itself was a powerful weapon, many sported smeared stripes of black dubbin on their faces. Others went further, mimicking the appearance of a skull by applying a thin layer of animal fat to their faces, dusting on white flour, and drawing rings of black dubbin around their eyes and mouth. The screaming horde's thunderous rush unnerved its adversaries. Still, they were met by a barrage of pistol shots and pikes, wounding and killing a few. Some Spaniards retreated to the far side, fumbling to reload pistols. Others clashed swords with the barbarous wave in self-defense.

Prior to boarding, Harker had offered words of encouragement to his men, '*Those petrified by terror are no match for unconstrained violence*'. Fueled by his sentiment, the raiders mashed and slashed their way through the front line before most of the defenders' pistols were ready to re-fire. Though slowed by fallen bodies, dismembered body parts, and a deck slick with blood, the onslaught was unstoppable.

Standing at the bow, Spanish Captain Rodriguez fired two pistol shots in the air. His aide, Julio, stood next to him furiously waving a white sheet, signaling surrender. "Rendición!" Rodriguez shouted over the roaring din.

"Enough!" yelled Harker, thrusting his cutlass high in the air. It was covered to the hilt in blood, some of which dripped onto his boot. He threw up his left arm as well, repeating his call, "Enough!"

The noise of battle died. Harker, his left eye covered by a crimson patch, looked around and smiled at his men. He walked toward Rodriguez with a confident swagger. His roughly bearded chin and bronzed leather skin were framed by long, jet-black hair flowing down below his neck in unruly strands. He was tall, strong, and menacing-looking. Battle scars etched on his face and arms spoke to his fearlessness, if not to the ruthlessness simmering beneath the surface. Most who dared challenge him met their end swiftly. Brutally. The fact that he once sailed with the legendary Drake also brought respect from his fellow pirates, though the Admiral had unceremoniously discharged Harker from his fleet.

As the pirate leader ascended the steps to the foredeck, Capitán Rodriguez nodded to his men, seeking to assure them their lives would be spared. He slowly removed his sword from its scabbard and held it flat, crosswise in his hands, palms up. Harker stopped within three feet. Rodriguez bowed his head, extending his arms and offering up the sword. By the time he looked up again, the bloody point of Harker's cutlass was rushing at his face.

Some of *Espíritu de Los Santos'* crew turned their heads as their captain's limp body crumpled to the deck. Two vomited. One involuntarily soiled his breeches.

Harker stood over Rodriguez, watching the man's last breath deflate his chest. He turned slowly toward the crowd, peering down on them from the ship's bow. Thrusting both arms in the air, he shouted in a heavily crusted voice, "No one challenges the *Red Knight* and walks away freely. Let no one doubt our resolve."

Julio knelt on the foredeck, head down and shivering as though awaiting his own end. Harker glanced at him, deciding he was too young to die this day. He descended the steps and walked toward the remaining Spaniards, all of whom had earlier dropped their weapons and pressed back to the taffrail. "Tesoro?" he asked of them [treasure?]. No-one moved. He walked up to one of the smaller men, swept him up by the armpit and crotch, and hoisted him overboard. His screams drowned with the splash.

"Tesoro?" Harker yelled, louder.

"Si Capitán." A grizzled old seaman stepped forward. He waved his arm toward the cargo hatch, nodding his head to suggest Harker follow.

Harker motioned to De Graaf, a hulking, half-Black, half-Dutch man who befriended him during their days with Drake. "Follow him. Let me know what you find."

De Graaf placed the tip of his sword against the old Spaniard, nodding in the direction of the hatch. Every bit as ruthless as Harker, De Graaf was less refined. Unpredictable. The Spaniard seemed to sense that. He moved briskly.

Harker pointed to two other pirates, indicating they should follow De Graaf. He scanned the eyes of the rest of his men. "Which of these Spaniards deserve to pay a price for challenging us?"

Two men were pulled forward, protesting vigorously. Beads of sweat glistened on their foreheads as Harker approached. "You are filth." He spit in one man's face. "You shall pay dearly for your actions." He ordered the men holding them to bind them to the mainmast. As they were pulled away, he addressed the rest of the Spaniards. "Habla Inglés?"

One man stepped forward, hesitantly. He was well-groomed, unlike an ordinary seaman. "I say Inglés, Capitán. Pequeño." He held up his hand, narrowing the gap between his thumb and index finger. Harker looked him up and down. The man was of medium build, dark-haired, and neatly shaven; probably in his late twenties. He wore a doublet over a surprisingly clean, white blouse. "Mi nombré es Cristiano. Soy tesorero. This," he waved his arm around the ship, "barco comercial."

Harker understood. This man was in charge of the financial aspects of the merchant ship. He pulled him by the arm to the ship's far side, not wishing to have their conversation overheard. "Tell me, Cristiano, cuanto dinero?"

"I not…cierto, Capitán. Quizás," his eyes peered upwards, as if counting, "acerca de 80,000 escudos y 120,000 reales: Ingresos de venta…sale, si? Pay for marineros, y dinero de las oficiales. I not know…ahorros", he reached into his pocket, "de marineros. Además," he held up two fingers, "dos cofres lingotes de plata…bars, si? Y uno de oro."

Harker maintained a stone face but inside his heart raced. He understood enough to know this was a small fortune. He would need to keep his men from learning the full value of the holdings, so that he might secure more than his rightful share. He sensed the treasurer might be helpful in that regard. The man would be spared.

———

Plymouth Harbor buzzed with activity as Garret approached the docks. Several merchant ships were at anchor, their goods being boarded and off-loaded by crisscrossing longboats. Nearby shipyards offered up the sounds of construction. The music of the waterfront filled her soul with happiness. And comfort. She'd come here specifically to meet with Musa and Caber, former crewmates.

Musa was a behemoth—dark-skinned, bald-headed, muscled and stern-faced; a man of few words, and fewer smiles. No one knew his origins for certain. Some said he was a former slave who dispatched his captors to gain his freedom. That was definitely believable. Perhaps even probable. He was easily the most feared and respected of all the men who ever sailed with Drake. His long, black-handled, double-edged axe was lovingly kept razor-sharp. He wielded it with ease and precision. The handle was painstakingly notched for each man who'd met his end at the blade. When not sailing, Musa was much in demand as an executioner. The authorities said it was for the cleanness and thoroughness of his strikes. In truth, it was more for the spectacle. He was the kind of towering, ominous presence that most landsmen never saw. And once they did, they were mesmerized. When he wasn't wearing his black executioner's hood, he favored a deeply soiled red bandana.

Caber wasn't near as tall as his closest friend. But he was wide as an ox and every bit as strong. His unruly red hair overwhelmed the top half of his head while his abundant beard drowned out the lower half. He was a proud Scotsman and a fierce competitor in Scottish games. His signature event was the Caber toss, at which he was undefeated. His nickname was favored by his crewmates. It was easier to pronounce than his real name: Farquhar. And more descriptive. Though financially well-off from his exploits with Drake, he had no family and no passions other than the sea. He and Musa had both taken the advice of Drake's brother, Thomas, leaving most of their share of treasure with the manager of Briscoe Bank in London. The banker sent them both a monthly allowance. It funded their lodging, food and entertainment in the many taverns and brothels in Plymouth.

The two friends were staunch supporters of Garret Connachan. They'd witnessed her courage and skill in battle and her onboard leadership. When Drake announced that 'he' (Garret) was in fact 'she', they had her back, dealing first-hand with those who dared challenge her presence and standing. That included a man named Harker, whom Musa had personally confronted. Their dislike for each other had only festered since then.

"Good morning gentlemen," Garret said, finding Musa and Caber hauling cargo on the dock. Despite their wealth, she fully expected they'd be here. She understood the innate draw of the harbor and the call of open water on veteran seafarers.

Musa turned, giving her a rare smile. "Cap'n," he exclaimed, grabbing her in his huge arms and lifting her off her feet with the bear hug she sensed was coming.

"Unhand me, you damned beast," she laughed.

Caber stood waiting, a wide grin on his face. "My turn, Cap'n." He too hugged Garret, but with surprising gentleness for a man of enormous girth.

"It brightens my day to find the two of you here. We have much to discuss."

"I be all ears," Musa responded, in a deep, growled voice. "I cannot say for Caber. His ears cannot be found in all that hair." They all shared a laugh.

"Are you up for a return to the Southern Seas, gentlemen?"

"Please," replied Caber. "How soon? Some tavernkeepers here

seem to have tired of me." He winked at Musa, who looked back at him knowingly. Caber was known for brawling with others to settle disagreements when he'd immersed himself too deeply in the local spirits. Damage to the taverns had become a source of concern for their owners. Though he was good to pay for the damages, the impact on their business and the frustration of making repairs was more than they cared to deal with. He was no longer welcome in more than a few places.

"I am all set, Cap'n," offered Musa. "I belong at sea. Especially the southern ones, where gold flows like water." His eyes twinkled with his smile.

"Excellent. We shall need a crew large enough to man three ships. I trust you shall bring me the best of those available." Musa and Caber nodded. Garret continued, "I am still seeking a complement of officers."

"Thomas?" asked Caber.

"I am afraid not. His responsibilities bind him tightly to Devon.

"William?"

"Perhaps. We shall see."

———

Following days of stripping cargo, treasure and supplies from *Espíritu de Los Santos*, Harker released Cristiano, Julio, and a dozen other Spaniards. They were divided among two longboats, with enough fresh water and provisions to give them a good chance of reaching land. Harker thought it important they spread word of his exploits. After all, fear had a way of creeping into men's minds, increasing their vulnerability—especially to him. He grinned as he watched the longboats depart.

It was only two weeks earlier that Harker took charge of what was now the *Red Knight*. At the time, he and much of the crew were painfully frustrated with their captain's lack of success in acquiring targets. And treasure. Harker himself fueled those flames. He knew how to get inside men's heads, to influence their thinking. Disgruntled men were easy to manipulate. It was a skill he'd finely honed. And it was complemented by his fighting abilities. Beating crewmates who disagreed with him tended to convince others to go along. Over several days, he challenged the ship's captain in front of the men, accusing him of incompetence. Their last confrontation led to the knife fight he sought all along. It took place on the main deck, circled by the crew. Harker ended it by wielding his dagger to leave a deep gash in the captain's temple. He considered that his trademark. Anyone who hadn't actually witnessed one of his killings would know, from the temple-gash alone, just who the killer was. It further burnished his growing reputation.

Following that death match, Harker renamed the ship. '*Red Knight*' wasn't a random choice. Since Drake had been knighted, this was Harker's way of aping that status. And red was the color of blood—a subliminal warning to vessels that might consider opposing him. It matched the color of the patch covering his left eye. Dull as a darkly overcast sky, the eye only ever aimed straight ahead. It was a long-standing source of pain for Harker. Emotional pain, not physical. Picked on, laughed at, beaten, and bloodied while growing up, his experiences eventually sculpted him into a fierce, finely-honed fighting machine. He found he could intimidate others simply by slowly, deliberately aiming his one-eyed head in their direction. The slower it moved, the more intimidating he appeared. It was a weapon; a mental one. But as his ambitions grew, he felt his benumbed eye presented an obstacle. Men refused to look straight at him, preferring to divert their gaze. He worried that might hinder his goal of one day captaining a ship. He needed men to look at him, not turn away. So it was sometime after parting ways with Drake that he decided to cover up the eye. The ruggedly sewn patch was held tightly in place by a black strap, knotted in the back. And it was behind that back that some of the crew took to calling him 'Dead Eye'.

Good fortune came mere days later to Cristiano and the other cast-offs from *Espíritu de Los Santos*. Spotted by a Spanish merchant heading to Spain on a similar course to the one their own ship had been following, they were soon on their way back to Spain. Nevertheless, Cristiano was concerned. Upon arrival, he would have the arduous task of informing King Philip of the capture of their ship, the loss of its precious cargo, and, most importantly, the slaying of his beloved nephew—Captain Luis Rodriguez. He cringed at the thought.

———

Particles of dust danced in the sunlight bathing the unopened letter bearing the Admiralty's seal. It arrived a day earlier but sat propped up on the desk in William Tovery's sparsely furnished room, awaiting his readiness. The joy brought on by the possibility that he might be assigned a naval warship was offset by the frustration he knew he'd feel if he were not. To steel himself for potentially unwelcome news, he'd let the envelope simmer until he felt fully prepared. That moment was now.

William hovered over the message nervously, his career either on the threshold of rising or the precipice of falling. He pulled back a chair at the table and sat, taking a deep breath. His hands shook a little as he reached for the letter and picked it up. The image of a warship was stamped in the deep-red wax seal. He unconsciously smiled at it, while noting the richness of the parchment—parchment of painfully uncertain value. He broke the seal and pulled at the overleaf to reveal the contents. As he began reading, his face turned pale. He hadn't made Post. As far as Her Majesty's navy was concerned, that meant he would remain a captain in name only; one with neither an assigned vessel—a 'posting'—nor a crew to lead.

Slowly, carefully, William refolded the demoralizing, valueless parchment that only moments ago had given him bright, albeit false, hope. He opened the drawer and placed it inside, on top of an older, similar letter. He stared down at it, committing himself to ultimately showing the Admiralty they'd made a poor decision. He would retain both letters, to one day remind them of their folly.

With the drawer still open, William thought deeply about all that this letter meant, beyond just the words themselves. His dream of commanding a naval vessel wasn't proceeding according to his desired timeline. Following England's victory against the Spanish Armada, there wasn't the same level of need for ships. As a result, many were being retired and fewer were being built. He understood that would extend his wait for an official posting. It could easily be a year or longer before the naval stock might be replenished or the rank of captains sufficiently withered. Even then, there was no guarantee he'd be given a command.

One thing William had already observed was that, despite the rigorous maintenance of a proper list of naval officers in waiting, politics often found a way of infiltrating the decision-making process. He hadn't come from nobility or a political family, so that wind never seemed to blow in his favor. His only connections were insufficient to give him a leg up on others. On the contrary, they were more likely to leave him under the Admiralty's feet. He'd already been passed over once for a man he knew was less qualified but better connected.

Not wishing to add to his collection of disheartening letters, William sensed he would be better served by navigating his own future. Signing on with Garret was one way to do that. It would provide him an active commission as captain of a sizeable, combat-ready vessel. Though it would only be a privateering ship, he could carve his own path, furthering his skills and reputation. Besides, he much preferred having Garret as his partner.

William closed the wooden drawer softly. He drew a sheet of parchment from atop his desk, took up a quill, and dipped it in bottled ink. He carefully quilled a letter of his own—to Garret—thanking her for her generous offer to join her small fleet and informing her he would soon be in Plymouth, on business, if she would care to see him.

———

He sensed the books filling the regal-like captain's quarters were what gave it its musty smell. '*I shall throw them out,*' thought Harker. Seated at the finely polished black-ebony desk, he admired the deceased Captain Rodriguez' heavy use of gold trim and black velvet throughout his quarters. King Philip's nephew obviously loved a fine ship, which was precisely why Harker chose it as his new flagship. The muffled sound of hammers and saws reminded him that battle-damage repairs were still being made. The ship's cargo had been transferred to the *Red Knight*, making this new flagship the faster vessel. He decided to rename it *Death's Head*, in mocked honor of the captain he'd slain. He would have De Graaf lead the *Red Knight*. The crew would be divided between them. They would soon need more men to keep the ships in proper fighting order.

Two days later, Harker's ships arrived at a remote island near the northeastern edge of the Caribbean string. Its harbor, partially secluded by a thickly treed peninsula, was suitable for finishing repairs and careening the ships. After anchoring the two vessels, the men floated their new treasures ashore, accompanied by a longboat filled with hogsheads of beer. A badly weathered skeleton lying askew on the beach prompted one crewman to label the place 'Skeleton Shore'. It stuck.

Harker was last to arrive, accompanying the final seaman's chest containing gold and silver coins. Eager crewmen hoisted the treasure from the longboat and carried it to where the remaining chests were assembled. Stepping onto the beach, Harker pulled aside Yosel. The man knew his math. "Once you finish the count, say nothing to refute what I tell the men. Understood?"

"Aye, Captain."

He passed Yosel ten pieces of eight. "For your silence." He looked him in the eye. "These pieces and your life."

The men were gathered near the trees. As Harker approached, he noticed there was vigorous discussion. It was driven by a suggestion that they bury at least part of their treasure here on the island, for safekeeping and future retrieval. Though he felt the idea had merit, he waited without comment until all the men were assembled. Most were seated. Beer was already well distributed.

"Silence!" Harker shouted. The noise quickly dissipated. He turned to Yosel and nodded, "Let the count begin."

The men watched studiously and drank their beer as two men opened the lid of the first chest and began drawing out its contents—escudos, reales, pieces of eight, gold and silver chains, jewels and other assorted valuables. The men cheered loudly and drank heartily in celebration. Yosel sat nearby, recording the items.

As the process dragged on, Harker could see the crew's interest turned increasingly to the consumption of beer than the counting of treasure. He smiled inwardly at the thought that their lack of focus served his interests. He was now certain that none of the men, not even Yosel, were aware that he and De Graaf surreptitiously secured two treasure chests in his private quarters the night before, while the men were drunk in celebration and passed out. Four Spanish prisoners were tasked with hauling the chests, their wrists tightly roped in front of them. When their work was done, De Graaf made them stand shoulder-to-shoulder, facing him. He slit their throats with a stunningly rapid slash of his freshly sharpened cutlass. It happened so fast they made no noise, except for the thump of their bodies hitting the cabin floor. He and De Graaf then dragged and hoisted the bodies overboard.

The counting continued throughout the afternoon and into the early evening as men came and went, relieving themselves as needed. Finally, Yosel gathered up his sheets and rose. He walked toward Harker, who was seated well off to the side, separate from the men.

"The count, Captain," said Yosel. He pulled a folded sheet from a pocket in his breeches. "And here is a list of the men's names."

"Remember," Harker reminded him, "not a word of dissent." He rose and stepped toward the now-inebriated crowd. "Gentlemen," he yelled. He waited while the men quieted and then lifted the sheets high. "I have the count!"

The men who were still conscious cheered loudly, clashing their tankards together in celebration. Again, Harker waited, patiently. When the cheering stopped, he continued, "I shall first read the names aloud. Say Aye if ye be here."

As their name was given voice, men responded. Those having passed out from drink were vouched for by their mates, amid howls of laughter.

"Thirty-two heads," Harker called out, stuffing the list inside his doublet. "Thirty-two shares then. Plus eight for the Captain [himself] and four for the First Mate [De Graaf]. Fifty shares in all." The math didn't work but none of the pirates were schooled or sober enough to know the difference. They knew only that their share would be one-fiftieth of the spoils, not the larger amount it should have been.

Harker glanced at Yosel, whom he knew understood the math didn't add up. He sent him a visual warning with his one functional eye. He then turned to the inventory sheets and ruffled through them. "Thirty thousand pieces of eight," he announced loudly. It was an egregiously under-assessed amount. Nevertheless, resounding and inebriated cheers erupted. No one questioned the count; especially not Yosel. "Dividing the total by fifty yields each man a share of six hundred pieces." Intoxicated with both drink and joy, no one but Yosel seemed to realize or care that their share of the treasure was absurdly low—to the benefit of Harker and De Graaf. Their inflated shares also included the unaccounted-for chests and other cargo which, in itself, carried significant value. Harker grinned. Rank, math skills, and paying attention to details, all had their advantages. But math and sobriety clearly ruled.

III

King Philip hung his head in shock. Cristiano had just delivered alarming news concerning the fate of *Espíritu de Los Santos'*, and that of its Captain, Luis Rodriguez. The Tesorero's carefully crafted recounting made Philip's beloved nephew out to be a hero—dying in combat while protecting his men and his ship. Still, it was a hard blow. Philip growled, waving his right hand madly in the air. "Leave me. Now!"

Cristiano withdrew. The King's aide remained in the room. Philip turned to him. "Bring me Valdez," he shouted, seething with the pain of loss. His pain had nothing to do with the loss of the ship or its cargo; they were replaceable. It was the loss of his nephew that hurt so deeply. His death would need to be avenged.

Jorge Valdez de Barragan was in his chambers preparing to meet with his officers. As a Maestre de Campo, he commanded a military tercio consisting of three thousand men. Tall, strong, and fierce-looking, with a three-inch-long battle scar across his cheek, others dared not cross him. Now in his mid-thirties and well-seasoned, he was a leader soldiers willingly followed. Even Generals respected him, treating him as their virtual equal. Perhaps that was partly in recognition of his close relations with the King. Their friendship grew from the many military briefings he'd given. Philip appreciated his candor, unfiltered assessment of battlefield conditions, and strategic counsel. He was here at El Escorial to brief Philip on developments in the Netherlands, where heavy Dutch resistance was thwarting Spain's efforts to achieve total capitulation. He was strapping on his cutlass when the King's aide knocked. "Enter," he called out.

"Pardon, Maestre. The King requests your presence."

Valdez tested the pull of his cutlass—it was smooth as silk. He took one last glance in the glass to ensure he looked his finest.

The King's aide announced Valdez and took his leave. The Maestre strolled into Philip's chambers as though he owned the place. And truly, he did, if 'owning' meant influencing the King on military strategy.

"Welcome Meastre. It is always a pleasure to see you."

"It is my great honor, Your Majesty." Valdez bowed.

"I welcome the more detailed briefing you and your officers shall provide on the morrow. But tell me briefly, what progress in the Netherlands?"

"The Protestants are a determined foe. Maurice of Orange has thoroughly routed Archduke Albert's foolish Burgundian Count at Turnhout. Fully half of the Count's troops have been slain; another five hundred taken prisoner. The Dutch benefit from the ample support of their English allies. I fear their support grows among the French as well."

"So, not well for us then."

"I am certain we shall prevail, but the war will not soon end."

"This continues to distress me."

"Parma is a fine General. He has my complete confidence."

"Good. Good." Said Philip, taking a seat on his high-backed, gold-trimmed chair. "Please, have a seat." Valdez sat across from him.

"I have challenges on other fronts, Jorge. Our colonies and ships in the Southern Seas continue to be attacked, primarily by the

English. They masquerade as pirates. I have lost faith in our naval forces' ability to maintain command of those seas. It is imperative we have a principal military leader in place to change our fortunes there and ensure our success. That is why I have called on you this evening."

Valdez nodded, "How might I assist?"

"You know of my nephew Luis, Captain of *Espíritu de Los Santos*?" Valdez nodded yes. "I have just now learned he was brutally attacked by English pirates. He fought bravely but was overcome by superior forces. He gave his life in saving his men."

"I am sorry to hear this. I know you favored him."

"I did, yes. And I shall honor his memory by acting decisively against the English. We must take every one of their ships that dares cross the southern oceans; whether merchant, naval or pirate. I wish you to take the lead on this."

"As you wish."

"I am appointing you Viceroy of Military Affairs for the Southern Seas. You shall establish a base on the Inagua Islands and command all naval forces. The two Islands are well situated to facilitate the interception of enemy ships in the area."

"You must know that Viceroys on the Main and the many islands will resent my appointment."

"I shall demand their support. Our fleets and merchants will also be alerted. They shall be open to inspection by your forces at all times. You are authorized to take command of any vessels you deem necessary to execute your mission."

"This is a most generous offer. How could I possibly refuse?"

"You cannot," Philip smiled. He rose, opened a drawer, and withdrew a gold ring with his image on its head. "Give me your hand."

Valdez rose and extended his hand. Philip placed the ring in his palm. "This shall serve as proof of your appointment. It is engraved on the inside." He waited for Valdez to look. "It reads: 'Al servicio del Rey' [in service of the King]." Valdez slid the ring on the third finger of his right hand. "Please, proceed with all haste, Jorge. But first, join me for a fine meal, and an exceptional Portuguese Porto."

———

"The ship's hull is sleek and narrow, as you requested," said the builder's architect. "A full complement of the finest sails adds to her unparalleled speed." He and Garret ascended the stairs to the foredeck. He pointed to the bow chasers, "Two chasers at the bow, two at the stern, and ten cannons on either side. She will not only be fast but also deadly."

"My compliments, Mr. Birch. You have fashioned a fine instrument. I shall do my best to honor its capabilities."

"I have no doubt you will." Birch leaned his hands on the rail.

Garret raised the urn her grandfather once gave her. Now fractured and lightly chipped, it contained a freshly cut rose she purchased earlier. "I christen thee *Pandora*. May your journeys be filled with the finest of adventures." She kissed the urn, touched it to the rail, and threw it far into the air. It tumbled over and over, letting loose the rose and splashing into the harbor. Bobbing for a moment, it soon filled with water and took its leave.

Garret drew the name for her three-masted flagship from Greek mythology. Pandora was earth's first woman, crafted to the specifications of Zeus. Legend had it she opened a jar, letting loose all of humanity's evils. That mirrored Garret's own desires—to unleash all

Hell on the Spanish. She believed it was they who assassinated her former lover, Pantas. She would deliver Hell to the villagers of Santiago del Príncipe as well, for having savagely massacred a dozen of her crew.

Her slightly smaller consort ship also borrowed a name from Greek mythology: *Athena*, goddess of wisdom and war. She named her third ship *Orion*, after the London tavern where she first shared the truth of her gender with Pantas, marking the beginning of their love affair.

"She is sea-tested and ready to begin her maiden voyage," Birch offered proudly.

Garret looked to the vast ocean beyond Plymouth harbor. Thoughts of Admiral Drake flooded her mind. She would now carry forward his legacy for the first time. "Did you know the Admiral was only a captain when my grandfather paid him to take me on as a midshipman?"

"I did not."

"He told Drake I was his son."

"Oh my."

"It was a family secret. For many reasons." Garret herself grew up believing she was Daniel Connachan's son, never having reason to doubt it. But a strange comment by retired Colonel Tyndale, her military tutor, led her to question Daniel. In response, he finally disclosed the truth. Though it came as a shock, Garret eventually accepted her reality. But she appreciated how presenting as male brought advantages, including sailing with Drake. That would never have happened otherwise. It changed her fortunes immensely.

"They tell me you were schooled at Ritchfield, like my son."

Garret smiled. It was an all-boys academy; another advantage she appreciated. "I was, yes." Though disruptive at times, Garret had proven to be an exceptional student with a brilliant, analytical mind. Her height and athleticism enabled her to compete successfully with the boys. Though often outperformed by her, none of her privileged classmates would ever have believed they could be bested by a girl. "Unfortunately, I ended up being expelled. Ungraciously, I might add."

"For what reason?"

"Some claimed I knifed a classmate, though I did not."

"That is most unfortunate."

"Perhaps," she replied. "It moved my grandfather to arrange private tutoring—in both academics and a range of military arts."

"Military arts?"

"Yes. My grandfather thought it best." Retired Colonel Tyndale had schooled her to the point where her combat skills were significantly advanced—well beyond those of her fellow mids on Drake's *Pelican*. And even beyond many of the crew's abilities. She continued, "He knew the risks I would face. Women are not generally welcomed aboard ocean-going vessels. He cautioned me to maintain my secret."

"That must have been difficult."

"Not really. Presenting as male was all I truly knew." She conveniently avoided any reference to the unexpected challenges her bodily changes had presented. They forced her to adapt quickly. "Besides, my goal was to prove myself in battle, making my gender irrelevant." She didn't mention having shrewdly manipulated Drake into extending opportunities to demonstrate her military skills. Her instrumental participation in the heroic charge at Sagres earned her the crew's unquestioned respect.

"Even so…" Birch let his words trail off.

Garret laughed, "Drake disclosed my gender to the officers and crew at the same time as my appointment to a captaincy!"

"I imagine it helped that he was so well respected."

"Indeed. And it freed me to be myself, which is why I am here today."

"Well then, both you and your ships are well prepared."

"I thank you, Mr. Birch." Garret placed her hand on his shoulder. "Your designs are exceptional."

As Birch left, Garret reflected. Although disclosing her gender ultimately proved good for her, it also significantly altered her relationship with her best friend, William Tovery. And others.

"Permission to come aboard, Captain." William was hailing Garret from a small boat now alongside the *Pandora*, having been rowed from shore by his old friend, Caber.

Garret called down, "What flotsam have you brought me today, Farquhar?"

"A questionable vintage, Cap'n. It does appear clean, however."

William smiled. He was finely dressed.

"Alright then, permission granted."

William climbed the rigging. Garret met him as he stepped onto the main deck.

"Welcome aboard, Captain Tovery," she smiled.

"Thank you, Captain Connachan." Though best of friends, formalities of the ship had to be followed. No first names; not at this point.

"Are you staying here in Plymouth?"

"I am. At Devon's Anchor. Quite well-appointed, I must say. Perhaps you might join me for dinner there later?"

"It would be my pleasure. And I would be in the best of spirits if dinner were to be a celebration of sorts." She grinned, hinting at her hope that William would accept her invitation to join her on the upcoming voyage. Ever since receiving his letter regarding his upcoming visit, she sensed it was not a mere coincidence. She felt confident he would accept.

"Let it be so," he smiled back. "I am here to express my desire to sail with your motley crew. Assuming you are still inclined to have me."

Garret felt an urge to hug him. Instead, she chose proper decorum. And a little humor. "I believe I still have an opening—for a cabin boy."

"Then I shall be honored to…" William stopped midsentence.

Garret laughed. "Oh, I am sorry. I forgot. I believe we discussed the role of Captain—second-in-command, rather than cabin boy. Would that be more acceptable to you?"

"Let us shake on it," William replied, "followed by dinner and a fine bottle of wine."

"I must inform Thomas at the earliest," Garret said, taking his hand. "No doubt he shall be pleased."

———

Spanish warship *Corona del Oro* began easing into open water. Viceroy Valdez looked back from its stern. The busyness at Cadiz Harbor had long since dissipated. He suspected most of the dock workers were already in the local taverns spending their freshly earned income. He scanned the many ships accompanying him on this voyage to the Inaguas. "The wide variety of vessels surprises me," he said.

"It seems our navy is not as well organized," replied Don Francisco Rivera de Mendoza, his 'Primer Tenient' [First Lieutenant]. "There is no benefit to be drawn from making every vessel unique. What would be the consequence if we did that with our primary weapons against the Dutch?"

"Chaos, I suspect."

The fleet carried well over a hundred soldiers, including five officers selected by Valdez from his tercio. Of those, Rivera was his most seasoned and trusted. Valdez turned and headed toward the bow. "I much prefer this ocean air to those putrid Dutch battlefields."

"Just so," replied Rivera. "And no corpses to step over."

"Not yet, anyway." They strode the main deck. Valdez continued, "The winds are stiff and the day clear. Hopefully, we shall make good speed to Islas Canarias."

"The men's interests are in Islas de Cabo Verde. They are partial to the hogs, chickens and other pleasures to be found in Ponta do Sol."

"We shall be stopping there for supplies, not entertainment."

"Of course," replied Rivera, hiding his disappointment.

———

Halim stood at the bow of the *Royal Adventure*, sailing north on the last leg of its return voyage to England. The Queen commissioned captain James McBride months ago to transport the then-interim Ambassador back to Indonesia. Halim reflected on his meeting there with Sultan Baabullah, at which he shared news of the agreement he and assassinated Ambassador Pantas negotiated. It consummated Drake's promises made years earlier—England would open active trading and station a few warships at Ternate. Though deeply saddened to hear of Pantas' death, the Sultan was delighted with the agreement; so delighted that he immediately appointed Halim as Pantas' replacement. Halim could hardly wait to set foot on English soil as the official Ambassador—without attachment of the 'interim' label. His thoughts were suddenly interrupted by a worried call from high on the mainmast.

"Ships ahoy. Spanish-flagged."

"What is your count?" yelled Captain McBride as he rushed to join Halim on the foredeck.

A pause preceded the lookout's announcement, "Eight. So far."

It wasn't long before shots were fired by the oncoming fleet— forward warning shots to *Royal Adventure*'s right and left. McBride wasn't surprised. "Lower the cross; hoist the white," he shouted. That was in keeping with his orders to protect the life of the Ambassador, at all costs.

Within the hour, *Corona del Oro* was alongside *Royal Adventure*, the two ships joined by grapples. Valdez was pleased at his good fortune; he was already fulfilling King Philip's demands. He climbed across with Rivera and three other soldiers, piped aboard at McBride's order. The English captain waited mid-deck as the Spaniard approached, hand extended.

"I am Jorge Valdez de Barragan, Viceroy of the Inagua Islands and advisor to King Philip II of Spain. I request command of your vessel."

"Regards, Viceroy. I am Captain James McBride of Her Majesty's ship *Royal Adventure*. Our mission is peaceful. We are transporting the Indonesian Ambassador to England, at the request of Sultan Baabullah. I therefore request safe passage. I am also required to remind you that you are now standing on English territory."

"We are in *Spanish* waters, Captain. I shall have your ship with or without your agreement. If you refuse, you and your Ambassador shall find yourselves in chains; in a rather unpleasant location." Valdez knew that would constitute a breach of tradition for officers captured at sea. He simply wished to make a point. "I trust you see the wisdom in accepting my request."

McBride glanced at the Ambassador. Halim nodded as though he were willing to concede. McBride turned back to Valdez. "This shall not sit well with Her Majesty."

"You may inform her to take that up with King Philip." Valdez motioned to his guards. They accompanied McBride and Halim back to the entry port. No bloodshed followed, only the transfer of precious cargo to *Corona del Oro*, both inanimate and human.

———

The King's messenger arrived almost breathless. "Wonderful news, Your Majesty".

"Please…proceed."

"Viceroy Valdez has captured England's *Royal Adventure*."

"I shall drink to his success," said Philip. He rose from his desk to pour a chalice of port, enjoying the immediacy of the return on his investment in appointing Valdez. "Continue," he said, retaking his seat.

"The ship was transporting Sultan Baabullah's Ambassador to England."

Philip lowered the chalice onto his desk. "Hmmm. An unfortunate complication." Detaining the Ambassador would pose a testy political challenge. Despite their current differences, Philip felt it best to maintain a healthy relationship with the Sultan. Trade with Indonesia was financially rewarding. He looked at the messenger. "Please send my compliments to the Viceroy. I shall inform him that the Ambassador's safety is of paramount importance until we determine our best course of action."

'As you wish," replied the messenger. He turned and left. Philip sipped his port, admiring his skillfulness at selecting the best people for the most difficult assignments. Valdez was a cherished resource.

Word of the *Royal Adventure's* capture found its way to Queen Elizabeth, through her agents in Madrid. She was with Sir William Cecil, Lord High Treasurer at the time.

"I am thoroughly appalled at the audacity of this newly appointed Viceroy. He has taken prisoner a foreign diplomat, not to mention an English-flagged warship."

Sir William shook his head. Elizabeth continued, "Please remind me, are we currently at war with Spain?"

"Most certainly not, Your Majesty."

"Precisely. Then why would Philip commission this Viceroy to raid English vessels sailing the Southern Seas?"

"There can be no good answer."

"This simply cannot stand." Elizabeth sat back down.

"We shall need to strike back," offered Sir William.

"In a measured way, yes. An eye for an eye, as they say."

"If this Viceroy is assigned to the Inagua Islands, I imagine that is where he will take and hold the Ambassador…and perhaps Captain McBride."

"Just so." Elizabeth sipped her tea. "The possibility that this news might soon reach Sultan Baabullah adds urgency to the matter. If we are to save face with him, we shall need to engineer the Ambassador's freedom. And punish this Valdez accordingly."

"Would that Admiral Drake were still with us, for that purpose."

"If I commission the navy to handle it, it will signal Philip that we are at war." She sipped her tea.

"We can ill afford to go over such a cascading waterfall of money and events. Any effort must surely be stealthy and deniable."

"Indeed. A privateer would be best." Elizabeth glanced out the window. "There is one who comes to mind—a brash and talented young woman groomed by Drake himself. A Captain Connachan."

"I have heard of this woman."

"She is quite fascinating." Elizabeth laughed. "She once turned down my request to serve as a military advisor."

"Surely she would be hard-pressed to turn down a second offer."

"This shall be her opportunity to prove her value in serving Queen and country."

IV

The two pirates dragged their small boat up the sandy beach and into the thick, green foliage at its edge. They made certain it was well hidden before taking the path to the nearby coastal village of Santo Pedro.

"Is this '*Phantom*' the same wealthy man who provided you with the zabra?" asked De Graaf, referring to their first small sailing vessel.

"He is," replied Harker. "His Cartageñian connections provide him access to the movement of Spanish ships through the Passage. He supplies the information; I capture the ships; we share the proceeds. That is our deal."

"Does he know we lost the zabra in that gale?"

"He has no need to know. Taking the *Red Knight* and capturing *Espíritu de Los Santos* allows us to repay him."

Harker and De Graaf arrived early at Santo Pedro's dingy little tavern, where Harker first met the Phantom. The place was frequented almost entirely by local fishermen. Its owner was once a fisherman himself. He'd tired of the often-fruitless existence of catching and selling fish. A small private room off the Tavern's rear served as his living quarters. To boost his earnings, he built a wooden shack in the back, with an opening near its top to let in air. Inside was a separating wall creating narrow spaces, each containing a bed of straw covered by a heavy blanket. The shack generated an increase in visits to the village and a surprising amount of income for the owner, while demanding only the occasional cleaning of soiled blankets.

Harker and De Graaf took a table at the back and ordered beer. It came heavily watered, as they knew it would. Though both pirates were large and imposing, De Graaf was the more conspicuous of the two. A man of mixed race, his skin color wasn't the deep black that signaled 'slave'; it tended lighter. His father was reputedly Dutch, his mother an African who plied her trade in the taverns—an environment he grew up in following his father's disappearance. His hair was oddly curled and a dark shade of brown. Like most sailors, he was tightly muscled, though more heavily so. His unusually large hands were roughened by the constant handling of rigging and the usual strains of ship-work. Easily over six feet, he was slightly taller than Harker, whom he befriended during their days sailing with Drake. But both were then, and now, resistant to the culture Drake established. They were independent, unencumbered, and carving their own path. Absent Drake's oversight, they found violence to be an excellent means of attaining the things they most desired, like the obedience of others. They'd grown fond of the tool—De Graaf even more so than Harker. He wielded severe punishment at even the slightest opportunity.

Felipe de Heredia y Ortega, aka the 'Phantom', ambled quietly into the tavern. Though wealthy, he was dressed as a fisherman. It allowed him to avoid raising undue attention among the locals. The two strongmen who accompanied him remained outside. He glanced at the tavern owner and waved for a cup of beer as he headed to Harker's table. He pulled over a chair. Harker and De Graaf remained seated. No handshakes were exchanged. "Buenas tardes." He sat. "I trust you bring good news."

Harker looked around as if to confirm no one was listening. He leaned forward, speaking quietly, "Fifteen [implying fifteen thousand] reales. Nearby." He pulled back quickly as the tavern owner approached with a tankard of beer. Ortega slid a coin across the table. The owner withdrew, appearing displeased with the amount of the payment.

Ortega turned to Harker, "The origins of this bounty?"

"*Espíritu de los Santos*. Returning to Cádiz."

Ortega knew the ship's captain—Luis Rodriguez, the King's nephew. They moved in the same social circles when he was in Cartageña. He chose not to share that detail with these two since it was he who alerted Harker to the ship's presence in the first place; it could prove awkward for him if any of the dots were to be connected. "Where is the captain of this ship now?"

"Perhaps in the belly of a shark," chuckled De Graaf.

Ortega was relieved. With Rodriguez dead, there would be one less link between himself and these two pirates.

"I believe the fifteen will settle my account," said Harker.

"Indeed. Perhaps we shall do more business."

"I choose to sail on my own account," replied Harker. He sipped his beer. "But I am always open to interesting opportunities."

Ortega drank, leaving most of the distasteful grog in his cup. He rose from his chair. Harker and De Graaf also rose. They would lead him and his bodyguards to a hidden, well-worn wooden chest containing the reales.

———

The rain descended as if from a wind-driven waterfall as Garret arrived at Richmond Palace, where two sentries greeted her. Once inside, she quickly shed her long navy-blue coat. One of the Queen's aides took hold of it. Within minutes, she was announced to the Queen and invited to enter the tea room where she sat. She removed her cavalier's hat, sweeping it crosswise in front of her as she bowed. Though it was a man's gesture, it was how she chose to greet those of high standing, including the Queen herself. She was wearing men's clothing, after all.

"Your Majesty," she said, rising. "It is an honor to see you again."

"Welcome, Captain. I am pleased to have you join me. Might I offer you a cup of tea?"

"Would you have any koffei, perhaps?" Garret had previously gifted the Queen some of the beans Captain Anton once gave her.

"I believe we might. I myself find the drink too bitter."

Garret smiled, "It does have a bite. Either way, a hot drink would be delightful. It is miserably cold outside."

"Well then," Elizabeth said, waving at an aide to prepare the koffei, "I hope this visit shall warm us both." Garret proceeded toward the chair to which the Queen now motioned. "Tell me, Captain, how did you take the loss of our dear Admiral Drake?"

"His death is a tragedy of the highest order. I doubt England shall ever have an Admiral to match his accomplishments. He was not simply my mentor; he was a much-loved friend."

"Were you at his side when he died?"

"No, sadly. I was with a small party, replenishing supplies."

The attendant brought a cup of tea, placing it on the small table next to Garret. "This shall warm you until the koffei is ready, m'lady."

"Thank you." Garret smiled at the attendant's addressing her as female, despite her dressing as male. Exhibiting her female assets while dressed in male clothing was clearly working as planned. "Unfortunately, Your Majesty, we were ambushed by local inhabitants. My men were massacred. I alone survived. I was on my way back to the fleet when the Admiral was buried at sea." She reached for her tea. "His death was not entirely unexpected. A sickness had consumed him for weeks."

"So I have heard." The Queen sipped her tea. "I had not heard, however, that you were attacked. That must have been frightening."

"It does focus the mind." Garret sipped her own tea. "It forces one to use every ounce of intelligence. And perhaps a touch of physical skill."

"Were you engaged in physical combat, then?"

"I shall say only that two men were…dispatched. At my hand. One sought to have his way with me." She said it matter-of-factly.

Elizabeth was wide-eyed. Speechless. "Things of that nature are not exactly elements of palace life."

"Even if they were, Your Majesty, I doubt they would be discussed in your presence."

"I suppose." Elizabeth sipped her tea. "You are a truly surprising woman, Captain. Would that there were more like you."

"You are too kind; I merely do as I was schooled." The attendant reappeared, this time with Garret's koffei.

"Apparently, *well*-schooled," Elizabeth concluded. She returned her cup to its saucer. "You know, the Admiral never did share with me how his men took the news when he informed them you were actually a woman."

Garret nodded her thanks to the attendant and turned to the Queen. "The Admiral went out of his way to ensure the announcement would be delivered thoughtfully and received in a positive manner. Those who knew me well, or saw me perform in battle, were supportive. Unfortunately, a few were not. In fact, one was particularly outspoken against me. A man named Harker. Thankfully, my good friend Musa confronted him."

"Musa? That seems an odd name."

"He is a large and imposing former slave. His African name means 'from the water'." She sipped her koffei. "Some of the men do indeed have odd names. A Scotsman, for example, is known for his skill at caber-toss. The men call him 'Caber' because his real name is Farquhar, which many find difficult to pronounce."

"I see."

"Seafarers frequently label each other. And for good reason. Suppose this Caber's real name were William. He might easily be confused with other Williams onboard the ship. But if you were to say 'Caber', then any crewmate would know the William to which you referred."

"Of course. Still, Musa seems a dreadful name."

"Yet behind that name is a most kind soul."

"That seems a little difficult to grasp…a large, threatening man with a kind soul." She sipped again at her tea. "Tell me, do all these men now accept you in your role?"

"Those on my crew do so, yes."

"Well then, you and I certainly have something in common— each navigating our own way in what can only be considered a man's world." She rolled her eyes and raised her eyebrows as she said it.

Garret laughed. "Perhaps we shall have a say in changing that."

They laughed together. Elizabeth again changed direction, "Tell me, what are your current plans?"

"I have assembled a small fleet at Plymouth. Three ships. I intend to return to the Southern Seas and, with your blessing of course, continue to make King Philip's accumulation of wealth a slower process than he envisions."

"Perhaps our interests cross, then." She shifted in her chair, leaning back. "Are you aware of the taking of the *Royal Adventure* by the Spanish?"

"I am not."

"It was captained by James McBride. He was returning from Indonesia with newly appointed Ambassador Halim."

"Ambassador Pantas' aide?"

"The very same. The Sultan was pleased with the outcome of our negotiations and sent word of Halim's appointment as Ambassador."

"I know Halim personally."

"So I understand. Apparently, you and former Ambassador Pantas were rather close," Elizabeth winked.

Garret was surprised by the comment. But then, the Queen was well known for having excellent sources of information. "We were close, yes," Garret acknowledged. "He was the first and only man with whom I shared deep affection."

"Dare I ask, just how deep?"

Garret blushed but recovered quickly. "He spoke of marriage."

"So did Philip!" Elizabeth's hearty laugh compelled Garret to join her. "He felt it would bring our two powerful countries together."

"How romantic," grinned Garret.

Elizabeth laughed so hard she could barely utter her words, "Not all proposals are created equal!".

Garret suddenly felt great affection for this woman. Though she was well advanced in years, and made a rather clownish use of oils, pastes and colors on her face, she brought an enviable strength to her leadership. The grand lady was thoughtful and decisive. And she did it all with a fine sense of humor that only those closest to her ever witnessed.

Elizabeth gathered herself and continued, "The last time we visited, you…gracefully…declined my invitation to serve me as a military advisor."

Garret smiled sheepishly. "I was young and impertinent."

"You are still very much in your youth," the Queen assured her. "And I find you to be focused, passionate and determined. Admirable traits for one so young." She took another sip of tea. "Do you recall what I said in response to your declination?

"I believe you suggested that you might one day ask me again to serve in some capacity."

"Indeed. And what else did I say?"

"If I recall correctly," Garret smiled, "you advised me to accept the next opportunity, even though I might question my ability to succeed."

"Wise words," the Queen smiled back. "I hope you follow them."

"But of course, Your Majesty. How is it that I can serve you?"

"King Philip has commissioned one of his foremost military

leaders to challenge our presence in the southern oceans—a Maestre de Campo named Jorge Valdez de Barragan. This is the same man who captured the *Royal Adventure* and took prisoner both Captain McBride and Ambassador Halim. We cannot let this stand. It is imperative that we free these two men." She paused as though searching for something. "We must also…neutralize…Señor Valdez." She let that sink in for a moment, looking Garret in the eye as if to communicate that 'neutralize' might actually mean 'eliminate'.

"I see," Garret nodded, suggesting she understood the implication.

"Philip has appointed him Viceroy of the Inagua Islands, which is where he is likely to be holding his captives."

Garret didn't respond. She was already contemplating the difficulties involved. Elizabeth continued, "I realize how challenging this mission would be for any Englishman—or woman for that matter."

Garret understood there was no turning down the Queen a second time. "I recall your having noted that, if one were to accept a challenging opportunity, one might then count on the full support of the person who extended it."

"And so you may, Captain. Determine what support you require and provide me with the specifics. You shall have my complete support. We have little time, however. Important lives are at stake."

V

"Damn these books," complained Captain McBride. He tossed one across the small structure he and Ambassador Halim were being held in. Halim held back a laugh. The books were all written in Spanish. While he could read them, McBride could not.

The two were being held captive on the larger of the two Inagua islands, under guard. Viceroy Jorge Valdez had chosen the south side of the island on the advice of a seasoned naval captain. The weather was apparently more favorable. It was also closer to the lake and its steady flow of fresh water. From that position, he would also have good access to ships heading to Hispaniola and on to Santiago or La Habaña, or even south to Cartageña. It was a suitably strategic location.

The island's small village already had a makeshift church and several wooden shacks. The residents were using sections of stagnant, shallow seawater and the evaporation process to produce salt. That and fishing were their primary occupations. They resented the fleet's incursion and their own conscription into the construction of residences for the Viceroy and his men. Valdez had also commissioned the building of a stone fortress, from which to defend the island. The village had quickly become a hotbed of activity, with food, supplies and slave labor being shipped in from larger, off-island population centers.

"Atención!" one of the prisoners' guards called out as Viceroy Valdez approached. McBride and Halim rose as he entered.

"Buenos días, caballeros." He continued in Spanish, "I trust you find your quarters here comfortable."

"Thank you, Viceroy," Halim replied, also in Spanish. "They are as good as we might expect."

"I have no desire to make your lives difficult or uncomfortable, gentlemen. You are my guests. Still, you must understand that you have limited freedoms. We must await my King's guidance on your return to your countries."

"Of course," replied Halim. "Thank you. I assure you, we shall cause you no trouble."

"Excellent. Then we understand each other." He paused for a moment, then directed his comments solely to Halim. "There is something the Captain can do for me. If you would, please, assist me with my English." Valdez had excellent English language skills but didn't care to let them know that. At least, not yet.

"Certainly."

Valdez continued, with Halim's assistance, "Capítan, I imagine that, since you were charged with the transportation of the Ambassador, you are well connected with your Queen. At the very least, you must be well connected within the Admiralty."

"I am proud of my standing, Viceroy."

"Then you must be well-informed of the various missions of England's ships; in particular, its naval vessels."

McBride was slow to respond. It didn't take a navigator to see where Valdez was headed. "I have limited knowledge."

"Yet you just assured me of your high standing." By his reaction, Valdez could tell McBride felt the noose tightening. His own foolish pride had just looped the knot.

"I am afraid it would not be prudent to discuss such matters with you," McBride replied.

Valdez stepped toward him, imposing the full height and weight of his muscular stature. "Do not play with me Capitán," he said, now in fluent English, "I shall have this information from you or things may become…"

he paused, smiling menacingly, "*less* comfortable."

He waited for McBride's response. None came. "Perhaps if I were to lean on the Ambassador, you might feel differently." Valdez had no intention of inflicting pain on Halim. He merely hoped the implication alone would be sufficient to get McBride to open up. Surely the captain would not wish to be held accountable by the Queen for any harm that might befall the Ambassador.

McBride hung his head, "You leave me no choice."

Valdez smiled; McBride had fallen for his ruse like an iron ball.

———

Thomas Drake, younger brother of the Admiral and executor of his estate, strolled into the foyer of Buckland Abbey, to greet William Tovery. The Abbey had been his brother's residence for several years. The Admiral's wife, Elizabeth, still resided there.

"Welcome William," said Thomas, with a gleaming smile. "What a joy to see you again." As they shook hands, he called out to Elizabeth, "William has arrived." The sound of her footsteps soon followed.

The three sat for tea and biscuits.

"I am so pleased to see you, William," said Elizabeth. "My husband always spoke fondly of you…and Garret Connachan.

"Your husband was an exceptional leader. I believe Garret and I were among his very first midshipmen."

"Just so." Elizabeth's eyes began to fill with water. "Your presence here today brings memories of better days," she explained. "Tell us, what brings you?"

"I have come from Plymouth Harbor. I shall be joining Garret on a voyage to the Southern Seas. She has three ships but only two captains. She would love to have Thomas join us as the third," he smiled, nodding to Thomas.

"And I would love to join you, were it not for my responsibilities here in Devon."

"We understand, Thomas. You may not be with us, but you shall always be among us."

"My brother would be proud to see the two of you sailing together again. And leading a fleet."

"He would be even more proud if he knew our orders have come directly from the Queen herself."

"That is wonderful," said Elizabeth. "Can you tell us more?"

William looked around, to ensure no servants were listening. "It is not for common knowledge…"

"Of course," Thomas and Elizabeth replied, almost in unison.

"King Philip has appointed a man named Valdez as Viceroy, charging him with intercepting any English vessels in the southern oceans—primarily in the islands surrounding Hispaniola, and along the Spanish Main. This Viceroy has already claimed the *Royal Adventure* as his first prize, taking prisoner Captain James McBride and Ambassador Pantas' former aide, Halim."

"I had news of Halim's appointment to Ambassador," said

Thomas, "though I had not heard he was taken prisoner. That is most upsetting."

"Her Majesty has charged us with rescuing the two men. She also asked that we…" he looked again for any servants, "*neutralize* the Viceroy."

"Oh dear," said Elizabeth. William could see she caught the not-so-subtle implication that the Queen wished to assassinate the Viceroy.

Thomas probed further. "But with only three ships? Will you not require a larger fleet?"

"We believe we can accomplish the mission stealthily. A larger fleet might draw too much attention."

"I see. Well, I trust you and Garret are capable of planning and executing a successful campaign. I have never doubted you before. How might I help?"

"You can certainly pray for us," William grinned.

"Indeed. You shall have both our prayers and our best wishes."

"There is something more we could use, of course.

"Please. Anything."

"A proper diversion would be most helpful to our cause. We suspect King Philip may have spies in the Queen's court. Given your connections there, we thought you might casually leak word of rumors that a large fleet of English pirates is preparing an assault somewhere along the Spanish Main. It would be helpful if that false information were to reach the King. No doubt he would inform the Viceroy to that end. Valdez would then be inclined to divert some of his forces from Inagua, where he is based, to prepare for an assault on the Main. That would turn the odds in our favor.

Thomas didn't hesitate. "I shall leave for London tomorrow and make my rounds."

"Thank you, Thomas." William rose. "I am afraid time is short. I must return to Plymouth. A pleasure to see you both again. Especially you, Elizabeth." She extended her arm. He took it and kissed the back of her hand. He then extended his hand to Thomas, who shook it. Elizabeth surprisingly approached, giving him a long, warm hug. "Take care, William. God be with you. And with Garret."

VI

The fleet officers laughed and swapped stories as they gathered on the breezy, sun-drenched deck of flagship *Pandora* at Captain Connachan's request. It was the morning after their departure from Plymouth and all were anxious to learn of their ultimate destination. William Tovery, leading *Athena*, was the only captain among them. No one was yet officially appointed to lead *Orion*. That position was reserved for someone who, in time, might step up and demonstrate the necessary leadership skills. For now, Douglas Wigmore was in charge of the vessel. Though a fine seaman, he was not captain-material. Not in Garret's mind. His manner was too harsh. She preferred someone with a more empathetic leadership style—someone who could rally the crew by winning their hearts not beating their backs.

Henry Blair, now engaged in conversation with William, was Garret's Master's Mate. He'd come highly recommended by Sir Walter Raleigh. David Webber, the new Master-at-Arms, joined the assembly last. He'd served previously with Blair. The two worked well together. Mr. Langton, interpreter for both Hawkins and Drake, was deep into a book he'd brought along. More introverted than the others, he preferred immersing himself in the written word, in any of four languages. Two promising young midshipmen had also been asked to attend. One was James Lee, son of Drake's former master-at-arms. The other was John Bowyer, son of a London-based merchant. Though Garret had interviewed others for the midshipmen positions, these two stood out for their character and integrity. Both were excited and honored to be part of this assembly.

Garret stepped onto the deck and invited the men to join her in her generously sized, wood-paneled, and well-appointed cabin. They shuffled in and began assembling around the center table. Most positioned themselves to avoid the morning light beaming through the larboard-side stern windows.

Garret spent the next fifteen minutes sharing the fleet's mission and some of the major details before turning to more general matters, "As Admiral Drake liked to say, '*None of us shall succeed unless we all succeed*'. Each of us must support our mission by executing our responsibilities according to plan. Nonetheless, conditions may unfold differently than envisioned. We must therefore be alert to changes and communicate them quickly and broadly, so that we might adapt in unison. Is this all understood?"

"Aye, sir," came the chorus.

"Excellent. Then let us ready our crews for every possibility." She turned to Webber, "With the Queen's support, we have no shortage of ammunition, Mr. Webber. I shall expect you to conduct cannon drills daily…at varying times—on short notice and regardless of weather conditions."

"Aye, Captain."

"Mr. Blair, we shall run several sail formations to learn how the ships react under all conditions. And we shall practice the tightest of maneuvers. Daily, if you please."

"Aye, sir."

"Masters Lee and Bowyer, you shall rotate every three days. The first rotation shall be with Master's Mate Blair, the second with Master-at-Arms Webber, the third with Captain Tovery, and the fourth with me. You are required to ask questions and seek clarity on anything you do not understand. Do not hesitate to disagree with us or challenge our thinking; we welcome all thoughts and opinions.”

“Aye, Captain,” the two mids responded, simultaneously.

Garret scanned the faces of her officers. “Voyages can be long and challenging, gentlemen. Time is a resource we must not squander. I expect the sharpest and most timely discipline from your men in carrying out your orders. Are we agreed?”

“Aye, sir.”

“Excellent. Then let us proceed with all haste.”

As the officers left Garret’s quarters, young Lee turned to Bowyer, “She may not be Drake, but she certainly has command.”

“So it would seem. Rather surprising, would you agree?”

“Not from what my father told me of her. She was the best of Drake’s mids. And heroic in battle. We are most fortunate to be sailing under her.”

“We shall see. She is a mere woman, after all.”

———

The *Red Knight* tilted close to the waterline, secured by ropes against which it fought. Most of the crew was in and around the water, scraping reluctant barnacles from the ship’s hull. Yaugaan De Graaf strolled the beach, casually supervising the careening.

An old rope secured to the main mast and tied to a distant palm bore the lion’s share of the ship’s weight. Constant rubbing against the roughened rear of the tree caused the splitting of a few strands, intensifying the pressure on other, already weak, strands. Within seconds, rapid shearing produced an unexpected snap. Those standing on the shore dove onto the sand, to avoid being whipped by the recoil of the failed rope. The added pressure on the remaining ropes, masts and trees created a resounding, creaking roar, warning of coming chaos. The ship's sway increased, accentuating the strain. The men careening the ship's bottom realized their moments were numbered if the beast were to break free. Though all scattered as best they could, two were crushed when the three-master finally groaned and gave way.

"Damn you all to Hell!" shouted De Graaf, to no one in particular and everyone in general. He ran toward the ship as it bobbed back into a near-upright position. Men splashed madly in the water while others raced onto the shore.

As the ship and men settled, De Graaf yelled out for all to hear, "Who was responsible for securing that rope?" No one offered themselves up. He knew the reason for that was his own brutal reputation for delivering punishment. He scanned them slowly with squinted eyes, shouting fiercely, "I shall have this man or you shall all pay a price."

One of the crew shoved forward a smaller man, barely five feet tall and scrawny. De Graaf walked toward him, evil on his mind. The man tried to run but someone tripped him. He fell face-first into the gritty white sand. Another crew member kicked him in the ribs. He grimaced, moaned, and slowly began pushing himself up. De Graaf was quickly at his side. The crew watched in silence as the quartermaster's enormous hands grasped the man's neck, pulling him up in the air, his feet dangling. While one enormous hand squeezed the neck, the other covered the top of the man's head, twisting it swiftly, more than a quarter turn. A scream rang out and then stopped as abruptly as it had begun. De Graaf dropped the man onto the sand. "Get back to work, you bastards. And get it right this time or by God, we shall have your shares."

A sailor next to the one who'd pushed the smaller man forward leaned toward his mate, "Ye be sure he was the one secured the rope?"

"Might as well o' been. He was a bloody nuisance."

De Graaf headed to the edge of the trees, where Harker was studying a rudimentary map of the islands and the Spanish Main. He'd pinned the map on the sand with stones, to prevent it from blowing away in the light breeze.

"I trust you dealt with the problem," Harker remarked casually, without looking up.

"The problem is no longer with us," De Graaf replied, matter-of-factly. He glanced down at the map. "Where to next?"

"Do you not find yourself tempted by the riches of Panama? We are so very close to that land of gold."

"A well-protected land of gold."

"Indeed," replied Harker. "Yet Isla Grande…here," he pointed on the map, "would prove an excellent base off the coast, midway between Porto Bello and Nombre de Dios. Still, we would need more than our two ships and perhaps another hundred men."

"Perhaps the French and Dutch pirates known to frequent Isla Tortuga?"

"My very thought. The island is far removed from Panama, yet where else might we find enough men to join us?" De Graaf didn't respond. If Panama was to be their target, then it was clear Isla Tortuga needed to be their next destination. Harker continued, "We shall head

57

there once the careening is complete. How soon will that be?"

"That is difficult to judge," De Graaf bemoaned. "These men lack many skills." He shook his head. "Perhaps five days. Seven at most."

"So be it. On to Isla Tortuga, within five days. Spare not the whip."

———

The luscious, flowered gardens on the grounds of El Escorial glistened brilliantly in the morning sun, following the overnight rains. King Philip strolled the pathway alongside his Austrian Ambassador. An aide ran toward him, breathing heavily, "There is news from our sources in England, Your Excellency." The aide glanced questioningly at the Ambassador.

"Speak freely," the King assured him.

"The Queen has set her sights on the Main. Panama, perhaps. A small fleet may have already set sail."

"Thank our sources. And find the next ship leaving for the Southern Seas. Have it carry word to Viceroy Valdez. It should sail to him directly, with no unnecessary stops."

"Si, Excellency."

The aide bowed and hurried away. The Ambassador turned to Philip. "Why would the Queen authorize such an assault, particularly with a small fleet? Does she not realize it would end badly for her?"

"We cannot be certain of her intentions. In any event, Valdez shall be well prepared...provided we alert him in time."

"I hear the man has a fine military mind."

"The finest. And a remarkable ability to lead his men to victory. If any man can rip the Queen's dress, it is him."

———

Garret's fleet was now three days into their stay on Isla de Saint Iago, one of the Cape Verde Islands. Though largely barren, it was well-positioned for ships heading to and from Europe, Asia and the Southern Seas. Her fleet was busy purchasing and loading supplies— stores of salt, palmettos, coconuts, rice, cotton cloth, wool and spices. The town of Saint Iago, for which the island was named, bustled with trading activity, the most significant of which was the merchandising of African slaves.

During the fleet's stay, local taverns were exceedingly busy delivering spirits and other comforts to thirsty sailors. While Captains Tovery and Connachan attempted to keep their men under tight control, most found ways to take full advantage of the taverns' offerings. And on this morning of departure, two men were missing, forcing an unwanted delay. Master-at-Arms Webber took Musa and Caber with him to search for them. It didn't take long; there weren't that many taverns. It was the third one they entered where they found the two stragglers passed out in a back room, both naked, though one still wore his boots. Musa took a nearby bowl of water and showered it on their faces. They startled awake, one falling off the bed. Scrambling to their feet, their privates swayed like synchronized, inverted metronomes. Caber couldn't help but laugh, despite the seriousness of the situation.

"You bastards grab your damn clothes. Now!" shouted Webber. The dangling duo quickly gathered their belongings, their heads pounding and ears ringing. They began putting their clothes on. "Don't bother," ordered Webber. "There be no time to dress."

Only moments later, five men exited the tavern and walked down the main street; two covering their privates with what they carried. Women laughed and passersby stopped to watch the naked, stumbling strangers, their butts blinding white in the mid-afternoon sun.

The stragglers were shortly on *Pandora's* main deck, facing Garret and covering their privates. There was no smile on her face. She looked at one, then the other. Both were completely disheveled—their beards and hair askew, and their clothes appearing ragged and soiled, as though they'd just been in a brawl. Although it wasn't a particularly pleasing sight, their mates were enjoying the moment immensely.

"May I ask, gentlemen, what gives you leave to discredit your crewmates and cause our delay?" asked Garret.

The taller of the two men smirked, still reeling from the spirits and events preceding his unconsciousness. "Just enjoyin' the fruits of the town, Cap'n."

"Aye," said the shorter man. "We were in good company. Slept too hard," he snickered.

The taller one coughed up a laugh. "We were not aware of the time. Sir."

"You shall make up the time we have lost." Garret turned to Webber. "See that these men scrub clean every slat of the foredeck, including the sides and the bottoms. I shall come by for inspection later in the day. The slats must be clean enough for these men to be served their supper on."

The two men cringed, their grins evaporating. They and their crewmates often defecated and urinated through those slats—all day long. This was to be an endless task, and they knew it. The thought of eating their food off the slats was enough to make one of the two lose the food he'd consumed the night before.

Garret turned and walked away, disgusted but grinning. Musa, a broad smile on his face, led the miscreants to the foredeck. The two slackards now held their belongings both between their legs and behind their rears.

"Weigh anchor, if you please, Mr. Blair," Garret called out. "Set sail immediately for the Southern Seas."

———

For a few years now, French pirates and privateers were frequenting the southern shore of turtle-shell-shaped Isla Tortuga. They were joined occasionally by Dutch brethren, finding common cause in raiding Spanish vessels. The island was now a refuge for those engaged in pirating. As *Death's Head* and *Red Knight* eased into the harbor, both flying crimson flags, pirates in the village hailed their arrival with an honorary firing of a single, ground-based cannon, set high in the hills above the small village. Harker ordered a like reply.

The ships were soon anchored. The stay-behind crew having been assigned, longboats began heading ashore. Harker and De Graaf were among the first landing party. They were anxious to let it be known they welcomed others to join them in a hunt for treasure. The vital piece of information they wouldn't disclose, however, was the target of their assault—Panama. It was unlikely to be a popular target since it was common knowledge that Drake's assaults at Nombre de

Dios had served to heighten Spanish defenses there. The destination would therefore remain secret until they were seaborne.

Alain Le Pen, the most feared of French pirates, strode down the beach to where Harker's longboat was about to ground. He was as fashionable a pirate as anyone had ever met. His broad-brimmed burgundy hat sported a small white feather. A V-waisted, brown-leather doublet covered his lime-green silk blouse topped with a white-ruffed collar. The cutlass at his hip gleamed in the sunlight, bright against his deep brown knickers. The green color of his stockings was slightly darker than that of his blouse. His black shoes were accented with brass buckles. The man was whip smart. And he was most curious about these two ships he didn't recognize.

As the longboats slid to a stop on the beach, Le Pen greeted the apparent leader, "*Bienvenue, mon ami.*" He smiled broadly, extending his hand. "*Je suis Alain Le Pen.*"

"*Bonjour, monsieur. Mon nom est* Harker, *s'il vous plaît.*" He shook Le Pen's hand. "*Mon intendant*, De Graaf. *Parlez vous anglais?*"

"*Oui, monsieur.* From where do you hail?"

"We make our way here in the Southern Seas. We find the Spanish to be rather…accommodating," Harker grinned.

Le Pen laughed. "What brings you to our lovely island?"

"It seems our ambitions exceed our present means. We are in search of, how do you say—*partenaires?*"

"Partners, yes," Le Pen nodded. "We are always open to proposals that might see us, *comment dites-vous*—singe the King's beard?" It was Harker and De Graaf's turn to laugh at the phrase they were so familiar with. It originated with Drake's flaming defeat of the Spanish at Cadíz.

"We sailed with 'El Draque' at Cadíz," volunteered Harker.

"*Incroyable!*"

"It was like watching a master painter at work. The Admiral was an artist."

"So he was," Le Pen replied, "though his medium was flames, not oils." There was more shared laughter.

Le Pen turned slightly, motioning toward the center of the village. "Come, let us discuss matters over cups of beer."

———

A powerful storm tore through the Inaguas, slowing the construction that was progressing so well. The fortress wall supporting the shore battery was already four feet high. The residence of Viceroy Valdez had been framed, though there was still much to do before it could serve as his headquarters. In the meantime, he'd taken an existing old wooden structure as his temporary quarters. Seated at a small table that served as his desk, his mind turned to the other Spanish viceroys in the region. He'd sent messages to those in Cartageña, Santiago, and other important Spanish cities, alerting them to his responsibilities and demanding their recognition of his leadership of all naval initiatives in the region. Though he imagined all would respond positively, he was wary of political appointees. They were generally known to say whatever one wished to hear, while secretly plotting a contrary course. In time, he would visit them face-to-face, to strengthen the bond he needed in order to be most effective. He counted on his orders from the King, his compelling physical presence, and his powerful influencing skills to bring them in line.

Through several conversations with Captain McBride, the most significant information Valdez obtained was that Sir Richard Hawkins—the son of Drake's mentor, Commander John Hawkins—was to leave England, cross the southern seas, navigate south along the east coast of the Spanish Main, and continue on to Magellan's Straits. It was supposedly a trading mission that might eventually take him to the East Indies, not unlike Drake's circumnavigation. Valdez suspected it was just another pirating venture. He would see to interrupting it.

Movement out the window of his quarters caught his eye—an unexpected, Spanish-flagged vessel arriving in the rain-drenched harbor. Two of his military officers were already on the beach, preparing to board a longboat that would take them to the ship. Valdez turned back to the parchment detailing the remaining work on his new quarters. It was currently the only thing that interested him more than military matters.

The unexpected ship that arrived in his harbor brought Valdez vital information. First, there was word that an English fleet was expected to be sailing for the Main. He wondered whether this might be Hawkins' fleet—the one Captain McBride had mentioned. The King had asked him to be alert to this threat and be prepared to defend Panama in particular since most of the Spanish gold and silver in the Southern Seas were currently stored there. Valdez had already dispensed some of his forces to the cities of Nombre de Dios and Porto Bello, to help them prepare for a potential assault. He was not uncomfortable sparing the forces. After all, his own island was an unlikely target. It was of no consequence as far as non-Spaniards knew. In addition, extending support to the viceroys in those two locations would surely help him gain their cooperation in the future.

The second item of information the unexpected ship had brought was contained in a sealed message King Philip addressed to him. It concerned the disposition of Captain McBride and Ambassador Halim. Philip wanted them retained until he could strike an agreement with the Queen of England for their exchange. He wasn't yet certain what he might bargain for in return. But he noted that England's loss of Ambassador Halim would be a blemish the Queen would need to resolve in order to keep Sultan Baabullah happy and her trading relationship with Indonesia in good order. He suspected she would be willing to give up much in exchange for the Ambassador's return.

Valdez understood, without having to be told, that he needed to ensure both men were well taken care of. And so far, they had been, thanks in part to McBride's willingness to share information. Valdez had a messenger deliver a container of fine beer and a note to McBride and Halim. The note read simply: *King Philip drinks to your good health.*

VII

They drew a crowd of onlookers from *Pandora's* decks. The sleek, gray missiles darted beneath the clear water, pierced it to fly briefly, and then gracefully slid back in, nose first, keeping pace with the ship which itself was making good speed. The crew pointed and smiled as the pod—some claimed as many as a dozen—continued pacing them for a good five minutes. It wasn't until a group of sharks appeared in the distance that the dolphins altered course.

"Back to work," shouted Blair as he approached Garret's cabin. Though it was already open, he knocked on the door to announce himself, "*Blair*, Captain."

"A moment, please." Garret placed the pages she'd been reading into a drawer and closed it. "Enter."

Blair walked in, looking serious. "Pleased to report we are making good time, sir. The winds are favorable and the men in good spirits."

"Excellent."

"We have just been signaled by Captain Tovery. One of his men has taken ill with fever. At times, he is delirious."

"Most unfortunate."

"Indeed. The last time I saw a mate go mad onboard ship, the crew were unwilling to breathe the same air. The mate was confined to the hold, in chains. It did not end well for him. The same could well be the case here, which is why Captain Tovery requests that Dr. Grant attend to him."

"By all means. Bring us alongside *Athena* and have Dr. Grant at the ready."

"Aye, Captain."

Garret quickly changed the subject. "Based on my calculations, Mr. Blair, and allowing for variable weather, I believe we may reach the Inaguas within a few days."

"I believe so."

"It is imperative that we approach the smaller island from the north, with minimum sail, to avoid detection by Viceroy Valdez' forces. Let us proceed to a position five leagues north of the islands before making our turn to the south. I intend to make a temporary base on the northern shore of the smaller island. From there, we shall scout the larger island to the south, in preparation for our assault."

"Understood. Five leagues north of the small island."

"With all due haste, Mr. Blair."

As Blair left, Garret reopened the lower left drawer of her desk. She reached in and withdrew Pantas' journal. His writing still brought her comfort, almost as though he were there with her. She searched for the dog-eared page she'd been reading when Blair interrupted. It recalled the night of Admiral Drake's wedding to Elizabeth Sydenham. She and Pantas arrived at the event separately, not wishing to bring undue attention to their relationship. At the time, only Pantas and Drake were aware she was a woman. Later that evening, she and Pantas strolled the grounds. He wrote about their conversation in his journal…

I am completely smitten by Garret. I find it increasingly difficult to be apart from her. She has not simply stolen my heart, she has placed it next to her own, embracing it as though it were a beloved pet. I cannot imagine a life without her by my side, for always. As we walked the grounds, I proposed that she and I return to Indonesia, where she could be free to live as a woman, rather than as a man. As my woman.

Garret could almost feel his touch and smell the greenery that surrounded them that night. Tears welled up in her eyes as she caressed the page and softly closed the journal. It was clear she wasn't yet fully recovered from the pain of losing Pantas. Nor was she convinced she ever would; his assassin's sword had virtually pierced her own heart. Still, she recognized the need to move beyond her sadness.

Garret shook her head, replacing her thoughts with the Queen's orders regarding Viceroy Valdez. Though she hadn't said it directly, the undeniable inference was that the man should meet his end…and by her hand! That would make her an assassin—just like the man who had slain Pantas. She would never willingly take anyone's life, other than in the midst of fight-or-die combat. Assassination was something different. Could she take the Viceroy's life, for example, as he lay in his bed, defenseless? That seemed so unfair, even if she had the nerve to do it. Better he were able to defend himself and be slain in doing so. Yet she understood Valdez was a well-seasoned military man. He might easily defeat her. Garret felt certain that was not a risk Her Majesty would wish her to take.

Another possibility was to have someone else assassinate the man. Musa perhaps? After all, he was an executioner. He would have no qualms about taking the life of a defenseless man. But was it right to ask him to do that if she, herself, were unwilling to? That didn't sit well with her. No, if it were to be done, she thought, it were best she do it personally. She would need to steel herself to become the Queen's hand-picked assassin.

———

It had been almost two days since the four ships sailed from Isla Tortuga—Harker's two, accompanied by two of Le Pen's. They were heading southwest, toward Panama, aided by unexpectedly favorable winds and relatively clear skies.

The sharp-eyed young spotter called down worriedly from *Death's Head's* crow's nest. "Ships astern. Two in number. Full sails." Though their country of origin wasn't yet clear, it soon would be; they were fast approaching.

Harker and Master's Mate Stevens hustled to the stern. "Spanish Navy," Harker offered. "Who else dares chase a fleet twice their size?"

"Shall we engage?"

"Signal De Graaf and Le Pen. Let us divide our ships, ninety degrees. Make the Spaniards choose—split and chase both groups or choose one to follow. More likely they shall hunt together, choosing either our two or Le Pen's. The two that are not being pursued can then circle behind and surround them before they realize it."

"Aye, sir."

Stevens signaled De Graaf and Le Pen. Within minutes, the two groups began separating. As time salted away, Harker waited anxiously for the Spaniards' response; for too long, he thought. They continued splitting the middle, probably wrestling indecision. It was nearly twenty minutes before they finally altered course. And Harker's guess was correct—the pursuers stayed together, recognizing they were better off two-on-two. They'd chosen to follow Le Pen's ships.

Harker ordered his sails reset to alter course, in preparation for ultimately encircling the Spanish ships. De Graaf followed suit on *Red Knight*, creating an almost one-hundred-eighty-degree line between themselves and Le Pen's ships.

Harker paced the deck, waiting for the Spanish sails to dip below the horizon—his inflection point to reverse course and trail them. That moment was agonizingly slow to arrive, as though time itself had suddenly paused.

Eventually, the white specs turned liquid, melding into the horizon. "Come about," Harker shouted harshly. The crew hastily rearranged sails. The helmsman spun the tiller, heeling *Death's Head* into a hard turn. Harker was pleased with the ship's maneuverability and the work of his crew. The men had clearly been whipped into shape—literally. He and De Graaf were both increasingly liberal in their use of the leather. Harker called out new adjustments to the helmsman, to maneuver into a chase position.

Early on, Le Pen had been signaled that whichever two ships the Spanish chased should alter course to starboard after losing sight of the other two. That would yield a shorter path for the trailing ships to close the gap on the hunters. Harker observed that Le Pen had done exactly that. His task now was to close within firing range of the Spanish before their assault on Le Pen began. But if it turned out the Spaniards were making a meal of Le Pen, Harker would leave the Frenchman to his fate; he had no desire to be Spanish dessert.

The two warships chasing Le Pen had been sent to the Main by

Viceroy Valdez upon learning an English fleet might be headed there. The flagship captain felt these four unflagged ships could well be the fleet they were searching for. He had no idea he was actually pursuing seasoned pirates. His full attention was now focused on Le Pen's ships, leaving his own two vulnerable to attack from behind.

Harker's smaller ships were faster and more maneuverable than the oversized warships. Having sailed with Drake, he knew how to take full advantage of his ship's abilities, the weather gauge, and the angles of the chase. "We are closing with good pace," he said to Master's Mate Stevens. "Spanish blood will flow."

With his sails fully sheeted, Le Pen spent much of the time with chains trailing in the water along his ships' sides, to carefully slow his progress without being obvious. His full sails would convince the Spanish he was at maximum speed, even though he wasn't. It was important he provide Harker with sufficient time to catch up, while still maintaining a reasonable gap between himself and the Spanish hunters. Hopefully, Harker would arrive before the Spaniards were raining fire on him.

"Friendly sails," Le Pen's spotter shouted excitedly.

"Welcome news," shouted Le Pen. It was now almost an hour since they'd lost sight of Harker's two ships. The French crews began hauling in their chains slowly, increasing their two ships' speed to give Harker more time, but not so much that the Spanish would give up the chase.

Death's Head and *Red Knight* were closing fast. The Spanish still hadn't spotted them since they were forward-focused, narrowing the gap with their prey. At Le Pen's command, the men on both of his ships pulled up all but their final chain on the larboard side. He ordered the sails adjusted and had both ships feign briefly to starboard before pulling the switch. The drag of the remaining chain enabled them to turn sharply to larboard. The sails flapped and then quickly refilled as their lines were pulled taut. The ships groaned heavily at the sudden shift, heeling to the turn and shearing the water as they emerged quickly into broadside position. It would enable Le Pen to engage with multiple cannons. Within moments, all peripheral sails were fully furled, slowing his ships.

Watching Le Pen's surprising maneuver, the Spanish realized they were closing too fast. In their head-on position, the only available weapons were their bow chasers. They would quickly be within range and under-gunned. The captain ordered sails altered to slow their progress and begin turning broadside.

Harker was now surging from behind, thrilled with Le Pen's remarkable seamanship. Between them, they would serve as opposing jaws of a hungry shark.

Le Pen opened fire, nailing down the range of the warships before they could complete their broadside turn. The shots were close but failed to strike either pursuer.

"Sacre bleu," swore Le Pen. "Recharger, immédiatement!" The cannons were quickly rolled back into position and reloaded but with less speed than the impatient Le Pen demanded. "Une malédiction sur vos mères!" he cursed at his gunners.

Nearing completion of their turn, the Spanish warships flung open their gunports. Their cannons were rolled fully through and secured. But moments before gaining broadside position, Le Pen's mighty guns breathed fire once again, followed by reverberating booms. The Spanish flagship was struck this time. Cannonballs shattered the sides, tore through sails and clipped the mainmast, sending wooden shards showering onto the main deck. Impaled sailors screamed in agony.

Spanish gunners were set to return fire, hoping to find the proper range with their initial volley. "Fuego a discreción!" came the call. The cannons roared and recoiled, belching smoke and fire but mostly missing their targets on the short side. With warship precision, the iron monsters were quickly reloaded, returned and locked into firing position.

Harker's undetected ships, now close behind, suddenly opened fire, scorching the side of the Spanish flagship near its stern. One lucky shot opened a gaping hole below the waterline. The Spanish captain, recognizing his ship might well flounder, sensed defeat was imminent. He signaled his second ship to retreat in haste. Unwilling to go down easily, he called for a second volley of cannon fire. It would be his final command. Le Pen peppered his ship with overwhelming deadly fire now that he'd perfected the range. The Spanish captain breathed his last, a ball shearing off the right half of his face.

Valdez railed at the messenger, "Maldiciones! Cómo es esto possible!" He waved his right hand furiously in the still air of his small, temporary quarters upon learning of the loss of his ship. He turned to Captain Rivera, "These naval captains are incompetent idiots."

Rivera turned to the messenger, "Are you certain it was a pirate fleet?"

"Si. Pirata."

"I can understand how English warships might have executed such an effective attack," noted Valdez. "But mere pirates?" He pounded his fist on the desk. "Utterly unacceptable."

"Surely to God these were not truly pirates," said Rivera.

"It can only be the Queen's trickery," replied Valdez. "The English are *all* pirates, whether they fly the Queen's flag or not." He turned and growled at the messenger, "Assemble the officers." The messenger left willingly.

Rivera rose to pour more port into Valdez' silver cup. "We shall need to save face with the viceroys on the Main, and in the islands."

"Indeed." Valdez reached for his cup. "Thank you."

Rivera poured port into his own cup while Valdez drank. "I suppose we could have sent more than two ships to each site."

"Perhaps. But for now, we need to find and strike these English pirates. It will send the Viceroys a strong message."

"How many ships can we spare?" asked Rivera.

"Make it six. That will leave us two."

"It will also leave us vulnerable to an assault on Inagua."

"The chances of that are small. It is more important that we convince the viceroys we can strongly defend the area."

———

William Tovery entered Garret's musty tent on the smaller of the Inagua islands. Garret rose, "Welcome back. I am most anxious to hear your news."

Under her orders, William's scouting party scouted the layout of Viceroy Valdez' installation on the big island. They approached overland from the north and remained in the hills for three days. Some monitored activities in the village while others quietly carved rough pathways from near the edge of the village to a desirable exit point From the bigger island.

"I must say, I was a little surprised," offered William. "The Viceroy has virtually emptied his harbor of warships. Perhaps Thomas' discussions at court have yielded an even better diversion than we hoped."

"Excellent. How many vessels remain?"

"Two warships—twenty-four and thirty-two guns—with little visible activity on deck. There are assorted smaller vessels; mostly supply ships from what I can tell."

"And the village itself?"

"It is busy with construction. A walled foundation is being built, though no cannonry is yet installed. They are clearly not expecting a frontal assault in the near future."

"Tell me about their military presence."

"We counted five long buildings under construction, likely to house soldiers and crew. I estimate they will ultimately accommodate several hundred men. At present, there cannot be more than fifty. Few were dressed as soldiers. We saw no guards stationed on the perimeter."

"And the prisoners? Were you able to locate them?"

"One small wooden structure has two guards posted outside at all times. I suspect McBride and Halim are being held there."

"And what of McBride's crew?"

"I am afraid there is no sign of them."

"Unfortunate. We might have used their support." Garret

paused. "And Valdez?"

"He has temporary quarters, with a single soldier posted outside. A more formidable structure is being built, which I suspect will serve as his headquarters."

"Excellent. Thank you, William." Garret's mind raced. "I suppose we have reasonable options, for either a land-based assault or an attack on the harbor."

"Or a combination."

"Indeed. Disabling the two warships could serve as a principal distraction to a land-based assault."

William jumped ahead, "Have you given more thought to the disposition of the Viceroy?"

Though still not entirely certain that 'neutralize the Viceroy' actually meant assassinating him, Garret suspected the Queen would have her dispatch Valdez right there in his quarters. "Tell me, William, what think you of the idea that we take Valdez alive? It might enable us to glean valuable tactical and strategic information."

"That would be a more challenging proposition."

Garret paused briefly. "It occurs to me that if we were able to take him alive, we might later ransom him back to King Philip."

"For gold?"

"Perhaps for territorial rights, here in the Southern Seas."

William scratched his hair. '*Lovely hair*,' thought Garret. "Well," he said, "if the Queen were supportive…"

"Yes. Of course." Garret understood that could prove tricky. Returning the Viceroy to Spain would definitely not be 'neutralizing' him. She changed the subject. "I imagine you have thought about our exit strategy from the village following the assault."

"I have, yes. An overland removal of McBride and Halim…and possibly Valdez…would take precious time, heightening our risk of capture by pursuing Spaniards."

"Indeed."

"Nonetheless, we prepared pathways that would facilitate such an exit and, at the same time, confuse the Spaniards."

"Evacuation from the harbor could also prove difficult," replied Garret, "considering the chaos that would be unfolding there."

"Just so."

Garret began clearing her map table. "Come, sketch out Valdez' settlement and the position of his warships in the harbor."

———

Captain Rivera entered the temporary quarters formally, as would any military officer. But Valdez would have accepted a casual entry. He considered the man a close friend. Their relationship began during their mission in the Netherlands. In time, Rivera became his primary advisor there. His intelligence and enduring loyalty were the primary reasons Valdez asked him to join him in the Inaguas. The man was older and known to speak freely, even when he might not agree with his commander. Valdez valued that greatly, believing it best to have someone unafraid to challenge his own thinking.

"Have a seat," Valdez said as he poured beer into a second cup. "How are things progressing?"

Rivera stroked his pointed gray beard, waiting for the pour to end. "I am pleased with our progress," he replied, referring to the foundation for the shore battery. He picked up the cup. "Within two weeks we shall begin installing the cannons. Military drills shall follow shortly afterward."

"Muy bueno. My compliments." Valdez placed his cup on the table between them. "I have a special assignment for you."

"As you wish."

"With our fleet and soldiers stretched thin, the time has come to call on my fellow viceroys. We need more ships and conscripts to align and strengthen our capabilities."

"I agree."

"Good. Then let us begin by approaching Viceroy Martinez in Hispaniola. The voyage is short and his resources are substantial—though he will no doubt claim otherwise. I shall provide you with a letter of introduction and a formal request."

Rivera nodded. "Perhaps while I am there, I should have Viceroy Martinez send word to the other viceroys that their donations are fundamental to our cause. It would save me further travel and time away."

Valdez shook his head, "Such a message from Viceroy Martinez is unlikely to have the desired effect. If we are to gain the support of the others, you must go in person, as my official representative. Then there can be no misunderstanding."

"I cannot disagree, yet my absence could delay completion of the shore battery."

"Then see that it does not."

Rivera nodded, sipping his beer. "It may be best that I commandeer a supply vessel for these purposes; otherwise you shall have but one warship at your disposal."

"Let it be so." Valdez rose from his chair, signaling the meeting was over. Rivera didn't bother finishing the remaining beer in his cup.

He rose immediately, saluting. "Thank you, sir. I shall leave on the morrow."

VIII

Nine men—and one woman—crouched quietly in the leafy jungle. Garret wiped beads of sweat from her forehead. She was glad the night was darkened by heavy clouds; it provided optimal cover for the assault. Nonetheless, stifling humidity and biting insects made the waiting difficult. Hopefully, the first explosion would soon initialize their assault.

Her team was positioned just beyond the guarded building where she suspected Captain McBride and Ambassador Halim were being held. Their release was her first priority. She glanced at the other guarded building, which served as the quarters of her second priority, Viceroy Valdez. Ten other raiders hid near it. Convinced Valdez held valuable information regarding Spanish military initiatives in the region, Garret had ordered he be taken alive. How long he would remain so was unclear. She turned to check on five other men spread out as a rearguard, for reinforcement.

With the prisoners freed and the Viceroy captured, Garret intended to return to the small island, to the northeast. Their winding escape route was thoughtfully carved by William's reconnaissance team. The main trail nearest the village would serve as the initial withdrawal path. She expected pursuing Spaniards would follow it. But there were two points at which William created virtually invisible exits—their entries being in an almost reverse direction, downhill from the main trail. Pursuers in a hurry would be unlikely to spot the detours. Still, a few of her quickest men would continue along the main trail, leaving evidence of their retreat to draw any pursuers' attention away from the first hidden exit. Those men would then take the second exit, two hundred yards further on. Both concealed paths led to longboats waiting at the northeast shore. Their pursuers would find only deserted shoreline at the end of the main trail, far removed from her longboats.

Garret's assault force included twenty men now on the water. Captain William Tovery and nine others rowed in one longboat, stealthily approaching one of the two warships anchored in the harbor. A black cape was draped over the length of their boat. Two men held it down, one at the bow and one at the stern. The cape had small openings to let in air and enable William to guide them. He whispered directions as the longboat neared the target ship's hull.

A second team led by Caber targeted the other warship. They would soon be scaling the side facing open water, to avoid being visible from shore.

William's boat pulled alongside the quiet ship. He scaled the side-netting barefoot. Once over the rail, he scanned the entire deck, spotting just one sailor. The man was up on the foredeck, urinating. William suspected others might still be onboard, possibly sleeping in their quarters. He signaled those still scaling the sides to maintain silence. Dagger in hand, he raced forward in a crouched position toward the pissing Spaniard.

On the other ship, Caber's entire team was already on deck, huddled closely together as they approached their target. A warship guard, his back facing them, hadn't noticed. The whispered whoosh of an axe slicing through the air sent his head and a portion of his neck spinning into the air and onto the deck, spraying blood everywhere. The man's body crumpled, spewing blood with the last pumps of a still-beating heart.

William wasn't as fortunate as Caber. The guard on the

foredeck suddenly turned toward him. In a split second, he drew his cutlass. William was leaping up the first few steps when the guard slashed at him. Attempting to alter his leap, William hit the side-rail and fell backward, losing hold of his dagger. The guard drew and threw his own dagger. William turned to avoid its strike but the blade sliced into his right side, just above the hip. Desperately trying to muffle the scream his body felt compelled to utter, he grabbed at the dagger's handle. The guard raced down the steps, his cutlass positioned for a killing slash. William closed his eyes in prayer, accepting his fate. But his would-be slayer paused. A short-pike thrown by one of William's men hit the assailant firmly in his chest. Its force sent it piercing through the man's back. He screamed in agony as blood oozed out, both in front and behind. One of the raiders fell upon him instantly, slitting his throat to silence the screams.

"Quickly," said William, cringing in pain, "set the charges." He used his right hand to apply pressure to the opening from which he'd extracted the offending dagger. Blood leaked through and over his fingers. His men secured the opening to the crew's quarters and set their charges.

On the other warship, Musa finished positioning a small barrel of gunpowder next to the mainmast. Others positioned smaller casings and slow-match fuses along the vessel.

"Let them burn," yelled Caber. The men lit the fuses and rushed to escape the imminent explosions.

William winced in pain as his men lowered him down the side of the ship. The unexpected boom of the initial explosion from the other warship drove pain through his ear canals. A sudden series of booms layered on the pain. The first warship was instantly ablaze, lighting the night sky with flailing orange jags that set the darkened clouds aglow. By the time William and his men were back in their longboat pulling hard away, the ship they'd set with explosives also erupted in ear-crushing blasts. They ducked, covering themselves from showering wood and falling embers. The force of the explosions propelled their boat away.

Valdez woke shockingly to the horrific boom of ships being torn apart. He hurriedly pulled on pants and boots, and grabbed his cutlass. Opening and rushing through the door, he saw numerous swords and pistols pointed his way. "Dios mio…"

Whatever other words he intended were muffled by a hand forcibly smothering his mouth. The assaulter placed a blade to his throat. "Your next words are your last," he whispered threateningly.

As the raiders swiftly ushered Valdez toward the escape route, his eye caught the body of his guard lying lifeless on the ground, bleeding profusely at the neck.

Half-dressed Spanish soldiers sprinted out of their buildings toward shore, their attention riveted on the flaming images in the harbor. The two guards tasked with watching McBride and Halim were also watching the brilliant flames compete to reach fire-lit clouds. Garret's cutlass went cleanly through the larger one's back, piercing his heart and exiting through his chest. Her dagger slit his neck, preventing him from making any noise. The crushing weight of his heavy, falling body almost forced the cutlass from her hand. The other guard was stabbed in the neck. He fell noiselessly to the ground.

Garret left her cutlass embedded in the big guard. She attacked the locked door to the makeshift prison with a thrusting kick. It only jarred the hinges. One of the larger raiders ran at the door, blowing it open with the full force of his weight. Black-faced raiders poured through the opening, grinning at the shock and fear on the faces of Captain McBride and Ambassador Halim.

———

The four ships in Harker's combined fleet anchored quietly in an isolated harbor on the northern side of Isla Grande, off the Panamanian coast. They were conveniently located halfway between the two Spanish treasure towns—Nombre de Dios and Porto Bello. Harker and De Graaf sat around a large but relatively flat rock, on top of which rough maps of Panama sat askew, pinned against the breeze. Le Pen approached. He sensed this might be his best opportunity to convince the other two that they should target Porto Bello. Harker nodded at Le Pen. De Graaf didn't bother acknowledging him. Le Pen chose to stand; it was a more powerful position.

"So," Harker posed to the others, "Porto Bello or Nombre de Dios?"

Le Pen responded first, "Porto Bello. The choice is obvious."

"I say Nombre de Dios," argued De Graaf. "We know it well."

"But what success did you have there?" challenged Le Pen. "Did Drake not fail at his attack on the treasure house?"

De Graaf was caught wordless. Harker jumped in. "There were reasons Drake diverted our assault. Reasons that no longer apply." His words brought a grin to De Graaf's face. "Still," continued Harker, "the Phantom has indicated the Spanish increasingly favor Porto Bello as the destination for their treasures."

"This 'Phantom' is a wise man," said Le Pen. "Porto Bello is newer, its defenses untested. Perhaps it is less prepared. The defense of Nombre de Dios is already well established."

"If we choose Nombre de Dios, we can go now," De Graaf countered. "With Porto Bello, we would first need to scout its defenses. That takes time." He glared at Le Pen. "Pirates are not a patient tribe."

"Mes hommes follow my lead no matter the timing," snarked Le Pen. He'd cast his vote for Porto Bello and wasn't about to be deterred by Harker's brash, dark-skinned second-in-command.

De Graaf rose slowly, his hand gripping his cutlass. "Do not test me, Frenchie," he growled.

"Enough," shouted Harker. "This is not a contest of wills. It is a contest of ideas. Let us be *reasoned* in determining which option serves us best." He paused. "I suggest we rest and reflect on our choice. We shall resume our discussion on the morrow."

Le Pen spat on the ground, turned, and walked away.

"Le Frenchie est stupide," De Graaf muttered.

The discussion resumed the following morning. Harker made the decision—Nombre de Dios. More than any other factor, he was persuaded by the need to preserve his valued relationship with De Graaf. Le Pen was expendable; De Graaf was not.

———

Back on the north shore of Inagua's smaller island, William lay prone in his tent. Dr. Grant finished tightly rewrapping the wound to his lower abdomen.

"Are you decent?" Garret asked from outside.

"I suppose that depends on whom you ask," William responded. "But feel free to take your chances."

Garret pulled back the tent's opening and stepped inside. Her eyes were immediately drawn to the fullness and firmness of her partner's pectoral muscles, the ripple across his abdomen, and the impressive size of his biceps. His skin glistened from the imposing heat and humidity. The sudden rise in her heart rate was unexpected. She hoped the color of her cheeks hadn't changed.

"You look sore," she said in an almost motherly way. "How are you feeling?"

"Like the dagger is still embedded, I am afraid." William attempted to sit up but winced in pain. Garret herself flinched.

"I suggest you remain prone for the next few days," counseled Dr. Grant. "It will speed your recovery."

William shook his head. "Bloody frustrating. I worry this might delay our return to England."

"Please excuse us, Dr. Grant," said Garret. The doctor nodded, gathered his supplies, and left. Garret sat on the stool he'd been using. She resisted an urge to place her hand on William's full, gleaming chest. "We need not return to England immediately." William looked at her questioningly. She continued. "For two reasons. First, I have unfinished business here, as you know."

"You mean taking revenge on Santiago del Príncipe."

"Yes. And," Garret added, "I have yet to determine the Viceroy's fate."

"I thought the Queen was clear? Disobeying her carries risk."

"Yes, yes. Her Majesty will be anxious to have us return with the Ambassador, though she will surely be shocked if we bring the Viceroy as well."

"Precisely."

"If we take him back with us, King Philip could well find England, and the Queen herself, behind this whole mission. She would be furious with me—with us—for exposing her in that manner."

"Precisely," agreed William.

"Captain McBride and Ambassador Halim are both anxious to return to England. I feel enormous pressure to accommodate their wishes."

"Indeed. So?"

Garret grinned. "Your injury offers me the perfect excuse to delay our return. It also gives me time to deal with Santiago del Príncipe, and to decide on the disposition of the Viceroy."

"I see." William smiled, though painfully. "I suppose I might find some relief in knowing I am not the sole reason for our delay."

Something in William's smile caused Garret to see him differently, for the first time—less a virtual brother and more a handsome young man. The entire time they served together as midshipmen, during which she presented herself as male, there was no room for amorous feelings toward him. Her natural default was to embrace William simply as a friend. Their friendship grew so deeply through the years that he seemed a virtual brother. But now, in this moment, she felt a transition back to one of friendship. A different kind of friendship, however. It was all rather confusing. Once again, she resisted the temptation to touch him. She rose from the stool. "These matters are confidential, of course. Just between us."

"Most certainly," he nodded. "Thank you for checking on me."

Garret took in one quick last look at this beautiful man and then left, feeling flushed.

———

Valdez sat alone in his tent, grateful it was large enough for him to stand and move around in. It was small comfort, however. He'd been humiliated—a Viceroy and former Maestre de Campo captured so easily and now held prisoner. He fought hard within himself to douse the fire of shame threatening to consume him. How could he possibly justify this to King Philip…assuming he might ever see him again? Had one of his own captains allowed this to happen to himself, Valdez would have immediately withdrawn the man's commission and forever held him in disregard. For the first time in his life, he felt humbled, and furious with himself. Nonetheless, he marveled at the degree of planning and execution with which the assault was carried out. The mastermind of it all was to be admired—militarily, and begrudgingly.

His thoughts were distracted by the lightly muffled voices of the guards outside. Musa and Caber nodded as Garret approached. "Good day, Cap'n," they said, not nearly in unison.

"Good day, gentlemen." She nodded toward the tent. "How is he?"

"A mite unhappy, I imagine," Caber jested. Musa laughed.

"I shall see him now."

Garret entered wearing a form-fitted, naval-like uniform. She'd decided long ago not to hide her female assets but instead to have men observe them. It led to one of two things—either they underestimated her, which inevitably worked in her favor, or they held her in higher esteem for having achieved all she had, given the obstacles she faced in being female.

Valdez was shocked. The mastermind who bested him was a woman, for God's sake! It only deepened his humility.

"Good Day, Viceroy. I am Captain Connachan. 'Tis an honor to meet you." She extended her hand.

Valdez was struck by how this woman moved with a rare combination of swagger and poise. She displayed an air of confidence with which he was so familiar—that of an officer. Though she bore a serious look, he found her face pleasant. He stood quietly for a moment, observing and breathing her in before returning her greeting.

"A pleasure to make your acquaintance, Captain." He bowed slightly and reached for her hand, to kiss the back of it as he would for any woman. But it wasn't extended that way. Instead, it was extended as a man would present his when expecting it to be shaken. His mind searched for the correct response. He grabbed her hand firmly, though comfortably, and shook it. Though not as rugged as his own battle-worn hand, Valdez noticed it was not that of a delicate, elite woman.

"Have my men treated you well?" Garret asked.

"They have indeed. They are clearly well-led." Valdez intended it as a compliment, hoping to avoid what could easily become an unhelpful relationship.

"I am curious—how does a former Maestre de Campo become Viceroy of an inconsequential island that produces nothing but a few hogshead of salt?" Garret's opening was carefully planned. Having already been briefed by the Queen on why he was assigned to the Inaguas, she sought to hear what the man himself would say, to judge his truthfulness.

"Shall we sit?" he replied, wishing to set the framework for a more casual conversation. He motioned to a small stool.

"Thank you, I shall stand."

"As you wish. A cup of water, perhaps?"

"Please, Viceroy, you are most thoughtful. But this is not a courtesy visit. I am here to interrogate you, as I am sure you understand."

He smiled, recognizing she saw right through his attempts to avoid her question. Still, he parried, "Tell me, how is it that a woman becomes captain of a small fleet and, clearly, an instrument of her Queen?"

Though she made direct eye contact, and offered a slight smile, Valdez could tell she was uninclined to respond. "I see," he nodded. "You wish an answer to your question before answering mine. Well played, Captain." He paused. She waited.

"You must understand; I am a mere servant of my King. He chose to post me in the Inaguas. Perhaps he was unhappy with my performance in the Netherlands."

Garret raised her left eyebrow and smirked with her lips closed. She said nothing.

"I see now why you have become a captain. You are a chess player." Valdez turned and walked to a small table, picking up a cup of water. He took a sip. "Let us be candid."

"By all means."

"We are both instruments of royalty. I am charged with protecting the interests of my King. And you are here to further the interests of your Queen. We can both be proud to have such confidence extended to us."

"Precisely what interests are you protecting?"

"Our peaceful settlements in the Southern Seas." He smiled, hoping it might soften her demeanor.

"And…?" she pressed.

'*Hmmm. No luck,*' he thought. "And the movement of our trading goods in the region."

"And how are you carrying out this mission of protection?"

"I am clearly not carrying out any mission at the moment," he laughed. It drew a smile from Garret. '*Ahhh,*' he thought, '*let the flirtation begin.*'

"Tell me, Viceroy—how does the protection you claim to provide result in the capture of an English vessel transporting the Indonesian Ambassador?"

Valdez recognized this chess player had just placed him in check. "An obvious error on my part, Captain." He now sensed this woman was as smart as any man he knew. And she had a strength of character he wished he could find in his own captains.

Garret took a deep breath. "Do you consider yourself a man of honor?"

"I do indeed."

"And would you agree it is honorable to tell the truth at all times?"

"To *tell* the truth, yes. Yet, in some circumstances, one might choose to *bend* the truth a little; to avoid an uncomfortable situation."

"Are you bending the truth now because you find this particular situation uncomfortable?"

Her words created an opening Valdez liked. "Most definitely not. I find your presence pleasantly comforting."

"Please, answer my question honorably. Are you bending the

truth?"

Valdez understood the dance was over. "I have broad license from King Philip in the matter of protecting the crown."

"Thank you for that." Garret changed direction. "Might I assume the Queen now has your sincere apology for taking action against Captain McBride's ship?"

Valdez sensed her question presented a body of deep water, with no bridge or boat to cross it—all while wearing metal armor. "Captain, please. I am a simple servant of the King."

"A servant, yes. Simple, no."

"May I take that as a compliment?"

"Take it as you may."

Valdez felt their discourse was becoming too confrontational. That needed to change. He knew the only path to furthering his interests was to forge a relationship with this challenging young woman. He chose to flatter her, circuitously, "So, Captain, you have not answered *my* question: How is it that you became a captain—and a hand-picked instrument of the Queen?"

"I had the great privilege of sailing with 'El Draque', as you Spaniards call him. Initially as a midshipman. I suppose he liked something he saw in me." A wry smile emerged on the Viceroy's face. Garret clarified, "At the time, he was unaware I was a woman. I imagine what he saw in me was the promise of a future leader."

"So you hid your treasures then?" Valdez teased.

"It was my grandfather's design. A rather long story, I am afraid."

Valdez reacted to the slight reddening in Garret's cheeks. "My apologies, Captain. I did not mean to imply…"

"Yes, of course," she nodded.

"So, you met the Queen through 'El Draque' then?"

"Yes. I had occasion to visit with her. She is a charming host."

"I have no doubt of that. The King is a fine man as well, though I imagine you picture him as an evil warlord—as I do her."

They both laughed. The ice between them fractured a little. The thread of commonality had opened the seam.

"Thank you for your time, Viceroy. We shall chat again, soon." Garret turned to leave.

"May I ask what your plans are for me, Captain?"

Garret stopped and turned back briefly. "They are evolving."

As she left, Garret reflected on the encounter. The Viceroy was well aware that his capture wasn't mere coincidence but rather a mission only the Queen herself could have set in motion. She grasped something else too—this was an intelligent, articulate man who could engage in wordplay as though it were just another form of battlefield conflict; and she loved a challenging discourse. Finally, she was confident she made her case—she was in charge and he would need to be truthful with her; she was not to be toyed with.

IX

The *Oportunidad* presented itself in wondrous fashion, its Spanish flag flapping hard in the stiff wind against which the three-masted ship fought forward. A two-masted consort vessel sailed alongside. They were pointed northeast against heavy seas, though the sky was broadly blue. The high clouds were swirled wisps, suggesting a south-southwest bent. The lookout in the hills on Isla Grande hailed the encampment below, waving a Spanish flag. He dropped the flag once, then raised and waved it again, indicating two ships.

De Graaf strolled to where Harker was seated on a rock near the shoreline. "Spanish vessels spotted. Two of them. Merchants. Bearing southwest. Heading northeast against the winds. Easy prey, it would seem."

Harker smiled. He lived for the hunt. And his crew could use the action. "Inform Le Pen. Ready all four ships. With haste."

"Aye, sir."

The unsuspecting prey were consumed with holding ground against an aggressively stubborn wind. Their crews hurriedly furled the largest of the sails. The spotter atop the mainmast was busy judging the direction implied by the streaming of the clouds as the ship frequently angled its course. By the time he noticed the oncoming fleet, it was closing rapidly, the wind at its back. The crimson flag on the lead ship sent a shiver along his spine. He'd heard that a dreaded pirate flew a red flag as a warning—submit or shed blood. This had to be a pirate armada. Four ships. The wind being too strong against him for his voice to carry, he thought it best to head to the deck below. The ship jerked suddenly in the gyrating water, causing him to slip. His forehead banged hard on a brace.

The spotter lay on the wooden floor of the fighting top, head throbbing, diamonds of light floating in his vision as he attempted to clear his eyes. He wasn't certain whether he'd actually blacked out and, if so, for how long. Rising to his knees, his head still clouded, he looked toward the oncoming fleet, shocked by the predators' closeness.

Some on *Oportunidad's* deck spotted the threatening ships closing before any word from the spotter. "Dios mío," exclaimed the captain. He screamed out orders, "Ready all cannons. Prepare to broadside. Alert the consort." A sudden terror inside raised involuntary dimples on his arms.

The initial shots boomed from *Death's Head's* bow chasers. They missed in the wind but one of the shots from *Red Knight* managed to hit the bowsprit of the Spanish flagship squarely, shattering it to oblivion.

The Spanish captain counted four vessels maneuvering into position with the wind at their backs. Two trimmed their sales, turning broadside, while the other two were moving into a flanking direction. His own crew scrambled. With their mainsails furled, his two ships were challenged to maneuver into a broadside position that would enable them to return fire.

Facing the ultimate decision—fight or surrender—the captain agonized over how his owner might ultimately judge his actions. But from his vulnerable position, he understood there was little choice.

Withholding fire might avoid raising the ire of the pirates who were destined to overwhelm him. Best to let them have the ships and spare his men.

"Izar la bandera blanca [hoist the white flag]," he shouted.

A shot unexpectedly rang out from his consort ship's bow chaser. He was appalled; that wouldn't play well with the pirates. Before his white flag could be fully raised, another volley of cannon shots assaulted his ship, one crashing its deck, another smashing into the mainmast. Other shots splashed harmlessly into the sea.

His consort signaled they'd been hit below the waterline. They were in danger of sinking. With *Oportunidad's* white flag nearing the top of the mizzenmast, the two flanking pirate ships came within lethal range. Boarding was imminent.

The six ships bobbed awkwardly in wind-churned waters. The Spanish ships were in the middle of the cluster. The consort vessel was floundering. Its crowded crewmen cowered in their longboats.

Harker, De Graaf and Le Pen boarded the flagship separately. Once gathered, they approached *Oportunidad's* commander, now surrounded by several pirates, many with battle-painted faces. The captain offered up his cutlass, hilt-first.

Le Pen was furious about his flagship being hit by the consort vessel's shot. He wanted blood. He drew his sword, swinging it upwards and knocking the surrendered cutlass out of the captain's hands. It ascended into the air, the bright sun glancing off its polished steel blade as it spun. Several men scrambled to avoid the weapon as it spiraled down, driven by the wind. Its point bounced off the deck, sending it sideways. One sailor was cut in the leg.

Le Pen stood nose-to-nose with the captain. Sweat ran down the frightened man's forehead. "Sacre bleu…qui a commandé ce coup?" Spittle flew with Le Pen's words, pitting the captain's face. Harker laughed as the Spaniard turned his head away from the unwelcome deluge.

"Un erreur, monsieur. Pas de mon bateau," the Spanish captain stuttered in French, hoping to appease Le Pen. He wiped his face. Le Pen didn't respond with words. He thrust his cutlass through the captain's left breast, turning and withdrawing it as the man collapsed to his knees and fell sideways onto the deck. His crewmen winced and gasped.

Harker looked around for the Spaniard next in the line of command. "Quien esta al mando ahora?" he shouted

One man was nudged forward by others—a small man, well dressed and clearly not a sailor. "I am the ship's owner," he said, in good English.

"You may have been," interjected De Graaf. "You are not now." The owner maintained an air of haughtiness De Graaf didn't like. "Are you not afraid?"

"I am not." His voice was arrogant.

De Graaf drew his dagger, inserting it swiftly and directly into the man's mouth. His scream was guttural as he too fell, writhing and kicking in excruciating pain, his boots wildly scuffing the hard deck.

Harker again scanned the Spanish crew. Judging by their looks, it appeared none had been particularly fond of the owner. Aside from the rushing howl of the wind and the agonized gurgling of the owner, silence prevailed. "What cargo have ye?" Harker called out, to no one in particular. The crew exchanged glances. None spoke, afraid to draw any attention. Harker decided to focus on one crewman in particular—an intelligent-looking man. He stared him down until it became clear to the man he had to speak now or face an unseemly fate.

"Please, señor, there are several items in the hold—molasses, sugar, gold coin..."

"Lead the way," Harker motioned, nodding to De Graaf to follow the man. He himself headed toward the cabins of the captain and owner, to see what information and treasures he might uncover there. The owner's incessant whimpering was unwelcomed at this point. "Someone fix that problem," Harker yelled, pointing to the squirming owner bleeding on the deck. He turned away and walked on. The whimpering stopped.

————

"This is completely unacceptable," shouted McBride. "I cannot abide staying on this Godforsaken island while you cavort in the Southern Seas for no apparent purpose. If you do not return us to England immediately, I shall report you to the Admiralty and seek appropriate charges against you."

Halim, standing next to him in the too-small tent, was shocked by McBride's harshness. He would have liked to intervene but didn't believe it was his place. Having first come to know Garret while serving as aide to former Ambassador Pantas, he felt badly for her. But he admired her diplomatic skills and was confident she would deploy them here.

"I understand your concern, Captain," replied Garret. "We are all anxious to return home. But Captain Tovery is in no condition to travel. I shall not leave without him. Nor can I sit idly by while there are other important initiatives to undertake.”

Then please, enlighten us—what initiatives of yours are more important than the Ambassador’s return?”

“I am afraid I cannot say. My mission is entirely between me and Her Majesty.”

“Might I see your letter of marque, then?”

“I am afraid you may not.”

“Then I say again,” McBride shouted, “this is completely unacceptable.”

“So be it,” Garret answered, calmly. “Good day to you then.” She turned to Halim. “May I speak with you privately, Ambassador?”

“By all means,” he replied, glancing at McBride briefly as if to apologize. The two left the tent with McBride barking profanities.

Garret and Halim walked away quickly as rain droplets began moistening their heads. The drops foreshadowed the storm brewing on the horizon, where darker clouds, heavily laden with water, rode toward them on a stiff wind.

“I am afraid I have been remiss in not properly congratulating you on your appointment to Ambassador,” opened Garret. “I have every confidence you shall accomplish much for our two countries.”

“Thank you, Captain. I am honored to have been chosen, though I wish it were not as a result of Pantas’ assassination. He was an exceptional man—a far superior Ambassador than I could ever wish to be. I miss him dearly.”

“As do I; though perhaps for different reasons.”

Halim smiled. “He loved you dearly. In all the years I knew him, he had never been happier than when you two were together.”

Garret suddenly felt the pull of Pantas' spirit. She remembered the dark, friendly eyes that initially drew her interest. But their time together already felt so distant. Though she still flipped through Pantas' personal journal on occasion, she'd done so less frequently in recent months. She was grateful to Halim for having given it to her long ago.

"Thank you, Halim. Now, I hope you understand, I have important business to take care of before we depart for England."

"Of course. We both serve our leaders. Your work here does not press upon my own personal interests."

"You are most kind." The growing wind blew traces of sand in her eyes. She turned her head and tried rubbing out the grit before continuing. "My men shall ensure you are well taken care of until I return. It may take a few weeks. If I am not back within one month, Captain Tovery should be sufficiently recovered to take you to England. He will not wait beyond that time. In which case, my fate shall then be in my own hands and those of the men who join me."

"May Allah be with you," Halim nodded.

Garret parted ways with Halim, reflecting on her conversation with McBride. Her response to his question about her initiatives was true in part. She'd artfully worded it to edit out the personal component of her mission, while still implying that the Queen had approved all of it. The missing piece Elizabeth was unaware of, and hadn't authorized, was Garret's intention to take revenge on Santiago del Príncipe. The villagers' massacre of her crewmates would forever haunt her. As the lone survivor, she felt an obligation to avenge their deaths. She would burn Santiago del Príncipe to ash.

———

As driving rain pummeled his tent, Valdez pondered his situation. Escape wasn't an option. At best, he could steal a small boat. But as a single rower, he knew he wouldn't get far before being recaptured. He deemed it best to remain a prisoner—a compliant one.

His recent meetings with Captain Connachan suggested their relationship was evolving favorably. He could build on that. Despite her youth and gender, she brought the same kind of strength and confidence to leadership as did he. Both recognized it as a skill they had in common. He also found their verbal repartee intellectually stimulating. He even sensed in her a gentle undertone of sexual attraction during their most recent visit. Gaining her friendship was critical to engineering his eventual return to Spain. He could definitely use this woman. In more ways than one.

———

Standing on *Pandora's* foredeck as it left the harbor, Garret couldn't help wondering what might unfold on the small island during her absence. William would be recovering under the diligent care of Dr. Grant. McBride would be stewing; perhaps even planting seeds of discontent among the men. Halim would be fine, probably enjoying whatever beauty and serenity the small island could offer.

As for Valdez? He was unlikely to pose a problem. There seemed little possibility he would attempt to escape. Still, she wrestled relentlessly with the question of what to do with him. Could she ethically eliminate him simply to cover any trail leading back to the Queen's involvement? Execution seemed unquestionably immoral under the current circumstances. And she was increasingly confident he could be a valuable asset in England's negotiations with Spain. Still, there was more here than she'd expected. She was developing feelings for Valdez—respect, obviously; but, admittedly, friendship as well. Or was it simply fascination? He was older, more experienced, highly intelligent, physically attractive, and delightfully engaging. Fascination or…infatuation, she wondered. She needed…no, *wanted*…more time with him.

X

It was one of Le Pen's men. Failing to properly secure the rope to his waist, he was flattened by the wind. As he slid across the deck, his shoulder hit the mast, causing his body to turn. Thrown airborne by the ship's sudden descent into a cavernous wave, the sailor spun away. His scream was terrifying but short as he dissolved into the grayness, swallowed whole by the raging sea.

Torrential rains continued slamming the pirate fleet. Howling gusts caused the ships to heel almost thirty degrees, straining the masts and shredding a sail that wasn't properly furled.

On the *Death's Head*, two men harnessed to the deck battled desperately with the tiller against crushing, sea-induced pressure on the rudder. The stays whistled in pain amid the haunting wailing of the wind.

On Le Pen's consort, the foremast cracked under surging forces. The top third of it leaned harshly, yanking hard against the rigging. The ship struggled, quickly separating from the rest of the fleet. Fortunately for Le Pen and his counterparts, only a small portion of their captured treasure was ever loaded onto the soon-to-be-lost ship.

Hours later, the storm now gone, Harker met with Le Pen and De Graaf onboard *Death's Head*. Le Pen delivered the sorry news, "One ship and near forty souls lost."

"Most unfortunate," replied Harker.

"Loss of the ship is not significant. We now have the Spanish merchant. 'Tis the loss of men that concerns me," noted Le Pen.

Harker looked to De Graaf, whom he'd assigned responsibility

103

for the captured *Oportunidad*. "Have any of the merchant's crew agreed to join our ranks?"

"Only a handful," replied De Graff. "But all of the eleven slaves they were transporting have joined us."

"I fear we no longer have sufficient forces to assault Nombre de Dios," remarked Le Pen. "An alternate plan is in order."

"There is no cause for concern," Harker replied. He wasn't at all dismayed. Yes, circumstances called for a change in plans; at least from a timing perspective. But the assault plan itself was sound. "It should not take long to augment our forces."

"How so?" tested Le Pen.

"Cimarrons," replied Harker. "The slaves who escaped their masters now make their life in Panama's jungles. They proved exceedingly helpful to Drake. I shall reengage with them."

"Can they be…" Le Pen began to challenge.

"In the meantime," interrupted De Graaf, "we have much treasure to count and distribute. And the men have earned the right to celebrate."

"Indeed," agreed Harker. "After that, they can rest while I take a small crew to meet with the Cimarrons. For now, let us make haste to Isla Grande."

Le Pen shrugged. He turned and left without saying anything.

De Graaf leaned into Harker. "Le Frenchie is not our friend."

"He remains unhappy with our choice of Nombre de Dios."

"Damn him to the seas. Were it not for need of his men I would throw him overboard myself."

"I have no like for the man either," admitted Harker.

"He dresses too finely to be a true pirate." The remark caused Harker to laugh. De Graaf continued, "One day I shall smear the man's finery with his blood."

———

With a crew of fifty men onboard *Pandora*, Garret was anxious to finally take revenge on Santiago del Príncipe. The village lay southwest of Nombre de Dios, near the mouth of the Francisco River on Panama's east coast. She intended to drown it in fire, thereby avenging her slaughtered mates. The fact that she was nearly raped during the massacre only deepened her determination to annihilate the perpetrators. She was traveling almost three hundred leagues simply to reap havoc. A knock at the door distracted her review of the map.

"Blair, Captain." He'd been asked to join her.

"Enter." She didn't bother looking up.

"Good morning, sir. Pleased to report we are making excellent time. We shall approach the mainland by the morrow." Garret looked his way and nodded. He continued, "Have you identified suitable anchorage?"

"I believe so. There is small harbor north of an extended peninsula." She pointed at it on the map. "It appears sufficiently remote to avoid notice." She dragged her finger along the coastline. "Approximately one and a half leagues by land, from there to the village. I imagine much of that passage will be through thick jungle. The crew's cutlasses shall require fresh sharpening."

"Of course. And the explosives?"

"Give each man a goodly amount of powder and fuse."

"As you wish."

While Blair was responding, there was another knock. "Enter," said Garret. She turned to Blair. "Thank you, Mr. Blair. You are free to go." Musa and Caber entered, nodding to Blair as he left.

"Morning, Cap'n," greeted Caber. "Sorry to bother you."

"No bother," replied Garret. "What can I do for you?"

"We would not be here, were it not important."

"I have no doubt."

"Musa and I have been discussing the mission."

Garret noticed Caber was shaking slightly. That was highly unusual. "And?" she asked.

"We are concerned for the women and children in the village. Killing them does not sit well." The words were uttered quickly. Caber paused abruptly.

Garret could see in his eyes the hope for agreement. She glanced at Musa. The enormous man always struck the deepest fear in his enemies; or anyone who might dare to cross him, for that matter. He was a fierce warrior, never hesitating in battle to separate a man from this world. Nor did he cringe when serving as an executioner. Most thought him a heartless behemoth. Yet here he was, head down, almost sheepishly joining Caber in support of their cause.

"You are right," Garret nodded. "Of course you are." She looked to Caber. "I suppose my focus on revenge has masked this unseemly consequence." The Scotsman breathed in deeply; she presumed to slow his pounding heart. She continued, "Honestly, it shames me that you had to bring this to my attention." She placed her hand on his broad shoulder. "Thank you. I shall revise our plan."

"Thank you, sir." Caber bowed slightly, as did Musa. They

turned and left—so quickly that Garret had to stifle a smile. '*How odd it would be for someone unfamiliar with these two behemoths to see them cower before me like this*,' she thought, '*or even to address me as sir*'. She knew that address was entirely appropriate. They were observing her rank, not her person.

She turned back to her map, though her mind wandered to a different place. She was ashamed at having missed this obvious outcome. Had she somehow become a less-caring individual than she fancied herself? She resolved to find a way for the women and children to flee the village before she obliterated it.

———

The sun beat down on the lesser Inagua Island, the still air and oppressive humidity cloaking everyone in a hot, moist blanket. It only served to worsen Captain McBride's mood. He'd had enough of sitting, doing nothing. His sole mission was to return Ambassador Halim to England and he felt compelled to do that now, rather than wait for the convenience of the brash, young—*female*—Captain Connachan. He walked with purpose to the shaded location beneath spreading palms, where the recovering Captain Tovery was sitting, reading.

William was mending well, though his bandage remained bloodied at its core. Any undue bending forced blood out through a roughly cauterized seam in his side.

"Captain Tovery, I must insist…"

"Good day to you as well, sir," William interrupted, mockingly.

"Yes, of course, good day," McBride backed up verbally, "How are you doing?"

"Rather well, thank you. Every day is an improvement. And

you?"

"I am deeply troubled. This endless waiting pains me. I find Connachan's absence unacceptable."

"*Captain* Connachan, if you please."

McBride chose to ignore the rebuke. "I must insist, respectfully, that you grant me a ship, so that I might return the Ambassador to England, per my commission." Though it was surely implied, he added, "Immediately; the Queen anxiously awaits his return."

"And you know this how?"

"Do not play with me, my good man. You know full-well the Queen desires our return."

"I am certain she does. Yet she is a woman of considered patience, as I have come to understand."

"Regardless, inaction is not the manner of the navy. Perhaps you have not learned that yet." McBride's intentionally sarcastic remark alluded to William's not having made Post. "I have been tasked to deliver the Ambassador, and I shall do that *now*."

William resented McBride's tone and remarks. Still, he remained calm. "Captain Connachan's instructions were perfectly clear—we are to await her return."

"Neither you nor Connachan outranks me. Indeed, I have been a Captain longer than the two of you combined. In Her Majesty's navy, no less; not as some mere privateer."

"I suggest you mind your words carefully, Captain."

"Understand, sir, that I do not recognize what you may believe is your authority."

"Nonetheless, these ships are not yours. They were commissioned by Captain Connachan and privately funded by her and other investors. Whatever authority you feel you might have as a naval captain does not extend to this fleet."

"Then I must exert my right as a distinguished captain of England's navy to commandeer one of these ships."

William was at a loss for words. He knew there was precedence for naval captains to commandeer private vessels. He hesitated to stand in McBride's way. If he did, the Admiralty might be upset. There could well be unfortunate consequences on the other side.

"I see by your reaction that you agree this is my right," continued McBride. "I shall take *Athena*. It is capable of sailing unaccompanied."

"That is my own ship, Captain. Have you no sense of honor?"

"It is no more yours than mine. As you yourself said, it is Connachan's ship—one she has merely asked you to command. I am now officially placing it in the service of Her Majesty."

"You cannot be serious."

"I assure you, I am. I shall have it ready to sail within two days. Ambassador Halim will accompany me." McBride turned quickly and walked away wearing a satisfied smirk.

William threw his book hard into the air, fuming at McBride's conceit and condescension—as though he were a better man merely by having made Post. After all, even the best of captains were sometimes overlooked when the Admiralty chose whom to reward with a posting to a new warship. '*Men are defined by their actions,*" he thought, *"not by their bloody titles.*'

———

The former Cimarrone guided Harker, De Graaf and six others

upstream along the rather pleasant Francisco River. Originally a slave who escaped to freedom, the man was later recaptured by his overlords. They sold him to a merchant whose ship was raided by Harker. It was then that he agreed to join the pirates, anxious to regain his freedom. He was still intimately familiar with the region surrounding Nombre de Dios.

Within the hour, they reached a turn in the river, where fellow Cimarrons commonly posted a lookout. At the guide's instruction, the men rowed ashore and secured the longboat. The guide then planted a white flag. The pirates drank water directly from the river and splashed it over their heads. They found shade and sat, waiting for contact.

It wasn't long before a Cimarrone lookout approached, long-pike in hand. Having observed them since spotting their approach in the longboat, he concluded their intent was peaceful. Harker's guide walked toward him. The two Black men spoke for a few minutes before the guide returned. "He will take you to his leader but he insists you leave your weapons here. Either that or we must depart now."

Harker was uncomfortable with the proposition. "Can we be certain his intentions are honorable?"

"It would be unwise to challenge him."

Harker considered his options. He withdrew his cutlass slowly and walked to the longboat, placing it inside. De Graaf did likewise. The two then left with the lookout. The guide remained with the rest of the crew.

Besides living as free men, the Cimarrons shared one other main objective—killing those who enslaved and treated their kind brutally. Though they'd dispatched several of them over the years, they were most proud of their success during Drake's raids. They not only slew their former masters but also helped Drake's raiders steal away their treasure. Harker was with Drake back then. The Cimarrons remembered him. Who could forget the man with the dead left eye, who fought as though he were possessed? They welcomed his invitation to once again challenge their former overlords, and rob them of their ill-gotten treasure. Still, they were concerned about a direct assault on Nombre de Dios. The town was well defended. They preferred to attack the treasure caravan. Harker needed to convince them his plan was better.

———

Several days passed before Harker and De Graaf returned to Isla Grande with news of Cimarrone support. They found Le Pen and the rest of their pirate band engaged in sport. A prisoner was tied to two trees, in a spread-eagle position. The pirates were taking turns using him as target practice, throwing daggers and pikes from fifteen yards away. They were drinking and howling at the hits and misses as the man wriggled to avoid being hit, or gushed blood and cried out in pain when he was.

As the next drunken pirate stepped up to take his turn, De Graaf shoved him aside. He drew his own dagger and turned sideways, aligning his shoulders in the direction of the heavily bleeding man. The pirates suddenly lost their voices. They watched in silence as De Graaf's eyes homed in on his target. "His neck," he shouted. A burst of cheering and laughter erupted from the inebriated horde.

The terror in the eyes of the half-dead man was matched in its intensity by the rapid increase in the twisting of his exhausted, bloodied body. Gleaming sweat coated his writhing skin.

The quickness of De Graaf's throw shocked the onlookers. The dagger sliced through the air like a pistol ball, finding the soft space between the Spaniard's clavicles in less than a heartbeat. Embedded up to its bolster, the knife forced the man's blood to spirt and bubble out the insertion. Another cheer erupted as the rowdy brigands threw up their arms in celebration. Beer from their cups showered the air. The near-dead man began choking on the blood flowing from his mouth.

Harker, ruthless though he was, walked toward the dying man in disgust. He used a double-handed thrust to crash his cutlass down and through the man's skull, deeming it best to end things quickly. It sobered the audience.

Harker turned to address the crew, "Killing a man in battle is honorable. Torturing him for pure sport is not." Though he was a pirate, Harker had no desire to do the Devil's bidding, certainly not of this kind. He walked away amid the silence. Passing by Le Pen, he nodded, "We need to talk."

De Graaf watched Harker and Le Pen walk away. Though he respected Harker, he thoroughly disagreed with the man's remarks. This was good sport, in his mind.

XI

Shadows morphed stealthily among the trees and primitive structures beneath a bright but dimming moon. Garret and her men retreated quietly, leaving small gunpowder cones leaning against the wood and palm-frond residences of Santiago del Príncipe. They settled into the nearby foliage and waited.

Thirty minutes passed. Light from the soon-to-rise sun dappled the clouds in pink and red, illuminating the village. The crow of a rooster caused sleeping residents to stir. An elderly woman exited her small lean-to, pulling on a dark, heavily worn shawl. Her eye was drawn to the large English ship in the harbor, its flag flapping in the wind atop *Pandora's* mast. Her instantaneous fear forced a shrill scream, alerting others. Shouts began echoing through the village as its residents scrambled in every direction. A few men ran toward two shore-based cannons, while most grabbed personal weapons. Women frantically pulled frightened and weeping children along a path leading inland through the jungle. As they rushed by, some detected men with blackened faces hunkered down by tiny pots of flaming oil. But their panic kept them running.

Pandora's gunports facing the shore popped open. The loud banging skimmed across the water, focusing the villagers' attention. Iron cannons rolled loudly forward at the shouted commands of *Pandora's* master-at-arms. It was all theater—a grand distraction from the direction of the coming assault.

Garret noticed the stream of escaping women and children coming to an end. Confident she could now proceed, she placed an arrow onto the knocking point of the string and against the frame of her bow. She pulled back slowly with her right arm. The arrow's tip was wrapped in thin threads of palm bark. She dipped it into the burning lamp oil, setting the bark ablaze. With precision, she aimed at the nearest powder cone. Her steady release sent the flaming arrow whistling toward it. The resulting eruption signaled her crew. They, too, readied and fired their arrows, most of which ignited other mounds of gunpowder.

The series of explosions shocked the villagers, drawing their focus away from *Pandora*. Turning toward the sounds behind them, they saw bright orange flames climb the walls of their rudimentary residences and spiral upward. Flecks of palm frond road the flames and heat high into the sky. A few villagers ran for water, to douse the fires. Others threw spears into the jungle—at invaders they could barely see. Those manning the two shore cannons fired abortively at *Pandora*.

Garret's men switched to arquebuses and pistols, methodically gunning down residents. She set her own sights on one villager in particular. His body shape reminded her of the man who tried to rape her during the massacre of her crew two years prior. She pressed lightly against the trigger of her arquebus to avoid altering its aim. The bullet struck her target in the chest, sending him sprawling onto the ground. She reloaded. '*One of them for every one of mine,*' she whispered to herself.

Cannon fire from Santiago del Príncipe echoed across the water, waking Harker. He scrambled out of his hammock and headed onto the deck.

Masters Mate Stevens, barefoot and still in linens, came

running. "What was that?" he asked, rhetorically.

"It seems to have come from the direction of Nombre de Dios," Harker answered. He wondered whether some other party was attacking the 'Treasure House of the World' as Drake often called it.

"That could well foil our plans," said Stevens.

"We were just near there. There was no sign of other ships."

Le Pen hollered across the water from his own ship, "Avez-vous entendu que [Did you hear that]?"

"Oui," Harker hollered back. "I suggest we investigate."

"Absolument," agreed Le Pen.

"Ready the ship," Harker ordered. "Alert the others to follow. With all haste."

———

Men were waiting to launch the longboat. William strolled toward them with Ambassador Halim, who would shortly be joining Captain McBride aboard the *Athena*.

"I regret that I must leave," said Halim.

"I too," replied William.

Halim withdrew a sealed note from inside his garment, handing it to him. "Please, give this to Captain Connachan upon her return."

William took the note. "Most certainly."

"Tell her I welcome the day when the three of us shall see each other again in London—with the Queen's blessing."

"I look forward to that," William smiled. "And please, if you can, send word to Admiral Drake's brother, Thomas. Tell him we are both well and have accomplished our mission, save for our return."

"I shall indeed." Halim extended his hand, which William

shook.

"To friendly seas, then," said William.

"Friendly seas," Halim nodded. He turned and stepped into the water alongside the longboat.

William looked out at *Athena*. Never before had a ship been taken from him—with or without arms. And by an Englishman, no less. He mourned its loss, well aware that Garret would also be displeased.

His thoughts turned to the Viceroy. He planned to check in on him. It was now part of his daily routine.

Within minutes, William was at Valdez' tent, opening the entry. "Good day, Viceroy. I trust you are well."

"I am, sir. Breakfast was acceptable, as always. The boredom, however, is not. Men of action and command, such as us, were not bred for…" he searched for the proper English word…"leisure."

William nodded in agreement, "We all wish to get on with our lives. And we shall as soon a Captain Connachan returns."

"Tell me, Captain, are you not enamored of this intriguing young woman?"

"We have come a long way together. I admire her greatly."

Valdez probed further, "Do you not have feelings for her—of a personal nature?"

William was taken aback, "I have not thought of her in that way. She is more like a sister to me."

"That surprises me. Do you not find her visually appealing?"

"It is more complex than you might imagine, I am afraid."

"How so?"

"When we first met, I understood she was male."

"So I am told."

"Our relationship was formed under that circumstance. By the time she and Admiral Drake chose to disclose her true gender, she was already my best friend. A *male* friend."

"I see. Well, in any case, I find her to be a most intelligent and articulate leader."

"She is indeed.

"It is unusual to see someone carry themselves with a woman's grace and poise, yet also with a man's swagger." Valdez changed course, "Would you care for a little water?"

"No. But thank you."

Valdez poured himself a cup and continued, "I can tell you that Captain Connachan's confidence and skill as a commander matches that of the very best captains I have known."

"She was well mentored by the Admiral."

"El Draque."

"Yes, Admiral Drake. He influenced both of us."

"So I gather."

The discussion paused, awkwardly.

"Is there something you wish to share with me?" asked Valdez.

William now realized his body language suggested there was something on his mind. Something important. Specifically, what was to become of the Viceroy himself? Garret still hadn't decided that. William wondered how he, himself, would handle things if the decision were his. He'd already befriended the man, and he admired him for his military success. So the thought of executing him didn't sit well. He doubted Garret would act on it, despite the Queen's obvious desire. In time, he would find out. But for now, those thoughts couldn't be shared with the Viceroy. He chose to deflect, "Let me ask you, as a gentleman and a man of honor, is it not unfortunate that war between nations pits good men against each other, for the selfish interests of their leaders."

"We are, truly, ammunition in our leaders' armories."

"Then what if our leaders' interests are less than honorable? Are we then *dis*honorable when acting in good faith to carry them forward?"

"A fair question," Valdez nodded. "Yet who are we to judge whether our leaders' interests are honorable or not? We may not grasp the full context surrounding their decisions. And if those decisions favor the nation's advancement, then one might argue they are honorable for that reason alone."

"But what if those interests are at the expense of another nation—one that views them as dishonorable?" William tested.

"As you yourself said earlier, some things are more complex than one might imagine." Valdez sipped his water. "Suppose England's interests are at the expense of another country and, for that reason alone, you feel they are dishonorable. If you then fail to carry out your actions in support of those interests, would not your Queen view that as treason?"

William's thoughts ran immediately to Garret's situation regarding the Queen's orders to execute Valdez. "She may indeed."

"Then what alternative is there?"

"I believe I would be obliged to counsel the Queen to change her thinking."

"Quite right—assuming you could gain an audience with her. Absent that, you are bound to execute your duty on her behalf."

William thought it unfortunate, and frighteningly ironic, that

Valdez had chosen to use the word 'execute'. He wondered whether the man had any idea that Garret was wrestling with *his* execution.

XII

The trek through the jungle, back to where they'd left their longboats, was a merry one for Garret's raiders. Their assault on Santiago del Príncipe was executed with precision. They decimated the village, spared the women and children, and left without major injuries. Some of the men even managed to secure valuables from the remains, though that was never part of Garret's plan.

Musa and Caber walked front-to-back along the narrow path.

"The Admiral would have been proud of the Cap'n," Musa volunteered. "Indeed," agreed Caber. "She has a fine military mind. I would never have imagined being led into battle by a woman."

"Like Joan of Arc," Musa laughed, huskily.

"Yet she not only carries the banner, she also joins us in battle. From the front!"

"She could ride into battle backward on a goat and I would still follow her." The two shared a hearty laugh at Musa's reference to the well-known image of a witch.

Their merriment was interrupted. "Sail ho, Cap'cn. Due north." There was no hesitation; everyone raced to the longboats.

It wasn't long before the raiders of Santiago del Príncipe were on the water, heading to their ship. Garret, still scanning the horizon, took in the distant sheets of white—four unflagged vessels headed their way. "No doubt they have spotted *Pandora*," she said aloud. Her ship was just now passing the far side of the peninsula, under Master's Mate Blair's lead.

"Make haste," she shouted to the men. "Lively now."

He could finally make out the flag of the ship they were approaching. "My, my," Harker said to Master's Mate Stevens, "The English have landed." He could see trails of smoke still rising from the mouth of the Francisco River. "What deed is this, I wonder?" It was now obvious that Nombre de Dios wasn't the focus of the English assault. But he was confused as to why this smoldering, nondescript village would be of any interest whatsoever.

"Shall we attack?" queried Stevens.

Harker thought for a moment. Judging from the English ship's appearance, it was either a warship or a well-outfitted privateer. Either way, was it worth an armed encounter? He wasn't certain. "Hoist the Cross," he said, deciding to approach bearing English colors.

Garret was already onboard *Pandora* when she saw the English flag appear on the lead ship of the approaching fleet. It wasn't long before *Death's Head* came alongside. Trumpets blew, welcoming Harker and Stevens aboard. Garret was shocked at how poorly dressed the two leaders were. They wore headbands, below which their long hair flowed in a disorderly manner. Their bland-colored shirts were soiled and torn, as were their pants. They both wore cutlasses on their left hip. Daggers were tucked into yellow-stained ropes holding up their breeches. As they came close, she sensed there was something familiar about one of them.

"They call me Harker." He extended his hand.

Garret shook it. She remembered him now; they'd once sailed together with Drake. But back then, his dysfunctional left eye was uncovered. He now wore a blood-red patch over it. She knew the man stirred sentiments against her when Drake first disclosed her true gender, but she was unaware he commonly referred to her as 'the witch', believing she seduced Drake in order to gain her captaincy.

Harker pointed to his partner. "This is Masters Mate Stevens."

"Welcome, Mr. Stevens." Garret turned back to Harker, "Quite the surprise to see you here."

"These waters are now my home. I find the Spanish to be generous hosts." He looked briefly to Stevens. "Though seldom welcoming," he laughed. Stevens laughed too.

Garret caught the implication; Harker was raiding Spanish ships, and maybe settlements. "Privateers?" she asked.

"The *most* private," Harker smiled wryly. Stevens grinned. "What about you, Captain? What brings you to attack a village of no consequence?"

"That, too, is private."

"Perhaps you are simply following your dear Admiral's footsteps. A veritable pirata himself."

"I am honored to follow Drake's leadership, though not his exact path."

Harker looked confused. "How so?"

"The Admiral was both officially and unofficially a member of the Queen's navy at times. I am presently charting my own fortunes."

"Then we have that in common. Perhaps you shall have an opportunity to join my fleet at some point."

Though offended by his condescending implication that she take a position subservient to him on some piratical venture, Garret remained calm. "I choose to set my own path, thank you."

"Well then, your path best not be in my way," Harker growled. "Otherwise, you may find yourself in an awkward position." As he said it, he moved closer, inserting his imposing height and size into her personal space. Musa's hand quietly, invisibly, gripped his cutlass.

Garret sought to be done with this unnerving imbecile. Still, she dared not look up at him. His towering presence, so close to her, would force her to place her head back almost as far as her neck would allow. That would display weakness on her part. She could step back, but that, too, would suggest giving into him. Or she could step to one side. None of these seemed acceptable. '*Match strength with strength*,' she thought. She stealthily drew her dagger from her belt. He was so close to her at this point that neither he nor Stevens saw it. She slid the tip of the dagger toward his crotch, feeling slight pressure against its tip. "Step back or lose it," she whispered, without raising her head in the least.

Harker stepped back. Garret surmised he didn't doubt her earnestness, recognizing the risk wasn't worth the potential cost. She withdrew the dagger quickly using sleight of hand to avoid anyone's notice. "I would offer you a cup of beer," she said, loud enough for those around her to hear, "but I am afraid we must be on our way." Though subtle, her snub was obvious.

Harker turned his head and spat on the deck. He looked down on Garret as though she were an impish child. "Like most *real* men," he said loudly, "I am not a fan of women onboard ship. They are a bad omen." He scanned the faces of Garret's crew. "Should any of you feel the same way, you are welcome to join me."

Garret sensed Musa might react poorly to the man's words. She put her hand lightly on his arm to hold him back, saying nothing. She looked at Harker, "You may take your leave now," she said, intentionally refraining from calling him Captain.

Harker again looked at Garret condescendingly. "They say a pirate's life is full, though short. I would add that a *pretender's* life is even shorter." He nodded to Stevens and turned to leave. Stevens walked backward behind him, hand on his cutlass, keeping his eye on Musa.

Garret waited until the two pirates were over the side. She suspected their paths might once again cross. If so, she would need to be prepared. "Weigh anchor, Mr. Blair. Let us make haste to Inagua."

———

Bursting into Captain Tovery's tent, the messenger gasped for air. "*Pandora*...has returned...sir." There was excitement in his voice.

"Let us go then," William said, rising and holding his wounded side. Though the bleeding had stopped days ago, he had no desire to accidentally reopen the wound. He followed the messenger out. They hastened toward shore, watching Garret's ship ease into the harbor.

The warm breeze wafted William's lengthy brown hair across his forehead. His bare feet sank comfortably in the soft sand. '*The sea has never looked so beautiful,*' he thought. The sun shimmered down on it from a late-afternoon angle. *Pandora's* gleaming white sails separated sea from sky, matching the white of the clouds streaking high above her. The English flag whipping in the wind warmed his heart. 'For England' he said aloud, to himself.

Valdez was enlivened by the commotion and talk outside his tent. '*Finally,*' he thought. '*Change has arrived.*' It would end the staleness of days that were sheer Hell for him. The only break in the numbing boredom was Captain Tovery's regular visits. He found the man to be good company. They'd developed a friendship. Still, he longed for something to do. Anything. Meaningful or not.

His thoughts turned to Captain Connachan. He was certain she would take him to England, as her prized prisoner. Even that seemed preferable to his endless days here on this island. Besides, he felt confident he would eventually be returned to Spain. Being valuable to both Queen Elizabeth and King Philip, he imagined an exchange could quickly be arranged.

Gliding ashore, the longboat offered up the gritty, sliding sound that Garret loved; it signaled change was underway. She stepped out of the boat into the shallow water, happy to be back on friendly soil, even if it wasn't English territory.

William greeted her with a wide smile, a nod, and a carefully managed handshake intended to avoid causing himself undue pain. "Good to have you back, Captain. I trust your mission was successful."

Though she understood William's need to engage her formally by title in front of the men, Garret found herself reflecting on the very casual nature of their last visit. He'd been bare-chested in his tent; unexpectedly alluring. She suppressed the thought. "The men are to be cheered. And rested."

"Indeed. Perhaps a celebration is in order?"

"I suppose," replied Garret, though she wasn't in a particularly celebratory mood after having taken so many lives. "And how are you feeling?"

"Ready to travel; both physically *and mentally*."

"Then let us waste little time in preparing our return to

England." She glanced briefly back at the harbor. "Tell me, where have you sent *Athena*?"

William shrugged, shaking his head. "There was nothing I could do."

"Damn McBride…," swore Garret, immediately realizing he'd commandeered the ship. "And damn his audacity. When did he leave?"

"Five days ago."

"With Halim?"

"Yes. The Ambassador felt obligated."

"They will arrive in England before us. McBride will surely spread his own version of events. It will not reflect well on us."

"Indeed," agreed William. "I believe we can be ready to leave within three days."

"Then make it two. There is no time to waste."

As they began walking up the beach, William asked, "Have you thought more about the fate of the Viceroy?"

"The simple solution is to execute him here and bury him on the island. It is, after all, what Her Majesty would have us do."

"Simple, yes. But not uncomplicated. I find him to be an intelligent and reasonable man—one with a keen sense of military honor and an admirable record of accomplishment. Not unlike Drake."

"That is my impression as well," Garret admitted, "though you have clearly spent more time with him. But we must not allow personal feelings to keep us from making the proper decision."

Wiliam didn't respond. They walked on in silence.

XIII

"We *cannot* proceed against Nombre de Dios," insisted Le Pen. "The Witch's raid has put the end to it." He pressed on, "Surely the village will now strengthen the defense of its storehouse in anticipation of a similar raid." Though he'd previously lost the debate to Harker and De Graaf, he sensed this was his opening to revisit attacking his preferred target. It's what brought him here to the *Death's Head*. "We must take Porto Bello instead."

"I will hear no more of this," yelled De Graaf. "Let us send a scouting party to Nombre de Dios'. Assess its readiness."

Le Pen could see from Harker's body language that he was inclined to agree with De Graaf. The Frenchman quickly volunteered an option he'd already formulated for that possibility, "Two of my men are Spaniards. From the Basque region. Their interests are more aligned with the French than with King Philip's. They can approach Nombre de Dios by boat, claiming pirates captured their fishing vessel and set them adrift. It would allow them to walk freely among the villagers and closely observe their defensive preparations."

Harker took a moment before deciding he liked the idea. "Let it be so," he replied.

Le Pen was pleased. He knew he could manipulate his men's assessment of the town's readiness, forcing Harker's hand and leading him to change their target to Porto Bello. But he didn't dare look toward De Graaf. The man was a powder keg. And not to be trusted. Not for a moment.

———

"Welcome back, Captain. Your presence is delightfully refreshing." After too many tedious days spent primarily in his tent, under guard, Viceroy Valdez was unabashedly happy to have young Connachan check in on him following her return.

"Thank you, Viceroy. You look well."

"Perhaps because I sense we shall soon leave the island. I find it quite smothering."

"I apologize for the delay. We are all anxious to move on."

"Might I be so bold as to ask again about the cause of that delay?"

"You may well ask, but it is not up for discussion."

"I see. Well, I presume all went as planned. You have returned unscathed."

"The mission was successful," Garret replied abruptly.

"Then you will celebrate with your men?"

"Perhaps celebrate is not the right word. But the men are certainly deserving of recognition."

Though anxious to learn what plans she had for him personally, Valdez wished to avoid appearing overly impatient. Best to refresh their relationship first, he thought; it might help influence his fate. "Would you care to sit?" He pointed to a small stool.

"Thank you, I shall stand."

Valdez remained standing as well. "I must tell you; I have enjoyed my conversations with Captain Tovery. He is a fine young man."

"Indeed he is."

"And fine-looking, I might add." Garret didn't respond. Valdez continued, "I understand you have known him for quite some time."

"Since our days as midshipmen with Drake."

"Ah, yes. A close friend then."

"We have been through a lot together."

"The two of you make a handsome couple," Valdez grinned and winked, implying there might be something more. He sought to understand the precise nature of their relationship.

"Our friendship is not of that stripe."

It was the response he hoped for. It left him an opening to seduce the woman—a door he immediately proceeded to walk through, "I find that surprising. You are an attractive young woman, and he is an attractive young man. Surely you must have desires beyond mere friendship. Life at sea offers few alternatives."

"We are simply friends, Viceroy," Garret insisted.

"Jorge; please."

"Jorge then," Garret nodded.

"Well," he smiled warmly, "that is welcome news for someone like me."

"How so?"

"Despite my current circumstances," he waved at his tent's stark surroundings, "I am an accomplished military leader. While that brings wealth and privilege, it also carries the disadvantage of frequently being far from home. Having a meaningful relationship with a woman is therefore rather difficult." Garret nodded her understanding but said nothing. Valdez continued, "Yet if I could find one, I would prefer it be someone such as you—intelligent and confident. And, of course, pleasing to the eye."

"You are too kind. Yet I have to wonder…are you speaking of a general longing or merely seeking to curry favor with me."

Valdez could tell from her smile that she was flattered. And her words suggested a willingness to engage. "I must be honest; I cannot deny a…certain interest."

"I see."

"I recognize I am a few years older," Valdez conceded, though he was easily ten years her senior. Garret stifled a laugh. "But I can assure you, I am a true gentleman. And robust for my age."

Garret could stifle it no more; she laughed aloud. "Robust is an interesting choice of words."

Valdez looked to the ground, "Perhaps an awkward choice, yes." He raised his head and looked at her, warmly, "Still, I am not an unattractive man." He instantly thought about the pale battle scar across his cheek. He ran his hand along it. "I suppose my scar might suggest otherwise."

"Your scar speaks to your fearlessness, Jorge. I have my own. Scars are not easily earned."

Valdez felt the fortress gates peek open. He stepped toward her cautiously, hoping she wouldn't step back. She didn't. He reached out slowly, gently touching her arm. "I should very much like to know you better. And differently." He smiled. His hand brushed softly down her arm, like a falling feather. He pulled it back as it reached her hand. "I hope one day soon we shall have that opportunity."

Her face slightly flushed, Garret cleared her throat. "I must take my leave. We have much to prepare; we shall depart in a few days."

"Might we speak again, perhaps on the morrow?"

"Possibly," she replied, turning and exiting the tent.

Valdez grinned. He was right where he wanted to be—in position to seduce this intriguing young woman. It would serve his interests well.

Garret walked toward her own tent, reflecting on the one thing she couldn't shake. Valdez had asked about her mission's success. Her purely factual response hid the burden her soul now bore. She was haunted with regrets. The assault on Santiago del Príncipe resulted in wives losing their husbands; mothers their sons; children their fathers. Families lost their homes. Her rigid focus on obtaining revenge had somehow obscured the broader downstream consequences of her actions. Those consequences were now a burden she realized she must carry for the balance of her life. She shook her head as if to fling that burden away. At least for a moment.

She mulled over the rest of her conversation with the Viceroy. She was surprised at just how forward he was. Perhaps that was to be expected. He was a military man whose very existence was almost daily in doubt—one who therefore needed to act quickly and decisively on things that mattered to him. But her surprise about his actions was actually pleasant. The gentleness of his voice was comforting. And his touch brought with it a certain warmth, not unlike the sensation she'd experienced weeks ago with a bare-chested William. She often thought about how imprudent an intimate relationship with William would be, given their dual command. But one with Viceroy Valdez would be even more complicated. She was in uncharted waters, and her navigational skills didn't extend this far. Nevertheless, there was no doubt Valdez would engage…if she let him. *'The man is nothing, if not charming,"* she thought.

The Queen's comment regarding the Viceroy immediately intervened: *"neutralize* Señor Valdez." She knew precisely what that meant, though it now seemed an impossible path to follow.

XIV

After three days in Nombre de Dios observing the town's readiness to defend itself, Le Pen's Basque spies returned to debrief him.

"Tell me," he asked, "how many warships in the harbor?"

The more articulate of the two spies responded, "Six. Two arrived recently, at the order of the new Military Viceroy appointed by King Philip—a man named Valdez."

"And the shore batteries?"

"The villagers say they have not been modified since Drake's assault."

"Not surprising," said Le Pen. "Drake attacked by land, not sea."

"In truth," the spy continued, "there is no increase at all in the military presence. The villagers complain about it. They say the soldiers are more interested in frequenting the taverns than patrolling the town."

Le Pen laughed. "Perhaps they drink to the King's health." But behind his comments, he suspected King Philip's increasing preference for Porto Bello over Nombre de Dios explained all this indifference."

"There was also much talk of the assault on Santiago del Príncipe," added the spy. "Women who fled with their children arrived in Nombre de Dios just days ahead of us. They blamed English marauders but could not explain their motivation; there was little of value in the village. The English simply burned the buildings, slew the men, and left."

Le Pen knew Connachan was behind the attack. Perhaps there

was some truth to Harker's claim that she was a witch. That might explain why there was no reason for her actions. Just pure evil.

The spy ended his report with a surprising remark, "The people in Nombre de Dios are oddly comforted by what happened in Santiago del Príncipe. They believe anyone planning to attack them would assume that the burning of the nearby village would put Nombre de Dios on high alert. That alone is likely to keep them from attacking."

Le Pen's feelings about his spies' report were mixed. Though he favored Porto Bello, their assessment suggested a ground-based assault on Nombre de Dios did have a reasonable chance of success. He decided to share the news with Harker exactly as it was, rather than color it to favor attacking Porto Bello. But he didn't want De Graaf around to lord it over him. He would wait to catch Harker alone.

They sat near the water's edge, under the shade of palm trees, looking out across the coral-blue sea.

"That is the fullness of their report," finished Le Pen.

"This is excellent news," replied Harker. "Nothing suggests we delay." He paused for a moment. "With warships in the harbor, a seaborne assault is unwise. Best we follow Drake's approach—land at night and attack from multiple flanks."

"I would agree," said Le Pen.

"Still, we must use overwhelming force. Drake's failure was at the impenetrable door of the storehouse. We shall breach it with a devastating blast of gunpowder."

Le Pen envisioned his men carrying away hordes of treasure. But then it hit him, "How can we transport the treasure without being stopped by the Spaniards? Surely we cannot carry it quickly through the jungle."

"The sea shall carry us," answered Harker.

"But how, with six warships in the harbor?"

Harker smiled wryly. "We shall take the Governor hostage."

"But how will you find him?"

"I have been to his residence before. With Drake."

"Was he there?"

"No. He fled. This time we shall target his home before he can leave."

"So, with him in our possession, his soldiers dare not attack."

"Precisely," exclaimed Harker. "We shall then commandeer the best warship in the harbor and set the rest ablaze."

Le Pen nodded, recognizing such a plan had real promise.

While the two conspirators began working through specific details of the assault plan, right down to the point of deciding which men would participate in which element of the raid, one man looked on from afar. The wind pushed back his knotted strands of hair. De Graaf watched with resentment at not being included in the conversation. It only deepened his distaste for Le Pen.

———

Water lapped warmly across her bare feet as Garret strolled along the damp, white sand. The morning sun was at her back, low in the sky, casting her shadow forward. She thought the dark image spreading out before her from her feet appeared too male, yet she saw in it her youthfulness, and the pleasing flow of her hair in the light breeze. As the water at her feet drew back to the ocean, she smiled at the birds seeming to chase it. '*This is the most wonderful region on earth*', she thought. There was a peacefulness here that served to wash away the horror of the many battles she'd participated in; the guilt she now bore over the devastation of Santiago del Príncipe; and the sadness of her personal tragedies. The sounds of the water and the birds brought serenity.

Being alone on such a treasured morning was refreshing. She'd learned from experience that leaders seldom rest. There was always some challenge to be addressed, questions to be fielded and answered, and decisions to be made—some life or death. The lives of her men depended largely on her ability to guide and protect them. So the stress of leadership was ever-present. It was only in these early morning walks that she could find the solitude to reenergize her being.

Her thoughts turned to the men in her life. First of Drake, the Admiral who mentored her and gave her authority to lead. She thought too of Pantas, her one and only love, whose memory was fading too quickly. The image of a strong, bare-chested William also crossed her mind. Again. Though she tried to suppress it, it refused to comply, constantly returning like the clear waves now caressing her feet.

And then there was Viceroy Valdez. He seemed the very essence of manhood—strong, sensitive, intelligent; a man whose presence alone filled any space he was in and commanded respect. She imagined his men looked to him with unquestioning loyalty and confidence. Her attraction to the man wasn't so much sexual as it was enchantment. Perhaps if she'd seen him bare-chested, as she had William, it might be otherwise. She understood how both he and William could captivate any woman, albeit differently.

The Viceroy's mere existence, however, posed an irrepressible dilemma—to execute him or not. She tried burying the thought, purposely stooping to pick up a smooth, flat, sand-colored stone. She threw it with a sharp, underhanded fling. It skipped along the relatively calm water, consuming her consciousness for a brief moment. But her mind quickly returned to Valdez. The Queen's desire to end him seemed the simplest way to deal with the situation. Yet it would only add to the black veins already scarring her soul.

She leaned toward taking the Viceroy to England. It might enable her to convince the Queen he could be a bargaining chip. She fought to suppress the sense that her emerging feelings for Valdez were pushing her in that direction.

Garret stopped, pressing her feet comfortably into the wet sand. The water flowed over them, warmly. *'The world truly is a serene place,'* she thought…*'absent the impact of man's presence.'*

She glanced toward the trees and walked on.

"And I shall be enjoying the company of both a buxom English lass and unwatered English beer!" replied Caber. Musa laughed. The two were deeply immersed in visions of their pending return to England.

Valdez, the prisoner they were barely paying attention to, stood in the warm sand beyond the lapping water, readying himself for a morning swim. He pulled his white cotton blouse off over his head and threw it aside. His thoughts turned to Captain Connachan. Delightful thoughts—of her auburn hair falling on his face as she lay on him, naked, his hands grabbing and pressing her buttocks firmly. He could almost feel the slow rhythm of their bodies and the penetration he knew would arch her back.

"Good morning, Viceroy," interrupted Garret from behind.

Valdez jerked at the sound. As he turned to face her, he sought to avoid displaying any guilt—crossing his arms, hand on wrist, to casually cover the giveaway. "Good morning, Captain. A pleasure to see you." He bowed slightly, hoping the bulge at his crotch might gently collapse. Apparently, it didn't go unnoticed by Musa, who sneered in disgust.

"We shall be leaving on the morrow, at break of dawn," said Garret. "I suppose you may be curious about your fate."

"So I am."

"I have given it much thought."

"Pleasant thoughts, I hope." Valdez smiled, raising his left eyebrow.

Garret appeared uninclined to follow his lead, perhaps due to the nearness of Caber and Musa. "You shall accompany us to England," she replied. "You may reside in the master's mate's quarters, befitting an officer of your standing. Under guard, of course."

"Thank you, Captain. You are most generous."

"Master's Mate Blair is the generous one," Garret replied.

Valdez stood there bare-chested, his battle scars obvious—a picturesque specimen of a modern military man. "Am I permitted to enjoy one last swim before we depart?"

"I see no reason why not." Garret looked to Caber. He nodded his concurrence.

Valdez began untying the rope holding up his breeches. "Thank you. I enjoy a refreshing morning swim."

Garret quickly averted her gaze and turned to leave.

"Will you not join me?" Valdez smiled, feeling the return of the bulge at his crotch.

"Most certainly not," she replied as she walked away. Valdez dropped his breeches and strolled toward the sea.

Garret walked several steps before hearing Valdez enter the water. She glanced back, suspecting that was precisely what he wished her to do. He was walking in slowly, the water now up to his knees. His skin appeared mostly pale in the bright sun, something she hadn't really anticipated since his face was so well tanned. His broad, muscular shoulders contrasted agreeably with his narrow waist. His firm buttocks appeared even whiter than the rest of him. She grinned. Turning away and walking on, she smiled at the sight. She felt her body temperature rise. '*There is, after all, some benefit to man's presence in the world,*' she thought.

XV

An enormous explosion drove bright orange flames soaring into the night sky, waking the residents and soldiers in Nombre de Dios and the guards stationed on the warships anchored in the harbor. It ripped the massive door off its hinges, thrusting it back into the storehouse in shattered pieces shrouded in smoke and flames. A ring of Le Pen's pirates looked on from protected positions. Within moments, they and a horde of Cimarrons began streaming inside the treasure-house, to gather whatever they could carry.

A dozen Spanish soldiers converged on the site, brandishing pikes and cutlasses. None had time to don armor. A few others set arquebuses and aimed pistols at the marauders, but their captain threw his arms in the air, palms forward, screaming to hold fire.

The town's governor stood in front of a group of pirates, waving both arms crosswise and echoing the captain's shouts to avoid shooting. His wife and daughter stood near him, restrained by a pirate wearing a red eye patch. Their bodies trembled; tears streaked down their cheeks.

"Lower your weapons or they die!" Harker yelled in broken Spanish. The soldiers hesitated. Their captain bent to one knee, placing his cutlass on the ground before him.

From their positions at the taffrails aboard the warships, Spanish guards looked on at the scene unfolding at the treasure-house. They were completely unaware that De Graaf and his men had scaled the far side of one of the ships. The pirates hopped barefoot over the rail, racing to the guards with cutlasses and pikes at the ready. De Graaf struck first, rushing the last steps and slashing his sword across the neck of the guard in the middle. There was no scream as the man crumpled to the deck. His fellow guards turned toward him but saw only their own fate. The pirates sliced at their necks and through their chests before they had time to react. It was over in a dying heartbeat.

"To the longboats," ordered De Graaf, pointing in their direction with his cutlass. Several pirates went about launching the boats and rowing them to shore. Shots were fired at them from one of the other warships, but the pirates scaling that ship quickly overwhelmed them and took control—just as their mates had on the remaining ships.

Onshore, Spanish soldiers parted, creating space for Harker and his men to haul chests of gold and silver down to the waterline. As De Graaf's longboats hit the shore, Cimarrons and pirates began loading captured treasure onto them until they could safely carry no more. The boats were rowed back to the warship De Graaf had commandeered and the treasure was loaded onto the large vessel. The process continued while the soldiers onshore remained powerless and frustrated.

When it became clear that the storehouse was largely emptied of its valuables, Le Pen signaled the pirates on the other warships. They descended to the holds, setting delayed explosives that would blow holes below the waterline. Only De Graaf's captured ship would remain afloat, to serve as the escape vessel.

The governor, his wife, and their daughter were rowed out on separate longboats with the last of the treasure. Harker, legs set wide in the boat, stood above the governor, pointing his cutlass at the frightened man. He sought to convince the soldiers onshore that they should continue holding fire or be the cause of their leader's demise. The governor remained quiet, wondering how best to resolve the crisis for his family.

The Spanish soldiers walked to the edge of the shore, following their captain. They watched the scene unfolding before them—ships aflame and the last longboat carrying their governor to the warship commandeered by the pirates. It was then that the Cimarrons unleashed a vengeful terror for which they'd long thirsted. They charged the soldiers, felling them with pikes, cutlasses, daggers, and pistols. The carnage soon painted the watery sand blood-red.

Deafening screams from shore skimmed across the water, drawing the pirates' attention. Many smiled at the Cimarrons' actions. The hacking and slashing were so vividly brutal that two younger pirates had to look away from the pure, unleashed slaughter of the most demonic kind. The former slaves then proceeded to set buildings on fire, adding to the panic and chaos of residents fleeing the town. Orange flames soared upward while dark smoke billowed across the harbor.

Still in the longboat, Harker looked down on the Spanish governor. "You shall be returned safely, with your family." The governor nodded his appreciation. "Mind you, there may not be much left to govern." Harker's men laughed at the dry humor.

Upon reaching the commandeered warship, the pirates scaled its sides, leaving the governor and his family alone in the longboat. Harker called out his instructions. "Weigh anchor! Full sails! Lively now!" He turned and smiled at De Graaf. "I believe Admiral Drake would be impressed. Perhaps even envious."

XVI

Sustained, grueling weather tested the crews' mettle as *Pandora* and *Orion*, battled back across the Atlantic. Robust, howling winds sent pelting rain and the tops of imposing waves streaming across their decks.

Garret sat alone in her cabin reviewing navigational maps. It was near impossible to determine their actual position with the skies so heavily clouded these last few days. Neither sun nor stars would lend their guidance, and there were no land formations to offer any bearing. She prayed the weather might break soon. In the meantime, she plotted their most likely location amid the vast, gray blending of ocean and sky. Her plotted circle widened generously with each day of uncertainty. Tracing a light curve with a freshly sharpened stick of charcoal, she was interrupted by the knock at her door.

"Enter," she said, not bothering to look up.

The wind flung the door wide as Blair stepped in, drenched and dripping streams of water. He fought to close the door behind him. "Sorry to bother you, Captain. We are fighting a fierce lady out there." He paused. "My apologies…a fierce *storm*."

Garret shrugged it off. It was typical sailor-speak. "Any damage to report?"

"We have lost a few unsecured items. Nothing of significance. A couple of minor sails were torn through early on. They can be repaired. Our progress, however, is unclear."

"So it is. God willing, the storm will soon pass." She looked up, "Is there something more?"

"Viceroy Valdez has asked to speak with you."

"Concerning?"

"He did not say."

Garret looked back to her maps. "I shall attend to him shortly."

"Aye, Captain." Blair turned to leave.

"Tell me, Mr. Blair, do we still have sight of *Orion*?"

"We do, sir, from time to time. She sails well."

"Good. Thank you."

As Blair left, Garret wondered what Valdez wished to discuss. She'd purposely chosen to visit him only a few times since leaving Inagua. Each time, she told herself the visits were merely welfare checks; yet they inevitably led to a deepening of their relationship. She worried about sinking helplessly into its depths.

Garret rolled up her maps, bound them, and set them aside in a chest. All in all, she thought, the Viceroy seemed comfortable, despite having turned down her invitation to take Blair's quarters. Instead, he chose a small room—a storage closet, really— nearest the ship's bow. In preparation for heading there, she tied back her hair and grabbed her topcoat.

"Will you need a line, Cap'n?" yelled one of the crew who saw Garret emerge onto the deck.

She took in the horrid elements and the severe rocking of the ship. Everything around her seemed fluid; nothing stable. Much like life itself, she thought. "I will," she shouted back.

Linked to the mainmast by a strong rope, the crewman nonetheless struggled to reach her, bearing another rope tied at one end to the mainmast. As she secured it 'round her waist, the wind and water whipped fiercely, as if trying to prevent the making of a knot.

Fighting the dreadful conditions, Garret slipped and swore her way across the deck toward Valdez' room. She was thoroughly drenched by the time she descended the steps and began unknotting her lifeline.

"I shall see him now," she yelled to the guard, despite his being only two steps removed. He knocked on the door for her. She quickly composed herself.

"Enter," Valdez called out above the storm's howl.

The guard opened the door. She hastened inside, removing her topcoat and hanging it on a hook. "Bloody frightful weather," she exclaimed.

"So it appears," replied Valdez.

Garret shook the excess water from her hair and wiped her face, finally looking his way. Despite his bare feet, Valdez appeared warm and comfortable. The white of his blouse seemed to brighten the room. Its sleeves were rolled up near his elbows. His tan-colored pants were neatly secured by a clean white rope. The man's thick hair was tousled, as though he'd been running his hands through it. His dark eyes sparkled in the lantern's light. "You look well, Viceroy."

"Thank you, Captain. I might say the same, though I notice you are wearing your hair differently." He flashed the disarming smile Garret was now quite familiar with.

"You wished to see me?" She unconsciously brushed back a strand of wet hair that fell along the right side of her face, tucking it behind her ear.

"I always wish to see you." He moved to a small shelf and began pouring a cup of wine, only one-third full. It was a challenging task, given the ship's sway. He raised the cup. "Would you join me?"

"I suppose."

He handed her the lead cup and poured another for himself, spilling the wine along its side as the ship lurched unexpectedly. Garret moved smoothly with the motion, maintaining her balance. Still, wine flowed over her cup's edge, running down her fingers. They both laughed.

"Perhaps we should sit," Valdez offered, pointing to a short bench. Garret nodded, moving toward it and sitting. He sat beside her, his left leg brushing up against her right.

"The reason I asked to see you is that I find myself in a rather difficult place," he opened. "I never imagined being held captive on a ship." He sipped his wine before continuing, "Especially at the hands of such a beautiful young woman." He grinned.

"Life bears many surprises."

"Which brings me to my dilemma. I am a man of action. The possibility of spending the remainder of my life in prison is unimaginable. I should prefer to die in battle, rather than succumb to the misery of constant confinement. Were you in my place, I believe you might feel the same."

"Honestly, the thought has never crossed my mind. But I suppose under similar circumstances I might feel the same way…if there were no possibility of escape."

"Precisely. Which leads me to what I see as two possible outcomes." He sipped more wine. Garret waited. "The first is that of being executed before a hostile crowd—obviously not something anyone would wish for. Still, it would be preferable to the second possibility."

"Which is?"

"Spending my remaining days in the dreaded Tower of London. At least execution would bring my misery to a quick end."

Garret sensed that either outcome would be a waste of a good man. She sipped her wine. The ship's movement sent it flowing above her upper lip. She wiped it quickly with the back of her hand, in a most unladylike fashion. "Is there no other outcome you might see?"

Valdez breathed in deeply. "There is something you might do for me."

"You need only ask."

"First," Valdez said, "I must share with you something I have kept concealed." He sipped his wine and then held the cup in both hands. "I am not simply my King's servant. Some would say I am his closest friend."

"I see. And what do *you* say?"

"It matters not what I believe. Nonetheless, I may well be a valuable bargaining chip for your Queen."

"That same thought has crossed my mind," she responded, pleased to know they were thinking along similar lines.

"I am relieved to hear that. I would need your help, of course."

"So it would seem."

"I imagine that, having sailed with El Draque, you have some degree of influence with your Queen."

Garret immediately wondered whether he also imagined it was Elizabeth who ordered his kidnapping. Or worse, his elimination. "Her Majesty takes some pride in my being a woman who commands men." As soon as she said it, she worried that her good standing might well evaporate upon returning to England without having executed the Viceroy.

The ship rocked violently. Both reached out to steady themselves. Wine spilled to the floor.

"I suppose having wine was not the best idea," she said once the swaying calmed.

"Tell me, Garret…" Valdez interrupted himself midsentence, "I presume by now I might address you as Garret?"

"Certainly not in front of my men."

"Of course. Of course. But surely in private…"

The Viceroy previously gave her permission to call him Jorge. And perhaps their growing relationship earned him a reciprocal right. Still, Garret worried about a potential inadvertent slip in front of the men. "Let me think on that."

Valdez proceeded anyway. "Tell me, Garret," he repeated, though more softly, "do you find joy in commanding men to do your bidding?"

"I enjoy command," she replied, sensing herself blushing. She took another sip of what wine was left, to hide it.

"As do I," he agreed. He looked at her directly. "Do you not find it difficult for people like us to share certain thoughts freely with others—thoughts of a more…personal…nature?"

"I suppose."

"I myself find it easier to be open with someone of comparable standing; someone inclined to empathize because their experience is similar."

Garret immediately recalled the day she disclosed her true gender to Pantas. How difficult that had been; yet how necessary to further their relationship. She wondered whether, at that time, they were of 'comparable standing', as Valdez put it. She thought not.

Valdez reached across and touched the back of her hand. She didn't pull it away. '*Must be the wine*', she thought.

He gripped her hand lightly, now peering searchingly into her eyes. "I feel compelled to open up to you." He paused. Her hand remained in his grasp. "Frankly, I have never been more smitten. Your presence warms my soul…such that I would willingly yield my command to you."

Garret, too, felt a certain warmth. How could she not? This striking, accomplished man's words were flattering. Yet what good could come of this? He was an enemy. A prisoner. Possibly even destined for execution. She couldn't allow herself to be taken by him, as she had with Pantas. It could only bring pain. She lowered her gaze to their hands, considering whether to withdraw hers. Instead, she let it linger. "I fear we are in challenging waters…Viceroy."

"Perhaps. But are we not wise enough to navigate them?"

Her pulse quickened. She brushed back the strand of wet hair that kept freeing itself from behind her ear. "Admiral Drake used to say, '*The most challenging times ask the greatest men to rise*'."

"Surely that also includes the greatest women. And, might I add, I am indeed rising." Valdez grinned.

'*Damn that smile*', she thought. '*It is thoroughly disarming.*' Her eyes descended to his lap, then quickly to the hand now caressing hers.

Valdez slowly withdrew his hand and delicately brushed her once-again-fallen strand of hair until it rested behind her ear. His fingertips then flowed smoothly to her cheek. "I have never been with a woman as beautiful as you."

Garret breathed deeply, to slow the beating of her heart and possibly deflect the Viceroy's advance. It seemed ages ago that she last shared such closeness with anyone. She could think of nothing to say.

Valdez placed his hand behind her neck, holding it there as he angled his head, drawing near. She quivered slightly as their lips pressed together. Her eyes closed by instinct. She savored the same physical sensation she once shared with Pantas. This man, over whom she had such power, now made her feel almost powerless. She felt his left hand grasp the other side of her neck. His kiss was warm; gentle. It lasted but a few moments yet seemed to sear itself into her memory.

Valdez withdrew slowly. She sensed he didn't wish to overplay his hand. He simply gazed into her eyes, his smile tender and adoring…'*Despite my wet hair*', she thought. Garret sipped the last of her wine while maintaining eye contact. It felt as though all the salt in all the world's timers was somehow suspended in mid-air. She put down her empty cup. "Well, that was unexpected."

"Though not unwelcome, I hope."

She blushed and took his hand. "You are a most charming man. I find myself a little outside my boundaries."

"It would be my pleasure to guide you beyond them."

Garret smiled. "I must go," she said, though not truly wanting to. She began to rise.

"Certainly," he said, also rising. "Thank you for coming. And listening. I hope you will come again, soon."

Now on her feet, Garret regained her composure, and her command. "I have no doubt another opportunity will present itself." She turned, threw on her topcoat, and left.

Valdez closed the door behind Garret, against the strong wind.

He walked to the bench and lifted the lead cup, sipping the last of his wine. '*There is still time,*' he thought. He knew if he could seduce her before reaching England, he could ensure her much-needed support. Gaining the benefit of her most private assets was simply a bonus. All for a worthy cause, of course—his life. And his freedom.

XVII

Chilling rain drizzled over the sailors scurrying *Athena's* deck as the ship arrived in Plymouth Harbor. Though happy to be home, several of the crew still resented being pressed into service by Captain McBride. His own crew had been transported to a Spanish prison somewhere in the islands, leaving him no choice but to force Garret's men into service. To a man, they would have preferred to wait for Captain Connachan's return to the small Inagua island. They hoped to sail with her again one day, assuming she ever made it back from the Southern Seas.

McBride approached Ambassador Halim on the foredeck as *Athena's* trailing anchor sought to grab hold of the harbor's bottom. Its sails were almost fully gathered and furled. "Welcome back to England, Ambassador. I must say, it has been a circuitous and rather unexpected voyage from Ternate."

"Indeed it has," laughed Halim. He looked out over the hills. "I am anxious to return to London. Will you be heading there as well?"

"Most certainly. I intend to report to the Queen post-haste and inform her of our experience. There is much to share."

"So there is." Halim steadied himself as the anchor grabbed hold, bringing *Athena* to a full stop. "What shall you tell the Queen regarding Captain Connachan's actions?"

"I shall give Her Majesty a clean account of the events on the islands. She shall decide for herself what to make of them."

"I thank Allah for Captain Connachan's assistance. Without it, we would not be here this day."

McBride also appreciated Garret's rescuing them. But he recognized the competitive threat the upstart young female presented to his own naval ambitions. "She was most helpful, yes. Yet I fear her decision not to return immediately to England could well have jeopardized the Queen's very mission. Her excursion to God knows where, and for what purpose, was not only risky but also highly disrespectful."

Halim appeared surprised at his remarks. McBride wondered whether the man might be too friendly with Connachan. It occurred to him that he would need to meet with Her Majesty alone, to avoid having his account undermined in any way. "Let us gather to disembark within half the hour, Ambassador. I shall arrange your travel to London. I am afraid we shall have to travel separately."

Halim watched McBride head back toward his quarters. He turned and scanned the harbor. Drake's Island was to his left. He wondered how the Admiral himself would have judged Garret's actions. Surely Drake would understand her need to take revenge on Santiago del Príncipe. Hadn't the Admiral himself repeatedly sought revenge against King Philip in his many military engagements? Nor did Drake withdraw from risky endeavors. On the contrary, the greater the risk, the more engaged he was known to be. His reputation was one of fighting with complete confidence that he and his men would ultimately succeed—as though he had some innate ability to compel the future to deliver his vision. Though Garret clearly drew on Drake's teachings, she was to be admired for her own accomplishments.

Captain McBride's comments left him concerned. He sensed a need to balance the Captain's account with his own observations. He would do his best to ensure the Queen would see things Garret's way…assuming he could gain an appropriate audience with her.

———

The tavern in Santo Pedro was full. The tables were surrounded by extra, well-worn chairs the owner kept in a pile behind the building. He'd brought them in to accommodate the many customers now assembled. Even still, several were standing. Cups of beer flowed freely. The news flowing ashore almost daily in this tiny village seemed to compel everyone to have a say on it. First came word regarding the capture of a Spanish Viceroy, though few knew anything about the settlement he governed. Closely on the heels of that, there was news of the burning of Santiago del Príncipe; and later, a pirate assault on Nombre de Dios. Speculation ran rife that pirates were feeling free to raid all Spanish settlements, potentially even Santo Pedro. Some said the pirates were Black slaves who managed to escape their masters. Others claimed they were English bastards, or perhaps French. Maybe even Dutch. To the tavern owner—a portly, bald-headed old man—it mattered little. What mattered most was that the debate over these questions demanded unprecedented consumption of his watered-down beer.

Felipe de Heredia y Ortega, the wealthy investor from Cartageña, left his small boat and headed toward the village center. As always, he and his two guards were dressed as fishermen, though they smelled otherwise. Some villagers sensed they looked familiar but didn't give them a second thought; it wasn't unusual for seasonal fishermen and buyers to pass through and do a little business.

The three Cartageñians approached the tavern without speaking. Ortega was surprised at the busyness of this ordinarily quiet place where he could meet without undue notice. He now worried this might not be the best time to meet with Harker, who knew him only as Fantasma—the Phantom, in English.

There being insufficient room inside the tavern, several men stood, and others sat, outside. Their clothes were soiled and torn. It was a poor village. Not even the tavern owner dressed well. While his guards waited outside, Ortega pushed his way through the entrance. The inside was dark and noisy. What little light there was filtered in through a tiny window that didn't face the sun. Men stood almost shoulder-to-shoulder. All the chairs were taken. Ortega scanned faces, hoping to spot Harker. The pirate was tall and might be easy to spot if he were standing. He wasn't.

Harker sat facing the entryway. He preferred to see who was coming and going—friend or foe. Spotting the Phantom, he rose and waved his arm. The man squeezed through the inebriated crowd. Harker pointed his pistol at a local seated near him and De Graaf, implying he should vacate his chair. The Phantom took the seat. No handshakes were exchanged; greetings were simply nodded.

"Perhaps we should talk outside," said the Cartageñian.

Harker shook his head, preferring the tavern's darkness. He pushed the departed man's cup of leftover beer toward the Phantom. It was a small gift; another cup might be hard to come by under the circumstances.

The Phantom glanced at the cup but didn't pick it up. His eyes turned to Harker, "I understand our lady [*Nombre de Dios*] has been violated." He favored speaking in a kind of code.

Harker and De Graaf both grinned. The former responded, "She is no longer a virgin. She has shared her treasures. And lost a stone or two in the act." He knew the Phantom was particularly fond of glittering stones.

"Excellent, though it often proves challenging to turn stones over."

Harker understood. Though the Phantom would keep the best of the jewels, he would convert some into coinage. "They say these stones weigh twenty-five [*implying twenty-five thousand pieces of eight*]."

"Perhaps they are wrong," replied the Phantom. "They have been scratched [*tainted by theft*]. That will no doubt reduce their weight [*value*] by half."

Harker didn't wish to be played the fool. "Another man [*a different buyer*] might be better able to restore them [*offer a higher value*]."

"Not half, then. Perhaps reduced by one-third. Call it sixteen."

"It should begin with a two."

"I cannot see past eighteen."

"And a half."

The Phantom paused, seeming to gather his thoughts. "And a half, then—provided these stones are in good order."

Harker raised his cup. The Phantom merely nodded. Harker drank.

"The usual hour, then? And place?" the Phantom asked as he rose to leave.

"As you wish," replied Harker. They would exchange jewels

for pieces of eight in the dark of night, well outside Santo Pedro.

XVIII

"Might I bring you something, Your Majesty?" The Queen was headed to her boudoir when her aide posed the question.

"Most certainly not," she replied, though too sternly, she thought. It was understandable; she'd just finished a disturbing meeting with Captain McBride. He recounted his voyage to Indonesia, his capture by Viceroy Valdez on the return passage, his imprisonment on Inagua, and his subsequent rescue by Captain Connachan. But he expressed grave concern about Connachan's unfathomable decision not to return to England immediately after freeing him. According to McBride, she undertook a separate mission—one she claimed bore the Queen's authority. Elizabeth was shocked; she knew that wasn't true. Garret had lied to the man. Whatever personal action she took clearly threatened the safe return of both McBride and Ambassador Halim.

The other piece of information McBride provided, also deeply concerning, was the capture and retention of Viceroy Valdez. Elizabeth had been as explicit as she dared with Captain Connachan regarding the need to dispatch the Viceroy. Ending his life in the Southern Seas would have given England, and her personally, the ability to deny any involvement. The last thing she needed now was to have this Viceroy arrive in England as a prisoner. If that were Connachan's intent, there would be bloody hell to pay upon her return.

McBride smiled to himself as he exited Richmond Palace. The Queen's reaction was precisely what he sought going in. Connachan may have believed she could pull off being a privateering agent of the Queen with better standing than him—a seasoned naval captain, no less. Well, she was wrong. She would now take more than a few steps toward the rear of the Admiralty's line. And rightly so—women should stay at home and tend to their children. That was the way of the world. It always had been.

The carriage awaiting him swayed and squeaked as he stepped into it. "To the residence, Mr. Friel," he shouted to the driver. He reflected on his decision not to bring Halim with him, concerned that the Ambassador was too friendly with Connachan. He grinned, recalling his recommendation to the Queen that she take a couple of weeks to arrange a suitable reception for the Ambassador. By that time, it would be too late for Halim's possible support of Connachan to make much of a difference.

———

The bell rang, announcing the arrival of the young messenger opening the door of Orion's inn. "Top of the day to you, sir," he said in greeting to the owner, George Tyndale. "I bear a note from the palace, for Ambassador Halim." He held it out.

George approached and received the message. He turned it over, noting the Queen's seal. "Thank you, my good man." He handed him a coin.

The knock interrupted Halim's Dhuhr prayer.

"A message from the Palace, Ambassador," George announced.

Halim rose from his mat, walked to the door, and opened it. "Thank you, Mr. Tyndale." He took the letter, giving George a small coin. As George left, Halim closed the door and walked to his small desk. He flipped the letter over in his hand, to see the bright red seal. It was definitely the Queen's. He'd seen it many times before while working with Pantas. He pulled back the chair and sat, breaching the seal and opening the letter. It was actually from Elizabeth's secretary, welcoming him back to London on her behalf. The letter included an invitation to join Her Majesty at a formal dinner, in honor of his appointment as Ambassador. The event would take place a fortnight from now. He was to feel free to bring an entourage, not to exceed five people.

'*A fortnight from now is not soon enough,*' Halim thought. He was concerned about any damage McBride's report might do to Garret's reputation between now and then, especially if there were no one to stand on her behalf. But what could he do? As Indonesia's ambassador, he simply served at the Queen's pleasure. He would need to wait until the dinner two weeks hence, to make his case for Garret. Until then, he could only hope that Garret herself might soon find her way to the Queen's door. Perhaps he might accompany her at that time. He decided to leave word for her at Plymouth Harbor.

———

Pandora and *Orion* were within a week of reaching Plymouth. The weather hadn't been favorable but wasn't expected to delay their arrival by too many days. Now that it was relatively calm, William Tovery came aboard the flagship at Garret's request. She was seated at her table scripting a note when he entered her quarters.

"One moment, if you please," Garret said without looking up. She wrote for several more moments while William waited.

Finally, she laid her quill on the table and rose. "So nice to see you, William." She said it with real meaning; their last visit was weeks back. "You look well."

"My wound seems fully recovered. But for the scar, of course." He smiled. "I feel better than expected. Perhaps it is the nearness of home."

"My spirits are high as well." Garret pointed to a chair. "I do worry, however, about the messages we deliver to the Queen. I am concerned about Captain McBride's likely presentation of the events."

"And no doubt the Queen's likely dismay over the unexpected arrival of the Viceroy."

"That too, yes."

William took a chair, Garret another.

"It is most unfortunate, Garret. Jorge is a good man—a natural friend, were Spain not our enemy."

"Just so. He has many appealing qualities." The last few words slipped out. Garret hoped William didn't think them odd, though the look on his face suggested otherwise.

"I imagine you wish to compare thoughts on addressing the Queen."

"You read my mind," she replied, relieved that William didn't inquire further about Jorge's 'appealing qualities'. She reached to pick up the sheets of parchment on her table. "I have prepared these notes on our mission. They do not include my answers to what might be her most challenging questions. Not yet."

"Drake taught you well."

Garret laughed, "Did I ever tell you I once overheard him verbally practicing his answers in preparation for Her Majesty's 'inquisition'?

"I, too, have heard him," laughed William.

Garret handed him the pages. "I welcome your thoughts."

William accepted them and began reading. Garret got up, poured wine into a cup, and set it on the table before him.

"Thank you," he said, without looking at her.

Garret poured her own cup. She watched William read, thinking how much alike their thoughts were on most issues. Perhaps that was due to their many shared experiences. There was comfort in having him available to confer with. She could always count on him to test her thinking.

William shuffled to the next page. Garret found herself observing him more as a fine-looking man than a partnering captain, or a virtual brother. As he continued flipping through the pages and reading, she studied his endearing face, his thick, curly hair, and his familiar mannerisms. There was a flair about him that she seldom saw in other men, though she couldn't quite define it. What *was* clear, however, was the complicated nature of her feelings for him.

William finished reading. He laid the pages on the table. "There is no mention of the assault on Santiago del Príncipe. Does that not concern you?"

Garret expected the question. "It was not relevant to the mission. I thought it best not to add an unnecessary tangent."

"It seems you have practiced that response," William grinned.

"I have, yes," Garret laughed. "But am I not right? There is no point bringing it up."

"In most instances, I would agree. But surely Captain McBride will raise it in his own report. You cannot simply ignore it."

"I never shared with McBride the reason for my departure, or my destination. I simply suggested it was between Her Majesty and me alone."

"But surely he shall ask her whether there was some other sanctioned part of her mission that caused you to leave Inagua."

"As commander of the fleet, am I not entitled to my own decisions?" Garret replied. "These are *my* ships, after all, not the navy's."

"Of course. Yet McBride will challenge your taking risks that could have led to unfortunate outcomes for the Queen's mission."

"I judged those risks to be minimal. The assault was against a poorly defended and surprised target. The fact that there were no casualties on our side proves the risk was negligible. If Her Majesty raises the matter, I am comfortable she will see it my way."

"Perhaps." William sipped his wine and returned the cup to the table. "I hope you are right. Still, she will not be in a pleasant state of mind once she learns we have returned with Valdez in hand. That, combined with your unsanctioned venture, could well tip her over the taffrail."

Garret laughed at the implied image. She composed herself before responding. "I trust my relationship with Her Majesty will prevent that. I once shared with her my experience during the massacre near Santiago del Príncipe. She will surely understand my motivation."

William's nod suggested he heard her but didn't necessarily agree. "Besides that one missing item," he said, "I believe your outline is fine. You have a flair for being precise and to the point."

"Thank you, William. Will you join me in meeting with her?"

"Certainly…if she will have us."

———

Having returned from their midnight exchange with the Phantom outside Santo Pedro, Harker and De Graaf assembled their crew on the shore of Skeleton Island, to divvy up the proceeds from Nombre de Dios. The men were loud and celebratory, having finished unloading the many chests that now lay scattered before them. Harker fired his pistol in the air, drawing their attention. Once he had it, he began, "In addition to the gold and silver before us, I am pleased to report that we have received five thousand pieces of eight in exchange for the jewels." A resounding cheer rang out, despite that amount being far less than he and Harker actually received.

Though most of the men accepted the five thousand as fact, Le Pen did not; he was no fool. "That cannot be true," he bellowed as the cheering subsided. "The jewels were worth five to ten times that amount."

Heads turned his way. Voices dulled to a murmur. Le Pen had just committed a cardinal sin, raising his concern in front of the men, rather than in private with Harker. The suspicious whispers would serve no one well. One of Le Pen's men suddenly drew his cutlass. Many of Harker's men drew theirs in response. Within moments, swords were drawn all around, accompanied by rising voices.

De Graaf stepped in front of Harker, his cutlass drawn and pointed directly at Le Pen. Shouting above the noise for all to hear, he directed his comments to the Frenchman he so despised. "You cannot question a man's honor without consequence. Draw your sword now or you and your crew shall leave here with nothing in hand."

Le Pen scanned the crowd, weighing his options. But there was no choice, really. He would have to engage. Though De Graaf was a much larger man, Le Pen hoped he had lesser skill with a cutlass. Still, even if he were fortunate enough to dispense with the brute, he might then have to deal with Harker as well. Or would he? Harker was a man of reason. He might accept the loss of De Graaf in order to avoid an all-out battle between their crews.

"Draw your sword, coward," shouted De Graaf, reiterating his demand.

'*Ben merde*,' thought Le Pen, realizing either he or De Graaf would soon cease to exist. Reluctantly, he drew his sword. The assembled pirates quickly shuffled back to give the combatants room. Voices began to break out, cheering on the man with whom they sided.

De Graaf grinned with a menace that chilled Le Pen. The Frenchman moved his left foot back, positioning himself defensively. De Graaf responded similarly. Le Pen began circling, wanting De Graaf to offer the first thrust. He planned to parry it and follow with a rapid riposte before De Graaf could resume a defensive posture.

The two men circled, judging each other's intent. To the onlookers, it seemed neither participant wished to engage. De Graaf jerked forward with a feint before quickly pulling back. Le Pen didn't fall for it. They continued circling in the hot sand. Sweat dripped from their bodies; whether caused by the heat or the fear of death was unclear. The circling continued, with no contact. The crowd groaned and began egging them on.

De Graaf's misstep in the thick sand gave Le Pen a small opening. He lunged, point first, at De Graaf's chest. It was the shortest path. But he failed to lunge far enough, managing only a slight puncture as De Graaf bent backward. The response came swiftly. A powerful upward-left parry sent the point of Le Pen's sword high. The

Frenchman held his grip but De Graaf finished with an elbow-raised, half-circle, sideways riposte that slashed across his left arm, hitting French bone. Le Pen screamed in agony as blood poured onto his blouse. He retreated on instinct, to gain time and stance. But he, too, tripped in the sand. He fell to one knee in a vulnerable position. His men were suddenly silent while Harker's cheered loudly.

To his surprise, Le Pen watched De Graaf step back. He was unaware the man had a penchant for watching his opponents endure excruciating pain for an interminable period. He'd even been observed prodding them to plead for a quick death.

Struggling to regain his feet, Le Pen stealthily grasped sand in his left hand. With his arm in searing pain, streaming blood, he was uncertain he could throw the dust. But he knew he had to try. He positioned his right side toward De Graaf, now needing to defend at all cost. Stepping back to give himself space, he prayed for an opening, however small. His blood dripped into the sand, absorbing particles.

De Graaf approached slowly. Le Pen continued his retreat. The men nearby shuffled back, giving more room. Le Pen finally stopped, waiting for De Graaf to get close enough. The space narrowed as time itself seemed to widen. Finally, Le Pen motioned his left arm forward. It didn't respond well. The sand he intended to throw fell sadly, mere inches in front of him.

De Graaf laughed voraciously. Then suddenly, unexpectedly, he leaped forward, slashing down hard toward the right shoulder. Le Pen arced his sword upward in defense but couldn't generate enough power to fully deflect the blow. The fierce downward thrust forced Le Pen's sword back across his left shoulder while the point of De Graaf's cutlass pierced his shoulder blade. Blood spewed upward as Le Pen once again stumbled to his knees. Some of his men chose to look away.

De Graaf stepped back, grinning. Le Pen drew a deep breath. He realized De Graaf was toying with him. The outcome was now inevitable; the only question was how, and how soon, it would arrive.

Not wanting a drawn-out blood-fest, Le Pen contemplated withdrawing his dagger and ending things himself. But he couldn't bring himself to do it. Instead, bleeding profusely and barely able to lift his weapon, he rose again. He stood wide-legged, for balance. Time salted away. Finally, he opened his arms, letting his sword fall to the sand in what seemed to him a floatingly slow motion. Wobbling as he stood, he closed his eyes, tilting his face toward the sky. The sweet sound of the ocean prevailed, as though the waves were arriving to escort him away. And still De Graaf waited, his bloody cutlass pointing downward.

"End it," Le Pen said bravely, his arms still extended, though his left wasn't far from his body.

De Graaf stepped in close. "I did not hear you."

Le Pen drew another breath, forcing himself to painfully utter the words one more time. "End it," he rasped. All but a few of his men dropped their eyes to the sand at their feet.

De Graaf spit in the sand. He turned and stepped away, letting his cutlass drop free. And then he stopped. He drew his dagger slowly. With a whirling turn, he threw it savagely at Le Pen's throat. He stepped back and watched as Le Pen's right arm seemed to jerk toward his neck. He fell to his knees, his eyes suddenly opening wide, capturing one last glimpse of his executioner, though the image never fully registered in his mind. He fell forward into the sand, coloring it red as the dagger penetrated further. No one cheered. Nothing moved—

men, waves, even time. There was only silence.

Harker stepped forward, moving between De Graaf and the fallen Frenchman. He raised his arms and faced Le Pen's crew. "This was a fine man," he called out loudly. "I am sorry to see him come to this end. It could have been avoided." He looked down at the body. "He brought this upon himself." He looked up and scanned the men's faces. "Let us end this matter here and now, and bury our brother honorably…at sea."

The wind blew. The waves returned. Time moved once more. Harker nodded to a couple of Le Pen's men to attend to his lifeless body.

As the crowd dissipated, Harker pulled De Graaf aside. The two walked away. "You have done what was necessary," Harker opened. "Our challenge now is to convince Le Pen's men to stay with us. We must work together toward that end. But recognize that those who were closest to him will present a threat. Keep your ear to the wind and your head turning."

XIX

To those onshore, the commotion was palpable. It started the moment the two ships approaching Plymouth Harbor announced their arrival with cannon fire. Some recognized them as *Pandora* and *Orion*.

Stories and rumors regarding the separation of Garret Connachan's fleet had filled the taverns ever since the much-earlier arrival of *Athena* under Captain McBride. There was even wild speculation that McBride had slain the female captain, of whom Plymouth residents were so proud. The hum of anxious conversation began sweeping the docks. A number of onlookers began placing bets on Captain Connachan's fate.

Garret stood at the foredeck, taking in the noise and activity as her crew hustled to furl and secure sails, haul anchor, and ready cargo for offloading. "You can smell the English countryside," she said to Blair, standing next to her.

"You can indeed. And English beer," he smiled.

Though she was pleased to be back home, Garret's bright enjoyment of the moment was dulled by her ever-present worry regarding the Queen's likely unfavorable reception of the news of the Viceroy's arrival on English soil. She took some comfort in believing she could persuade the Queen to use him as a bargaining chip—returning him to Spain in exchange for an English foothold in the Southern Seas. She would suggest Las Vírgenes islands. Discovered by Cristobal Colon (known by the English as Columbus) the islands were originally named *Santa Ursula y Las Once Mil Vírgenes*, in honor of Saint Ursula and the legend of the eleven thousand virgins. Lying east of Hispaniola, they were strategically well-positioned among the trailing islands.

Garret's thoughts returned to the present, "The deck is yours, Mr. Blair." She turned to retrieve the Viceroy from his quarters.

"Good day, Captain Connachan," Valdez said as Garret entered. She understood the reason for his formality—the guard standing nearby to accompany them was all ears. "A good day indeed, Viceroy," she replied, watching him stuff the last of his few belongings into a canvas bag on his hammock. "I see you are ready to depart."

"I am indeed, though to what future is unclear."

Garret noticed he was nicely groomed, his thick hair brushed, his beard short and trimmed. He was wearing the regular seaman's clothes he'd been given, to help maintain the secrecy of his identity.

"You shall accompany me and Captain Tovery to London. Under armed guard, of course. We shall seek a timely audience with Her Majesty. I have no doubt she will be most interested in meeting you." Inside, she cringed at her harmless little lie.

Valdez said nothing but nodded furtively toward the guard. Garret caught his meaning. Despite his being her prisoner, their relationship had unexpectedly become awkwardly amorous. They needed to be discreet. "Give us a moment please," she said to the crewman.

"Aye, Captain," he replied, turning and heading to the main deck.

Valdez recognized this could well be the last time he might be with Garret in private. He enjoyed their visits during the Atlantic crossing. Their conversations ranged from childhood and family memories to political realities—a kind of *intellectual* intimacy. Still, there'd been no deeply physical engagement. Though not for lack of effort—he'd made more than one subtle advance. But Garret always dictated the pace. He presumed she sought to maintain some degree of emotional separation due to their complicated circumstances. He felt a need to attempt one last seduction, knowing her support was crucial to avoiding long-term imprisonment, or even execution. As a military commander, he was used to marshaling every resource at his disposal. That now included Garret. He moved toward her, opening his arms. "May I?"

She stood motionless, saying nothing. Her rising heart rate assured her she wanted him. Physically. If circumstances were different, she would have him. But her mind stilled her craving—he was, in this moment, potentially poisonous fruit.

Valdez took Garret's silence as a welcoming signal. He closed, placing his head alongside hers and wrapping his arms gently around her back. She accepted them but didn't reciprocate. He kissed her on the cheek and then drew back slowly, his arms still holding her. "Whatever happens, please know that our time together has brought me enormous pleasure. I wish for so much more…though I envision so much less."

Garret smiled warmly, as would anyone who cares deeply for another. "Perhaps our story has not been fully written." Almost unexpectedly, her hand raised itself and ran along the beard that defined his sharp jaw. She quickly gathered herself and pulled away. She swung her right arm toward the stairs.

Disappointed, but not totally surprised, Valdez grabbed his canvas bag and headed out ahead of Garret, feeling optimistic. She would have his back, of that he was confident. But now he could only hope she would be convincing enough to negotiate his freedom. That would enable him to once again serve his King. And perhaps even take revenge on those who so badly embarrassed him—possibly including Captain Connachan herself.

While Garret and Valdez were in conversation, a longboat drew alongside *Pandora*, bearing a military officer, an English flag, and the Queen's standard. The officer and two of his men were piped aboard. They now waited on deck for Captain Connachan.

As she and Valdez reached the main deck, Garret spotted the soldiers. She appreciated what she believed was her official welcoming party. They must have expected her arrival shortly after McBride's. She thought it odd, however, that the officer was stone-faced.

"Greetings, Captain Connachan. I am Lieutenant Nightingale, here at the request of Her Majesty, Queen Elizabeth."

"Greetings, Lieutenant."

"I am afraid I have been authorized to take possession of you and your prisoner." He said it quietly. Garret presumed that was to avoid creating an uncomfortable situation on deck. The Lieutenant handed her a sealed authorization document signed by the Queen's Secretary.

Garret unsealed and read the note. She handed it back to the officer, maintaining her composure. "I do not understand why this is necessary."

Nightingale deflected, "You are required to accompany us, Captain. I trust you shall not trouble me in that regard."

Garret hesitated only briefly. "Mr. Blair," she called out, "you are now in charge. I shall be leaving the ship at this time. Mr. Valcour shall accompany me." Surely Blair would sense something was amiss—her departing the ship this early, leaving without him, referring to the Viceroy as 'Mr.', and using the French-sounding name 'Valcour'. Hopefully, he could read between the lines.

"Shall I follow you to London, Captain?" Blair called back as he approached.

"No, thank you. Please be certain the crew is attended to."

"Will you not be addressing them, then?"

"Tell them the press of business demands I leave for London with all haste. I shall send word following my arrival there."

"Aye, Captain,"

"And give Captain Tovery apologies for my early departure."

"I shall, sir. Safe travels, then."

Garret rode in the carriage, seated opposite Nightingale. She judged he was of medium age. Clearly not an accomplished man, she thought—not in any military sense. Neither his look nor his poise communicated the confidence of a successful officer. He had more the air of an errand boy. She challenged him. "Are you not sufficiently informed to tell me what this is all about?"

"I have only my orders, Captain. You shall be taken to the Tower and held there for a time."

Garret surmised that her pending imprisonment at the Tower of London was a direct result of Captain McBride's reporting. It did not bode well for an opportunity to present her case to the Queen. She reflected on the Tower. It once served as the principal residence of England's rulers, dating back to its construction by William the Conqueror. But over time, despite new sections being added, the original structure had fallen into disrepair. Though it had a history of housing visiting dignitaries, many of its current residents were prisoners. Rumor had it some were tortured, even murdered, within its walls.

Her thoughts spun back to McBride. '*Damn him*', she thought, convinced he informed the Queen that the Viceroy was still alive, and might well be arriving on *Pandora*. Her Majesty would not have received that news well, given her desire for his clandestine assassination. Garret despaired over her likely inability to message the Queen from the Tower, to lay out her exchange proposal.

"What of Mr. Valcour?" Garret asked Nightingale. She was uncertain just how much he knew about Valdez, if anything. Best to keep his identity and origin secret, she thought.

"He, too, is being taken to the Tower. The guards shall be questioning him."

Garret shuddered inwardly about the methods those guards might employ. It disturbed her. She knew she needed to get word to William, and perhaps Thomas, as soon as possible. "Am I entitled to message my associates?"

"That is not part of my orders, Captain."

"Can you not make it so? It is not a challenging request."

"I am afraid not. I follow my orders to the letter."

'*Which is precisely why you are nothing more than an errand boy*,' thought Garret.

Valdez sat uncomfortably in the creaking, flatbed wagon following Garret's carriage. He realized he hadn't heard the clop of horses' hooves in some time. Strangely, it brought him a sense of comfort. He needed that. The guards had handled him roughly; no doubt to demonstrate his fate was entirely up to them. The rope tying his hands behind him was course and uncomfortable, scraping against his wrists. So any comfort he could find was welcomed.

He was also relieved. The ring King Philip gave him was safely stowed in a small pocket inside his boot. He placed it there as a precaution while packing for departure. The guards would surely have taken it if they saw it on his hand. It would have raised questions in their minds about his relationship with the King. He wondered whether that would have led to his being treated better, or perhaps worse. He felt a need to test these men, without letting on who he was, or that he spoke excellent English. He nodded to one of them, "Agua? [Water]?"

"Damn village idiot," replied the guard.

"Agwa, agwa," said the other, as though he were a monkey uttering the sounds. Both guards laughed. A third guard knocked their prisoner fiercely upside the head.

Valdez said no more. He already had everything he needed to know. These were not intelligent, disciplined soldiers. He felt he might be able to use that to further his interests, at the right point in time.

———

"What do you mean, she left early? She would not leave without me," insisted William.

"The Queen's guards accompanied her," Blair replied. He'd come aboard *Orion* specifically to deliver news of Garret's sudden departure. "I imagine Her Majesty was anxious to see her."

"Even so, she would have had them wait for my accompaniment."

Blair shrugged. It was clear to William he had nothing to add. He feared Garret's abrupt departure might be the result of an unhappy response by Queen Elizabeth to McBride's likely reporting of events. He decided to proceed immediately to London. But first, he needed to send word to Thomas, Admiral Drake's younger brother. As their former fellow midshipman, Thomas was close to, and fond of, Garret. He would ask Thomas to meet him in London, confident the younger Drake could wield helpful influence if it were required. He would send messages both to Buckland Abbey and to Thomas' flat in London.

———

With his two prisoners secured in the Tower, Lieutenant Nightingale sent word to his commander, who passed it along to the Queen's Secretary. The Secretary intended to wait a few days before alerting the Queen. She'd informed him earlier that there was no rush. He wasn't certain why.

Elizabeth's reasoning was simple. She wished to teach Garret the consequences of failing to follow explicit orders. Though she liked the brash young commander, there was no accepting this level of insolence; especially since it now placed England in an awkward position. How could she possibly explain to King Philip that she was holding his cherished Viceroy prisoner?

Elizabeth had been clear with her Secretary—Captain Connachan was not to be beaten or interrogated in any way. But she consciously avoided expressing the same sentiment regarding the Viceroy. She did not wish anyone, including her Secretary, to know that the Spanish prisoner was anything more than a minor player. She needed to suppress this whole matter for the time being. It was important that word of Valdez' arrival on English soil not find its way back to Spain inadvertently. If mayhem befell him in the Tower, so much the better.

XX

The rising sun's gleaming light was intentionally captured and held by the elaborately designed grounds of El Escorial. The compelling beauty frequently caused King Philip to contrast his landscape architect's work with that of the many paintings gracing his palace walls—those of masters like Botticelli and da Vinci.

The primary reason he enjoyed these morning walks with his two dogs was the peace they brought him. But that peace escaped him this day. He'd risen earlier than usual, unable to find sleep. Troubling news was flooding in from the Southern Seas; most specifically, the raid on Nombre de Dios and the capture of Viceroy Valdez.

As far as Nombre de Dios was concerned, this was the final straw. The town and its mule trail were favored targets of El Draque. And now there was another raider. Philip knew the town's days as the focal point for his treasure trade must soon end. He would increasingly shift resources and investments to Porto Bello, making it the principal port for the shipment of precious metals.

Preliminary reports from Nombre de Dios indicated the assailant was an English pirate; a man known only as Harker. His ship was said to fly a blood-red flag. The man himself apparently wore a patch of a similar color over his left eye. There was some speculation he might also have been responsible for the decimation of nearby Santiago del Príncipe and, more importantly, the kidnapping of Viceroy Valdez.

It was the loss of his beloved nephew, Luis Rodriguez, that moved Philip in the first place to appoint his close friend Jorge Valdez as Military Viceroy. And now Jorge was gone as well. The man was a highly accomplished military leader and trusted advisor. But it was their friendship that made his capture even more painful. Philip couldn't fathom how such a fine military officer could have let that happen. Not only had Valdez established a military base in the Inaguas, but he also had a fleet of warships at his disposal. And there was nothing on those islands to be gained by pirates. Or anyone else.

Philip wasn't buying the speculation that it was Harker who kidnapped Valdez. He doubted pirates had the necessary capabilities. No, he suspected the real perpetrator was one of his major enemies—England or France. Or perhaps the Dutch. In fact, they might have the most interest in capturing him since his knowledge of Spain's military initiatives in the Netherlands was extensive. Yet how would they even know Valdez had been assigned to a base on an obscure island in the Southern Seas? Someone from his inner circle must have leaked word to his enemies. A damn spy in his own house! He would not rest until he could find and punish the traitor.

There was no indication of what happened to Valdez following his capture. Since he was taken alive, there was no reason to believe he was later slain. Tortured was more likely…to obtain every last ounce of intelligence. But at some point, his usefulness being exhausted, Valdez might well meet his end. Philip knew he needed to act right away.

The more he thought about it, the more convinced he became that the Dutch were responsible. This was a virtual assassination attempt by a nation-state. It could not go unpunished. He would deal them a vicious blow.

Philip stooped to pick up a small branch laying on the ground. He rose slowly and threw it far, for the dogs to chase. Watching them race down the tree-lined path, he imagined the stick being the

Netherlands and the attacking dogs his own military forces. He smiled for just a moment, before turning and heading back for breakfast.

———

Bruised and near lifeless, the petty thief lay in spread-eagle position on the hard floor of his cell, each limb secured by ropes attached to iron rings deeply embedded in the stone walls. He'd been savagely beaten by the guards who dragged him here for brazenly knifing a street merchant. They'd beaten him for fun, not necessity.

The loud sound of approaching guards made him wince. But it seemed they weren't coming to deliver another beating. They were bringing new residents to this dingy row in the Cradle Tower, which had only recently been opened to accommodate criminals.

The young but rugged-looking guard stationed outside the prisoner's cell had been told to expect new arrivals sometime this day. One was said to be a woman who'd been captaining a ship. He assumed that story was made up; women didn't even serve on ships, let alone captain them. Perhaps she had a small fishing boat. But as the group appeared in the dingy, gray hallway, he found the woman unexpectedly well-dressed. Definitely not a fisherwoman. He smiled at her as she glanced his way. She returned his smile. He looked briefly at the other prisoner with her. No one had told him what this man did or who he was. Nor did he care. If the man gave him any trouble, he would beat him without hesitation. That was the way of things here in the Tower.

He pulled open the heavy, creaking door to an empty cell. One of the soldiers bringing the two prisoners shoved the male inside. The guard slammed and locked the door. They all moved to the adjoining cell, where he once again opened the door. A soldier grabbed the woman's buttocks, squeezing it hard as she walked in. She showed no reaction. The guard locked the door behind her.

Garret and Valdez were surprised to find themselves in adjacent cells. The accommodations were cold, damp and hard. There would be no comfort here, aside from each other's presence. Yet they were uncertain whether they could, or should, converse. Happily, their young guard didn't appear to care, though Garret suspected he would be most interested in listening to a female voice…even though hers was now a little gravelly from barking orders in heavy seas.

Garret and Jorge chose not to share anything of real substance. She spoke mostly about the brighter side of life in London. Valdez simply peppered her with questions, responding to the visual images she painted.

It wasn't long before Garret decided to engage directly with the young guard, hoping to put him at ease and perhaps draw a little empathy. It seemed he had an eye for her. That was a weakness she could exploit. "Might I have some water, please?" she asked, sweetly.

"Indeed," he replied, seemingly happy to accommodate her. He left for a few minutes, returning later with a wooden bucket of water. He dipped a long, narrow ladle in the water and lifted it through the small window in the cell door. "Your water, ma'am."

Garret grabbed a cup sitting on the wooden stool nearby and brought it to the window. The guard began pouring. "Thank you kindly, sir," she said. "Tell me, are you from London?"

"I am, ma'am. Born and raised here. Me dad is a wheelwright. Does a right-fine job, he does."

"How come you to this place?"

"Me dad. He builds wheels for carriages. The captain o' the guards is a customer."

"Have you been here long?" She sipped her water. It tasted stale, though unlike the deep, wood-flavored staleness of the water onboard ship.

"A couple o' years, ma'am. It pays enough." He put down the bucket.

"You live nearby, then."

"With me dad," he nodded. "Me mom is long gone."

"I am sorry to hear that."

"She was a frail, sickly woman. A good mum, though."

"Is your dad pleased you work here?"

"Not truly. He tried teaching me his trade; it was not for me."

Garret changed course. "Will we be fed soon?"

"A couple of hours, ma'am. My relief will bring it." The guard clarified, "Sometimes he can be late."

"What might we expect to be fed?"

"Cold broth and a small loaf."

"That does not bode well for my health. Am I to be here long?"

"That is not for me to know."

"I see." Garret paused for a moment, now ready to ask a favor. "Is there anything more you might bring me? Some fruit perhaps? I have a coin to pay for it."

The guard glanced down the hallway, apparently to ensure no one else was present. He turned to look at Garret through the opening. Maybe it was her auburn hair, brightened by the light of the sun that was low in the sky and shone through the high window of her cell; or perhaps it was her green eyes and pleasant smile; or possibly just the money. Whatever it was, it seemed to work. "I shall see, ma'am. It is frowned upon. On the morrow, perhaps."

"Fruit for me as well," chimed in Valdez from his cell next door.

The guard didn't respond.

———

Its dreaded crimson flag absent from the mainmast, and its sails tightly furled, *Death's Head* wrestled with the churning waters of a stormy sea. It swayed near uncontrollably in the howling gale. Two other ships accompanied her: the aging *Red Knight*, and the *Cutthroat*. The latter was the Spanish warship Harker & De Graaf captured at Nombre de Dios. Since De Graaf had slayed Le Pen to quiet his dissent, Harker granted his partner's request to captain the warship. De Graaf chose Cutthroat as its name—something one of his crewmates suggested. He liked the sound of it.

Though challenging, this was far from the worst storm these two pirates ever faced. And it wasn't long before the skies began to lighten, though they remained overcast. The wind slowed but was still brisk. Fortunately for Harker, none of the three ships incurred anything other than minor damage.

The small fleet was heading toward Hispaniola, hoping to intercept vessels transporting valuable goods and treasures back to Spain. They'd been at sea a few days already without success. Harker signaled De Graaf to join him on the *Death's Head* as soon as the calming winds would permit. That didn't happen until the following morning.

Breakfast consisted of salted pork, biscuit, and cups of watered beer. When they were done, Harker cleared the table and laid out an old map. It was soiled, discolored, worn at the edges, and torn in a few places. He quickly set a few weights on top to secure it. "I believe we are somewhere in this area." He drew an imaginary circle.

"About twenty leagues south of Las Vírgenes islands," noted De Graaf.

"From the most southern tip, yes."

They continued perusing the map in silence for a few moments. Harker finally stood erect. "These waters are too quiet," he said. "We must soon find a target or face the crews' wrath."

"Perhaps our luck will turn as we near Hispaniola," replied De Graaf. "There should be a healthy flow of Spanish ships."

"Another possibility is Ponce, on the southern shore of Isla San Juan Bautista." Harker pointed to it. "There are likely to be merchant vessels in the area." De Graaf nodded, noncommittally. Harker continued, "Let us head west-northwest." He drew his finger in that direction and stopped at Ponce. "With luck, we shall find a stout target along the way."

"When we do," De Graaf responded, "I should like to lead the attack." He was anxious to begin fashioning his own reputation.

Harker looked him in the eyes, as though taking his measure. He stood erect once again. "I suppose you have earned that right, my brother. I shall defer to your lead. But do not disappoint me."

"I will not. You have my word."

"I pity the captain and crew you encounter," Harker grinned.

De Graaf grinned back with a joy-filled sense of anticipation. "I shall devour the first vessel we lay eyes upon, no matter her flag."

———

The young prison guard's relief arrived well after sundown. He carried the meager meal Garret was told to expect—cold soup and bread. Even with the meals for her, Valdez, and the third prisoner combined, there was barely enough food to provide meaningful sustenance for just one of them.

The relieving guard was a career man in his late forties. Short, bald and overweight, he was living a sedentary life. And eating well. He regularly filched portions of prisoners' food for his own consumption. His bulbous, heavily veined nose suggested he drank spirits as much as he ate. Dark warts on his face tended to turn away the heads of others. It was no wonder he felt more comfortable in this grim, gloomy world where he bore unrestrained power over the prisoners. He was their overlord and meal ticket. They were his dogs, completely beholden to him for their welfare.

"Feed that piece of garbage," he shouted at the young guard, who snapped to his orders. The young man entered the cell of the third prisoner. He knelt, poured soup into a wooden bowl, and tore the bread into small pieces. He dipped them into the soup before shoving them into the sickly man's mouth. Once he'd swallowed them all, the guard held up the prisoner's head, so he could finish the cold soup. The guard then stood, bowl in hand, and exited the cell. The older guard checked the knots on the prisoner's ropes, ensuring they were still tight. Before leaving, he spit on the captive. Because he could. He locked the cell door on his way out and glanced back through its window, smiling at the spread-eagled prisoner's discomfort as he writhed agonizingly on the floor.

Valdez was to be next. The young guard entered his cell. The older one followed, drawing his sword and pointing it at the Viceroy, "On your arse, filth!"

The chains attaching his wrists to the wall clanged as Valdez slid to a seated position. The young guard grabbed his ankles and secured them in bracelets that were also attached to the wall by chains. He placed the meal near the Viceroy's feet.

Sensing this prisoner might be a Spaniard, the old guard pushed the younger one aside and stepped toward Valdez. He leaned down to look him in the eye. "You smell like fish," he growled, before spitting in his face. He sneered and placed the loaf in the cold soup before moving the bowl far enough away that Valdez couldn't reach it, except with his face. For good measure, the old guard spit in the bowl. He laughed and kicked Valdez in the ribs before leaving the cell. Valdez winced at the kick's impact but stifled any sound.

The two guards moved on to the next cell. The old one smiled wryly; female prisoners were rare. When they did show up, he enjoyed all they had to offer. It was the most welcome aspect of his job. Constrained and beholden to him for the things they needed, he found them open to serving his very special needs.

The young guard placed Garret's food on the floor and attached her ankle bracelets. He looked back to the older guard, "Shall I unlock the shackles from her wrists, so she might eat in a proper manner?"

The old guard frowned. "Be gone," he said, nodding toward the door. As the younger man walked out, the old guard used his right foot to slide the food beyond Garret's reach. He headed back to the cell door and watched the young guard walk the hallway and turn the corner. Waiting until he heard the sound of footsteps descending the stairs, his loins began to fill with emotion. The young guard's descent signaled the festivities could begin. He drew inside the cell and closed the door.

The old guard turned and stood for a moment, looking Garret up and down. She was young, clean, and pleasant to look at, despite the look of annoyance she bore. In all his many years here, he had never seen the likes of her in his dark kingdom. And he was her master. She was about to learn what that meant. Food and water had to be earned.

XXI

The roast chicken was cold but it would do, thought William. He was beyond hungry. He picked up his utensils and cut in, thinking about Garret and her unexpectedly early departure from Plymouth Harbor. Before following her to London, William dashed off messages to their former shipmate, Thomas—one to Buckland Abbey and another to his London residence. The message implored Drake's younger brother to meet him at Orion's Tavern, where he now sat, eating.

Orion's was always Garret's preferred base when she was in the city. William had hoped to find her here. But when he arrived, he found she wasn't. Nor was there any word of her whereabouts. He immediately sent a messenger to Richmond Palace, inquiring as to her possible presence there. Unfortunately, no word had yet come back on that. He placed another forkful of chicken in his mouth, savoring its saltiness. His only other thought as to Garret's whereabouts was that she might have been called to visit her mother, whom he understood had a lengthy malady of madness.

As he reached out for his cup of wine, the door to the tavern opened. "Thomas!" he exclaimed, rising from his chair, "What a joy to see you."

Thomas strode his way, wearing a board smile that lit up his face. "Tis a great pleasure to see you as well, William."

As they hugged each other heartily, fond memories of their days sailing together flooded both their minds. Those memories now seemed so long ago but nevertheless felt as though they were only days away.

Following his legendary brother's death, Thomas had taken a different path. He was now busy managing the deceased Admiral's substantial property holdings, businesses, and other assets, as well as being active at Her Majesty's court when necessary. He pulled back a chair. "Is Garret here?"

"I am afraid not," replied William, retaking his own seat. "She departed *Pandora* hastily once we anchored. The Queen's guards accompanied her. Mr. Blair indicated she was heading to London. I presumed the guards were escorting her either here, or to Richmond Palace. Have you received no word from her?"

"None at all," Thomas shook his head.

"Tea, sir?" interrupted George Tyndale, the tavern owner.

"Please," replied Thomas. He reached into his pocket for a coin as George placed a cup on the table and began pouring. "I thank you," he said as the owner finished. Thomas handed him the coin and watched him leave. Turning back to William, he continued, "This is most surprising. Garret was never one to disappear without a word."

"Indeed."

"If she has gone to her home, I am afraid she shall find rather tragic news. Her mother has taken her own life. The poor woman never knew anything but suffering. I hoped I might see Garret first, to deliver the news myself."

"I am sorry to hear that," replied William. "Garret seldom spoke of her mother." He changed course, "Tell me, do you think you could inquire at the Queen's court regarding Garret's possible appearance there?"

"Most certainly. I shall also send a courier to her residence, to see whether she has shown up there. I cannot imagine where else she might have gone."

"I do hope we find her soon. The men are confused and concerned over her wordless departure. I shall need to return to Plymouth shortly, to calm and secure them."

"Of course," replied Thomas. He sipped his tea and placed the cup on the table. "So tell me, William, how was your voyage? I am most anxious to hear the details."

"Where to start?" pondered William.

"By the way," interjected Thomas, "I should disclose that I am Garret's lead investor. I shall need to report back to the others regarding the return on our investments."

William was shocked. Garret hadn't said anything to him about there being investors. And he knew only modest treasure was taken from Santiago del Príncipe. Not only was that treasure nowhere near enough to satisfy hungry financiers, but it had already been distributed among the crew. And in truth, treasure-seeking had never been the principal purpose of their mission. It would be awkward to share that with Thomas at this point. He chose to sidestep the issue. "You may recall that we were charged with finding and freeing Ambassador Halim, who was captured and held by King Philip's commander of military operations in the Southern Seas—a man named Valdez. The King appointed him Viceroy of the Inagua Islands."

"I do recall that, yes. And I learned a few days ago that Halim had returned, albeit with Captain McBride. May I presume your mission was successful then?"

"I am afraid our results may have differed from Her Majesty's expectations." William noticed the look of confusion on Thomas' face. "We freed the Ambassador," he assured him, "but we also took the

Viceroy prisoner." He sipped his tea and continued, "Unfortunately, the Queen's preference apparently went beyond that."

"Can you say more?"

William glanced around to ensure no one was listening. "Garret swore me to secrecy on this point, though I imagine she would understand my sharing it with you…provided it goes no further."

"No to worry, William. It shall be secret between us."

William leaned in, lowering his voice. "The Queen's desire was for the Viceroy to meet his end in the process. Garret chose otherwise."

"Oh, my." Thomas leaned back for just a moment. Then he leaned back in, speaking softly, "If that is true, certainly Her Majesty had good reason. She is a thoughtful woman." He paused, as though searching for some other explanation. "Perhaps Garret misunderstood."

"I do not believe so."

"Was there a written order?" Thomas shook his head immediately after he said it. "No, I take that back. Her Majesty would never provide a written order for something of that nature."

"Precisely," replied William.

"So what has become of this Viceroy? Valdez, you say?"

"Yes, Valdez. Jorge Valdez de Barragan. A former Maestre de Campo. Prior to his appointment to Viceroy, he led a tercio in Spain's campaign in The Netherlands. A fine gentleman, I must say. I had the pleasure of getting to know him while he was our prisoner. We brought him back with us."

"And where is he now?"

"With Garret, I presume. They left *Pandora* together, along with the Queen's guards."

"I see. Well, the first thing I shall do on the morrow is visit the palace."

"Thank you, Thomas. I appreciate your assistance. I worry
Garret may be in great need of it."

Thomas left the tavern processing all he'd learned. Something
wasn't right. He'd heard nothing from his sources at court about
Pandora's arrival, or the capture of a high-value Spanish officer.
There'd been prior news of Ambassador Halim's arrival, so why would
there not have been exciting news upon the return of Captain
Connachan, who'd been responsible for freeing Halim? A storm cloud
of worry began forming in his mind. He knew Her Majesty didn't look
fondly on those who failed to follow her instructions to the letter.

———

The breeze-assisted evening chill stiffened his aging bones,
despite the blanketing of his dark cloak and the generous layers of fat
that typically kept him warm. The old guard clopped along the
cobblestones with the prisoners' bread in his sack and a black kettle of
lukewarm soup in hand. The half-asleep guard stationed in front of the
Cradle Tower rose at his bark, quickly opening the door but not
bothering to look at him.

Passing through, the old guard could almost taste the coming
excitement of this night. The thought of soon enjoying a generous
reward from his new female prisoner caused his privates to quiver.
He'd been unable to find much sleep prior to coming; his recollections
of toying with her the night before repeatedly played back in his mind.
But that toying was just a light touching. A subtle message about
giving and receiving. This night would bring much greater pleasure. He

already had a full-payment plan in mind.

Topping the stairs, the crusty old guard frowned at his young counterpart. "Be gone," he growled. "I have this." He waved his hand, dispensing with the younger man.

As he exited the Cradle Tower, the young guard couldn't help thinking his replacement had nothing good in mind. The last time there was a female prisoner, the old guard had been clear—she was not to be tampered with. He considered her his personal property. And what a price that poor woman paid, notwithstanding her rather distasteful appearance. The old guard went easy on her initially. But in time, the wart-faced beast ravaged her virtually every night. He saw the evidence himself each morning. She was always freshly bruised, and sometimes bloodied. In time, her clothes were so shredded that they sheltered little of her disgusting frame. By the time she was released, the poor thing seemed barely human.

He worried for this new female prisoner. In the brief time they'd interacted, he'd grown fond of her, even smuggling in fruit for her. And why not? She was pleasant-looking and spoke kindly to him, showing interest in who he was. The thought of the old guard taking advantage of her made him cringe. But what was he to do? Nothing, really. He crossed the grounds, trying to erase an unwanted image from his mind.

The old guard hurriedly delivered meals to Valdez and the other male prisoner, not bothering to spite them this time. He was even generous in his apportionment of their bread and soup, thinking it best they were occupied while he enjoyed his encounter with the woman.

He set the bread and soup kettle on the floor outside Garret's cell. It would remain there until he was fully satisfied that she sufficiently rewarded him. As he inserted the key and unlocked the cell, Valdez called out, knowingly.

"Remember, you bastard…you shall pay for your actions."

The old guard chuckled, hearing the clanking noise emanating from Valdez' cell. It sounded as though he were thrashing in frustration.

Garret sat expressionless as the repulsive brute entered. His broad smile exposed several missing teeth. The ones remaining were darkly and variously colored, and crooked as pickets in an old fence. Memories of his foul breath wafted through her mind.

She was well aware what was about to unfold. The thought of it sickened her. She watched as he withdrew his sword, a ravenous look replacing the smile on his heavily warted, pasty-white face. "On your knees, wench," he ordered. He approached slowly, as though savoring the moment.

Garret bent to her knees, as ordered. Watching him approach, she noted that the sheath supported by a leather strap running down from his shoulder, and across his chest, was missing its dagger. His keys jangled on the other hip. The bulging presence at his crotch repulsed her.

She recognized her movements and options were limited by the length of the chains attached to the shackles at her wrists and ankles. She needed the man to be close enough before pressing her attack. From her kneeling position, however, there was no possibility of a kick to the groin.

The old guard leaned down, grabbing her wrist shackles and pushing her arms against the wall. He sniffed her hair loudly. Garret turned her head. He proceeded to lick the side of her face with a tongue that smelled of rotting flesh. Garret couldn't bear it any longer. She wrestled to her feet, pressing her back against the wall.

The guard rose, roaring with laughter. "You wish to play, do you?" He stepped back to give himself room and then withdrew his sword.

"Enough!" yelled Valdez upon hearing the man's words.

Garret's arms hung loosely at her side, giving the chains as much slack as possible. Still, the guard was too far away.

"You shall learn not to fight," the guard growled. He extended his sword to the center of her chest, just above her breasts. She felt its freshly sharpened tip pull back hard against her buttoned blouse, popping a button and exposing her left breast. The sword left a thin reddish line threatening to bleed any moment. The guard smiled, dragging the tip of his sword to her right side this time, exposing her other breast. He stood motionlessly, staring at Garret's perky white treasures, each one accented by a taught, pink-encircled nipple. "You need to earn my favor," he said, without moving his eyes. "But I shall let you choose how. Surely a woman such as you has a preference."

Garret shook her head sideways. "I cannot hear you," she said softly, hoping to draw him closer. The guard finally looked up from her breasts, saying nothing. A grin rippled across his warted face. He let go of his sword. It clanked hard on the floor. He loosened his waist-rope, letting his darkly soiled pants slide to his feet. The man wore no linens. His excitement was obvious. He stepped out of his pants and moved toward Garret, reaching to grab her wrists. With the speed of a lizard's tongue, she jerked her arms upward and forward, close together, fists wrapped. Her knuckles crunched the guard's larynx, snapping his head forward but his body backward. He stumbled, falling to the floor in a heap, unable to utter a sound. Seeing both he and his sword were beyond reach, Garret pulled back tightly against the wall. The guard squirmed briefly on the ground, his right hand at his throat. His face appeared even paler than normal. He struggled back to his feet and walked, hunched over, to grab his sword.

Garret expected the worst. He would seek violent retribution…and be more guarded with his next approach. She stood quietly defiant. Her eyes peered into his, daring him to come closer. She shifted her weight, putting her left foot forward and pulling back her right hand as though prepping to strike him with it. She hoped he would fall for her deception, enabling her to surprise him with a leg blow to the testicles. The method had worked well in the past. But she worried about his sword. In addition to threatening harm, it enabled him to maintain distance. She pondered attacking his right wrist, to free the weapon. Perhaps she could grab it once it fell to the ground. There were really no other choices, of that she was certain. She would make her decision as the brute approached, led by both his sword and his now slightly less-rigid member.

Valdez suddenly called out again, "Stop this now, you bastard!"

The guard reacted instinctively to the voice, turning his head toward the cell door, his worried look suggesting he thought his superior was yelling at him. His momentum carried his body forward, in Garret's direction. She spotted her opening and drove her right boot forcefully into his exposed testicles, leaning back to give the blow maximum force. His shattered larynx stifled the scream his body fought to deliver. His sword fell to the floor as he doubled over in agony, grasping his scrotum. Garret propelled the iron shackle on her wrist forward, crushing the bridge of the man's nose. She heard the cartilage give way. Blood sprayed everywhere as the guard's head flew backward while his feet slipped forward. His head slammed hard onto the cell floor. He lost consciousness.

With the guard down, Garret reached for the closest leg of the man's pants, to which the keys were attached. They were beyond her grasp. She stretched out in a different direction, straining for his sword. The tip of her middle finger pressed down on the edge of the handle but she was unable to drag it toward her. She dropped her bottom to the floor, checking to be certain the fallen guard hadn't regained consciousness. Sliding her foot slowly along the floor, she felt her boot contact the hilt. She turned the foot sideways, attempting to maneuver the boot's toe into the hilt. It wasn't working. She pulled her leg back, removed the boot, and then used her foot to methodically drag the sword toward her. Sweat dripped down her temples—not from exertion but rather from worry that another guard might have heard the commotion and would come running. She needn't have worried; commotion was not uncommon in the Tower. And the only other guard was sleepily stationed outside the Cradle Tower's entry.

Finally, with the sword close enough, Garret grasped the handle. She reached out and pointed the sword's tip through the key ring on the guard's pants, drawing the keys toward her. Grabbing and fumbling through them quickly, she found the one that unlocked her shackles. Once freed, she listened intently for the sound of someone approaching. There was none.

Garret dragged the guard closer to the wall and shackled him there. She ripped off a section of his ragged shirt, stuffing it into his mouth. She stripped off a longer section and tied it around his head to secure his mouth shut, in the unlikely case that he might regain his voice. She rose up and took one last at the brute below. 'Bastard!' she whispered, kicking mightily against his privates.

Valdez looked shocked when Garret peered through the window of his cell door. She unlocked it, entered, unchained him, and handed him the guard's sword. They left the cell.

"What about him?" Valdez said, motioning to the third prisoner as they passed his cell door.

Garret turned and glanced through the cell-door window. She saw the man spread-eagled on the floor, ropes tied to each wrist and ankle, and threaded back through the wall anchors.

"Wish him luck," she replied.

"Are you sure you want to do this, Garret?" Valdez queried with an unnecessary whisper. "Would you not be better served by calling on your Queen's mercy?"

"My handling of the guard leaves us no choice." As she said it, she wondered how many guards they might encounter between here and the Tower gate. Then it struck her—the ropes holding the third prisoner offered an alternative. "Wait." She turned back to get the keys and then unlocked the man's cell.

"What are you doing?" asked Valdez.

Garret dashed into the cell, telling the man to remain perfectly quiet. "Help me untie him," she said to Valdez.

While they worked furiously to untie the prisoner, Garret

shared her intent, "We shall tie these together and use them to scale the wall." Valdez looked at the cell window, high up the wall. Garret followed his gaze. "Not to worry. You shall find a way through it."

When they finished loosening the ropes, Garret gathered others from a nearby pile. She instructed Valdez on tying a blood knot. They quickly knotted the ropes together, end-to-end. When they were done, the length appeared to be about thirty feet. Garret secured one end to an iron ring in the wall with a slip knot. She hoped there might be sufficient length remaining to allow for a reasonably safe jump. But first, they'd need to cross the moat.

Valdez hoisted Garret up the wall until she could pull herself onto the sill of the cell window. She reached back. Valdez threw her the rope. She knew the next part would be challenging. There wasn't enough room on the sill for the two of them. She threaded the rope down the side of the tower and moved into position. Holding the rope with her left hand, she slid her legs partially out the window. Reaching down with her right hand, she helped Valdez scramble up the wall. As he grabbed onto the sill, Garret glanced at the third prisoner. He'd been stretched so tightly for days that he could barely move. There was no way he could mount the wall. His face bore a resigned look—he was free, but he wasn't. "Good luck," she mouthed to him.

Garret turned her head to look down the rope outside the wall. To her dismay, it seemed far too short in the darkness. But there was no going back. She would descend as far as she could and then push away from the tower wall with her feet. It seemed possible her momentum would send her out over the moat—a wet but workable landing.

She tested the rope. It held. Ever so slowly, she began placing increased weight on it. Though it groaned, it seemed firm enough to hold her. The greater risk would be the anchor in the cell wall. Carefully, she began walking down the wall, intending to jump if the rigging gave way. When the rope's end was at waist level, she stopped briefly to look down. The drop appeared to be twenty feet. She knew landing in the moat could cause a loud splash. Going in vertically was the only way to minimize the amount of her body breaking the water's surface, thereby lessening the noise. But she was uncertain of the moat's depth. She knew she'd need to spread her arms wide immediately after hitting the surface, to slow her downward thrust. The whole dismount worried her. But again, there was no choice.

Valdez watched Garret holding at the rope's end. He glanced back into the cell where the sword lay on the floor, forgotten. 'Dios mio', he whispered. He turned back, looking down at his accomplice.

Still holding the rope, Garret pushed off with her feet. She swung out, away from the wall. It wasn't far enough. Her momentum returned her. She pushed her legs hard against the wall, gaining momentum. '*One more time*,' she thought as she swung out. When her momentum began taking her back to the wall, she bent her knees tightly and then pushed off it as hard as possible. She let go as the rope reached its outward apex. Down she went, hands at her side, toes pointed straight to the water. She entered with a sound-sucking splash. Spreading her arms, arching her body, and folding her knees to avoid hitting bottom, she sensed she'd submerged about five feet beneath the surface. The ice-cold water seemed to sting. Her eyes still closed, she felt something float against her but dared not think what it might be. She propelled herself upward, finally thrusting her head above the surface.

Garret gasped for air. The smell of raw sewage raced down her nostrils and into her throat. She gagged and stroked her way to the far side of the moat, head above water, anxious to pull herself out of the floating filth. By the time she reached the edge, Valdez was near the rope's end. Climbing out of the moat, Garret watched as he pushed away a couple of times, just as she had. And then down he went, into the putrid, cold muck, with a full-body splash that made her cringe. He bobbed up quickly and began heading to the edge, flailing to stay afloat. Garret reached out. He desperately grabbed her forearm and then climbed the edge.

Valdez rose to his feet, smeared by stinking ooze. Garret smothered a laugh. They scanned the area, seeing and hearing no one.

"This way," mouthed Garret, pulling at his arm.

They ran down dark streets until they glimpsed the outline of a person, then quickly turned left and began walking, as though they were mere street people. Wet, cold, and smelling like days-old scraps of raw meat festering in the sun, they walked as quickly as they dared, breathing heavily and trying to avoid undue notice.

"Where to from here?" asked Valdez.

"The future," whispered Garret.

XXII

Although it was cold, the night sentry at the Cradle Tower preferred stationing himself outside. The air inside was too stale for his liking. So unless it was drenching rain, this was his station. He also preferred the solitude and tranquility of nighttime. It brought him peace, especially compared to the daytime moaning of prisoners inside the Tower walls. But night duty also brought prolonged stillness—and frequent drowsiness, during which his head jerked occasionally to reverse an imbalance.

The unexpected creak of the Tower door sharpened his consciousness. He turned, shocked to see a prisoner emerge, crawling on all fours. Leaping off his stool, the sentry drew his hickory stick and beat the would-be escapee senseless, wondering how he managed to free himself from his cell.

Grabbing the frail man under his arms, he dragged him inside and up the stairwell, swearing at his dead weight. Upon reaching the hallway to the prisoners' cells, he spotted three open doors. The coolness of an instant sweat enveloped his entire body. He let go of the dazed prisoner, drew his sword, and walked warily toward the first open cell. Glancing inside, he saw it was empty. He quickly checked the next cell; also empty. It was the third cell where he found the old guard bloodied, gagged, and laying on the floor, shackled to the wall. He smiled; he never liked the ogre. The man was a bully. He walked back to his beaten prisoner and hastily secured him in his cell, anxious to have a go with the fat bastard lying unconscious.

Returning to the third cell, he approached the half-naked slab of humanity on the floor. He kicked the butt hard until the mass of flesh finally growled and stirred.

"Wake up, ye bloody bastard," the sentry ordered. He kicked the heap once more, for good measure and pure enjoyment. The old guard's eyes squinted open. The sentry knelt to unlock the wrist-shackle but didn't bother to remove the guard's gag. "Get ye dressed and meet me outside, fool." He spat near the guard's face as he got back up and left.

The beaten old guard felt a deep throbbing in his head. Everything either ached or screamed pain—head, nose, neck, crotch and backside. He reached slowly and gently for his nose, finding it differently angled and caked in dried blood. Sitting up, he grabbed at his pants, wincing in pain. '*Bloody Hell*,' he thought as the fog in his mind cleared, revealing a memory of being hit by his female prisoner. He drew his pants on painfully, staggered out of the cell, and hobbled down the stairwell, to join the sentry waiting outside.

The Constable of the Tower was livid. The sentry and the wretched old guard, who had rudely interrupted his sleep, now stood before him in his quarters, having shared the news. Their heads hung down. The guard had dried blood on his face around his shattered nose. He struggled to breathe, let alone speak. The Constable had only disdain for the bastard and his revolting appearance. He vented physically with a powerful slap to the side of the guard's head.

"You are a complete disgrace," he yelled, showering the man with spittle. "You shall pay dearly." He turned toward his door in a hurry, intending to alert the guards at the Tower's main entry. But he turned back first. "Stay right here," he ordered, "I am far from done with you."

A bell rang out harshly in the cold night air. Word spread quickly. Tense commotion filled the grounds and ran along the Tower walls as the search for escapees unfolded. But there was no sighting …for tens of minutes. And then there was…

"A rope!" one of the guards yelled from beyond the Tower walls. "Outside the Cradle Tower!"

"Assemble the guard," the Constable shouted. Several men ran immediately to the gate, some bringing horses. "Find these bastards. Do not dare return without them. I want them both. Alive."

————

They had no money, no weapons, and no means of transportation. Garret squelched a chuckle at the thought that they were now, literally, on equal terms with the beggars eking out their meager lives on London's streets and alleyways. But at least there were others on whom they could rely. Garret suspected William, or perhaps Blair, might search for her at Orion's Tavern—the place she usually stayed while in the city. It was near the Thames and commonly visited by seafaring men of higher standing. The owner, Geoge Tyndale, knew Garret well because of her frequent visits. Over the years, he'd seen her transform from presenting as male to becoming the woman she truly was, without choosing to judge her; at least not that she knew. Garret was confident she could count on his help. After all, she always paid him well. She'd once heard him bemoan that his customers' ability to pay was often a function of their success at sea. Since that ebbed and flowed like the tides, she knew a reliable payer like her was a premier customer.

"This way," whispered Garret, pulling at Valdez' arm. "I have a friend nearby." Heading in the direction of the tavern, they barely spoke, to avoid drawing attention. They chose dingy alleyways over wider streets wherever they could.

"Dios mio," Valdez exclaimed in a loud whisper after tripping over an unseen body splayed out on the ground. The sleeping vagrant barely reacted. They came across several others along the way, finding their occasional groaning and unintelligible mutterings disturbing. Garret recognized it was the first time she'd taken real notice of hapless beggars, and of just how many there actually were. In some way, they disgusted her. Yet the more of them she encountered, the more she began to feel for them as fellow humans. Yet there was little she could do for them given her circumstances. She simply chose not to make eye contact. It could easily bring on undesired and potentially challenging engagements that might draw the attention of anyone pursuing them.

Nearing Orion's Tavern, Garret noticed the outside lantern was unlit. And there was no light emanating from within. Nevertheless, upon reaching the door, she quietly attempted to open it. As expected, it was locked. Garret thought it best not to knock; they could wait until the owner opened. She judged it wouldn't be too long. She and Valdez headed off to find a secluded spot down a nearby alleyway, like two vagabonds seeking solace in a precarious and cruel world. Finding an uncluttered spot, they sat.

"What if William is not there?" whispered Valdez.

"He has to be," answered Garret. "There is nowhere else in London he would search for me, or stay himself."

A mumbling beggar approached. "Food?" he queried.

Valdez waved his arm. "Away with you."

The beggar wavered slightly, trying to maintain his balance in the stillness. Either he didn't hear or didn't understand the command.

"I said, be gone." Valdez waved his arm more aggressively. The beggar took it as a threat. He wobbled backward, his beady eyes now squinting directly at Valdez' face. Quickly, he charged with a sharp stick of wood in hand. Valdez tried scrambling to his feet but the beggar was already on him, slashing wildly with the weapon. It pierced Valdez's forearm as he raised it to deflect the blow.

"Damn you!" Valdez exclaimed. He grabbed the man's right bicep, pushing his arm backward fast and hard. He felt and heard the crunch of the man's shoulder separating. The wooden shiv dropped out of his hand as he screamed in pain. Valdez put his left fist straight into the man's jugular, transforming the scream into a gurgle. The beggar fell, reaching for his throat with his left hand. Valdez reached for the shiv. The beggar scrambled to his feet and hobbled quickly down the alleyway gasping for breath, his right arm hanging low at his side.

Garret observed the fray with mixed feelings. From a fighter's perspective, it was a work of art. Valdez wasted no motion; just two lightning strikes and it was over. He was clearly well-seasoned in combat. She admired his ability to take immediate control of the situation, though she felt a pang of sorrow for the poor beggar.

"This may come in handy," Valdez said. He stuffed the shiv into his rope-belt and then grabbed his arm to stanch the small flow of blood.

"So would a change of garments," Garret smirked, wishing deeply to be rid of her foul-smelling clothes.

Exhausted, the two escapees eventually dozed off. Their sleep was uneasy, their nerves skimming the edge of being discovered.

The girl's tangled, dirty-brown hair hung over and around a sweet but filthy face. Her clothes were grimy and ragged. The old, worn shoes covering her feet were far too big for her. Nor did they match. She'd rescued each from a different pile of trash. For as long as she could remember, her life was one of searching through rubbish, begging on the main streets, and sleeping on the backstreets.

She stopped. Two figures she didn't recognize were huddled close against the wall of a building. She moved in closer, for a better look. It appeared one might be a young woman—with a not-unpleasant face but for the two smears of muck. An inexplicable feeling of belonging coursed through her body. She knelt, quietly placing the cup she'd been holding on the ground near the woman. The two coins in it shifted position but made little perceptible noise. She sat for a while before her head finally rested against the woman's shoulder.

Garret awoke, startled, her mind in a haze. She saw the girl but couldn't instantly pull together the puzzle pieces that might explain her presence. When the fog inside her head dissipated, she realized the little urchin was merely seeking warmth and comfort. She placed her arm around the girl and fell back asleep.

With dawn about to break, Valdez awoke to footsteps approaching on cobblestones. He nudged Garret just enough to wake her. Placing his hand softly over her mouth to keep her from speaking, he spotted the girl snuggled up against her. It made him pause. But there was a more pressing concern at the moment—two dark figures at the far end of the alleyway, possibly Tower guards. Slowly, he and

Garret rose.

The girl stirred, instinctively grabbing her cup. She got up, looking in the direction Valdez was focused. Pulling at Garret's sleeve, she nodded as if to lead them away. The three walked casually, to avoid drawing undue attention from the two distant shadows now approaching. After turning the corner, they quickly pulled off their boots and ran barefoot toward the end of another alley, footwear in hand. When they turned the corner, Garret laid flat on her stomach, moving her head along the dirty but dry ground, to the edge of the old stone building. She peered down the alleyway and waited. It wasn't long until she heard the faint steps of the two men approaching their corridor. They emerged as live shadows. One turned in her direction and stood there a moment. Garret froze, hoping he couldn't make out her head in the dark and distance. Every moment of stillness seemed to raise the sound of her heartbeat. She dared not move but worried the dawn's emerging light would surely give her up if the man in the distance remained much longer. Luck broke her way. The man turned and dashed off to catch up with his partner.

Garret, Valdez and the girl sat, resting against the building. "What is your name, little one?" Garret asked, stroking the back of the girl's head.

"They call me Scrapper, mum."

"Who calls you this?"

"My friends."

"And where are your parents?"

"Have none, mum. Just me friends."

Garret's heart went out to this miniature person, guessing she might be nine or ten years old. Her matter-of-fact pattern of speech suggested she was well-adapted to her current existence, if not comfortable with it. She didn't seem to know any better. But Garret did. A girl her age deserved something more.

"Thank goodness for the dark," Garret said, running her hand through her hair in a fruitless attempt to freshen it. The hair chose not to cooperate. Its movement simply wafted a moat-like stench into the air. Garret rose, dusting dirt off her clothes, though it hardly mattered. "Let us see if the tavern is open."

Valdez felt a pressing headache. Probably from the lack of food, he thought. As they walked along, he glanced at Garret. Her empathy for the street urchin was obvious. Almost motherly. And as dirty as Garret was, with her hair badly straggled, her face still captured his interest. He reached out and swept a strand of misbehaving hair behind her ear. "You are quite the sight," he said.

"I am not alone in that," Garret answered back.

———

William Tovery noisily descended the wooden stairs to the main floor of Orion's Tavern, planning on a hearty breakfast. He'd slept uneasily. The light of a soon-to-appear sun entered the window, illuminating the room. He welcomed the new day, hopeful it might bring him closer to finding Garret.

The tavern owner hadn't yet opened the door for business when William greeted him, "Top of the morning, George. Biscuit and tea, if you please."

"Morning Captain. A moment, if you please."

William pulled back a chair and sat at the table. "I am in need of a horse this morning."

"I shall arrange it. It may be half the hour. Might I ask where you are headed?"

"To see a friend," replied William. Though the owner knew Garret, there was no sense uttering her name. It would only generate further, perhaps awkward, discussion. "Am I the only guest this morning?"

"There is one other gentleman. A man from Lincolnshire, in town on business." George placed the tea and biscuit on William's table. His head turned in the direction of a knock at the door. He walked to the entry.

Garret was about to knock again when she heard the owner unlocking the door. He opened it, looking askance at the street beggars before him, clearly catching their foul-smelling scent.

"Get ye away. We are not…"

"George—tis I, Garret."

George paused, looking at her with squinted eyes. "Oh my," he exclaimed, opening the door wide. "Come in. You look in horrible condition, if I may say."

"A long story, I am afraid." Garret walked in, the girl beside her, Valdez following. "This is my friend, Jorge," she gestured toward Valdez, "and my other little friend." She nodded down at Scrapper and then glanced back at George. He had a curious look on his face. She presumed he wondered what she was doing with a Spaniard…and both of them looking the beggar.

"Garret!" William exclaimed, rising from his chair with a look of shocked surprise. "What on earth has happened?"

"William. What a joy to see you," Garret called out. She, Jorge and Scrapper approached. George closed the tavern door.

Valdez nodded to William, "Good morning, Captain."

William nodded back and turned to Garret. "I hope you don't mind if I refrain from greeting you with a hug," he said, smiling.

"Of course. Parfum de moat," she laughed. Garret turned to George. "Are there rooms?"

"There are, yes. I presume you shall want a basin and water?"

"Please. Thank you."

"Will you be needing anything else, Captain?"

"Would there be any fresh clothes perhaps?"

George looked distraught. "Just my own garments, I am afraid."

"I have fresh clothing that might be passable for you," offered William, "Jorge will need something larger than I can provide."

"I shall check with a friend, for these two," George interjected, pointing to Valdez and Scrapper.

"Excellent. But please, leave no word of our names," said Garret.

"As you wish." George rushed off to retrieve a large jug of water.

"I am anxious to hear all that has transpired," William said. "But please, address your needs first."

"Thank you, William," replied Garret. "All in good time; though time is rather precious at the moment."

———

His carriage slowed to a stop. Thomas opened the door and

stepped down onto the cobblestones, seeking to address the posted sentry personally. Having been to Richmond Palace often, he knew the man well.

"Best of the morning to you."

"And to you, Mr. Drake."

"I am here to meet with the Queen's Secretary." Thomas had no desire to drag the Queen herself into this. Certainly not yet.

"Do you have a meeting arranged, then?"

"I am afraid not. It concerns an urgent matter that has just arisen."

"I see. I believe the Secretary is somewhere on the grounds at the moment."

"Fine. I shall find him."

"Of course."

William gave the man a coin, conferred briefly with his coachman, and walked onto the grounds. He listened to the clop of the horses as the driver sought to make a turn and reposition the carriage to a staging area, for later departure.

Strolling the park-like setting, it took William several minutes to locate the Secretary. The man was seated on a bench in the gardens, quietly reading. "Good day, sir," Thomas offered, doffing his hat.

The Secretary looked up, nodding hello but saying nothing. His grimace conveyed the frustration of being rudely interrupted. Not a particularly friendly man at the best of times, Thomas knew he reveled in the leverage his role gave him. He had a way of making others feel subservient, regardless of their standing.

"Might I have a moment of your time?"

"You may. But *just* a moment, if you please. I have pressing business to attend to." Thomas imagined that was nothing more than a display of power. The man was clearly just reading his book and enjoying the pleasant morning.

"Thank you. I have a simple inquiry. I understand Captain Garret Connachan has returned from the Southern Seas. I was informed she traveled here immediately following her arrival, to meet with the Queen."

"I am afraid you are misinformed."

"Pardon me?"

"You are mistaken. The Queen has not received the Captain."

"But I was told…"

The Secretary interrupted him, angrily. "Must I repeat myself? The Queen has not met with the Captain."

Sensing the man wasn't being entirely open, Thomas knew he needed to tread carefully—the Secretary was key to gaining any access to the Queen herself. "I am sorry," he said, "Might I inquire whether Captain Connachan has met with anyone else here at the Palace?"

"You might. Yet the answer remains the same. The Captain has not come to the Palace."

"Well, then," Thomas began, "would you happen to know…"

"You test my patience," interjected the Secretary.

"Of course," Thomas demurred. "Thank you for your time." He turned to walk away, convinced the man was withholding information.

"Shall I tell the Queen you were here?" asked the Secretary.

Thomas turned back. "No, thank you. Please not to bother her."

"As you wish." The Secretary went back to reading his book.

There could be only one other possibility, Thomas thought, as he hurried back to the main gate. If Garret had left *Pandora* in the company of the Queen's guards, but not come to the Palace, then she must have been taken to a different location. Her failure to execute Valdez, and then bring him to England, loomed large. It was highly likely Her Majesty was displeased. He feared that could mean Garret was taken to the Tower. The place had a troubling reputation. Prisoners were commonly held there, some prior to execution. A few reputedly never made it to their beheading, or hanging, for reasons unknown. But would Her Majesty dare treat Garret in that manner? He doubted it. Yet where else could Garret be? And for what other reason would the Queen send her guard to meet and accompany Garret, if not to bring her straight to the Palace or secure her at the Tower?

Thomas' thoughts turned to the Secretary. His insistence that Garret hadn't been to the Palace was certainly believable. His intentional withholding of her whereabouts, however, appeared to be a cover. Thomas realized he needed to get to the Tower right away, to inquire after his friend.

The impressive stone walls and storied towers emanated strength, Thomas thought, as the Tower increasingly filled his view. He prayed Garret wouldn't be there yet found himself hoping she was. At least then he would know her situation for certain. And perhaps he could help.

As his carriage drew to a halt, Thomas opened the door and stepped down. The sentry at the gate approached. He was curt. "State your business."

"I wish to inquire about the recent arrival of a prisoner. A

Captain Connachan."

"And you are?"

"Thomas Drake—the Captain's agent."

"Wait here, if you please."

The sentry turned and walked toward a guard, with whom he conferred briefly. The guard then headed to the Constable's office.

"We have a visitor at the gates, sir," announced the guard. "He claims to be an agent of Captain Connachan."

"I see," Constable Clutterbuck replied. "Please, bring him." Seated regally at his oversized, ornate desk, Clutterbuck was deeply interested in meeting this visitor who might have information to help him apprehend the two people whose escape threatened to shine an unwelcome light on him. They may have even put his command in jeopardy—a station he'd held for nearly a dozen years. He found it quite agreeable. And it paid handsomely. He knew he wasn't the most militarily skilled officer but he prided himself on being politically skilled. He'd purchased this particular command precisely for the combination of political power and societal standing it offered.

It was several minutes before the guard returned to the gates and spoke with the sentry, who then approached Thomas. "The Constable shall see you," he said. "Follow the guard." He waved his hand dismissively in that direction.

Thomas trailed the guard to the Constable's quarters. He observed the place was well-appointed. The Constable himself, though quite overweight, was discerningly dressed, his gray hair and beard finely sculpted.

"Thomas Drake, Constable," announced the guard.

Clutterbuck rose. "Thank you, you are dismissed," he replied. He turned to Thomas, extending his hand, "Good day, Mr. Drake. I am Constable of the Tower, James Clutterbuck."

"Good day to you as well, sir."

"Might I ask…are you related to the Admiral?"

"He was my dear brother."

"Well then, this is truly an honor. I admired your brother. He was the finest Admiral England has ever known."

"Thank you, Constable. I had the pleasure of serving with him, though he treated me no differently than any other sailor," Thomas smiled. "He loved his men. No doubt like you, he would stop at nothing to ensure they were well-served, well-fed, and well-led."

The Constable appeared to enjoy the indirect compliment, whether or not it was deserved. "So I have heard. How is it I can help you today?"

"I am a friend of Captain Garret Connachan, who also sailed with my brother. I should like to see her."

"And why is it you have come here?"

Thomas noted Clutterbuck didn't deny Garret's presence in the Tower. "She recently returned from the Southern Seas. One of her officers informed me she was met at anchor by the Queen's guard. She was escorting a prisoner back to England. I was told she brought him here."

"I see." The Constable paused. "A prisoner was indeed escorted here recently by Her Majesty's Royal Guard."

Again, thought Thomas, no direct denial of Garret's being brought here. If the Constable knew something, it was clear he didn't wish to share it. Best not to press too hard. "Might I see this prisoner?"

"I am afraid he was here only briefly. Tell me more about this Captain Connachan."

"A fine young woman," replied Thomas. "Intelligent and pleasant. Auburn hair. Green eyes. She and I served together as midshipmen. A first-rate seaman and a damn fine swordsman."

"Do sailors not say that a woman onboard ship is a bad omen?"

"They do, yes. But not this woman. She earned the crew's respect. Her gender was never an issue."

"Hmmm." Clutterbuck paused. "I was not informed that the prisoner was accompanied by a woman. I shall have to inquire." He extended his hand, signaling the end of the meeting. "I am afraid I have an important matter to attend to. I shall, of course, let you know what I find."

Thomas thought the ending too abrupt. He shook the Constable's hand, surmising he was being toyed with. He considered asking where Valdez had gone but sensed Clutterbuck was unlikely to be forthcoming. "Thank you, Constable. I shall be most grateful for any information you can provide—as my brother would have been, were he here with us." Thomas hoped the reference to his brother might signal to this reluctant Constable that his cooperation could bring him the support of Drake's family, perhaps even a generous gratuity, if he were later forthcoming with word of Garret's situation.

Clutterbuck stepped outside his quarters to watch Thomas exit the Tower gates. It appeared Drake's brother accepted that Captain Connachan was never here. Disclosing she'd escaped under his watch would only have invited trouble. Nonetheless, he thought it best to remain on good terms with the deceased Admiral's brother. Knowing such a man could prove politically valuable at some point. He made a note to kindly message him later, stating he could offer no further information on Connachan.

————

In the hour following the arrival of Garret, Valdez and the girl at Orion's Tavern, William thought deeply about their situation. His primary worry was that the Royal Guard might decide to take possession of *Pandora* and *Orion*. He needed to circumvent that possibility. It was imperative that Garret have a means of escaping the country, if necessary. He arranged for a messenger to be sent to Master's Mate Blair, whom he'd ordered to remain in Plymouth.

He wrestled with two other significant concerns. One was whether Garret might ask him to join her and Valdez in their flight from capture. That would be a big ask, effectively making him a partner to her crime. It would certainly shut down his naval career. And tarnish his family's fine name. But at least there was still time to weigh his options.

The other pressing concern was how best to deal with Valdez. Perhaps a case could be made that the Viceroy escaped on his own, taking Garret hostage. But if he and Garret were found to be providing Valdez with assistance in avoiding capture, their actions would be deemed treasonous—a foundation for execution. Though he believed Valdez should be left to fend for himself, he worried that Garret had grown too fond of the man. It could easily distort her judgment. He worried this was the more difficult of the two problems to resolve.

And then there was the added complication of the little girl. He chose not to give that further thought.

XXIII

Standing near the top of the mainmast, *Death's Head's* spotter leaned forward, squinting his eyes. He was now certain the distant image barely visible in the light mist was Isla San Juan Bautista. "Land ho!" he shouted down to the deck, excitedly. "Two points to larboard."

Harker didn't bother to respond. His ship and its consort, *Red Knight*, already had their bearing. They trailed well behind *Cutthroat*, per his agreement to let De Graaf take the lead on their next prize. They'd spotted it earlier. Unless De Graaf signaled him to engage, Harker intended to maintain a spectator position. The fact that Isla San Juan Bautista was nearby was of only passing interest.

De Graaf wasn't focused on the island either. He watched the growing white sails of his prey skim the water's edge, presuming they'd recently departed the port of Ponce. It occurred to him that Harker was right; these were excellent fishing waters for ravenous pirates. And here was their potential meal—a lone, two-masted merchant, not yet fully sheeted. "Two points to starboard," he yelled, adjusting his intercept course.

There seemed little possibility his target could outpace him, especially since he had better advantage of the wind. He thirsted for a decisive, bloody battle that could spark his reputation as a brutal predator. It would facilitate future conquests. "Hoist the crimson," he shouted. In moments, the blood-red flag unfurled, flapping forward in the stiff breeze.

Several grappling hooks soared over the side of the Spanish

merchant, descending like vultures to a dead carcass. *Cutthroat's* crew yanked hard against the ropes, pulling the hooks to catch the vessel's taffrail. The two ships were shortly drawn together, enabling face-painted pirates to stream over the rail and scurry like cockroaches.

Recognizing his ship's vulnerability, the merchant captain had frozen his cannons. He hoped for a non-lethal boarding in return; his crew were seamen, not soldiers. Lightly armed and deeply frightened, some ran below deck, ahead of the oncoming wave of savage raiders.

Pikes were the leading edge of the pirates' charge, thrown as though shot from an arquebus. Two merchant seamen were pierced through cleanly, promising them an agonizingly slow and painful death. Seamen with pistols fired back in response, grazing a few marauders but failing to prevent the inevitable. Blades quickly clashed in a screeching symphony of steel on steel, sparks exploding off the blades. The dissonant music of battle morphed as the gouging of bodies layered in muffled sucking sounds and screams of agony. Cracking bones added to the cacophony. Blood rained red, seeming to mock the foolishly brave seamen giving their all to defend a soulless wooden vessel.

The beleaguered merchant captain looked on from the foredeck. He had no stomach to watch his men suffer further in this sickening bloodletting. He raised two pistols in the air. Their shots barked out above the fray, one after the other. His aide stood beside him, furiously waving a white flag like a conductor gone mad. Few of the pirates acknowledged the surrender, choosing instead to finish their opponents. The profuse flow of blood only seemed to intensify their thirst for more.

"Halt!" yelled De Graaf, raising both arms, his cutlass in his right. The red splatter covering him reflected the dispatch of two sailors to their final destination. His left arm oozed blood from beneath his ripped shirt. He approached the surrendering captain, his face blackened for battle and striped in white. Seamen and raiders alike parted to give him room.

Watching the ominous-looking pirate leader ascend the steps to the foredeck, the merchant captain withdrew his sword nervously with his left hand. It clanged on the deck as he let it fall. The sound was soon echoed by the descent of his surviving men's weapons. A sudden wave of silence gave life to the moans of the wounded and the rhythmic beat of De Graaf's boots landing heavily on each stair.

Drops of fear-filled sweat beaded profusely on the captain's forehead as the pirate captain closed in.

"You dare oppose me?" De Graaf screamed, so loud that his words carried across the water to the deck of the *Death's Head,* bringing a grin to Harker's face.

The captain bowed his head. "Forgive me. I…" His words were lost to the air as De Graaf swung his cutlass cruelly through the thick of the captain's neck. The soft crunch and the spray of blood caused the captain's aide to vomit. De Graaf turned to the aide and waited until he looked up. It was a short look, ending with the aide's head falling off his shoulders to join his captain's on the foredeck. The ship's sudden sway caused both heads to bound down the steps, leaving a red trail to the main deck.

De Graaf turned to face the men below. He thrust his arms high in the air, causing his men to cheer raucously. Drawing in a deep breath, he savored his first victory as a captain. Finally, when he dropped his arms, everyone stopped to listen.

"My fellow warriors," he opened. The men smiled and cheered. "My bloodthirsty pirates," he yelled, thrusting his cutlass high in the air. Again, the men cheered, raising their own weapons high. De Graaf let the noise trail off before lowering his sword and raising his left hand to bring complete silence.

"We have earned the right to the riches of this ship. But first, let us search below deck for the cowards who chose not to fight." He pointed and swept his sword in the direction of half his men, indicating they should head below.

While awaiting arrival of the cowards, De Graaf scanned the crowded deck. Everyone could hear pistol shots and a brief scuffle emanating from below. Moments later, shabbily dressed prisoners filed out, hands gripped behind their heads. Two were dragged. One young man was in tears. They were all ushered to the rail, at the point of swords. De Graaf nodded to his men. They proceeded to skewer the cowards and hoist them overboard. Their screams ended in gurgles.

De Graaf raised his arms high, palms forward, requesting silence.

"I wish to address the remaining crew of this ship," he shouted. "You have fought bravely this day. I commend you. You shall make excellent pirates, should you choose to join us. You can then fight for yourselves, rather than for overlords." He paused to judge their reaction. "Should you choose not to join us, you shall share one of two fates—be set free on a longboat or remain prisoner." He didn't bother mentioning his intention to use prisoners for occasional sport— torturing them variously for his crew's entertainment. "But you must choose now," he continued. "If you would be a pirate, step to larboard."

The captured seamen exchanged glances, their futures hovering on a sword's edge. A few began shuffling to larboard. Some already on that side crossed to starboard. The repositioning continued, though not for long. When it ended, just under half had chosen a baptism to piracy. The rest were too numerous for one longboat to hold.

"There being too many of you," De Graaf said to those on the starboard side, "I shall allow only twelve to go. The rest shall remain prisoner. Decide among yourselves."

The captives huddled. They were soon arguing and shoving one another. No decisions were being made. De Graaf grew tired of waiting. "You," he yelled, pointing to one of the captives. "Here," he ordered, pointing to the deck in front of him. The bloodied, disheveled, middle-aged man glanced first at his fellow sailors. He didn't step forward right away. Two of De Graaf's men stepped in, shepherding him forward. Dirty and sweating, the man appeared surprisingly calm thought De Graaf, especially having just witnessed the slaughter of his Captain, the Captain's aide, and the cowards from below deck. Perhaps he thought his end would come quickly.

"Choose a man," De Graaf instructed.

"Que?"

"Choose," De Graaf howled, pointing toward the captives.

The man looked back to his crewmates clearly uncertain whether he was choosing one for the longboat or a death sentence. He locked eyes first with a friend, then with a man he despised. Finally, he pointed to a man who only recently joined the merchant crew—a badly wounded sailor.

De Graaf nodded to his men. Two of them pulled the wounded seaman forward. He was in his late teens. Portuguese.

Something shiny flickered. De Graaf tore open the young man's shirt to take a look. A small crucifix hung on a thin leather strap around his neck. "Tu nombre?" De Graaf asked.

"Manuel," said the teen, looking straight into De Graaf's eyes.

"Do you pray to die today?"

"God will decide."

"Am I not your God in this moment?"

The young man seemed unafraid. "God's will shall be delivered through you."

De Graaf admired the teen's spunk. He turned and faced the man who selected him. "You have chosen poorly, my friend." He turned to the guards holding him. "Secure him to the mainmast." They pulled the man away. He didn't bother to struggle.

De Graaf pointed to Manuel. "Clean him up. I have need of a man such as this." Two pirates escorted Manuel toward the group of seamen who'd chosen the pirate life. De Graaf pointed to another captive who hadn't. "You. Here." He pointed to the deck in front of him. The designated man approached, not needing any accompaniment.

"You are?"

"Francisco."

"Your rank?"

"I am contramaestre."

"In English."

"You would say, boatswain."

"I see. What cargo shall I find on this ship?"

"We carry sugar and molasses to Spain."

"And silver?"

"Enough to purchase supplies."

"How much?"

"I cannot be certain."

De Graaf peered deeply into the man's eyes. He seemed to be telling the truth. "Choose one," he said, pointing again to the captives.

"Please. This is not my place. You choose for me."

"Choose," De Graaf insisted.

Francisco pointed to an older man with a scruffy, gray beard.

De Graaf looked at the chosen man. He bore no visible signs of having engaged in battle. De Graaf presumed he'd hidden somewhere above deck during the siege. "Come forward," he yelled.

The older man approached. De Graaf queried him. "No blood?"

"No, capítan. I not fight. I old."

"Old and worthless," muttered De Graaf.

"No, no, Capítan. Marinero." Apparently, the old man didn't understand the word 'worthless'.

De Graaf called out to the captives. "You shall choose which of these two men goes free." He directed his cutlass to Francisco and the old man, and then waited for a decision. The captives murmured and argued.

"What are they saying?" De Graaf asked one of his pirates who was fluent in Spanish.

"This man Francisco is not well-liked. They say he holds himself above them. Still, some believe he is more able to share in the rowing."

De Graaf grew impatient. "Enough! Decide!"

A moment later, one of the captives spoke up. "The old man stays." De Graaf understood; the old man was expendable.

The selection process continued until twelve men were identified. They gathered near the taffrail to disembark while their less fortunate brethren were taken below deck. Once the twelve were provided a modest supply of fresh water and hard tack, they descended into a longboat. Several grabbed an oar and began pulling.

"Not until I give the signal," De Graaf said to his men. They waited anxiously with pistols loaded. De Graaf watched until he judged the boat was far enough away that some of its occupants would likely survive.

"Fire at will," he said calmly.

Shots rang out at the bobbing boat. Its occupants ducked, though its oarsmen rowed harder. Some of the men were hit or grazed by the spray of pistol balls. Two jumped overboard. The pirates laughed heartily at the humor in all of this. They reloaded to have another go.

De Graaf turned and walked away from the rail, listening to the pops from his men's pistols. Shots continued until the longboat was too distant for their liking. No one could be certain how many of the seamen survived. De Graaf cared only that there was at least one—to tell the tale of his brutal assault; an account that would surely be embellished in the telling.

XXIV

The messenger dismounted his tired mare outside The Sea Horse tavern. His first inquiries upon reaching Plymouth made it clear that the men he sought were well known and likely to be found at the harbor. He'd been directed to two taverns in particular, this being the second. The creak of the door was drowned by the bell's ring and the clamor of voices as he walked in. The dingy place smelled of stale beer and pungent fish. His eyes were still adjusting to the darkness when he spotted two shadowy hulks seated off to his right. He walked to their table. "Pardon the bother," he said. "I am looking for a man named Caber."

The Black colossus pushed back against his chair and rose, threateningly. "Who asks?" he growled.

The messenger darted his eyes at the other man—the still-seated, bearded redhead whom he suspected was the one he sought. He looked back, and up, to the hulk now towering over him. "I have a letter," he said shakily. Reaching into his doublet, he withdrew the note and extended it in his hand. No one moved. The messenger looked left and right, confused at what was happening.

The Black man stepped forward, pressing his enormous frame against the extended hand. It was all the messenger needed. He dropped the note, turned, and scrambled out the door.

"You be leaving something behind," shouted Musa. Caber and several onlookers laughed.

Musa looked down at the lonely-looking message on the floor. He turned to Caber. "Tis yours. You be pickin' it up."

Caber chuckled. He bent down and grabbed the note. Turning it over, he recognized Captain Tovery's seal. He placed the message on the table and took a swig of beer before picking it up again. The corner was now wet from the spillage of the prior hour's boisterous drinking. He unsealed the parchment. The writing seemed hurried. He took a few moments to decipher the words. When he was done, he folded the note and inserted it in his doublet.

"Cap'n Tovery wishes us to gather the mates. Quietly. We are to ready the ships and sail for Cardiff. He intends to meet us there within two weeks." Musa nodded. Caber continued, "I shall inform the men. You secure the supplies. Say nothing of our destination to anyone."

"What about Blair?"

Caber paused to think. "I imagine the Cap'n would have us inform him. Perhaps he thought the messenger would have an easier time finding the two of *us*." They both grinned, recognizing they were famous—and infamous—here at the docks. They rose simultaneously. The sound of their chairs scraping against the floor went virtually unheard in the noisy tavern. Caber left a coin on their table and walked to another, where crewmates were drinking beer and laughing loudly.

Musa exited the tavern. The clouds obscuring the late afternoon sun were beginning to shed their heavy load. He pulled the collar up on his sailor's coat and breathed in the fresh, salty air that blew in his face…and fired his soul.

———

Nearing the crest of a hill, three horsemen and a child slowed to a stop. The one in the lead, with the child seated behind, pulled the reins to the right. Her shabbily groomed mare turned to the side. The rider gazed at the distant city, sensing it might well be her last look at it. An anchor of sadness weighed on her heart.

William edged his horse next to hers, "Let us hope for better days."

Garret nodded in agreement but had no words to offer. A horde of memories flooded her mind—of Drake; of Pantas; of the Queen; of her beloved tavern…all things she'd now lost. She wondered what was to become of her life, realizing she might never be able to come home again; if London ever really was home for her.

Pulling the reins to her left, Garret guided the old chestnut brown mare's head back in the direction she wished to go: Cardiff…perhaps six days hence. Maybe seven. She hoped they would make good time. She also hoped to avoid raising suspicions among those they might come across. Being dressed in William's clothing helped; the Queen's guards would be searching for a woman. And even if the guards were to come across them, passing herself off as male wouldn't be challenging. She'd presented as male on Drake's circumnavigation of the globe and was well adept at navigating in arguably the most challenging of men's worlds—the one at sea.

William pulled his horse alongside Garret's. "Tell me," he said, "when we get to Cardiff, will you want me to sail with you?" The look on her face suggested to him that she was surprised he even needed to ask. Perhaps she was too consumed by her own situation, and that of the little girl, to have given much thought to his dilemma. He waited, hoping the real implication behind his words would set in.

Garret shook her head. 'I am so sorry, William. I have been

quite thoughtless, have I not?"

"You have much on your mind."

"I do, yes," she shrugged. "Though I must say, the thought of your not sailing with me brings me great pain. I have no closer friend."

"There is great risk in it, for me."

"Indeed. You would become a turncoat on my behalf."

"Just so."

They rode on for several paces before William continued, "I am torn myself. And truly, I worry most for my family. For their reputation."

"As you should."

"Your own thoughts on the matter might influence me," said William.

"I trust you are not expecting me to make such a decision for you."

"Not at all."

Garret paused to think. "Let your heart lead you, William."

"Just as you always have," he smiled.

They rode side-by-side for a few minutes, neither speaking. Finally, Garret added another thought, "Once your decision is finally made, I suggest you never revisit it. Rather, make it *be* your best path."

"A fair point," William replied, nodding.

"Just know that I feel blessed to have shared our partnership thus far…and would welcome its continuation."

William looked at Garret, noting the sadness in her eyes. He had no desire to disappoint her. Or himself, for that matter. Losing contact with her would haunt him. He felt a sudden, unfathomable urge to spend the rest of his life alongside her. If not *with* her.

The four rode on. Having overheard Garret and William's conversation, Valdez once more contemplated his own future. His scheme to seduce Garret in service of his interests hadn't gone as planned. And it seemed perfectly clear she no longer had any influence with Queen Elizabeth. Her only value now was in helping him flee the country. But, he conceded, there might be something more. Having pulled through a challenging escape together, he sensed their relationship was changing. Was he actually developing feelings for the woman? '*No*,' he thought. '*I cannot go there.*' He shook his head to clear his mind.

His thoughts turned to Spain. If he were ever to find his way back there, how might he best explain to King Philip the events that brought him to this place? One thing he knew for certain—he needed to get off this hostile island. With or without young Connachan.

He wondered whether Garret now pondered *his* situation. If so, would he depart Cardiff with her, or be left behind in some prison? He wondered briefly what he would do, were the situation reversed. It seemed clear he would take her along…at the very least to fulfill his sexual desires.

———

The rocking of the ship and swaying of the lantern hanging in his quarters comforted De Graaf as he sipped his beer. Returning his tankard to the table, he continued reviewing the inventory of the proceeds from his recent capture. Though not large in coinage, they were not insignificant. Unfortunately, it would take some time before they could exchange the sugar and molasses for coins.

After providing Harker and his crew with their entitled share, he worried that the watered-down remainder for his own men would annoy them beyond measure. He contemplated hiding a portion of the goods from Harker—a technique his fellow pirate commonly used himself. But Harker was no fool. Nor was he a trusting soul. If he were to discover a portion of the treasure was withheld, the two would surely face confrontation—a possibly deadly one. That was not something he desired; certainly not this early into his captaincy. Best to deal with his men's annoyance by finding another ship to raid. And soon. In the meantime, he thought he might provide the men with a little celebratory entertainment. The Spaniard they tied to the mast earlier would serve that purpose well.

A commotion on the main deck interrupted his thoughts. Perhaps the men had started without him, he thought. He took one last swig of his beer and headed to the door. Opening it sucked in a raucous wave of tension-filled air. He hurried onto the deck, shoving his way through the huddled mass of his crew. They encircled two men about to engage in combat. The larger one accused the other of stealing an ivory-handled dagger from one of the captives. The smaller man denied it, holding the dagger in question in his right hand.

The larger man waved his cutlass menacingly, seeming to like his chances against the dagger. The two began circling, each seeking an opening. De Graaf welcomed their settling the disagreement in this fashion, trusting the more skilled of the two would win the day. What better way to reinforce the importance of honing combat skills? Still, he wondered at the decision of the smaller man—Spriggs. He'd chosen not to draw his cutlass. And his dagger was no match for his opponent's lengthy blade. The two continued circling, the larger man grinning.

Spriggs held his dagger low and wide—an abnormal throwing position. He wanted the bigger man to believe he had a commanding advantage, giving him a false sense of invulnerability. It might dull his sharpness. Stopping suddenly, he hurled the dagger sideways and upward. It wedged itself deeply into the bigger man's chest, causing him to stagger backward, eyes wide. His left hand reached as if to withdraw the dagger from his chest. But his movement seemed slowed by the blurriness of a clouded mind.

Spriggs drew his own cutlass. He leaped toward his opponent, who dropped involuntarily to his knees. With two hands on the hilt, Spriggs whipped the sword diagonally at the big man's throat. Blood showered over those nearest the action and onto Spriggs himself. His rival fell sideways onto the deck, blood gurgling from his partially severed neck. He stepped onto the dying man's right wrist, the one nearest his fallen cutlass. Looking around, he addressed the assembly, "Be there others who question my ownership of this dagger?" Everyone looked at him. Many shook their heads. No one questioned his ownership.

Spriggs bent down and withdrew the dagger cleanly from the fallen man's chest, causing more dark-red blood to pump from the incision. "I claim this cutlass as well," he exclaimed, picking up the man's sword. It was his right, as every pirate knew.

There was a brief silence on deck as the pirates absorbed what had just transpired. De Graaf shattered the quiet. "Clean up this bloody mess," he yelled.

A few observers came forward, struggling to lift the body. Sticky red fluid smeared their hands, arms and chests as they unceremoniously boosted the seemingly dead man up and over the taffrail. One of the lifters thought he heard muttering as their crewmate tumbled into the sea, turning the surrounding water a murky pink.

De Graaf's eyes followed the action. As they did, he noticed *Death's Head* approaching. The *Red Knight* followed closely. He would soon be celebrating his first victory as captain, with Harker.

XXV

The near-full moon competed with streaming clouds for dominance of the sky as Garret, William and Valdez ambled into Taunton, with Scrapper in tow. Tired and hungry, they pulled up at a small, stone-faced inn with two rooms, only one of which was available.

"There be but one bed in that room," said the owner.

Garret looked to William. He shrugged. "We shall take it," she said to the man.

"The four of you?"

"Yes."

"I be havin' ta charge ye an added fee, then."

"That will be fine."

"Meals be separate," he grunted.

"Indeed."

After settling in, the four sat down at a too-small wooden table, to eat. While the innkeeper prepared their meal, they discussed things other than their current dilemma. It wasn't until the innkeeper brought the food and took his leave for the evening that they lowered their voices and began discussing the matter at hand.

"I imagine we shall arrive at the harbor within two days, provided the weather is agreeable," said Garret. "I trust the ships will be ready for a prompt departure."

"I am confident they will," replied William. "The men are quite capable."

"We shall need funding, of course. Thomas can help with that."

"Who is this Thomas you refer to?" asked Valdez.

"Drake's brother—a fellow midshipman when we first sailed with the Admiral," replied Garret.

"I see."

"He now manages the affairs of his brother's estate. We both use Briscoe Bank to handle our financial matters. I shall write him a post-dated note against my own holdings, which I believe the Bank will honor. I am confident he will provide us immediate funding in exchange for the note."

"You say 'us' as though we are all in this together," said William.

Garret looked at him, worried that he'd decided not to accompany her. "I shall understand if you choose to stay behind, William. But again, that would be at your desire, not mine."

"You misunderstand me. I have given this much thought. My mere presence here with you and Jorge makes me fully complicit. I cannot arrive at a different conclusion." Garret nodded in agreement. William continued, "By questioning your use of the word 'us', I was referring to Jorge's inclusion." He turned to Valdez. "No offense, my friend. I am simply assuming our time together shall be short." He took a swig of beer.

"No offense taken," Valdez replied, though his expression suggested otherwise.

Garret went on, "Before we left London, I sent word to Thomas, asking that he join us in Cardiff. Unlike us, he will have taken the main road. So he may already be there."

"I hope he is," said William. "By the by, I believe I failed to mention that Thomas visited the Tower to inquire about you. I assume he arrived sometime after your escape."

"I hope his appearance there poses no future difficulties for him," replied Garret.

"Certainly no more than those facing us," William frowned.

Garret and Scrapper shared the small bed in the room that night. William and Valdez slept on blankets on the hard floor. No one bothered disrobing. Still, Scrapper needed no confirmation of the fact that Garret, though dressed like a man and carrying herself that way, was most certainly a woman—one she greatly admired for seemingly being in charge of these two men.

———

De Graaf boarded the *Death's Head*, pages of parchment grasped tightly in his hand against the breeze. He knew his accounting of the cargo from the captured merchant would be foremost in Harker's mind. Spotting him at the foredeck, he headed that way with an exaggerated swagger. Harker's crew cheered him, raising their weapons. He drew and raised his own cutlass. The cheers increased.

Ascending the steps to the foredeck, he sheathed his cutlass. The two pirate captains grabbed each other's right forearm. Harker spotted the pages in De Graaf's left hand. "Congratulations on your first capture. No doubt the first of many," he said.

"Let it be so."

"You look in fine spirits. I imagine your pages bear good news."

"Perhaps. You shall be the judge of that."

Harker looked to the horizon, taking a deep breath of the salty air. "I have no bond with any God," he said. "But surely one favors me."

"We should review these pages in your quarters," said De Graaf.

"Just so."

"The inventory was prepared by two of my men," De Graaf said, placing the sheets on Harker's desk. "I believe everything is in good order. Your personal share is noted here, at the bottom of the page. Your crew's share appears on the next."

Harker chose not to look at the documents. "My crew shall expect a full share."

De Graaf didn't respond. He pointed to a line item on the first page. "I have made allowance for the wounded men here, in accordance with their injuries." He slid his finger further down the page. "I allotted eight shares for myself." He turned to the second page. "The balance is split between our crews, here. I gave mine a slightly larger share."

"My men will not accept this difference."

"Your men are not bloodied," argued De Graaf.

Harker looked De Graaf up and down slowly with his one good eye, taking the measure of his junior partner. He moved one step toward him, their noses now mere inches apart. Tilting his head slightly, he spoke each word as though it were a sentence on its own, "You - have - no - right - to - challenge - me - on - such - matters." A dark menace shrouded his voice. He reached down to pick up the pages and then sped up his pace, "My crew will have full shares."

A moment of silence followed. Harker glanced at De Graaf,

sensing his partner elected to swallow the words he wished to express.

"My men will not be pleased," volunteered De Graaf.

"Your men are mine, lest you have forgotten."

Harker's dark mood dissolved just as quickly as it had appeared. "Come," he said, "let us celebrate our success with a tankard." He wrapped his muscled arm around De Graaf's shoulders—as though they were still the best of friends

———

The rain landed hard on Valdez. Having risen before dawn, unable to sleep, he'd decided to take a short walk. That was before the rain started. He now regretted his decision. Hurrying back to the inn, his mind revisited the thoughts he'd been having. He was torn between his desire to return to Spain, perhaps on a merchant vessel, and his feelings for Garret—sexual or, possibly, otherwise. He knew he needed to engage her before reaching Cardiff. He ran onto the porch, opened the door to the inn, and hurried inside.

Garret, William and Scrapper were seated at a table enjoying hot tea, warmed bread, and boiled eggs. Valdez removed his coat and hat, shaking off the water before hanging them on a hook. He ran his hands over his face and hair, draining off the excess water.

"Top of the morn, Jorge," said Garret. "You picked a fine time to be dashing about."

"This damnable English rain chills my bones," he replied.

"Come, share my tea." She slid her cup toward the empty chair and waived at the innkeeper for another.

"How is it that England has become so formidable a nation when this incessant rain begs one to stay inside and accomplish nothing?"

"We are a hardy people," offered William as Valdez sat, pulling the cup closer. "We find the rain to be cleansing. Indeed, we welcome its appearance; it brings life to our surroundings."

"From a military perspective, it is most unwelcome," countered Valdez. "It muddies the battlefield, making our weaponry heavier, more difficult to transport, and less reliable. Our prolonged mission in the Netherlands bears proof of that."

"Then perhaps the rain shall deter Spain from also invading England," William responded, with a chuckle.

Valdez chose to change course, "This weather can only lengthen our travel to Cardiff. Let us hope it slows the Queen's guards as well.

"I am unconcerned," remarked Garret. "Her Majesty will have little desire to push for our speedy capture. Better for her that your presence in England remains unknown. Otherwise, it shall complicate her already challenging relationship with your King."

"Nonetheless," William interjected, "best we get an early start." He looked at Valdez and smiled, "Rain or not." He took one last sip of his tea and rose from his chair. "I shall ready the horses. You three finish your meal."

"Thank you, William," replied Garret.

William put on his coat and hat and walked out the door. Valdez saw an opening to broach the sensitive matter of his future, despite Scrapper's presence. He judged the girl was too young to be of any concern.

The innkeeper entered the room, bringing another cup and more hot tea. "Eggs then, sir?"

"Yes, thank you," said Valdez. As the innkeeper turned away, Valdez reached for Garret's hand. He squeezed it softly, meeting her eyes. He withdrew his hand quickly, not wishing the innkeeper to notice. As far as the man knew, he thought, Garret wasn't even a woman.

Scrapper winced at Valdez' hand movements.

"I have been thinking on what happens next," said Valdez. "Once we are at sea," he smiled at his presumption that she would take him along, "you shall be without a home—but for the ship itself, of course. I, on the other hand, still have a home. In Spain. For the sake of argument, what say you return me there?" He didn't wait for a response. "And join me there for a time." Scrapper noisily devoured her bread like a hungry colt, though Valdez suspected she was taking this all in.

Garret fully believed Valdez bore true feelings for her. So his suggestion to join him came as no surprise. But as fond of him as she was, she had no desire for a life in Spain. Or *any* Spanish colony for that matter. She was English. She would always be English; despite her Queen having seemingly disowned her. "You are a special man, Jorge," she said softly. "I admire your strength and character."

"And my obvious charms," he responded, with a twinkle in his eyes.

Garret smiled back. "But, let me ask…were our situation reversed, would you choose to live in my home in England, with me in charge and you there to do my bidding?" She watched as surprise painted his face.

"Perhaps you misunderstand…"

"There is no misunderstanding," she interrupted. "I am a leader, not a follower."

The innkeeper returned with the eggs. Valdez thanked him and watched him leave. He turned back to Garret. "I apologize if I have offended you." He paused briefly to taste his eggs. "May I be frank?"

"I would have it no other way."

"Perhaps you are already well aware." He glanced briefly at Scrapper before returning to face Garret. "I have feelings for you."

"And I for you," she assured him, without hesitation.

"Then let the world be damned. We shall have our way with it."

"If only it were that simple." Garret scanned the room. No one besides Scrapper was present. She placed her hand gently on Jorge's. "I cannot spend my life in Spain. Nor can I imagine being welcomed there—especially having sailed with El Draque."

"Then choose an island in the Southern Seas. There are several possibilities."

"All Spanish," Garret lamented.

"But what other option is there? I cannot be forever imprisoned on an English ship."

"No. Certainly not."

"Although…it might give us more time to…" he looked toward Scrapper and then back… "otherwise engage."

Garret blushed at the implication. She pushed back from the table, rose, and walked next to him. She leaned over and kissed him on his cheek. "You shall have your life," she whispered. "But it shall be your life, not mine."

She turned to Scrapper, who now looked on with great interest. "Come, little one, let us attend to our duties."

Valdez gazed down at his eggs. They were suddenly as uninteresting as his fate appeared to be. He wondered how it was that Garret managed to turn the tables—his toying with her had somehow mutated into her toying with him.

<h1 style="text-align:center">XXVI</h1>

Its great stone walls emerged hauntingly out of the drifting fog. More than ten feet high and six feet thick, they proclaimed strength. Garret knew from her days at the academy that Norman conquerors constructed Cardiff Castle and its walled grounds on the site of Roman ruins dating back to the first century AD.

Reaching the gate, she looked on as William conferred with the sentry. They soon rode slowly onto the grounds and past the Norman Keep, where prisoners were held from time to time. At Shire Hall, William dismounted and entered alone while Garret, Valdez and Scrapper waited outside. It wasn't long before he returned to join them. He mounted his horse. "They say two English-flagged ships arrived three days prior."

"Pray they be ours," replied Garret.

"I inquired as to whether a Black behemoth was among the crew. They said I might find such a man at the inn nearest the harbor." He drew his horse in that direction.

"Any word of Thomas?"

"I am afraid not. If he is here, he had no desire for it to be known."

As they rode to the inn, William turned to Garret, "No doubt we shall find our crew enjoying the tavern."

"Hopefully not too much. They must be ready to sail within a day or two."

"Perhaps we shall find Thomas with them."

"One can only hope."

The Seafarer's Inn was as raucous as any other harbor tavern. No one inside noticed the slight-looking individual who entered and scanned the place, followed by a somewhat larger man.

"You there; you damned brigand," the smaller one shouted above the noise, drawing a cutlass and pointing it at a large Black man. "Stand and be measured!"

All heads turned. Voices quieted. The Black man in the soiled red bandana rose slowly, like a whale breaching the sea. A menacing grin materialized on his face. His hulking frame, over six feet high and seemingly three wide, dwarfed his challenger. Several men stepped back to yield room. The shuffling of feet and sliding of chairs dominated the sounds within. The Black man's companion—a heavy-set, red-headed Scotsman—remained seated. The shape of his mouth mimicked the Black man's grin.

Onlookers stared at the challenger, whose pleasant young face communicated surprising confidence given that these next few moments might well be the last. They were shocked when the fool sheathed the cutlass and strode stone-faced toward his opponent. The Black man placed his hand on his dagger. The challenger stopped...and then smiled, arms opening wide.

The Black lifted his challenger off the floor with a mighty hug, A genuine smile replaced his menacing grin. A collective sigh wafted through the tavern as the men relaxed.

The red-headed man rose to greet the challenger's accomplice, who approached from behind, hand extended. They too shook and nodded hello, with smiles.

"Such a tiny man," growled the Black, placing his challenger back on the ground. "One might think you a mere woman!" The few patrons who recognized the challenger laughed aloud.

"Those are fighting words," challenged Garret. "I demand you take them back."

"Or what?" replied Musa, frowning.

"Or I shall demote you to powder boy."

"Aye Cap'n Connachan. You are not a mere woman. You are a most distinguished one." He bowed graciously with a giant sweep of his right arm, as though he were a gentleman. The crowd roared, most still not realizing Connachan was indeed a woman.

Garret laughed as she tapped Musa on the shoulder. "Arise, fool. Thou art forgiven."

———

Three unflagged ships emerged from the horizon framing the southern harbor at Isla Tortuga. Originally home to only a few handfuls of Spanish settlers, the small village here was fast becoming a favored stopping point for privateers and pirates of all kinds—primarily French but also Dutch, English, Black and mixed race. For them, it was a safe harbor, since it was out of mind of Spanish authorities.

The small fleet's appearance was hailed aloud, bringing the village alive. Its residents were always invigorated by the approach of ships, particularly vessels sailing low in the water; it meant they were heavily laden with cargo or, better yet, the spoils of victory. Such arrivals portended celebrations in the taverns and along the main thoroughfare, putting money in the pockets of shopkeepers, tavern owners, and obliging women.

Harker and De Graaf each disembarked their own ship to board a longboat. De Graaf arrived onshore first and waited. Within minutes, Harker's longboat ground onto the sandy beach. He jumped into shin-deep water and smiled broadly at De Graaf. Striding toward him hurriedly, he wrapped his arm around his partner's shoulders. "Let this be a day to remember, my brother—one filled with food, beer, songs, and buxom lasses. Many lasses!"

"Indeed," replied De Graaf, "But food first."

The two laughed as they and their entourage proceeded toward the center of the village. The men sang with dissonant voices, some bolstered by favorable memories of prior visits. Handfuls of women eagerly followed, hoping to score coins and jewels. The crowd giddily descended upon their preferred tavern—the Gente de Mar.

Inside, the tavern was soon standing-room-only. Watered-down beer spilled as tankards were raised, clanked together, and waved in the air to the rhythm of bawdy songs. Women wearing colorful attire writhed on fervid laps and shoved food into hungry mouths. Their artfully crafted frocks exposed plumped-up bosoms and welcoming legs—white, brown, and all shades in between. The revelry raged on as the sun fell from the sky and drowned in the harbor. Several men, spent and intoxicated, ended up passed out in chairs, on hallway floors, or in back rooms…some missing their pants.

Harker rose. He glanced back at the two young women still laying in his bed. No doubt they were expecting a generous return for having doubled his pleasure. He reached for his pants and threw two gold coins and a small jewel onto the bed. One woman grabbed for it all. The other screamed and pulled her hair. Harker shrugged as the battle raged on. He put on his clothes, boots and cutlass, and then left to find De Graaf.

He went first to the room next to his own. Opening the door, he found a different man and woman within, fully entangled, both groaning.

De Graaf shouted in the distance. Harker closed the door and followed the sound of his partner's voice to the tavern, where De Graaf was the target of a dark-haired young woman.

"Damn you and your bloody pittance," she yelled, slapping his face hard. De Graaf laughed, throwing a small coin in the air for her to catch. As she reached for it, he landed a crushing blow to her left cheek, sending her head sharply to the right. She fell to the floor, landing splayed out and motionless, and bleeding from the impression of De Graaf's rough metal ring.

"You bloody fool!" said Harker, sensing De Graaf was sheeted to the wind. "We want them coming back for more, not fearing punishment."

"There be…many others," mumbled a bleary-eyed De Graaf. "This one left me wanting."

"Others yes. But how many will care to please you, or any of us, after hearing of this?"

De Graaf hung his head, stared vacuously into his tankard, and waved his arm, suggesting he was done with the conversation.

Harker turned, motioning to a couple of nearby crewmen who were still conscious. "Take care of the woman," he said, nodding her way. He gave them three pieces of silver. "One of these is for her."

As the men dragged away the disoriented woman, Harker pulled back a chair across from De Graaf and sat. "I have interesting news," he said. De Graaf didn't react. "Not much happens in these waters without the women soaking it in." De Graaf stared blankly into his tankard. Harker went on anyway, "They say a Spanish Viceroy has gone missing. Name of Valdez. King Philip sent him to direct military affairs in the Islands. Word is he was kidnapped; perhaps even killed. Supposedly by English pirates."

Since De Graaf didn't appear to be drinking anymore, Harker grabbed his tankard, took a sip, and returned it. "I suspect old Philip might pay handsomely for the Viceroy's return. Or even for news of his whereabouts."

De Graaf grunted, apparently too far into his cups to care. Harker persisted, "Tis hard to believe pirates would do this. For what reason?" he asked, rhetorically. He leaned in. "Do you recall when we came across Connachan and her ship near Santiago del Príncipe? I suspect she may be behind this. She is as much the Queen's lapdog as was Drake. Perhaps the old painted lady put her up to it. After all, the Viceroy would be the biggest threat to her greedy interests in the Southern Seas." Still no reaction from De Graaf. Harker didn't care. "If we find Connachan, we may well find the Viceroy. Or even retrieve him. Easy money, brother. Easy money."

A girl came by to refill De Graaf's tankard. She poured the beer. De Graaf sat motionless, seemingly mesmerized by the flow of the grog. Harker nodded to the girl. She unhitched a tankard from her belt and poured a watered beer for him as well. He gave her a silver coin and watched her leave.

Harker leaned in again. "We need to find Connachan." Sipping his beer, he looked around the dimly lit room. As far as he could tell, no one was listening. "After we left her, she sailed northeast toward Hispaniola. But there are too many Spaniards there. She would have chosen one of the islands beyond. They say Valdez had a base on the larger of the two islands north of Hispaniola—the Inaguas."

De Graaf lifted his head briefly. It swayed like a leaf in the wind. Harker went on, "Was I the Queen's lapdog, and she asked *me* to kill the Viceroy, I would head to the north side of the big island. Anchor there, go overland, and find him." He leaned back.

De Graaf's head tilted forward, eyes closed. Suddenly, it dropped, hitting the table nose-first. Blood trailed out a nostril. The server heard the thud and turned to see what happened. She brought a rag to clean the mess.

XXVII

The harbor at Cardiff was abuzz. *Pandora* and *Orion* were the principal loci of activity. Anxious to set sail, their crews rapidly boarded and stowed the last of the needed supplies. But they had no knowledge of their destination. Garret had sworn her officers to secrecy on the matter. There could be no trail; no hint that the authorities might sniff out.

While the ships were being readied, Valdez shared a table at the inn with Garret, William, and the man he'd already heard much about but never met—Thomas Drake. He moved his leg briefly as Scrapper came by, sweeping the floor. She'd been put to work by the innkeeper in exchange for a small coin. Valdez redirected his attention to Thomas, who was providing details of the arrangements he'd made on Garret's behalf. The man was clearly intelligent, he thought.

"Briscoe's [the bank] was quite concerned with my request," said Thomas. "Luckily, Langton's father chairs the Board. He was most supportive. So we have arranged the funding you need."

"Excellent news," replied Garret.

"Most of your financial assets are being transferred to the bank's affiliate in France, to avoid any constraints Her Majesty's administrators might impose; at least until I can reason with her concerning your situation."

Garret grasped his hand. "I do hope you can convince her."

"Indeed." Thomas sipped his beer before continuing, "I have also spoken with the manager of your various estates. He agreed to establish a trust as the named owner. While he shall retain day-to-day management of the properties, Briscoe's French affiliate will nominally serve as trustee."

Garret nodded. "I cannot thank you enough, Thomas. This takes an enormous burden off my mind." She glanced at the legal papers Thomas pushed toward her for signature.

"I am happy to be of assistance. I shall take the documents back to London, to complete the arrangements. God willing, I might also be granted an audience with Her Majesty, to discuss your situation."

"Thank you again. That would be greatly appreciated. I shall write a brief note you may hand her."

William interjected, "I wish you would choose to sail with us again, Thomas."

"Would that I could, William. I am afraid my feet have grown roots."

As Garret signed the documents, Thomas turned to Valdez. "I must admit, Viceroy, your presence here raises many questions— friend? enemy? Your own countrymen might ask: traitor?"

"They might indeed if they knew I were here. I suspect they do not." He sipped his beer. "Thankfully, my reputation in Spain is that of a hero. And I remain loyal to my King. But my enemies have always been Dutch, not English. I find I only have *friends* here in England." He smiled, looking in turn to Garret and William.

"I can assure you, Thomas, Jorge is a good man," William volunteered, "You would feel the same, had you gone through all that we have."

"I shall take your word then."

Garret, signing the last of the documents, added her own thoughts. "The man is a complete bore," she smiled. "With no military to lead, he has but one mind." She secretly winked at Valdez. He shuddered at the thought that she might be referring to his desire for physical intimacy. He sought to quickly defuse that.

"I long for a return to my position," he explained. Garret grinned.

"And what position would that be?" asked Thomas.

William interrupted. "Yes, please clarify, Jorge. Your last position was that of directing military operations against foreign vessels—including English ones."

Garret put down her quill, looking at Valdez intently. All eyes were now focused his way. "A fair question," he replied shifting in his chair. "My life has been one of service to my country. I am required to carry out the King's wishes, whatever they may be. Absent that role, I am uncertain who I am."

"You are much more than your role might suggest," Garret offered in support. "You are a man of knowledge. Of integrity. One with a sense of mission. You have the gift of being able to make friends easily. And admirable skill in influencing others."

Valdez looked at her with an amiable grin. "I do indeed seem to be able to influence many…though some are not so easily persuaded." Garret returned his grin.

Thomas collected the documents and slipped them into his portfolio. "Well then," he said, "let us share one last drink before I depart."

———

Standing at *Pandora's* stern alongside Scrapper, Garret watched longingly as Cardiff dissolved into the gray horizon.

Consumed earlier by thoughts of her childhood, her grandfather, and her life at Ritchfield Academy, she now found herself pondering her future. Would she ever return to England? If so, would she be welcomed back or treated like a criminal? She felt an urge to speed up time, to see the outcome. Instead, she sighed deeply and returned to thoughts of the present. She was glad William was again sailing with her, captaining *Orion*. He was her comfort zone. Her confidant. She was happy, too, that Jorge was with her, though what to do with him was still unclear. Even her feelings for the man were foggy. Was she attracted to him because of his strong presence, his intellect, and his obvious leadership skill? Or was it some unconscious thirst of a more physical nature? Whichever, it was in no way the same feeling of infatuation she'd had for Pantas—the handsome young Indonesian Ambassador. Jorge was perhaps a decade older than both she and Pantas. And she now felt so much older, and wiser, herself. No, her attraction to Jorge was more intellectual than it had been with Pantas. But the man's apparent enchantment with her, coupled with his occasional artful touching of her body, left her with a sensation that was clearly carnal at its root. Did she even dare go down that path?

Garret shook her head and looked down at Scrapper. The girl seemed to be enjoying her first experience on the sea as it rocked beneath them, its breeze blowing her hair freely.

"Farewell, London!" Scrapper exclaimed as the countryside vanished. London was *her* homeland; she knew nothing really of England. Garret smiled knowingly, placing her hand on the girl's head.

Blair approached from behind, interrupting them. "She sails fine, Cap'n. Coming on six knots now and craving more. The crew's repairs have served us well."

Garret appreciated when Blair brought good news. He more often came to her with problems and complaints. "Excellent, Mr. Blair. We shall follow our usual path to the Western islands. Now that we are at sea, you may spread word that our ultimate destination is Isla Tortuga."

Blair appeared shocked. "Pardon if you will, Cap'n. I find that rather surprising."

"How so?"

"They say Tortuga is a welcome stopping point for dubious privateers offering up cargo of questionable provenance."

"Pirates, you mean." It was a statement, not a question.

"I suppose."

"Are we not pirates ourselves?"

"Surely not! We serve at the Queen's pleasure."

"Not this time, I am afraid. We have neither a letter of marque, nor her verbal authorization. We now sail on our own account."

Blair shook his head in apparent disbelief. Garret sought to console him. "It is a life of freedom, Mr. Blair. We are now free men. And women, of course." Though she was teasing him about being pirates, Garret was troubled by the reality that they couldn't rightly be considered privateers. Certainly not in the traditional sense.

"God be with us," moaned Blair.

Garret was tired of the dour man's company. She wished to change the conversation. She smiled at Scrapper, taking the girl's chin and lifting it upward so that their eyes met. "Now that you have a new life, what say we find you a new name, dearest?" Scrapper smiled back. "An exciting new life such as this is worthy of a new name,"

Garret emphasized. She never liked the name 'Scrapper' for the girl. Looking up, Garret watched as Blair stomped off in disgust.

———

He waved as farmers in the field stopped their labors and stared. His stylish four-horse chaise, with a coachman and two uniformed footmen, obviously made for an unusual sight. '*They look like live scarecrows,*' thought Thomas.

Making its way through the countryside back to London, the carriage slowed as it entered a turn into a heavily wooded section. Within minutes, six uniformed royal guards approached on horseback, two abreast, their pace quick. The leading guard on the right raised his hand and shouted, "Halt, if you please."

"Whoa," cried the coachman, pulling hard on the reins. The carriage rattled to a stop. The tall guard dismounted, handed the reins of his horse to another, and approached the carriage door.

"Good day, sir. Might I inquire as to your heading?"

"Good day to you as well," replied Thomas, "We are off to London. I have business there."

"Might I ask the nature of your business?"

"You may certainly ask," replied Thomas, somewhat perturbed, "though I do not believe I am required to answer." It was a lawyerly response.

"Quite right. It is no matter, I suppose," said the guard. "However, I must ask—is anyone with you, besides your coachman and footmen?"

"I believe you can see I am alone."

The guard stepped on the foot rail and raised himself to the window, quickly scanning the inside. "Indeed. Quite right. I shall need a moment, if you please." He stepped down and walked to the back of the carriage. Thomas stepped out to follow him. The coachman came down as well, to stand alongside Thomas.

One of the footmen at the back stepped down, allowing the guard to take his place. The tall man mounted the back. He spotted the large trunk secured to the top. "Open this trunk," he said to the other footman.

Thomas worried that the documents inside bearing Garret's name and signature could easily implicate him in her escape. "What is the meaning of this?" he asked promptly.

"We are under orders to search for an escapee from the Tower."

"And you believe he may be hiding in my trunk?" It was a mere four feet long.

"One can never be certain."

"Then let me assure you, no one is suffocating in my trunk."

"Nonetheless, I must see for myself."

"What is your name?" Thomas demanded.

The guard stepped down from the carriage and walked toward Thomas until they were almost nose-to-nose. "I have no patience for your meddling, sir." There was menace in his voice. "You will comply with my request or I shall take you prisoner."

"Do you know who I am?" Thomas asked matter-of-factly, to indicate he wasn't intimidated.

"You could be the Queen's nephew. It would be of no consequence."

"I am Thomas Drake, brother of the Admiral. You would do well to mind your manners with me."

The guard paused. He stepped back to get a better look at Thomas. He turned to the coachman, who nodded back affirmatively. The guard stood speechless for a few moments. "My apologies, sir. And my deepest sympathies on the passing of your brother. He was much admired. Please, be on your way."

"I thank you," nodded Thomas.

As the guards rode off, Thomas watched and waited. He took a deep breath as he reentered his carriage; only his brother's good name had spared him. He smiled at the thought of his brother's influence being so strong even now, well after his death.

XXVIII

Charcoal-colored clouds and intense winds drove drenching rain at them horizontally. The gale sprayed off the tops of soaring waves as their ships descended into the chasms below. Heading for Inagua, Harker and De Graaf found themselves in the teeth of a demon ocean. *Death's Head, Cutthroat* and *Red Knight* were reduced to mere toys. A hapless sailor screamed in terror as the wind swept him overboard and spun him away. Ships' masts and ropes moaned under the pressures, yet somehow refused to give up their hold. Waterlogged helmsmen fought physically and mentally to maintain a bow-first direction into the howling winds and cascading walls of water threatening their demise. "Bloody Hell," Harker screamed to Masters Mate Stevens. "She's a damned witch of a storm."

"She be the worst I have seen," Stevens hollered back.

"Let us get the best of her!"

"Aye, Cap'n."

The morning sun shone brightly above light clouds at Garret's back as she stood on *Pandora's* foredeck, looking west. She contemplated the emerging, near-black line layering the horizon. It didn't bode well. Her current course would have her colliding with what was unquestionably a great storm. Uncertain of its precise direction, she needed more time to gauge its progression relative to *Pandora's*.

Master's Mate Blair came alongside. "I am baffled, Cap'n. In all my years, I have never seen such a thing. It spans the entire horizon."

"Just so," replied Garret. "Let us buy ourselves time. Furl all sails, if you please."

"Furl all sails," yelled Blair. The crew responded immediately. Several men scurried up the rigging to douse the sails while others manned the clewlines. Within minutes, the canvas sheets were furled and secured tightly to the yards. The tall ship slowed, moving only with its original momentum until the ocean itself took charge. There was quiet now, as all hands stopped to observe the ominous dark line separating sea and sky.

"What say you, Mr. Blair? Two leagues? Less?"

"Perhaps less, Cap'n."

"Now that we are calmed, let us measure how quickly the height of the black line grows. Have the lookout keep its measure and note whether it disappears at either end of the horizon."

"Aye, Cap'n."

Jorge Valdez approached as Blair left to join the young lookout in the crow's nest. "An interesting sight, is it not?"

Garret remained focused on the horizon. "The Chinese have a saying, '*May you live in interesting times.*' Though many think it a blessing, 'tis said in irony. *Un*interesting times are those when nothing of note transpires—times forever lost to history. *Interesting* times are those when chaos and uncertainty reign; where battles are fought and history is made. We can only hope this is not an interesting time for us."

"So you intend to avoid it, then."

"Evil surely hides within its darkness. We shall do all we can to elude it."

"I fear you may be eluding *me* as well," replied Valdez. "We have been at sea for some time now, and I am still uncertain what your plans are for me…and for us."

"You choose an awkward time for such a discussion."

"I find my impatience grows by the day. We must talk soon."

Garret turned toward him. "There are no simple answers, Jorge. Have you even pondered for a moment how you might handle the situation if our places were reversed?"

"I have indeed. There is not a doubt in my mind." His words were soft and warm.

Garret understood—he would take her with him wherever she might wish to go. '*It is so easy for a man,*' she thought, '*But how very difficult for a woman.*' She turned to leave. "I must attend to my duties."

"Of course," replied Jorge, nodding. "Once things clear up, let us make time to attend to our *other* interesting topic."

Valdez watched as Garret headed to the main deck. Still intent on seducing her for selfish interests, he resisted the constant pull of a deeper relationship…and wondered what her own thoughts were on the matter.

———

The Queen's messenger entered Orion's Tavern bearing a note for him. Thomas broke the seal and opened it. It was beautifully written he thought, though not in Her Majesty's own hand…

Dearest Thomas,

I have received your letter of the twenty-first. It was always my

It was precisely what Thomas hoped for. He placed the letter inside his doublet, contemplating how best to shape his discussion with Her Majesty regarding Garret's dilemma. He had only two days in which to perfect it.

———

The crew of the *Death's Head* were exhausted. Many lay on the deck in damp clothing, absorbing the beauty of this warm, calmed night. It had finally delivered the mercy they prayed for.

The ship was eerily silent, save for the sound of water softly caressing its sides, and the occasional creak of wood and rasp of ropes. The skies offered up a slivered moon, a mass of sparkling stars, and a few wisps of cloud.

Harker stood silently on the foredeck, surprised at how well his ship had withstood the storm's savagery. He spotted the north star beyond the stern. The ship needed to reverse course but he thought it best to give his sailors time to convalesce before asking more of them. For now, he simply scanned the horizon, seeking signs of *Cutthroat* and *Red Knight*. There were none. He hoped De Graaf had survived. If so, they would surely meet as they neared Inagua.

Harker turned and strode to the helm, seizing the wheel. Its weight felt good in his arms. It seemed to connect his soul directly to the sea, reminding him just how much he cherished sailing these waters. Despite their occasional violence, they had provided him a handsome living.

Further to the east, in the coming dawn, *Cutthroat* bobbed in open water, its sails still fully furled and secured. Its foremast presented a visible fracture requiring repair, at least until it could be replaced. De Graaf had no desire to tempt the sea by endeavoring to sail on to Inagua. Instead, he decided to turn to Isla Tortuga for repairs. Neither he nor Harker were aware that the *Red Knight* had succumbed to the storm. Its crew would never again join them…except perhaps on the dark side.

XXIX

Thomas Drake's eyes were drawn to the manservant carrying a silver service with tea and biscuits into the private room where he sat opposite the Queen. The sitting room felt sterile, lacking the warmth and pleasantness of his own private study. He glanced back at Elizabeth. She seemed tired. Perhaps stressed. He sensed that beneath a face heavily caked in some strange white substance, she bore the etchings of innumerable challenges endured over countless years. She hadn't responded to his opening remark about the situation in Ireland. Perhaps it was the manservant's arrival that gave her pause.

"I feel your brother's presence, Thomas." Elizabeth smiled. "The Admiral and I often sat in this very room while he shared his most engaging stories with me." She sighed. "I feel a great loss."

"Tea, Your Majesty," offered the manservant, placing the tray on a small, ornate table. He took the pot and poured hot, fully steeped liquid into the two cups.

"Thank you," said Thomas, picking up his cup after Elizabeth did hers.

"We shall have the room please," the Queen instructed.

While they waited for him to leave, Thomas watched Elizabeth sip her tea. It was clearly too hot. She returned it to the saucer.

"I agree," said Elizabeth. "It is most unfortunate that we find ourselves at war in Ireland. Rest assured, we shall honor your family's holdings there once hostilities have ended."

"Thank you, Your Majesty. That is a great relief to my family."

"Now tell me, for what reason have you *really* come to see me?"

Thomas smiled at how insightful the woman was. "Tis a rather difficult topic, I am afraid."

"You are among friends." Elizabeth smiled back.

"You must know that I have sailed in the past with Captain Garret Connachan."

"I do, yes."

"For all the time I have known her, she has struck me as a person of the highest order. My brother once said that, next to you, she is the closest woman England has to France's Joan of Arc." Elizabeth didn't comment. She nodded humbly. Thomas continued, "He also said Garret bore the kind of intelligence one sees only once in a generation."

"Just so," replied Elizabeth. "For all she has accomplished, it is hard to believe she is still so very young."

Thomas noted she hadn't offered up anything regarding Garret's current situation. He wondered whether she knew anything at all. Yet she must, he thought. He sipped his tea and continued. "You may not be aware that on her recent return from the Southern Seas, she was accompanied by a certain high-value Spaniard."

Elizabeth was expressionless. Thomas chose his next words carefully, "For reasons unknown, she and the Spaniard were apparently imprisoned in The Tower shortly after arrival." The Queen's face remained a blank page. He pressed further, "I attempted to visit her there but was informed she never arrived, although the Spaniard had." He stopped, not wishing to stroll too far along the plank.

"Go on," said Elizabeth, reaching for her cup.

Thomas braced himself. "I subsequently learned that she and the Spaniard escaped." Elizabeth sipped her tea. And waited. Thomas saw he had no choice. "I feel compelled to disclose that I have knowledge of the circumstances surrounding their escape."

Elizabeth placed her cup carefully on the table. "Please, tell me."

"Captain Connachan draws the attention of many men, as I am certain you can imagine."

"I can, yes."

"It seems the guard fancied having relations with her… against her wishes."

"I see. Quite troubling."

"She had no choice but to vigorously oppose his efforts. The guard was rendered unconscious. Fearing the consequences, Garret felt the need to escape, for which she sought the Spaniard's assistance."

"I am appalled, Thomas. No one deserves such treatment, least of all a woman. And where is the Captain now?"

Thomas hesitated, uncertain of the Queen's intentions and now deeply worried about his own involvement. "If I may, Your Majesty." He reached into his doublet and withdrew Garret's sealed note. He placed it on the table. Elizabeth made no effort to reach for it.

It wasn't until Thomas left that Elizabeth picked up the note. She hadn't expected Garret would be the topic of his interest, or that he would be delivering her message. She appreciated his not having inferred that she herself had ordered Garret's imprisonment. But she was distressed by what he'd shared with her. She'd been explicit with her Royal Guard that Garret was not to be mistreated while imprisoned. Someone would pay for that.

———

Together in her cabin, Garret and Scrapper sat, playing cards. "I believe I have a new name for you," Garret said, laying down a knave and looking Scrapper in the eyes.

The girl's face lit up. "Tell me, please."

"It begins with an 'S', to honor the name by which you have lived your young life," Garret explained. "But it is derived from your *new* life, here on the world's oceans." Scrapper was all ears as Garret continued, "It is a *water* sign from the Zodiac, which speaks to the sun's movement through the stars." She spotted a teaching opportunity. "For what do we use the stars?"

"For navigation."

"Precisely. And you shall navigate your life on the seas under your new name."

"Please," Scrapper begged, "What is it?"

"Before I answer that, you should know that the name reflects what I find to be your very nature—your emotional strength and your innate sense of the world around you."

"Please mum, I can wait no longer."

"The name is Scorpio."

Scrapper frowned, thinking how odd it sounded. Garret reacted, "I shall call you Scorpi," She reached out and touched the girl's shoulder.

That was better, Scrapper thought. She smiled, placed her cards face-down on the table, and rose to embrace Garret in a lengthy hug. "Thank you, mum."

Garret suddenly experienced a feeling she imagined her grandfather may have felt when holding her as a child—a purity and warmth she'd never felt before. It brought a sense of belonging; of shared lives; of the very meaning of life itself. The moment was interrupted by a knock at her door.

"Blair, Cap'n."

"Enter," said Garret. She let go of Scorpi.

Blair walked in. "Pardon, Cap'n. I am pleased to report the storm travels north. I believe we can proceed sou' sou'west without peril."

"Thank you, Mr. Blair. On to Isla Tortuga, then. Full sails if you please."

"Full sails," Blair acknowledged with a bow and a nod of his head.

Watching Blair leave, Scorpio thought how special it was that Garret had such power over men. Perhaps she herself might one day have such power. Hadn't Garret said only moments ago that she had 'strength?

———

"Land ho!"

"Where away?" yelled De Graaf.

"Eight points to larboard, Captain," came the call from *Cutthroat's* crow's nest.

Saint Iago, thought De Graaf. Spanish territory. It meant they would soon be nearing Hispaniola, to the northeast. And just beyond that lay Isla Tortuga, their safe zone. His mind turned to Harker. Where was he, De Graaf wondered. Had he survived the storm? And if so, where would he head? Would he press on to Inagua, as planned? Following his own ship's repairs, he too would sail for Inagua, hopefully to join him there.

De Graaf wasn't entirely comfortable being alone—the sole leader of his pirate crew. He knew he and Harker were better off together—a stronger, more potent force against their prey. But if Harker hadn't survived the storm, De Graaf knew that would open the door to taking over the mantle of 'most feared pirate' in the Southern Seas. The thought made him smile, warming a cold heart.

———

"A Spanish merchant, of that I am certain," said Harker, looking out across the sea. "Let us take her. The crew is in need of fresh meat—a just reward for having battled the great storm. And won."

"Aye Cap'n," replied Master's Mate Stevens. "Full sails!" he shouted. "Bearing six points to larboard," he instructed the helmsman. They would gather the wind gauge, whisking them quickly to their target.

The gap between the two ships now sufficiently closed, Harker shouted his orders, "Hoist the Crimson. Ready the battery." Within moments, the blood-red flag flapped briskly atop the mainmast. The ports slammed open. Ten cannons rolled out their noses, announcing the pirates' intentions.

Harker's prey was already prepared. It delivered a robust round of cannon shot. One ball hit *Death's Head's* mainmast, shattering off pieces and ripping through the sails. Sharp wooden shards showered over the deck, cutting and scraping a few pirates, though not seriously injuring any.

"He wants a fight," said Harker, to no one in particular. "Reply the cannons, Mr. Stevens," he shouted.

"Aye sir, all cannons." Stevens turned and hollered, "All fire at will!"

As the black-iron monsters roared, flames streaked in the direction of the Spanish-flagged vessel. Smoke billowed and reversed like a sucked-in cloud. The cannonballs mostly splashed short and wide. One managed to crash through the ship's side, just above the gun deck. Both ships reloaded and exchanged more fire, filling the narrowing gap with smoky gray clouds. The pirates readied their grappling hooks. Pistol shots pelted down from elevated positions and streamed horizontally at men on both decks.

Some of the merchant sailors slashed at the ropes attached to hooks now clawing their taffrail. But there were too many. The pirates began hauling the merchant ship close, readying boarding planks. Several frightened sailors prepared for the inevitable, grabbing cutlasses and reloading pistols. Pirates hastily crossed the planks and poured over the taffrail, cutlasses waving and pistols firing. The two sides immediately enmeshed in riotous bloodletting. Screams and shouts pierced the air, even above the noise of pistol shots and clashing metal.

Harker's men were better prepared and more experienced in combat. Harker himself was particularly lethal. After firing two pistols at the heads of his opponents, he drew cutlass and dagger, slashing at bodies in front and to his right. Opponents on both sides fell to the deck, spurting blood, some missing body parts. Men who tripped over bodies or slipped on the slick red ooze were mercilessly impaled by their more fortunate assailants.

The spotter atop *Death's Head* peered down at the massive crowd and lifeless bodies filling the deck as the pirate horde pushed ever forward. A few sailors near the rear disengaged, preferring to find shelter. One scaled the taffrail, intending to leap into the water below. His quartermaster, furious at the display of cowardice, slashed the jumper's leg, leaving a spray of blood and severed foot trailing him into the sea.

In part from sheer exhaustion, the brutal engagement ended amid the screams and moans of the wounded. Harker, covered in blood splatter and bleeding from his arms and legs, spotted his defeated counterpart. He headed that way, stepping over bodies, some moving, some not.

The merchant captain cringed at the sight of the large, bloodied warrior with the eye patch approaching with a face contorted in anger. He bent low, laying his sword crosswise at his feet, and then rose slowly.

Harker used his forearm to wipe sweat and blood from his face. He closed tightly on the frightened captain, smelling and feeling the shorter man's quick breaths pulse against his neck. "Men do not fight this hard when little of value is onboard," he observed. The captain stayed silent. "I wish to see what treasures my men have bled for."

"Of course. I am Capítan Pereira. I shall take you to the hold."

"Pereira? Portuguese?"

"Si, though I now sail under a Spanish flag."

"Then I shall spare you," Harker replied. "It is only Spanish captains I choose to dispose of."

"Graçias." Pereira stooped to pick up his cutlass offering it hilt-first to Harker.

Accepting the weapon, Harker's eyes were drawn to its jewel-encrusted handle. The cutlass seemed more wall-ornament than weapon-of-death.

"This way, please," said Pereira, sweeping his left arm in the direction of the cargo hold.

Harker followed with two of his men. The rest of his crew stayed on deck, looking to free wounded opponents from their misery.

XXX

She sat in the chair next to the side table, with Garret's note in hand. Her manservant left, having finished lighting a fire to warm the room. Elizabeth felt another warmth—the one in her heart for her spirited young agent. She remembered fondly the moments and laughs they'd shared in the past. Feeling a sudden urge for tea, she placed the letter back on the table and picked up her teacup. Its contents were too cool for her liking. She set it back down, took the note, and turned it over in her hands.

Elizabeth was proud of Garret. Surrounded by superstitious and uncivil miscreants, she somehow navigated her ascendance to a captaincy on Drake's fleet. Elizabeth shook her head, amazed at the improbability of it all. And yet, given her assignment to 'neutralize' Viceroy Valdez, Garret had foolishly chosen to return him to England's shores, just as Captain McBride predicted. Elizabeth dared not countenance such misbehavior.

Even more worrisome was her concern that King Philip might learn of the Viceroy's arrival in England. If so, he would surely believe Elizabeth herself was complicit. That could easily lead to all-out war between their two nations. Her hands were already fully occupied with military efforts in Ireland. Responding to a Spanish assault would overtax both her treasury and her military forces. That concern led her to order the immediate detention of the Viceroy, to prevent word of his presence from spreading to Spain. Garret was to be detained as well, for misbehavior. But she never intended Garret's imprisonment to be anything other than short.

As she toyed with the note, Elizabeth pondered the Tower

guard's unwanted advances on Garret. She would have loved to watch the young Captain exact a suitable price on her assailant. The mere thought of it brought her a pleasurable feeling. Under the circumstances, Garret's actions were understandable. Admirable even.

Though Elizabeth was grateful for Thomas having deftly broached the matter without bringing any dishonor to her or Garret, she now faced a dilemma—how to proceed given all the complications. She still hoped this valiant young woman might one day join her inner circle of advisors. But Garret was now an escaped prisoner, in partnership with a Spanish commander. Not only that but King Philip's rage was to be avoided. This ranked alongside the more challenging problems she'd ever faced.

She now noticed she was unconsciously twirling Garret's note. Sighing deeply, she broke the seal and unfolded it.

Your Majesty,

It pains me greatly to know that I have disappointed you in the matter at hand. I imagine Captain McBride has informed you of his displeasure with what transpired. That is most unfortunate. I would have preferred delivering my own thoughts first.

Once our prize was acquired, it occurred to me it might have significant value, which argued against its being neutralized. I firmly believe your Spanish friend might grant us certain holdings in the Southern Seas in exchange for its return, facilitating the westward expansion of our empire.

I apologize for being so brash in my actions, and for causing you the frustration you must be feeling. That was never my intent. I hope we might one day reconcile our differences.

> *I remain, your humble servant,*
> *Garret Connachan*
> *Captain. For England.*

Elizabeth read the note twice, appreciating the subtleties in Garret's words. Had anyone intercepted the message, they would have been unable to determine the nature of 'the prize'. She folded the note, mulling Garret's suggestion—exchanging the Viceroy for an English settlement that Spain would formally recognize and honor. It had merit; England needed a secure base in the Southern Seas.

She rose from her chair with the letter in hand and walked toward the crackling fireplace, contemplating the situation with King Philip. Perhaps she might convince him that an ambitious young captain had simply made an impetuous decision to kidnap the Viceroy, believing it would advance 'his' career. That would enable her to shift the blame, yet still negotiate the terms of exchange with Philip, all while masking Garret's involvement. She stopped before the fireplace, welcoming its bright, warm flames. She threw in Garret's note, watching it flash and disintegrate, ensuring the secrecy of its contents.

———

The knock at her door startled Garret. Her breakfast done, she was now so intensely focused on her navigational charts that she'd lost all sense of time. She let go of her circular viewing glass and leaned back. "Enter," she called out.

Valdez strode in like the military leader he was, with a

commanding presence, self-confidence and his usual no-nonsense attitude. Garret observed he was once again wearing the ring given him by King Philip. She hadn't seen it on his hand since before they'd landed on English soil. She just assumed the guards took it from him.

"Good morning, Captain," Jorge announced loudly as he closed the door. He did that commonly, so that anyone within hearing distance would assume his visits were all business. They weren't. And yet they were. Valdez approached with a warm, broad smile, lowering his voice, "Such a beautiful sight to begin my day."

Garret rose and smiled. He grasped her gently with strong, comforting arms. "You flatter me," she stated. "I sense you may be seeking something in return."

He pulled backed, holding her biceps in his extended arms while searching her eyes. "Have you something you wish to offer me, then?"

Garret blushed. "What did you have in mind?"

Jorge leaned in, slowly sliding his left hand to the base of her neck. Her soft, auburn hair flowed over the back of it. He placed his right hand on the small of her back, pulling her toward him while angling his head. Their lips met.

Garret wrapped her arms around the back of his broad chest, savoring the feel of his muscular body for a few moments. She soon placed her hands on the front of his chest and pushed back, gently.

"Dios mio! Do you greet all your captains this way?"

"Only those who would have me." He grinned.

"And you think I shall?"

"I have grand dreams."

Garret sighed, gazing deeply into his eyes. "What am I to

do with you?"

"I can think of many things."

She frowned. "Your behavior is rather unbecoming of an officer."

"On this ship, I am simply a man. A smitten one, I might add."

"Really? I had no idea." Garret decoupled from him, not wanting to take things beyond the line she'd drawn in her mind.

"Must I chase you, then?"

"Certainly not. But you may join me…for koffei." Garret turned and walked to her credenza. She withdrew a nearby pot from its perch above three candles and poured its dark contents into two cups. She brought them to her table.

"How long until we reach Isla Tortuga?" asked Jorge.

"Mere days I believe; subject to wind and weather."

"Then I must assume you are ready to share your plans for me once we arrive."

Garret sipped her koffei and placed her cup on the table. "Do you trust me?"

"I trust you have the best interests of your country in mind. I am unclear what that portends for me."

"What options do you believe I have?"

"Setting aside my favored option for the moment," he replied, "I imagine you could allow me to return to Inagua."

Garret laughed.

"Just so; quite unlikely." He sipped his koffei. "Another possibility is that you release me on Isla Tortuga, upon my promise to never to take up arms against England."

"Is such a commitment even realistic?"

Jorge evaded the question, "I imagine some on that island—people of a certain persuasion—would not favor my presence there."

"You mean pirates."

"I do, yes."

"So that option also seems unworkable."

Jorge nodded. "I suppose you could hold me prisoner here…for whatever mischievous purposes you might have in mind."

"Is that what you are here—a prisoner?"

"At the very least, I am your *personal* prisoner, to do with as you please."

Garret smiled. "We are fast running out of options, are we not?"

Jorge looked at her quizzically, offering nothing more. "Have you exhausted the possibilities, then?" she teased.

"Well, if you choose not to return me to Spanish territory, set me free on Isla Tortuga, or hold me prisoner on *Pandora*, might I assume my original offer is still under consideration?"

"Remind me of the specifics of that offer."

"I propose we retire to a Spanish settlement, there to live out the remainder of our lives. Cartageña perhaps."

To Garret, the thought of living in a vibrant city like Cartageña held a certain charm. But she shook her head, no; it wasn't for her.

"Then please, share what you have in mind."

"You are a truly special man, Jorge. But," she paused, "you are even more special to your King. And perhaps equally valuable to my Queen."

Jorge's eyebrows rose in surprise. "You see me as a mere property to be exchanged? A bargaining chip?"

"You are so much more than that, Jorge. But, as you yourself once acknowledged, I serve my Queen."

"Still? After she imprisoned you?"

"I firmly believe she simply wished to discipline me."

"I am confused. For what evil deed would she discipline you?"

"For not carrying out my mission in the manner intended." Given his years in the military, Garret was certain Jorge understood there were times when prudence in the moment might dictate a diversion from the mission. He would also know that taking an alternate course could easily frustrate a superior who wasn't in situ at the time.

"I see." He paused. "And how is it you failed in your mission?"

Garret didn't answer. Not verbally. She stared at him blankly, suggesting he put the pieces together himself. She waited.

"Dios mío!" He shook his head, rose from his chair, turned, and paced a few steps in the opposite direction. "She would have you take my life?" Again, no response from Garret. Jorge searched her eyes. "Why?" he asked. "Why did you choose otherwise?"

Garret looked away. It was suddenly clear—she did have deep feelings for Jorge—deeper than she'd let herself believe. Perhaps it began when they first met. At the time, she only wished to see what information he might share before his execution. But that initial conversation gave her pause. She found him both intellectually stimulating and charming. And his distinguished good looks were disarming. It was in that long-ago moment that she wavered on carrying out the Queen's wishes, thinking there had to be a better way. Though things hadn't gone as planned, she didn't regret her decision. The man brought her the kind of happiness she hadn't experienced since her days with Ambassador Pantas.

She breathed in deeply, peering down at the cabin floor to compose herself. "I saw something in you," she explained in a near-whisper. "Something that…touched my soul."

Jorge walked toward her and knelt to one knee, taking her hand in his. He looked into her eyes. "It touched both our souls."

Alone in his small cabin following their visit, Jorge sat pensively, replaying the session in his mind. She was having none of his offer to take up together on some Spanish settlement. When he first suggested it weeks ago, it was merely a ploy to seduce her. It served his broader interests—removing an English player from the chessboard and placing her beneath him. Literally.

He had to admire how artfully Garret backed him into the very corner she'd already landed at. But in the end, her emotions disclosed her true feelings for him. He remembered thinking at the time, '*This is it. She has fallen for me. I shall soon taste this fruit.*'

From the very beginning, his intent was to seduce her in service of his own interests. But he now wondered whether he was skirting the edge of actually wanting her…for the woman she was.

XXXI

It first became visible from the shore of Isla Tortuga when the evening sun began flattening on the western horizon. Only a handful onshore recognized the vessel as one of Harker's ships. A buzz of anticipation swept through the village, especially among the local shopkeepers for whom pirates were a welcome source of low-cost goods and lavish spending.

The first of De Graaf's men began disembarking in the dark. They rowed ashore with an energetic chorus of song that skimmed loudly across lapping waves. The men's spirits were high, in expectation of a bawdy night bursting with beer, food and women, in whatever order they were presented.

De Graaf was still onboard *Cutthroat*, ascending the steep stairwell from the ship's hold. He was comfortable he now had a good mental picture of the cargo, to compare against its appearance when he returned. "Not a soul enters the hold," he barked to the three men carefully chosen to stand guard this night.

"Aye Cap'n," they replied.

De Graaf firmly believed *three* was the right number. If there were only two guards, they might conspire to steal some of the cargo. That was much less likely with a third party involved. Nor were these three known to share a friendship. That, and the fact that one was a deeply loyal, long-time mate of De Graaf's, further minimized any risk.

"I shall return later," he lied, clouding any potential plan of thievery with added uncertainty. He walked to the entry port and descended to a waiting longboat attended by several of his men. As he stepped heavily into the swaying boat, the gold and silver coins in his pockets jingled. Their noise brought to mind a particular woman he intended to visit—a black-haired, dark-skinned beauty who demanded the highest price for her services. He fully expected she would make herself available at the first opportunity. After all, he'd been quite generous with his gratuities following their last engagement, unlike with the other woman who so gravely disappointed him.

Once onshore, De Graaf strolled the middle of the main street with a newfound swagger, feeling for the first time as though he were master of this place. Dressed entirely in black from his bandana to his boots, and followed by his entourage of hell-bound pirates, he radiated a menacing, demonic impression. But that didn't deter two local women flanking the entrance to the Gente de Mar. Intrigued by his appearance, they leaned in provocatively, baring ample skin to gain his curiosity. Both had long, dark hair flowing softly around generously displayed breasts flanking bright-colored bobbles nestled invitingly in their décolletage. Their lips were tinted bright red, their brows excessively darkened. As De Graaf ascended the two steps to the entryway, one of the women stepped forward, caressing his upper chest and smiling suggestively. He grabbed her head roughly and drew her face to his, giving her a hearty kiss before pushing her away, gently. She was not the woman he sought. He tucked a silver coin behind her bobble. The woman smiled and rubbed her hand slowly along his crotch.

As De Graaf entered, his nose caught the pungent blend of uncooked fish, stale beer, and roast boar. He pushed his way through the thick crowd of thirsty patrons and skillful women. The off-key singing and boisterous yelling seemed to stifle whatever it was the man next to him was saying. He walked directly to a table where a woman was dispensing beer. The two men seated there rose, yielding the table.

De Graaf slammed down a gold coin. "Bring me your best," he said to the server.

"Drink or woman?"

"Brandy, if you have it." He felt a worthy celebration was in order.

The server took the coin and left, returning shortly with a full olive jar and one tankard. She poured liberally. De Graaf took a healthy swig of the golden liquid. It burned his throat. He scanned the room, looking for his woman.

Partially obscured from De Graaf's view by the flowing crowd, the tall, dark-haired object he sought attempted in vain to rid herself of a drunken, filthy pirate with designs on her. The boor pressed his hips against hers, cupping her breast. His tongue sought to lick her face. She turned her head to dodge it, catching a whiff of the man's foul, fish-laced breath.

"Give it me," he yelled, reaching out and grabbing her waist. His hand suddenly jerked at the hard yank of his hair, his neck twisting sharply. De Graaf slammed the man's face forward into the nearby wall. A tankard fell from his hand, splattering beer on bystanders. The boor's nose broke, sending blood spewing down the wall and onto his feet. His knees buckled as his body collapsed onto the floor. Consciousness would return later.

The dark-haired woman smiled at De Graaf—a beautiful, warm smile that hid awkwardly shaped teeth, a couple of which were missing. He nodded silently, drawing her body toward him. She placed her arms around his neck and kissed his lips, playfully thrusting her tongue between them. "Bienvenido de nuevo, mi mal hombre."

De Graaf didn't mind that she spoke only Spanish. He understood enough of her words. Especially those that mattered most. He knew she just welcomed his return and used her nickname for him: 'Badman'. He liked the moniker. "Quiero tu Tesoro," he replied.

Pulling her by the hand, he led her to his table and handed her his tankard. He picked up the olive jar and then began muscling his way through the crowd, with her in tow. They proceeded to a room in the back. He flung open the door.

"Blast ye!" said the pants-less sailor inside. He turned toward the intruders. "Be gon…" He stopped mid-sentence, recognizing his captain. Quickly reaching for his breeches and boots, he made a hasty exit. A half-naked woman followed him out, protesting as she went.

———

It took almost an entire day for his men to transfer the cargo from the captured Spanish vessel to the *Death's Head*. When they were done, Harker walked Captain Pereira to the edge of his now-empty ship. The bodies of his fallen crew had been weighted down and unceremoniously offloaded. The deck had been scrubbed clean by some of the Spanish crew, under guard.

"I thank you for your cooperation, Captain Pereira. The ship is once again yours. I trust you have sufficient crew remaining."

"Gracias, Capítan. We shall find our way."

"Where will you go?"

"Hispaniola. Mi casa."

"I wish you well, then," replied Harker. He turned to leave but then paused. "Should we meet again, I trust you shall choose more wisely regarding the defense of your ship."

Pereira frowned. "So I shall."

Harker wasn't buying it. He suspected Pereira would seek to make his ship less vulnerable, so as not to be overtaken. Nonetheless, he offered his hand. The two shook.

Harker and his men crossed over to their own ship just before the grappling hooks were removed by Pereira's crew. The two vessels began separating.

"On to Inagua. Full sails. Lively now," ordered Harker, smiling to himself. Sometimes letting a small fish go meant catching it again later, when it was even bigger. He looked forward to that day, wondering whether Pereira would dare challenge him, or make it an easy taking.

———

Scorpio maneuvered on the deck, wielding her sword in a make-believe confrontation with an imagined adversary. The wooden weapon was a gift made by one of Garret's crew. She slashed and thrusted, backed off, turned, and arced her arm upward to defend an illusory blow. She then followed an imaginary parry with a riposte. The crewmen watching her smiled. The feisty little thing's hair flowed in the breeze as she skipped along the deck, slaying the many make-believe warriors who dared challenge her. Several swordless lessons from Garret had clearly provided her both foundational skills and confidence.

"Land ho," came the call from the crow's nest. "Five points to larboard."

The crew's attention fell away from the 'Battles of Scorpio', moving immediately toward the sighting. Though the land wasn't yet visible from the deck, they knew it would soon emerge from the horizon.

Blair watched as Garret exited her cabin and strolled briskly onto the main deck. "Isla Tortuga, Cap'n," he said, pointing at the hump just beginning to surface in the distance.

"Thank you, Mr. Blair. Well done. We shall soon see what this peculiar place has to offer."

"Peculiar indeed," Blair mumbled under his breath. The place was reputedly a pirate haven. He was troubled by the thought of Garret's potentially sailing down that dark path. He walked away intentionally, putting space between himself and the captain whose motives he now questioned. He also resented her too-close relationship with the Spaniard, Valdez. As much as he respected her skills, he assured himself this would be his last voyage with her. He wanted no part of any piracy.

Jorge approached Garret. "How familiar are you with Isla Tortuga?" he asked.

"Only a little," Garret replied. "They say it is not actively controlled by your country, which explains why it is now a stopping point for ships from many nations, some with dubious reputation."

"I am told it is nothing but a cauldron of those who illegally attack Spanish merchants."

"You mean attack ships that deliver slaves and abuse native peoples to enrich their King and finance his wars on other nations?" Garret replied, teasingly. Jorge looked at her, without debate. She imagined he valued their relationship above winning an argument.

"Have you the slightest idea of the nature of the men on this island?" asked Jorge. Garret offered no response. He continued, "They are without discipline. No sense of service to others. They live only in the moment, drinking and whoring away ill-gotten gains. You shall find no civility here."

His words gave Garret pause. All she wanted was a place that might serve as a temporary base while she worked to restore relations with Queen Elizabeth. And, as far as she was aware, this was the only settlement in the Southern Seas without the presence of Spanish officials or military. If Jorge were correct, she wondered, could she and Scorpio find comfort here?

Garret looked out over the sea as the island's hump grew in size. She could see why the Italian, Cristobal Colon—whom the English referred to as 'Columbus'—had named it Turtle Island. Its appearance was vaguely reminiscent of a turtle's shell. And from this distance, it seemed as docile as a turtle as well. That was misleading.

———

After a few days of leisure, soaking in every vice Isla Tortuga had to offer, De Graaf and his crew were as collectively disheveled as they'd ever been. Drunk and exhausted, they had few things on their minds, other than more drinking and sharing body heat with the locals. They tended to prefer both their drink and their women darker. The darker the beer, the less watered-down it was. The darker-skinned the women, the fewer inhibitions they seemed to have. Fewer expectations too—nothing but a few pieces of eight and a sprinkle of trinkets.

De Graaf arose mid-morning, his head pounding. The stale air in the tavern wasn't helping. He needed clean air and an early swim to freshen his hair, his skin, and his undergarments. He dressed and sheathed his cutlass before heading outside to the main street. The morning was warm and clear, with just a slight breeze. His boots felt heavy in the hard-packed, sandy grit. As he shuffled along, he noticed there were only a few people on the street. It was as though even the residents of this small village had joined in the pirates' late-night partying and were similarly in need of extended rest.

Nearing the shore, he saw one of his smaller boats approaching. The two men inside were pulling heavily on the oars against relatively still water. He stood watching as the boat slid ashore and the men jumped out. One ran to him directly.

"We may have a problem, Cap'n." The sailor paused, gasping for air. "Two ships approaching. English flags."

"Damn," groused De Graaf, thinking how unprepared his men were and how little time they had to ready themselves. He suddenly wondered where the Hell Harker was; if he were even alive. "Are you certain? No crimson flags?"

"No, Cap'n. White. Red Cross. Definitely English." The sailor now had his hands on his bended knees, gathering his breath.

"Come, we need to roust the crew. Now." The men hustled down the main street, calling out, "Sail ho. Men at the ready. Sail, ho."

Inside the small shacks and buildings, weary men began to stir—French, Dutch, English, African, it didn't matter—all were brother pirates. They dressed and gathered their weapons. Most were still in a haze but recognized the need to shake it off. There was no uncertainty about the phrase 'men-at-the-ready'. Action lay ahead. Full wits required.

Men soon began pouring onto the street, many stumbling. De Graaf stood atop a wooden box. Already tall in stature, the large Dutch-African man towered over the assembling crowd. His arms held high and wide, he waited patiently for the men's silence before barking instructions. To those gathered on the street, viewing him with the sun in their eyes, he struck an evil image—a darkened devil ascended from Hell. The other pirate captains who'd ventured onto the street begrudged the man's commanding presence. Whether they would choose to follow his instructions depended entirely on what he had to say. They were anxious to hear it.

XXXII

Harker was now convinced—the two ships visible on the northern horizon and sailing toward him, fully sheeted, were Spanish warships. Their bearing suggested they'd come from the Inaguas, site of the now-missing Viceroy's military base. He, himself, was headed to the north of the big island. But that plan was now suspect; he could only lose a confrontation with two well-armed combat vessels. It called for a change of course—perhaps a return to Isla Tortuga. That was the nearest safe harbor, where like-minded pirates might collectively present an unwelcome challenge for these warships. "Mark a new heading, Mr. Stevens," he shouted. "Sou' sou'east. Full sails. Lively now!" He waited for *Death's Head* to respond.

Several men scrambled up the masts; others readied the clewlines. The helmsman spun his wheel and held tight as the ship leaned hard into the turn.

"Press on, damn you," Harker swore, not liking the time it was taking. He walked toward the stern, keeping an anxious eye on his trailing predators. There was no question; they were gaining on him. "Kilburn!" he yelled to his Master-at-Arms, "Ready the stern chasers." They were his only realistic deterrence.

"Mr. Stevens," he cried. "Join me here. Now." Stevens ran the short distance from mid-deck.

"What think you, Stevens?"

"Even at our best, Cap'n, we cannot maintain the gap. They will close on us."

"My thought as well," acknowledged Harker. "No time to hesitate, then."

"What have you in mind?"

"Unload the heaviest supplies from the hold. All but the treasure."

"Will that be enough, Cap'n?"

"We shall see. If not, we shall float the cannons."

"The cannons?"

"Aye. They are not worth our capture. The battery can be repurchased. We shall hold our treasure 'till the last."

"Aye, Cap'n." Stevens headed mid-ship, shouting as he went, "All hands to the hold. Lively now!"

Harker looked on as the last barrels of sugar plunged into the blue water. He cursed the wind. It seemed to favor the warships. They were still gaining. There could be no holding back. Not now. "Float the cannons, Mr. Stevens," he shouted. To soften the shock and doubts of his crew, he quickly added, "At best, they will only delay the inevitable."

"Aye, Cap'n. Cannons overboard." Despite their reticence, the crew flooded the gun deck, feverishly dismantling their only mechanized means of mayhem. Some formed a line, furiously shuffling cannonballs up the stairwell and over the rails. Once separated from their carriages, the iron gun barrels were hoisted to the main deck and swung overboard. Their violent splash was strong enough to shower those nearest the rail. Other heavy components followed, splashing into the water and descending to their embedded eternity.

Harker could see the fear on his men's faces. No doubt they questioned his sanity—placing them at the mercy of winds and warships. No one could like these odds.

A variety of vessels lined the harbor at Isla Tortuga, four of them were two- and three-masters. Garret noticed none were flagged. That was telling—these were pirate or, at best, privateering ships. She worried how they might respond to two oncoming English-flagged vessels. "Lower the flag, if you please, Mr. Blair," she instructed. "Signal *Orion* to do the same. No need to generate opposition."

The opposition was already mobilized. Pirates were manning their ships and readying guns. There being no shore battery, the ships' cannons were the settlement's sole defense. Anchors were weighed as several ships maneuvered into broadside position, presenting *Pandora* and *Orion* with a formidable anti-welcome.

Coming within range of hostile cannons, Garret and her crew heard the whacking echoes of dozens of wooden gun ports banging hard against the sides of the defending ships, exposing deadly black iron. She wondered whether these miscreants even noticed her flags had been lowered. If so, they hadn't taken it as a positive sign. "Furl the sails!" she called out. "Haul anchors."

De Graaf ordered the firing of a single warning shot. The cannonball soared high in the air, propelled by a flash of orange and trailed by a heavy cloud of smoke. It splashed harmlessly into open water, well in front of *Pandora*. Uncertain what the protocol might be, Garret sought to signal non-aggression. With her bowsprit facing the harbor, she ordered the firing of two bow-chasers—one shot each to larboard and starboard, signaling no threat. If that failed to gain their acceptance, the only remaining option was to hoist a white flag. But she worried that might give the wrong impression. She awaited their response.

There was only stillness for a few minutes as the stand-off persisted. One by one, De Graaf's counterparts responded to his questioning signal. There was general agreement—these two ships didn't appear to be a threat. De Graaf ordered a turn to face *Pandora* head-on. As the turn neared completion, the anchors were hauled.

Garret drew a deep breath in relief. "Raise the top foresail," she ordered. They would approach slowly. William Tovery followed suit on *Orion*. The two ships slowly entered the outer harbor, while most of the pirate ships angled to new broadside positions, their gunports remaining open.

Upon reaching the outer edge of the inner harbor, Garret and William ordered preparations to secure their ships. Everyone appeared anxious to enjoy whatever this village had to offer. Surely there would be beer and fresh food, judging by the number of ships.

Garret signaled William to board *Pandora*, wanting to confer with him before releasing the men. As he came aboard, she and Valdez greeted him. Scorpio approached, wooden sword in hand.

"Good day Captain. Viceroy," William said, turning to both in sequence, and nodding.

"Best of days, William. We are entering an interesting time…and place," Garret replied, referring to the fact that they were now neither navy nor privateers. Nor pirates. "God be with us."

"Just so," he replied.

"Welcome Captain," said Valdez, extending his hand to William. The two friends grabbed forearms and shook.

"I see your beard has gone awry," observed William. "And

your apparel appears rather sad." He chuckled. "Not your usual fashion, if I may say so."

Valdez laughed as well. "No point proclaiming the arrival of a Spanish Viceroy. I am but a simple seaman." As he said the words, he felt the slight press of the King's ring now secured inside a pocket in his boot. He dared not wear it in the village.

"You are most certainly anything *but* a simple seafarer," offered William, "though your soiled bandana would suggest otherwise."

Garret elected to interrupt the levity, "I believe we should send an emissary in advance, with a flag of truce."

"A *blood-red* flag of truce might be in order," jested William. They'd all heard that some pirates, beginning with Harker, had taken to flying that color as a warning to their prey.

"You may well be right," Garret replied. She motioned to Blair. "Find me a piece of red cloth."

"Aye, Cap'n," Blair responded, begrudgingly. He turned and left. "Red cloth be damned," he muttered.

"It is most important we not be viewed as representing England, or as any threat to the inhabitants," Garret continued. "I believe we should send Musa and Caber in advance. They are perhaps best able to present themselves as fellow…seafarers."

"Agreed," replied William. "Good choices."

"Fine, then. I shall instruct them accordingly. Let no one leave either of our ships until those two make contact and signal all-clear."

"Certainly," responded William.

"In the meantime, let the crew complete their preparations. We shall soon see what this place offers us."

De Graaf and some of his men assembled onshore to greet the eight men approaching by longboat. He soon recognized the two large ones seated at its stern. They'd sailed alongside him and Harker, under Drake. He recalled how, back then, both men supported the witch's promotion to Captain. He was there when the taller of the two, Musa, even threatened Harker if he didn't get on board with Connachan's appointment.

This was not a welcome crew. He suspected the witch chose to stay behind on her ship while these two made peace with Tortuga's pirates. He didn't say anything to his men, however. It wasn't the time for that. He needed to think further about what to do regarding the witch.

Musa and Caber stepped out of their longboat as it slid onto shore. "Greetings," said the latter, extending his hand. "We hail from the ships *Pandora* and *Orion*, Captains Connachan and Tovery."

"Caber, I believe," said De Graaf. He turned his head. "And Musa," he nodded.

"Farquhar," corrected Caber.

"Too hard, my friend. You shall always be the Caber." De Graaf turned to address his men, "I have sailed with these two. They are fine seamen."

As they shook forearms, the other pirates took special note of the newly arrived giants. It was rare to see one as tall as Musa or as wide as Caber. They made a formidable, though odd-looking, duo— one Black, one ginger; both with hands like bear claws and arms like cannons.

"Your flags are English," noted De Graaf.

"Merely for recognition," replied Caber. "The captains be English but we sail on our own account, without Royal orders. We go where we please and feed on those we choose. We prefer Spanish food." Those nearby laughed.

"Pirates then?" queried De Graaf.

"So it would seem," replied Caber, without hesitation. It was more ruse than truth…per Garret's instructions.

De Graaf masked his suspicion, "Then come, join us. We shall drink to your arrival."

"I be devilishly thirsty," Caber smiled. He motioned to one of his oarsmen to wave the red flag, signaling *Pandora* and *Orion* that all was well. For his part, De Graaf had his men signal an all-clear to the pirate captains still manning their ships.

The motley group of strongmen strode along the main street, passing by mostly disheveled and weather-worn wooden structures. Bothered chickens squawked their discontent. De Graaf, wishing to demonstrate his prominence here on the island, raised his arm around Caber's back. "You shall have a taste of my tavern. It may be small but it has all we need to celebrate the hunting of Spanish dogs."

"How is it that Spain allows this island to remain beyond its control?" asked Caber.

"Ahhh. A fine question. We disposed of the Viceroy King Philip sent to shut us down," De Graaf boasted. "The poor dupe never had a chance."

Musa squelched a laugh at the irony in De Graaf's shameful claim. It wasn't pirates who thwarted the Viceroy but rather he himself, along with Caber, Garret and William. And the Viceroy was, in fact, nearer than De Graaf could have imagined. But that was not to be shared. Garret's counsel echoed in his mind, '*Simply make merry and accept their leader for the fool he is.*'

———

The men who delivered Musa and Caber to the village rowed the longboat back to *Pandora*, to confirm the crew would be welcomed ashore. Those onboard cheered the news, looking forward to celebrations in a village with at least one tavern. Whether there might also be willing women was a major point of speculation…though not in Captain Connachan's presence.

Valdez headed to Garret's quarters. Before disembarking, he wanted confirmation they were of a similar mind concerning how he would be presented to the locals. Everyone was supposedly clear that he was not to be referred to as 'Viceroy'. It could jeopardize his very existence. But Garret further agreed to inform the crew that, were anyone to inquire as to his role, they should respond that he was a navigator's aide. In truth, he knew little of the subject. But, in preparation, he studied her maps and other relevant material to familiarize himself with the intricacies of nearby islands, prevailing currents, and common navigational methods. He was comfortable he could hold a decent, albeit short, conversation on navigating the seas with anyone but a real navigator, if it came to that.

"Enter," Garret answered to his knock. She shooed Scorpio away with her astrolabe, which she'd been instructing the girl on.

"Good news from the village, I understand," Valdez said as he entered.

"I suppose we may consider the news good," replied Garret,

"though doubtless some of the men shall soon be the worse for it."

Valdez smiled. He was quite familiar with how Spanish military men abused their leave by drinking too much, fighting with others, and engaging with women. He had no reason to expect otherwise from English sailors. There was no alternative, really. It was near impossible to maintain any sense of discipline in settings such as these. "I came to confirm the crew is fully aware of our story regarding my role on the ship."

"Not to worry, Jorge. I have spoken directly with William and Blair. Everyone understands that you are nominally *Pandora's* navigational aide. As it was in England, you shall be referred to only as Valcour. It is more French than Spanish. Should anyone call you Valdez, you can claim it is a common error since your father hailed from the Basque region.

"Excellent. I thank you."

"Blair will accompany you to shore. I believe that is best."

"Might we meet at a tavern later?"

"I think not."

"Are you intending to stay on *Pandora*, then?"

"I am, yes."

"For how long?"

"I may bring Scorpi ashore in the coming days if William believes conditions are not unfavorable."

"I see." Valdez was disappointed. He'd been looking forward to spending an evening onshore with her, in some quiet place where they could be alone. It would offer a chance to explore just how intimate she was willing to be. It had been far too long since he was last pleasured by a woman. But there was also another option. "Perhaps I should stay with the two of you.”

“If you are to have any presence at all onshore, it would be best to go now. If you go at a later time than the rest of the crew, your presence as a newcomer will be more obvious, drawing more scrutiny.”

“Fair point,” Valdez nodded. “It seems you have thought of everything. That comes as no surprise.” He knew her reputation among the crew—nothing escaped her attention.

“Go and have your fun, Jorge. We shall be here when you return.”

“Might I ask, have you some way of getting word to the King that I am available…as your bargaining piece?” He said it with disdain.

“I do, yes.” Garret didn’t expand further.

Valdez could see she had no desire to disclose any specifics. He would have to trust her. “Well then, I shall be on my way. But first…” He stepped toward her, taking her head in his hands. “I accept your suggestion to have some fun.” He looked deeply into her eyes, “But that shall not involve another woman.” He moved his face toward hers. She met him halfway. They shared a warm kiss. It was enough, he thought. For now.

“Is he your lover?” Scorpio asked after Valdez left the cabin.

Garret laughed. “Perhaps he feels that way. I, however, am uncertain. We shall see.”

“I like *William*,” replied Scorpi.

“As do I, dearest. But William is like a brother to me.”

As Scorpi returned to toying with her astrolabe, Garret pondered Jorge’s inquiry about getting word to King Philip. There was risk in her plan for that. William was to find someone in the village who might serve as a suitable conduit. He would need to determine whether that person was trustworthy enough to avoid putting Jorge in harm's way.

———

Death's Head found new life after tossing her cannons overboard. The gap between her and the two predatory Spanish warships was finally widening. Harker was relieved. He now expected to arrive safely at Isla Tortuga within a day or two; wind and weather permitting. He would then look to purchase replacement cannons from other pirate captains, although he knew the price would be dear. No problem, he thought, that cost would be deducted from his crew's share of the treasure.

His mind turned to De Graaf's situation. It was now several days since the storm separated them. He didn't imagine *Cutthroat* had been lost at sea. It was a sturdy vessel and De Graaf was an excellent seafarer. But he did wonder whether his partner might also have encountered the same Spanish warships he himself had just evaded. He hoped not. Together, he and De Graaf were a formidable force. He did worry, however, about the man's unpredictable nature and fits of rage. But he valued his fearlessness in a fight and his ability to command his crew. The beast was an asset.

The only other thing giving Harker pause was De Graaf's growing reputation as a ruthless pirate captain. It could ultimately lead to a contest between the two of them—something that would threaten the end of one of them. He needed to keep the beast close, and friendly. Being apart like this didn't help.

"The counters, Cap'n," interrupted Master-at-Arms Kilburn.

"Bring them, then."

Two guards waited outside while Kilburn shepherded in the two counters. Although an earlier inventory was conducted by two others, Harker ordered this second count. He claimed it was to ensure accuracy. The truth was, he sought to cloak the count in a fog of confusion. It worked in his favor.

One of the counters held out their tally, "Here are the numbers, Cap'n."

Harker grabbed the parchment and studied the figures while they waited. Within moments, he looked up at the two men. "Your numbers do not add up."

Both counters appeared puzzled. They'd spent two days taking meticulous inventory. One spoke up, "I assure you, Cap'n, we have counted every item. Twice, in fact. There can be no mistake."

"Then you had best hope your numbers are correct." He laid the sheets of parchment on the table. "I shall compare this to the earlier count. If anything is found missing, you shall forfeit your shares." He grimaced. "Perhaps more."

"We have taken nothing Cap'n, I swear." Sweat began beading up on the man's forehead. "This is the complete list of what is stowed. The guards assured us they let no one in or out, prior to our counting."

The other counter jumped in, "They also checked us as we left, to ensure we carried nothing with us. Please, sir, ask Mr. Kilburn."

"Secure these two men," Harker ordered. "Until I confirm their count, I want them locked up and guarded."

"Aye, Cap'n." Kilburn nodded. "Guards, take these men to the gaol." A short verbal commotion followed as the two protested their detention.

After all the others left, Kilburn asked, "Have they stolen some of our treasure?"

"It may well be. I shall know more once I study the records." He looked down at the documents and waved his right arm dismissively. He had no desire to continue the conversation.

Harker watched Kilburn leave. He smiled at the thought of making the count whatever he wished it to be. He could summarily accuse the two counters of theft, have them executed, and keep an undisclosed portion of the treasure for himself, without any questions being raised. Being a pirate captain carried many privileges, he thought; especially for those who were quick of mind and comfortable with math.

The next step, thought Harker, was to divide the spoils from Pereira's ship among the crew. De Graaf and his men had no right to share in that. Nevertheless, he would reserve a cut for De Graaf himself. In Harker's world, there was never any loyalty that hadn't been purchased.

XXXIII

Three riders appeared at Buckland Abbey—palace guards, sent to deliver a note from the Queen. One dismounted and walked toward the entryway. The riders' approach had been caught in advance by Thomas' manservant, who opened the heavy door and waited until the messenger ascended the steps. "Good day, sir. Welcome to the Drake residence."

"Thank you, my good man. Is Thomas Drake available?"

"He is, sir."

"Might I see him? Her Majesty has sent word."

"But of course. May I see the note?"

The messenger took the sealed parchment from his doublet. "I have been instructed to deliver it in person."

The manservant recognized the Queen's seal. He'd seen it often while the Admiral was still alive. "Certainly. One moment, if you please." He turned and headed to the study, where Thomas was reviewing papers.

Not waiting to ask, the messenger stepped inside the foyer. He marveled at the opulence of what was once Admiral Drake's home. There were several pieces of intriguing artwork on display, seemingly brought from various ports around the world.

Thomas' manservant returned shortly. "Accompany me, if you please." The other palace guards remained outside while the messenger followed down the hallway.

"The Queen's messenger, sir," the manservant announced.

"Please, come in," said Thomas, rising from his chair.

"Thank you kindly. My name is Bremmer. Lieutenant Bremmer." He bowed briefly before approaching the desk where Thomas now stood. "With the Queen's compliments, sir." He handed him the note. "She trusts you shall keep the contents in strict confidence."

"Most certainly," replied Thomas. "Would you care to stay for tea Lieutenant?" He pointed to a chair.

"Thank you, but I must return with haste, to assure the Queen you have received her letter."

"Travel well, then. And thank you."

"You are most welcome." Bremmer bowed once again and took his leave.

Thomas sat, anxious but optimistic. He broke the seal and opened the letter. It was written in Elizabeth's own hand.

Dearest Thomas,

I am most grateful to you for delivering the letter from our mutual friend [referring to Garret]. *I have given the matter much thought. I believe we have an opportunity to reap benefits from what our friend has presented. I trust you shall convey these thoughts, along with my assurance that our friend shall once again be graciously welcomed in my presence. However, it would be best if our friend were to come as their grandfather originally intended.*

With all my affection,
E.R.

Thomas understood the Queen's last sentence to mean that she wished Garret to visit the palace presenting as male. He imagined Elizabeth wished to minimize, if not avoid, any controversy surrounding her meeting with a woman she had once imprisoned. '*Her Majesty is nothing if not brief and inconspicuous*,' thought Thomas. He wondered how quickly he might get word to Garret, confident she would be quite pleased.

———

The rain began plinking *Pandora's* deck. "Time for a change," said Garret, bringing Scorpio's lesson in swordsmanship to an end. "Let us retire to my cabin for some reading while we wait out the coming storm." Judging from the color of the clouds and strength of the breeze, this was unlikely to be much more than a brief watering.

"Must we stop?" Scorpio frowned. She enjoyed having a weapon in hand, even if it was only this wooden cutlass. For so long, her lessons had simply been movements with imaginary weapons. That had been at Garret's insistence. She'd told her it was best to first master control of her movements before adding the weight of a sword, pistol or dagger. Now that she'd learned several tricks and maneuvers, she thoroughly enjoyed deploying them with a physical weapon. But she hoped it wouldn't be long before Garret might let her use a real sword.

"That is enough for today, dearest. We shall turn our attention to reading. And a little mathematics."

Scorpio frowned. Mathematics wasn't her favorite subject. In truth, it was probably her least favorite. Unless it was geometry. She loved navigation and geometry was a big part of understanding it. She followed as Garret headed to their shared cabin.

As they walked along the deck, Garret thought about how different these days onboard ship must be from the experiences the men were availing themselves of onshore. She had no desire to be around them at times like this. She disliked seeing them inebriated. And she found it demeaning to see women baring themselves in temptation, to earn trinkets and coins. That was not an environment she wanted Scorpio exposed to. But it occurred to her that the girl might well have seen similar behavior in London's alleyways. Perhaps she shouldn't be overly concerned. Regardless, she would wait for William to return, hoping he might bring word of a suitable residence, somewhere on the outskirts of the village.

Her thoughts turned to Thomas. Before leaving England, she'd asked him to send word to Isla Tortuga if the Queen were open to her return. Until then, she would remain here. If a suitable residence were not available onshore, she would have one built outside the village, where she and Scorpio might enjoy some privacy and avoid the excessive behaviors in the town itself. She and William had already discussed constructing temporary quarters for the men as well.

Despite the increasing rain, she stopped to take a long look at the island. This was far from home, she thought—in more ways than mere distance.

<h1 style="text-align:center">XXXIV</h1>

De Graaf stirred. The rain and wind had awakened him. Though it was early in the afternoon, he was still in bed, as was his custom. He preferred the late-night tavern life that commonly ended just before dawn. His stomach growled, messaging its hunger. Sensing he'd be unable to fall back asleep, he rose from the bed and splashed his face with water from the hammered copper bowl on the nearby table. He ran his wet hands through his long hair, pulling it back and tying it in a knot before grabbing his black bandana, which he noticed smelled not unlike a dead squirrel in humid heat. He submerged it in the water, rubbing it vigorously with a soap block. He rinsed and wrang it out before wrapping it around his head. He put on his clothes, stuffed his dagger in his waistband, holstered his pistol in his bandolier, and thrust his cutlass in its scabbard. He was nothing if not prepared. Just like every other pirate he knew.

Descending the stairs, De Graaf noticed four men at a table near the back. Two he recognized instantly—Musa and Caber. A third looked vaguely familiar. The face of the fourth was obscured from view. He strolled to an unoccupied table in a different corner at the back and sat. A tavern girl came by to ask his pleasure. "Beer and eggs," he replied, placing a silver coin on the table. The girl took the coin, turned, and left. He glanced over at the four men and nodded. He now recognized the somewhat-familiar one as William Tovery. The fourth man, the one he didn't know, had a scruffy beard and tussled dark hair, yet he bore the posture of a man who was used to being in charge. His complexion suggested he wasn't English. A Spaniard, perhaps? That seemed odd.

De Graaf turned his gaze to the tavern door as two men walked in. '*Always best to keep an eye on who was entering,*' he thought. He sat quietly and, without peering their way, tried to overhear the conversation of the four men. The tavern girl returned with a tankard of warm, watered beer. He nodded his thanks and took a deep swig.

"I suppose we have no alternative then," said William. He was responding to Caber's comment that there were no empty residences here; certainly nothing suitable for Garret and Scorpio. "We shall need to pick a location to build temporary residences. I prefer we keep the men as close together as possible. There is too much bad influence in this village to do otherwise." As he said it, he lowered his voice, "I shall inform Captain Connachan."

Musa and Caber nodded. Each drained their grog. Caber grabbed a chunk of bread as the two left. Valdez, apparently not wishing to have the rough-looking pirate with the black bandana overhear them, changed chairs so that his back was to the man. "What can you tell me about Garret's plan for me?" he asked William, his voice barely above a whisper.

"Has she not said anything to you?"

"Only that I am a pawn in some game she has chosen to play."

William was convinced Jorge had feelings for Garret. Either that, or he was playing her well. Though it bothered him, he still liked the man. Nonetheless, it wasn't his place to provide Jorge with information Garret herself chose not to share with him. "Do you trust her?"

Valdez paused, his face blank.

"Garret is a person of honor," William went on. "Given all that has transpired, surely you have no reason to doubt her."

"No," Valdez admitted, "though I may not always agree with her."

William smiled. He understood Jorge's uncertainty. "We shall find a way to make things work."

"In whose favor?"

"Well, certainly England's," he smiled. "But also yours."

"How so?" Valdez sought to probe as deeply as he could.

"I cannot say. Certainly not without her concurrence."

Valdez clearly accepted that but shook his head anyway. "I am more than a little frustrated." He'd said it a little more loudly than William would have liked. He didn't want the nearby pirate overhearing their conversation.

"Be patient, Jorge. She will share her plans for you in good time."

"I am used to *setting* plans, not following those of others," Valdez stated. "I have commanded thousands, yet here I am commanding no one. It is particularly emasculating at the hands of a woman."

Again, too loud, William thought. He chose not to respond but felt a need to defuse the situation.

De Graaf's eggs arrived but their delivery failed to distract him from obliquely eavesdropping on the conversation. Two surprising words he was certain he'd just heard were: 'commanded thousands'. Did this unknown man have a military background? It seemed possible, despite his common clothes. He needed to learn more. He picked up his fried eggs in his right hand and shoved them into his mouth, then grabbed his tankard and washed the eggs down with another large gulp of beer. Tankard in hand, he rose and walked to Tovery's table. "Good day, gentleman. Tovery is it not?"

"Do I know you?" William asked.

"Yaugaan De Graaf. We sailed with Drake."

"Of course. Have a seat, if you please."

De Graaf sensed William's remark was disingenuous. But he pulled back a chair anyway and sat.

"This is Monsieur Valcour, our navigator's aide."

"My pleasure," De Graaf said, extending his hand. "What brings you to Tortuga?" He'd already heard Caber's story but wanted to hear Tovery's version.

"Looking for a place to rest up."

"This may not be the best place for that," replied De Graaf. He sipped his beer. "At best, it is friendly only to those sailing on their own account." The look on Tovery's face suggested he grasped the implication—that the place could be hostile to those sailing on behalf of Kings, Queens and wealthy merchants. "We bring the proceeds of our travels here and leave some behind for the villagers," De Graaf continued. "But you two came under an English flag."

"We answer to no one," William offered.

The way he said it, De Graaf sensed Tovery wasn't enjoying their conversation.

"We are men of free will, William added.

"Privateers, perhaps? For the Queen?" probed De Graaf.

"Privateers on our own account."

"Not pirates then," De Graaf replied, with disdain. "And how long do you privateers intend to stay?"

"Only until we do not." William looked away, dismissively.

De Graaf squinted his eyes, looking first at Tovery and then at the man introduced as Valcour. He spit on the floor and then rose, his chair scraping noisily as he pushed back on it. "Take good care, gentlemen," he said, menacingly. "This is not a place for men who would search for courage."

———

Standing at the bow in drizzling rain, Harker counted the surprising number of ships anchored in the harbor as *Death's Head* approached Isla Tortuga. Spotting the *Cutthroat*, he relaxed about his partner's fate. He looked forward to reconnecting with De Graaf.

As he continued scanning the many ships, one in particular caught his eye. He knew he'd seen it before but couldn't immediately place it. No problem, he would find out who captained it soon enough. "Hove to," he called out, ordering a slowing of the ship as it neared the harbor's outer edge.

Within half the hour, *Death's Head* was anchored and secured. Harker and his crew were in good spirits, despite the wet grayness of the air. Guards assigned, he disembarked to the stern of a longboat. As others noisily filtered in, Harker caught the name painted on the stern of the ship he'd spotted earlier—*Pandora*. 'The witch's ship', he grumbled—the woman whom he surmised once put a spell on Drake to gain her captaincy. But what in damnation was Connachan doing here? And why was she not flying her blasted English flag? Had the ship been captured by a pirate who now claimed it as his own? It was all quite interesting. He was anxious to catch up on the news with De

Graaf.

Garret rose from her chair, where she'd been reading with Scorpio. Through the stern windows, she'd earlier caught Harker's ship emerge like a ghost from the grayness. It was now anchored nearby. She approached the window, watching several men disembark to a longboat. One already seated at the stern wore a blood-red eye patch. He was gazing up at her ship. She wondered whether he saw her through the window.

Her cabin was silent, its air suddenly chilled by the nearness of her nemesis. Time itself seemed to stretch in the moment. Harker's arrival brought unwelcomed insecurity to her decision to find even a temporary residence on Isla Tortuga. Still, she was confident of her crew's abilities, both as sailors and, if necessary, as warriors. She'd never felt truly threatened by anyone, even her enemies. Yet here was a man whom she worried could be serious trouble. He was devious and unpredictable. She couldn't quite label her feelings of discomfort. Not fear, really. More just anxious uncertainty.

As his longboat passed by, Harker focused on the windows of the captain's cabin at *Pandora's* stern. Through the drizzle, he could see a shaded gray silhouette in the dark windows. He searched for any sign that it might be the witch. One thing was certain—if she were here, it would not end well for her. He'd given her fair warning the last time they met, off the coast near Santiago del Príncipe.

———

"I should like to meet that pirate in a dark place," said Jorge, still bristling from De Graaf's intimation that he was in want of courage. "Just him and me. He would learn something about disrespecting others."

William placed his cup back on their table at the Gente de Mar. "I suspect if you were to meet him in some dark place, it would not be him alone," he responded. "De Graaf is simply the lead animal of the pack."

"Indeed. But to confuse the pack, you need only dispose of its leader. This man is unlikely to have had any formal training in military arts. Any number of men who have served under me could quickly dispense with him."

William understood Jorge's reaction; military commanders were unaccustomed to having their courage challenged. Rather than fan Jorge's flames further, he sought to defuse them, "Most pirates prefer to take what they want through fear and intimidation rather than actual physical force. Truly, his words mean little."

"He had best keep them to himself. I am not one to back down from a challenge."

"Just so. But for now, I have another matter to attend to—finding someone of influence in this village."

William waved to catch the tavern girl's attention. She was in her mid-teens and of mixed color. Perhaps half-European, half-black. Her long, thick, and dark hair framed a pleasing face. She saw William's wave and came to the table. "Will there be something else, sir?"

William put a silver coin on the table. "I have a question," he said. "Does this village have a Rector?" A frown emerged on the girl's face. She was clearly unfamiliar with the term. "Someone in charge?" he clarified.

"There is," she replied, glancing down at his coin disapprovingly.

William recognized the game she was playing. He placed a second coin on top of the first. "I presume he has a name then."

"He does, sir. But he prefers not to let it be known."

William smiled at this brash young girl's attempt to maximize her payment for providing what he wanted. The coins meant little to him. He pulled another from his pocket but held it in his hand this time.

The server seemed to catch his implication. "He goes only by 'Prince'."

"And where might I find this *Prince*?" The girl said nothing in response. William waited. But not for long. He added one more coin to the pile.

"He owns the tavern."

"Is he here, then?"

She darted her eyes upstairs, without saying anything.

"And how shall I recognize him?"

The girl looked down at the pile of neatly stacked coins. She smiled and waited once again.

"You are a skillful bargainer." William reached into his pocket. "But this shall be the end of it." He placed a fourth coin on top of the pile, ensuring all four were perfectly aligned.

The girl wasted no time. She scooped up the coins and placed them in her apron. "Look for a heavy-set man; scruffy, gray beard; black hat with a white feather. He chooses to wear a sky-blue coat and white gloves."

"Thank you," said William. "Perhaps I shall have another koffei."

The tavern girl nodded sweetly, then turned to leave.

"What is your name, girl?" asked William.

"Catherine," she said, turning toward him with a smile. "They call me Cath." She nodded, turned, and left. William watched her go, his eyes lingering on her budding young figure. '*Brash and smart*,' he thought. '*Not unlike Garret.*'

XXXV

Standing on the rain-slicked cobblestones at Plymouth Harbor, Thomas Drake watched the warship *Mercilus* sail into open water, heading for the Southern Seas—specifically, Isla Tortuga. Captain James Wenman, a hero in the battles against King Philip's Armada, was in charge. He carried with him Thomas' sealed letter to Garret, explaining that she would indeed have the Queen's support in negotiating terms for returning Viceroy Valdez to King Philip.

Thomas understood there were still several potential storms between Garret's temporary island home and this harbor. First and foremost was the continued well-being of the Viceroy himself. Even with Garret's protection, there was always the uncertainty associated with seafaring life—the vagaries of the weather, the actions of rogue players on the high seas, and the potential for sickness—all of which concerned him. King Philip's willingness to participate in such a negotiation, and agree to England's terms, was perhaps an even bigger hurdle. Still, it was encouraging that the Queen herself was supportive of Garret's plan. Praying it might unfold as intended, Thomas lingered long enough to watch *Mercilus* pass through the visual limits of the rain-filled air, taking his heart with it.

———

Word that *Death's Head* had set anchor sent De Graaf strolling calmly to the shoreline. Harker's longboat was already sliding ashore when he arrived. The men jumped out, their boots splashing in the clear, shallow water. They pulled the boat high onto the beach.

"There be no room here for pirates," shouted De Graaf.

Harker turned his way…and smiled. De Graaf approached, extending his right hand. The two men shook forearms.

"It is good to see you, my friend," said Harker. "I am anxious to hear of your travels following the storm. But first, let us get out of this rain." They turned and headed to the Gente de Mar.

"We have some familiar English visitors," offered De Graaf. "William Tovery is in the tavern at this very moment."

"I saw *Pandora* in the harbor. Is the witch here as well, then?"

"Not that I have seen."

"I hope she is. I should like to have a few moments alone with her," Harker grinned. "Perhaps I might instruct her on a woman's proper place onboard a vessel."

De Graaf laughed. "I imagine she would be a challenging romp. You would be well exercised."

"You encourage me even more, sir." Harker threw his arm around De Graaf's shoulders, laughing. "In the meantime, perhaps another woman shall do."

"There be a young serving girl in the tavern who might draw your fancy. She may well be ready for her first entrance." Both men laughed heartily.

———

The gradually lightening clouds finally finished dispensing their water. Garret suggested to Scorpio that they return to the main deck. The girl quickly closed her book and followed Garret out the door.

"Might we go to the village today?" Scorpio asked as they reached the deck.

Garret looked down at her knowingly. They both longed to set foot on Tortuga's shore. She bent her knees, bringing herself to eye-level with Scorpio. "I wish to go there as well, dearest. But first, we must be certain it is safe for us. This is not London, I am afraid."

"But I made my own way in London," Scorpio challenged. "I am not afraid of anyone."

Garret had to smile. The girl was so self-assured—as though there were nothing she couldn't deal with. It reminded her of herself when she was younger. "It shall not be long," she assured her. "Let us wait for Captain Tovery's return."

"But I don't want to wait," Scorpio pleaded. "Can we please go now?"

On any other occasion, Garret might have been persuaded. But having seen Harker pass by in his longboat earlier, her concern was heightened. "I am truly sorry, Scorpi. You know I would take you if I were convinced you would be safe. You must trust me; it will not be much longer." She rose and looked out over the harbor toward the village, hoping William and Jorge might soon return.

———

The Gente de Mar was now astir. Recently awakened pirates from various ships had responded to early afternoon pangs of hunger and followed their noses to the smell of food. A few enterprising women were also afoot, making their presence and availability known. Tovery and Valdez were still at their table in the corner, waiting for an appearance by Prince, owner of the tavern and, arguably, the nominal leader of this pirate colony's more-permanent residents.

Harker, De Graaf and their entourage entered boisterously. This was a place they'd enjoyed since first coming here more than a year ago. Seeing them walk in, some of De Graaf's men rose from their seats, making their tables available for the two leaders. Harker acknowledged the men's deference before choosing one.

"Now where is this girl of whom you spoke?" he asked, taking a chair and scanning the tavern.

"On her way, now," replied De Graaf. He'd waved for her before they even sat down. Having earlier tipped her well, he assumed she would come quickly. And she did.

"What might I bring you?" Cath asked.

"My friend here wishes to know what you have available." De Graaf nodded toward Harker.

"We have boar, chicken, eggs, cheese, bread…"

Harker smiled at her. "I am thinking something other than food."

Catherine was familiar with the desires of men returning from long stints at sea. "Shall I fetch you a woman, then?"

Harker looked her up and down, liking what he saw—a pretty face, long dark hair, big eyes, and a pleasing physique. Even more enticing, her age suggested she was not 'used goods', as the other women in the tavern appeared to be. He liked the idea of introducing her to life's greatest pleasure. "I have someone better in mind, my dear."

"I handle the food and drink; not the men."

Harker and De Graaf laughed aloud. The chase was on. "Well, perhaps you are ready to handle a real man," said Harker. De Graaf snorted.

"I shall bring you a beer. You can decide on food, or women, while I am gone." She turned to go.

Harker reacted instantly, grabbing her arm. "We are not done here."

"Food, then?"

"Name your price."

"I am not on the list of offerings," she replied, yanking her arm from his grip. She turned again, to walk away.

Harker rose quickly from his chair, sending it falling behind him. "Come back here," he yelled. "We are far from done."

The commotion caught the attention of the crowd, including Tovery and Valdez. Jorge began to rise. William grabbed his arm. "Not our fight," he cautioned. "The odds here are against us."

Cath stopped and turned nervously toward the scruffy-looking Harker.

"Ahhh," said Harker. "Come," he motioned, smiling. "I am ready to place my order."

She walked toward the table hesitantly, stopping just out of Harker's reach.

"I shall have my meal. First." He retook his seat

"And what might that be, sir?"

Harker looked straight at her chest. "Breasts," he said for effect, letting the comment hang in the air for a moment before looking her in the eye again. "*Chicken* breasts. For now." De Graaf chuckled at Harker's wit, unable to squelch his reaction.

"And you," asked Cath, turning to De Graaf.

"Just the beer," he replied. "It fuels my imagination."

Cath turned and left. She walked toward the kitchen, her body shaking, tears beginning to moisten her eyes.

XXXVI

The splotches on the peeling, soiled-white paint on the walls seemed to deepen and expand with the intensity of the early afternoon light filtering into his room through a dusty window. Prince sighed, feeling the woman lying on her side next to him had overslept her welcome. Nonetheless, he cupped her breast in his right hand, relishing its soft fullness and taut nipple. It spawned an immediate response between his legs. He squeezed his hand gently, causing the woman to roll slowly onto her back.

A loud shout emanating from the tavern below interrupted his thoughts. It was followed by a sudden quiet. That was a worrisome sign. He preferred the tavern's usual happy hum—the sound of profit. Experience taught him abrupt silence such as this was the precursor to a potentially dangerous situation. His tavern was far from immune to damage at the hands of inebriated pirates. In the end, someone always paid for the repairs. Still, it was an inconvenience he didn't welcome. He needed to intervene.

Prince rose, now flaccid at his groin, and dressed quickly. He finished by putting on his well-worn, powder-blue coat. Once a piece of finery, it now showed its age in stains, rips and frayed seams. Still, he felt it conveyed an air of superiority over the men who lived in or frequented his village. And, after all, this was his village to lead. Nothing went on here that he didn't either know about or have a direct hand in. Even the pirates paid him homage since he was the one who best filled their most pressing needs. Due to the need now at hand, he dispensed with his usual white gloves.

The woman in his bed snorted, suggesting she'd returned to her sleep. He shook his head as if to make her magically disappear. She didn't. He put on his yellowed wig and black hat, and rushed out of the room to see what the commotion below was all about. He had no idea it was Harker who had silenced the sound of money.

"There," said William quietly, nodding toward the staircase. "The man we seek."

Valdez watched as the oversized, aristocratic-looking gentleman in the blemished blue coat descended the creaking, wooden stairs. The man seemed out of place in this small, seaside village laced with grimy, disheveled pirates and uncouth merchant seamen. "How does a man such as this end up in charge?" he asked rhetorically, judging the man by his ostentatious but sullied appearance.

Other heads turned to watch Prince descend. He nodded to the assembled crowd, clearly relishing their attention. "Please, gentlemen, proceed as you were. Drink heartily," he spoke the last two words loudly, with a smile and a wave of his right arm. Several in the crowd laughed, easing the tension in the room.

"I see," said Valdez, answering his own question. "He is a showman."

"Indeed," replied William. "Big presence. Small appendage."

Valdez laughed. He leaned in, "I do not trust men of his ilk. They often hide the truth behind their choice of words. All bluff 'n stuff. No substance."

"Unfortunately, we require his assistance. I doubt there is another way to safely get word back to your 'friend' that you are still among the living."

"What possible contact would this man have with my *friend*?"

"Through seafaring merchants," answered William. "They buy pirated goods at low prices and resell them to others elsewhere at market prices. There is good profit in that. Some suspect your friend himself takes a share."

"That cannot be true," countered Valdez. "Philip is a fine man. He would never participate in such deception."

"I shall take your word for it, then. Still, seaborn merchants at some level will have the ear of your friend's contacts, if not your friend's own ear as well. At this point, they are the only path along which our word can travel. Paying this showman to have them deliver our message would seem to be our best course."

Prince made a point of checking in with the customers in his tavern, particularly those who were captains. It wasn't just their spending he welcomed; it was also the knowledge they brought—of all that was happening in the Southern Seas. He prided himself on being the most well-informed, self-appointed figurehead of an island settlement by seeking information of all kinds: what ships were traveling through these waters; the nature of the goods being shipped; what recent captures had been made; what pirated merchandise was available for purchase; what goods were sought by merchants; what prices were being paid; what captains were sailing which ships; what was happening politically around the islands, and what news was current back in Europe. Information had value, and he fancied himself highly skilled at converting that value into gold and silver. So it was only natural that he scanned the tables as he descended the stairs, looking for both familiar captains and others he didn't know, who nonetheless bore the look and swagger of a captain.

He easily spotted Harker. The man with the blood-red patch had been here before. He was seated next to De Graaf. When here together, the two were frequently loud and spent heavily. He approached their table, smiling at one of the tavern ladies and swatting her firm buttocks as he walked by. For women like her, he provided rooms where they could deliver their services. In return, they handed over his share of what they received from their clients. At his insistence, they were also adept at gleaning information from the men they serviced—information that might be of value. If it were, he was known to reward the women generously.

"Good day to you, Captains," he said, nodding first to Harker and then De Graaf, in accordance with their standing. I trust all is well, and that you are in good hands."

"I crave the hands of that young tavern girl." Harker nodded toward Cath. "She seems uninclined to share them with me."

Prince glanced in the direction Harker motioned. His heart beat errantly. "I am afraid she is rather new to serving, Captain. Far too young, as yet. She is also my niece." He glanced around, "I shall find you a woman worthy of your time. With my compliments, of course." He looked briefly for a woman and then turned and saw the disappointment on Harker's face. He imagined the pirate craved his niece even more, knowing she was prohibited fruit.

"Perhaps at a future date," Harker suggested.

Prince didn't respond. He looked back and waved at one of the experienced women, moving his hand quickly to indicate she should come right away. De Graaf saw the woman and cringed. It was *his* woman. He understood her profession but had no interest in sharing her with Harker. He pushed back from the table, stood, and intercepted her as she approached, grabbing her firmly by the arm. He pulled her away into the now-animated crowd.

Prince watched in dismay, recognizing the need to find an alternative that might satisfy Harker's interests. "Give me a moment, Captain," he said, turning and rushing away to find another.

Now on his own, Harker scanned the patrons' faces. He paused, thinking he recognized a familiar one, but wasn't certain. The moving crowd obscured the man.

He was suddenly distracted by the young tavern girl delivering his food. "Thank you kindly, my dear," he smiled, hoping he might earn her favor by easing off his prior intensity. He gave her twice the money required, as a display of good faith. And future interest.

"Thank you, sir," said Cath, returning his smile.

Harker could see she didn't wish to cause any ill will or commotion in her uncle's establishment. As she turned to leave, he called out, "What be your name, girl?"

"Catherine, sir."

"A regal name. Quite fitting."

"Thank you." She bowed slightly and left.

Picking up the over-cooked chicken and biting into it, Harker was finally able to catch the face of the man he thought he might know. He now recognized him as William Tovery, originally a midshipman during their voyage with Drake. The two had their differences. Harker knew the man was friendly with the witch—Connachan.

His gaze turned to the man seated next to Tovery. He didn't appear English. His hair was dark and his skin more browned than even the most sea-tanned English sailor. He looked more like a Spaniard.

Dressed as an ordinary seaman, he appeared older than most crewmen. What's more, there was an aura of strength about him. It wasn't just his broad shoulders or the way in which he moved; it was the look and character of his lightly scarred face that suggested something more. A military man, perhaps. But a Spanish one? That seemed odd given he and Tovery were having a rather friendly conversation.

De Graaf returned to the table with a tankard in hand. Harker once again tore ravenously at the less-than-willing chicken. "Did you run out of food on *Death's Head*?" De Graaf laughed.

Harker swallowed, washing down his mouthful with a swig of grog. His gaze was still riveted on the man with Tovery.

De Graaf turned in that direction. "I see you noticed our old friend, Tovery." His emphasis of the word 'friend' seemed to Harker an obvious mockery of the relationship they shared.

Harker took another bite, asking with his mouth full, "Do you know the man with him?" Some of the chicken followed the words out of his mouth.

"Valcour. A navigator's aide."

"Navigator my arse. He has more bearing than that."

De Graaf took a closer look at the man, pursing his lips as if to agree without committing. "Perhaps."

"Valcour, you say? French?"

"Maybe. Maybe Basque."

"Does it strike you as odd that those two should be so close?"

"There be many strange friends in this village," De Graaf smiled and winked.

Harker smiled back. There was truth in that. But this seemed different. "Something is going on there. I am uncertain what, but I sense they are scheming."

"You would know," said De Graaf. "You are among the best at it." He sipped his grog.

"What was the name of that Viceroy the Spanish King sent to Inagua? The man he chose to lead his military forces in the Southern Seas?"

De Graaf shook his head, indicating he didn't remember…if he ever knew at all.

"Valcour?"

De Graaf shrugged. "Perhaps. But if that were him, and if Tovery captured him, then why would the two be sitting there as friends? It makes no sense."

A buxom tavern woman came by, having received a gold escudo from Prince. Her blouse was open to her navel, revealing ample assets. She placed her hand on the back of Harker's head and slid onto his lap.

"Perhaps," replied Harker, not losing a beat. He squeezed the woman's buttocks. "We shall see." As he spoke, more chicken left his mouth, landing on the table. The woman laughed, wiping his mouth with the soft brush of her fingers.

Prince approached the table where William and Valdez were engrossed in conversation. "Gentlemen," he said, "welcome to my establishment. This is your first time here, is it not?"

"It is," replied William. Valdez sipped from his tankard.

"Welcome, then. I am the man others call Prince." He extended his hand. "I own the tavern. Some say I own the village," he chuckled, though it seemed clear his message was delivered with serious intent.

"Captain Tovery," said William, shaking Prince's hand. This is my navigator, Monsieur Valcour."

Valdez shook Prince's hand, noticing how soft it was. '*This man has never done hard labor*', he thought.

"I hope you are enjoying yourselves, gentlemen. Is there anything I might do for you?" Prince asked

"There may well be," William replied. "But please, have a seat. Tell us about this village of yours."

XXXVII

He'd waited patiently at his table. Now, watching William Tovery descend the stairs, he wondered just what the man had discussed with Prince. He saw Tovery nod to his associate, 'Valcour', who rose to join him. They left the Gente de Mar together. Harker waited a few more minutes before heading up to Prince's quarters with De Graaf.

Prince heard the heavy footsteps of two men approaching. The sound was ominous. He checked his two French pistols on the table beside him, confirming they were loaded. Focusing on the door, he placed his right hand on one of the pistols. The knock he expected came quickly.

"Who is it?" he called out nonchalantly, masking his trepidation.

"Harker and De Graaf."

Though he'd always treated these pirate captains well, he was now alone in his room, with his hard-earned money. And vulnerable. "I am otherwise engaged. What is the purpose of your visit?"

"Tis a matter of business."

"State your business, then."

"We wish to discuss the intentions of the newly arrived English privateer," answered Harker.

Prince knew he was referring to Tovery, who'd just left. He also sensed frustration in Harker's voice; pirate captains were obviously unaccustomed to being questioned. He sought to tread carefully since his discussion with Tovery was in confidence. And paid for. "How is that *your* business, if I may ask?"

"What happens here is of great concern to us." Harker paused before adding, "And to our many associates who frequent your tavern."

Prince caught the implication. "I shall be downstairs in half the hour. We can speak then."

Harker responded without hesitation, as though he'd expected that response. "We are prepared to pay you for your time *now*."

"What is my time worth to you?" Everything was for sale, Prince thought—at the right price.

"Two escudos."

"You have much to learn, Captain."

"Four, then."

"Very well," replied Prince, not wishing to risk pressing further. "Give me a moment." He took the pistols from the table and tucked them into the band under his coat. He walked to the door, unlocking and opening it.

Harker didn't bother to acknowledge Prince. He pushed through the door and strode to the window while De Graaf paid the tavern owner. He peered out the window, seeking to confirm that Tovery and his 'navigator' were indeed gone. The street was dusty from the breeze, and fluid with the scattered movement of people and animals. His eyes spotted his targets walking toward the harbor.

Harker shifted his gaze to *Pandora,* now convinced the witch was there. He hoped there was something of value in the ship's hold. He was also in need of cannons. He would soon take it all from Connachan. She needed to be put in her proper place—a box interred somewhere in the woods. She was not worthy of a sailor's burial at sea.

Prince closed the door. "Thank you for your consideration, gentlemen. What would you care to know about this privateer?"

———

The seawater pressed between the boards, leaking lightly into the longboat carrying Tovery, Valdez and six oarsmen. Only Valdez seemed concerned. But he stifled any comment, thinking it best not to alert seasoned seafarers over fears they might laugh at.

It was late in the afternoon when the boat rubbed alongside *Pandora*. Garret had seen it coming. She and Scorpi walked to the taffrail. Despite the girl's companionship, Garret had been feeling a kind of loneliness—a longing for the company of other adults. She hoped William and Jorge were bringing news that there was a place to stay in the village. She had no desire to spend her entire time confined to *Pandora* while awaiting word from Thomas, or from the Queen herself.

Assuming Her Majesty approved, they could proceed with returning Jorge to Spain, in exchange for English title to an island here in the Southern Seas. Her favorable standing with Elizabeth would then be restored. That wasn't merely the best-case scenario, it was the *only* scenario in her mind. If it didn't come to pass, there were significant questions regarding her future. As an escapee from an English prison, there was literally no chance she could ever return to enjoy freedom in her home country without the Queen's support.

William was first to step through the entry-port and onto the deck.

"Welcome back, Captain Tovery. Your smile portends favorable news."

"I suppose that depends on how you define favorable."

Garret turned to Valdez, "Viceroy," she nodded. Though no crewmen were on the ship, she still liked to maintain a degree of formality when officers boarded. Even these two. She smiled inwardly at just how smoothly she was able to separate her official role from her personal feelings for Jorge in particular. Whatever those feelings were. "Shall we retire to my cabin, to discuss the matters at hand?"

"Just so," replied William. Valdez nodded.

Scorpio followed as they headed to Garret's quarters. She always enjoyed the intrigue of Garret's dialog with her officers in the cabin. But she was unusually excited about this particular discussion, feeling it could lead to her visiting the little village that was so close, yet so removed.

———

"So, do you trust this man Prince to arrange delivery of Jorge's letter to the King?" Garret had just finished refilling the cups of wine on the table and now sat. Her cabin was relatively warm, its great stern windows capturing the full light of the sun as it neared the water's edge.

Valdez reached for his cup, injecting his own thoughts, "In this village, it is impossible to trust anyone. Yet what choice is there?"

"I believe we can trust him," William chimed in. "He trades not only goods and services but also information. He may well make more money from exchanging information than from selling food, drink and other pleasantries in his tavern. He has relationships with countless merchants, privateers and pirates who ply their dark trade in these seas. His dealings with them serve everyone well. Were he not to be trusted, he would not be alive today."

"How much has he requested for his services?"

"Forty escudos. Half now, half upon receipt of a reply. Another twenty for the captain of the merchant vessel he chooses, though I suspect he shall keep a portion of that for himself. He also requested another ten for his silence in the matter."

Garret thought for a moment, feeling *Pandora* sway gently with the harbor's pulse. It wasn't the man's asking price that gave her pause. "Merely seeking payment for his silence raises concern. It suggests he might well share this information with someone offering an even higher price."

"Then perhaps we pay him something beyond his request, as an expression of good faith," offered William.

"In return for which," added Valdez, "we might ask that he alert us if anyone else *does* seek information regarding our plans." Garret and William nodded their agreement.

"One more thing," added William. "There are snakes here in the village—one named Harker, the other De Graaf.".

———

Following his meeting with Prince, who was most forthcoming, Harker was now convinced—the man he'd seen with Tovery— 'navigator Valcour'—was indeed the kidnapped Viceroy Valdez. Why else would Tovery have sought Prince's help in getting a message to King Philip?

What he couldn't understand was why Tovery and Valdez were on friendly terms. King Philip appointed Valdez to direct military affairs in the area. And the man was known to be a close friend of the King. That would make him the perfect hostage for the English—one Philip would pay handsomely to retrieve. Yet Tovery's apparent friendship with Valdez suggested the two were conspiring against the King. Why else would Valdez be walking around freely, posing as a navigator? It brought to mind his long-ago statement to a highly inebriated De Graaf—'*Find Connachan and we find the Viceroy*'.

It seemed highly likely the three newcomers intended to bluff the King for ransom money. Which brought another thought to mind—capture the Viceroy and collect the ransom himself. That would be even easier money than sacking a village. He could assault *Pandora*, take the witch for quick pleasure, and kidnap this Valcour. Even if Valcour wasn't actually the Viceroy, he would suffice for the ruse and ransom.

<h1 style="text-align:center">XXXVIII</h1>

"So it begins," said Garret. She and Jorge stood on the deck, looking out over the dark, quiet harbor, watching William leave on a longboat with six oarsmen and the escudos Prince requested for his services in delivering a message to King Philip. William was to meet him at night's peak, at his remote cabin in the hills far from the village.

"Indeed," replied Jorge, "Yet there is much ocean to cover between now and the receipt of any response from the King." He turned to look Garret in the eye. "Perhaps we might find something interesting to do in the meantime."

William listened to the calming sound of water lapping against the sides of the longboat with each orchestrated stroke of the oars. He took note of the vast array of stars filling the warm night sky. Though life was challenging, the stars always had a way of bringing him peace. He patted the sealed letter tucked safely inside his doublet. Though uncertain what Jorge had written, he had no doubt it was consistent with their discussions. After all, the man was now his friend.

What he was more curious about was where Garret stood in all of this. If she had deep feelings for Jorge, as he suspected, then how could she bring herself to use him as a pawn in this game? Among other things, it would mean the two would ultimately have to part. Unless, of course, she had designs on going with him. But William didn't believe for a moment that Garret would give up everything she had, and everything she stood for, to become 'the Viceroy's woman'.

He recognized that he, himself, had mixed feelings for her—somewhere along the continuum between friend/sister and potential lover. It pained him that Jorge had chosen to stay behind with her while he alone delivered the sealed note and escudos to Prince. No doubt Jorge had designs on an evening of intimacy with Garret, though he chuckled inwardly at the thought of Scorpio's presence presenting a slight challenge.

Regardless of whatever future Garret might foresee with Jorge, William hoped she would always remain part of his own life. In some way.

Prince gazed out the window of the weathered and isolated little cabin overlooking the sea below. At the shoreline, he watched a group of sailors pulling their longboat onto the sand. How fortunate he was, he thought. This was an easy haul that would serve his interests well. Though he was here alone, he had no fear for his physical well-being. He prided himself on being able to judge a man's character. Captain Tovery struck him as a man of integrity. Besides, the Captain would have nothing to gain by threatening him.

He sipped beer from an old lead cup, watching three men begin their climb to the cabin while the rest remained behind. It would only be a handful of minutes before he would have their gold in hand…and the letter for which he'd already arranged delivery to King Philip.

———

It was time, thought Garret; the man who was now her only ticket back to freedom in England had earned the right. She and Jorge had waited patiently until Scorpio was asleep in her cabin. They walked barefoot across the deck to his quarters, his arm around her waist. The door creaked as he opened it. This was the first time she'd ever entered his space. In the dim light, she wasn't surprised to find it in good order; he was a highly disciplined military man. Everything was in its place—right down to the items on his desk, where she imagined he'd earlier penned his letter to the King. She turned to him as he followed her in.

Jorge smiled as he took Garret in his arms and pulled her body close. His original plan to seduce her for his own interests was about to pay favorable dividends. But things had changed significantly since then, and he knew it. Initially thinking of her as a mere tool—and plaything—he recognized his interest in the young Englishwoman had evolved. It now went well beyond her use as a tool to regain his freedom; and even beyond her physical attraction. He had to admit, he found himself enamored with the woman simply for the person she was. Perhaps it was their shared experience in escaping the Tower of London that marked the turn. Whatever it was, the possibility that he might soon return to Spain now brought him a mix of joy and sadness. Leaving Garret would be more difficult than he'd ever envisioned. While he once toyed with her in suggesting she join him—setting a false pretense to gain her support—he now suspected there was also a hint of wistfulness in that offer.

Though perhaps not hopelessly in love with her, his heart was clearly tacking in that direction. And this was their first real opportunity to be truly alone. He placed his hand on the back of her neck and brought his lips to hers. They shared the warmth at some length, their bodies moving with *Pandora's* gracefully slow rhythm.

Garret was finally prepared to give herself fully to this man. Though more than ten years her senior, he had something younger men did not—a certain seasoning; a comfort with who he was in this world;

a confidence of character and intellect; and unquestioned command of others. But, most importantly, he seemed to care for her deeply.

He'd been patient with her through all this time, never pressing her for more than she was comfortable giving. She felt the strength of his arms and chest, and wanted him in a way she'd never before wanted another man; not even Pantas. Her love for the Indonesian Ambassador had been a young love—a sense of wonder in the coming together of two souls. An infatuation, really. This, however, was different. She had never allowed Jorge to take her, as she did Pantas. She'd only ever been casually physical with him. And he'd respected that. Yet here she was, ready to give her all to a man she admired, respected, and now craved physically in the moment.

'*The future be damned*,' she thought. Whether they might stay together in time had no bearing on her desire to share herself with him now. She slowly began removing his leather doublet. That only intensified the warmth she already felt inside.

XXXIX

They arrived silently in the early morning hours, under a thinly slivered moon—nine barefoot pirates in one longboat, now gently rubbing *Pandora's* hull. Harker placed his index finger to his lips, reminding his men to ascend noiselessly.

It was just past midnight when his lookouts had earlier informed him there'd been no visible activity on *Pandora* for at least an hour following Captain Tovery's departure. The ship came under close surveillance shortly after Prince informed him of the upcoming exchange with Tovery. The main lookout said the person onboard, whom Harker assumed was the witch, was joined on *Pandora* in the late afternoon by a crew of eight, but that only one stayed—the navigator. To Harker, that meant Connachan was now alone with Valcour, or whatever name Valdez was going by.

There was reportedly a child onboard as well, though that was of little concern. Harker intended to secure the ship, capture the Viceroy, and bring the witch's captaincy to an end. Finally.

It was now time to deliver payback for the lengthy list of slights Harker held. He never condoned Drake's support of Connachan by hiding the truth of her gender from the men. In his mind, that put their voyage at risk. Drake later added insult by appointing her captain. And when Harker shared his concern about the witch's presence with other members of the crew, Drake's henchman, Musa, assaulted him physically. For all that, he would now take the witch's life, her ship, its cargo, its cannons, the Viceroy, and perhaps later, her crew. He would even take her most personally intimate treasures as well; that was the pirate way when it came to women.

Ascending the ship's side, his mind continued burning at the thought of Garret's being made captain. Sailors needed to *earn* that right, not obtain it by seducing a superior. In the pirate world, no one handed the role of captain to a pirate except the men he was to lead. And they only did so if that man had already proven himself to be daring and successful in both strategy and combat. That was a lesson he would soon carve on the witch's chest.

He glanced down at the men following him up the side. This night's mission had so much to offer, which was why he'd carefully selected each of them. They represented the most brutal and heartless members of his crew, though admittedly not the brightest. All of them now scaled *Pandora*'s hull like a scurrying swarm of black roaches.

———

Scorpio awoke in the dark. She wasn't sure why; the ship's creaking seemed normal. As she turned over in her hammock in Garret's cabin, a movement at the window caught her attention. A leg with a bare foot moved up along the window's right edge. The hair on her arms rose, pulling up tiny bumps on her skin. She glanced toward Garret's hammock. It was empty. Where was she? Then she remembered—Viceroy Valdez was with them. Perhaps they'd gone to the main deck, so as not to disturb her. She waited until the foot swayed beyond view, then scrambled quietly out of her hammock. Heading to the cabin door, she noticed Garret's cutlass and pistol on the table. She grabbed both and ran barefoot to the deck.

There was no sign of Garret or the Viceroy. She ran stealthily to Jorge's cabin, hoping they might be there. The door creaked as she opened it; too loudly, she thought. Despite the darkness, she could see the outline of what looked like two people in the hammock. That seemed odd. She ran to them, hastily whispering in Garret's ear, "Someone is boarding."

Garret awoke instantly, startled and naked. She nudged Jorge, "We are being boarded." She hopped out of the hammock, followed quickly by the naked Viceroy.

Scorpio was wide-eyed, watching both dress hurriedly. She'd never seen them like this before. Something was going on here, though she wasn't sure exactly what. But both quickly had their pants on.

Garret stretched her arms into a blouse. She accepted the two weapons Scorpio presented. The pistol was already loaded. Jorge, bare-chested, loaded his own pistol.

"Scorpi," Garret whispered, bending down to look her straight in the eye, "you must take care. Hide here and remain quiet until I return. We shall take care of the intruder." Though Garret suspected there might be more than one intruder, she didn't wish to alarm the girl.

Jorge waved at Garret, frantic to get to the main deck before any invader could gain an advantageous position. Barefoot, they crouched forward—panthers on a floating wood forest. Jorge peered around the corner. He spotted two figures approaching along the starboard side, another on the larboard. All three appeared threatening. This wouldn't be easy, he thought, reaching into his pocket for a gold coin. He had just one chance to create a possible distraction. He hand-signaled Garret so that she might understand his plan. She was to take the man to their left.

Jorge threw the coin high in the air toward the stern, ensuring it would hit the deck behind the men. One of the pirates noticed a glint of moving light, which his eyes automatically followed. All three of them turned their heads at the noise of the coin bouncing off the hard deck. Jorge leaped forward, making room for Garret to head left. He fired his pistol at the head of a pirate who was already turning back toward him. A dark hole appeared instantly in the man's left temple. His knees buckled. His partner's eyes followed the motion. Valdez slashed his cutlass across the second brigand's throat, his eyes opening wide with shock while his blood spurted profusely.

Having ended two invaders, Jorge felt the same thirsty demon inside who always came to him in battle. His adrenaline raced, his eyes searching for another victim. He couldn't wait to engage. Nor would he have to.

Garret felt bloody spittle hit the side of her face as she fired her pistol at the pirate approaching fast from her left. The ball passed through the man's shirt, entering his left breast. The blast made him stumble backward. He raised his cutlass with his right hand, bringing it down toward Garret's shoulder. His strength failed him on the slash. Garret deflected the blow with her sword, her right elbow high in the air. It enabled her to follow with a thrust directly into the pirate's throat. Thick, dark blood bubbled out. The man's eyes closed. He fell hard onto the deck.

The sound of other pirates approaching instantly refocused Garret's attention. She had no idea how many she and Jorge were up against, but she would do everything humanly possible to keep them from getting to Scorpi. To draw them away, she sprinted toward the foredeck, where she would have the advantage of height over anyone coming at her.

———

Musa lay flat on the shore, sleeping off his night of drinking. He woke to the sound of the first shot skimming sharply across the water from the direction of *Pandora*. It startled him. He rose, pistol in hand. Caber, lying next to him, also sprung to attention. They saw a flash and then heard the sound of a second shot. They rushed to haul a small rowboat down to the water. Jumping in, they headed toward *Pandora*, both straining hard at their oars, in pace with each other. Both worried for their captain, uncertain they would arrive in time to help.

———

Jorge saw his next adversary closing quickly with his pistol raised. He dove and rolled, pulling his dagger deftly from his waistband as the invader's shot glanced off the deck next to him. Rising to one knee, he hurled his dagger into the pirate's groin. It wasn't his intended target, but it would do. The man screamed in agony, grabbing at the dagger while Valdez slashed his wrists with a cutlass. The intruder fell sideways onto the deck, his head crashing hard against an oak barrel on the way down, knocking him unconscious.

Jorge experienced the sudden feel of cold steel entering his back near his right trapezius. He saw the tip of the blade exit through his pectoral muscle. Despite the excruciating pain, he turned jarringly to his left, jerking the weapon out of the hand of the shocked pirate behind him. The unbearable pain caused him to lose hold of his own cutlass. He tried scrambling to his feet, blood now pouring from his chest. The cutlass remained embedded in his upper torso.

Two men faced him, both grinning at the sight of the blade piercing out from his chest. With a swiftness neither seemed to expect, Jorge drew a second pistol from the waist of his trousers, firing it at one. The hot ball buried itself deep in the man's heart. He would bleed out quickly. The second man reached for his dagger. Jorge was now defenseless but for his wits, and they were beginning to dull. With the light in his eyes turning dark, he saw his assailant was no longer alone. One more strolled into view—the man he recognized as De Graaf. The dark street on which he once hoped to encounter this villain was instead a dark ship, growing darker by the moment.

———

Garret stood wide-footed at *Pandora's* bow, ready for battle. Two pirates came at her quickly. She finished reloading her pistol and chose to hold her cutlass with her right hand. Fortunately, she'd learned to shoot both right- and left-handed. Though she preferred using her right, she was comfortable with either.

As she raised her pistol, the two men scrambled toward the stairs on either side of the foredeck. The man to Garret's right wore a dark eye patch. She recognized him immediately. Choosing to focus on Harker, she kept the dark image on her left at the corner of her eye. She aimed her pistol at that image, hoping that by keeping her head directed toward Harker, the other pirate might not fear the pistol. She pulled the trigger lightly, without moving her head or hand. The pirate fell backward down the stairs in agony, bleeding from the stomach. Garret dropped the pistol to focus fully on her next assailant.

"Ahoy, Connachan," Harker grinned, with visible menace.

"Here we be, mano é witch. Cutlass on cutlass. Let us see who deserves to be a captain. And who does not."

Garret contemplated Harker's significant size advantage. The confrontation would be challenging. His pistol remained in his bandolier. It seemed he preferred carving her up—having her feel the pain of a slow death. Knowing he'd survived numerous battles as part of Drake's crew, she didn't underestimate his fighting ability. She would need to outsmart him. That was *her* advantage. Her only advantage.

———

Having heard several pistol shots, Scorpio could no longer bear to remain hidden in the corner beneath the Viceroy's coat that she'd thrown over herself. She rose, suddenly recalling there was a second pistol in Garret's cabin. Slowly opening the door of the Viceroy's quarters, she peered out. Men were engaged on the larboard side. The path along starboard looked clear. She ran hurriedly to Garret's quarters, finding the extra pistol and her own short cutlass—an extended dagger, really— that Garret had recently given her. Before leaving the cabin, she peeked out the door. No one was coming. She approached the deck, trying her best to minimize the noise.

Scuffling and screaming now surrounded her. She moved her head and eyes carefully around the corner. Horror unfolded—Viceroy Valdez was on his knees, the point of a sword emanating from his chest. Two large, frightening men stood across from him, the smaller one with a dagger in hand, the other a cutlass. She judged the man with the cutlass to be the bigger threat. Taking careful aim, she pointed Garret's pistol at him and pulled the trigger. It clicked. The chamber was empty.

De Graaf and the other pirate heard the sterile click of the pistol's hammer. Both looked that way.

Jorge, now barely breathing, reached out, grabbing and yanking the ankle of the smaller man. He fell sideways, banging his head harshly on the deck, his dagger skidding away, beyond reach.

De Graaf turned quickly, slashing his cutlass mightily at Jorge's outstretched arm. His blade descended so forcefully that it sliced through the bone, splitting the forearm in two. Blood spewed from both severed ends.

De Graaf's eye caught the flash of the Viceroy's ring as it reflected the moonlight. He knelt and removed it from the separated hand, placing it on his third finger. It fit snugly. The sight of Valdez laying near-motionless, in obvious agony, made him smile.

His accomplice returned to his feet, grasping his throbbing head. De Graaf turned to see where Harker was.

Scorpio pressed her back against the wall, hoping to remain unseen. There was no sound coming from Jorge. And no movement. For the first time in her life, she uttered a prayer…to a God she didn't even know.

———

Garret contemplated Harker's patch. It had to affect his depth perception. And it meant he had a blind spot on his left side. She searched for a way to take advantage of that.

He came at her slowly, a foreboding sneer on his face. His cutlass was in his right hand, pointed toward her. She gave ground, hoping he might lunge forward. He didn't. Instead, he continued slowly, appearing to savor the moment.

Garret feigned to her right, expecting to draw his gaze and his sword to his strong side. It would enable her to attack the blind side.

Harker simply smiled. "You underestimate me, witch. Just like every man before you who tried the same trick."

Garret didn't respond. Her focus was on the fight, not the babble. She knew the foredeck was going to confine her maneuverability. And she no longer had the height advantage it initially offered. She headed down the stairwell, jumping over the fallen pirate and taking position on the deck. As she did, she saw De Graaf standing over Jorge, blood dripping from his sword. She felt a sudden emptiness. She was now alone. And outnumbered. With no time to reload her pistol. A quick glance for an invader's fallen pistol came up empty. Only Harker's was within range. She prayed to God he didn't decide to reach for it. But there was some comfort in the fact that his own arrogance might keep him from doing so. '*Cutlass on cutlass*,' he'd said.

Garret watched as Harker stood on the foredeck, laughing as though her rush down the stairwell represented a fearful retreat. He probably sensed she lacked the courage to face him. '*He will learn otherwise*,' she thought.

Musa and Caber were closing fast on *Pandora*. Turning his head toward the ship, Caber spotted two figures at the bow, the smaller of which looked like Garret. "Stop," he said softly enough for only Musa to hear. The boat slowed. He drew his pistol, using both hands to aim it. The smaller figure was no longer visible. He could hear the other one laughing. Breathing slowly, he took final aim and squeezed the trigger lightly. The shot whizzed high in the air toward the bow.

Harker turned to his left at the sound of a distant shot, just as the ball streamed past his head. Garret spotted her opening. She flung her cutlass at him, her arm finishing fully extended in his direction as she released the grip. The blade flew into his right bicep, pinning his arm to his chest. He screamed in pain, losing the grip on his own weapon. Garret scaled the stairs, again leaping over the bloodied pirate who'd fallen there. Reaching the foredeck, she stretched out for Harker's dropped cutlass. He managed to kick it away while staggering backward.

Musa's pistol shot followed Caber's, missing Harker and embedding itself in the taffrail. He and Caber returned to rowing with intensity.

With Garret scrambling for his cutlass, Harker put the pain in his right side out of mind, to focus on her. He struggled to clutch his pistol with his left hand. Its butt faced right, making it difficult to reach without excruciating pain from the cutlass impaled in his right arm.

Garret finally grabbed his cutlass and leaped toward him as Harker drew his pistol. She slashed sideways, cutting his left hand at the back of his wrist. He screamed and fell back awkwardly, tripping over his feet. Garret quickly straddled him, thrusting his own cutlass to the edge of his throat. "You have lost, pig." She grinned. "To a woman, no less." They were the last words Harker would ever hear.

———

Scorpio peered around the corner at the two men near Jorge. She watched in tears as De Graaf, still kneeling, took another trophy from the Viceroy, carving off the right ear with his dagger. Jorge growled weakly, his life fast leaking away. Scorpio couldn't contain her scream. She buried her face in her hands.

De Graaf heard the girl's scream. He glanced her way, quickly judging she was no threat. Bloody ear in hand, he rose and looked back toward the bow, near where he'd heard pistol shots. He saw Connachan standing over one of his mates, though he couldn't tell which one. Looking around, he saw no other movement. Had all the others been lost? That seemed impossible. And what about Harker? Where was he?

Garret wasted no time. She scooped up Harker's pistol and checked to see whether it was loaded. It was. Before heading down to the main deck, she scanned the ship. There were two intruders near the entry to her cabin. She took aim at the one standing and holding his head—the clearer target of the two. She squeezed the trigger. The shot passed directly through the back of the man's neck. He collapsed onto the deck.

De Graaf ducked at the sound of Garret's shot. Retaking his full stance, his eyes glimpsed a fast-approaching rowboat. He was about to be outnumbered. He tucked the Viceroy's ear into a pocket in his doublet and peered for a moment at the lowered head of the young girl nearby. There was no point taking her, he thought. He strode confidently to the rail above his longboat before slipping down the side of the ship. Recognizing he'd be unable to row the longboat away from the two men approaching in their smaller rowboat, he slithered into the still water like a thick, black eel.

———

Garret scampered down the stairs to the main deck, watching as De Graaf went over the rail. She ran toward Jorge, avoiding the scattered bodies of dead pirates. Thick, dark blood covered the deck around Jorge's upper torso. His breathing was labored. His head lay sideways, exposing a missing ear. "My God," cried Garret, falling to her knees in the sticky, still-warm blood. She placed her hand on his cheek. "Stay with me, Jorge." Tears streamed down her face as she saw him wince slowly, in debilitating pain. Scorpio came quickly to her side, also in tears.

Garret sensed Jorge was desperately trying to say something. She leaned in, placing her ear next to his lips.

"So…much…pain," he mumbled.

"What can I do?" Garret sobbed.

"I am…done," he winced. "End me. I…beg you."

"No Jorge, no," Garret cried softly, wiping his face. "I love you. Stay with me." Scorpio wailed at the thought.

"Please," Jorge whispered, his face now ghostly white, "…end it."

Garret's body shivered as the inevitable suddenly became real—Jorge would perish. There was no changing that. But he clearly wished to die on his own terms—having her end his agony. She kissed him, wiped her tears, and looked around. Blurred eyes obstructed her vision as tears raced down her cheeks. She spotted a pistol near Scorpio and pointed to it. "Hand me that," she said.

"No," the girl protested. "Please. No."

"There is no choice, dearest." Garret's voice broke. "We must end his pain." She sniffed heavily.

Scorpio, sobbing and mad, reluctantly pushed the pistol toward her. Garret picked it up and checked to see whether it was loaded. It wasn't. She struggled to load the ball, her hands shaking uncontrollably. Scorpio buried her head against her knees.

Garret leaned in again, whispering in Jorge's ear, "I love you." She stroked his hair. "I shall always love you."

"And…me," he muttered. It seemed to be all he could manage.

Garret kissed his face. "God be with you." She rose and wiped away tears. "Cover your ears, Scorpi."

"No!" screamed the girl. "No. Please, no."

"It is his wish, Scorpi. To be with God."

Scorpio placed her hands over her ears, weeping heavily, head buried. Garret aimed the pistol at Jorge's head. Through her still-blurred eyes, she watched the glimmer of light in his disappear with the pistol's crack.

The bang brought Jorge instant peace, the image of Garret seared in his darkness.

Musa and Caber, now alongside *Pandora*, were securing their rowboat when the shot rang out. It hurried them up the side.

XXXX

William Tovery watched as Prince turned to place Viceroy Valdez' sealed letter to King Philip, and the bag containing gold escudos, on his desk. "I shall provide the remaining payment when you deliver any response from the King." He paused to make certain Prince was paying attention. "But only if word of our transaction has not found its way to others." A distant pop emanated from the direction of the harbor, catching his attention.

Prince smiled broadly. "I have already discussed delivery of the message with a trusted merchant. He has delayed departure, awaiting only our payment." As he spoke, there was a second pop.

"I must take my leave," said William. The two shook hands.

"Fare thee well, then," offered Prince as William turned and left.

More shots followed as William raced along the winding pathway, trailed by two of his men. He worried what might be afoot. Yet another pop rang out as they descended the maddeningly steep hill.

"That makes seven, I believe, Cap'n; if I heard them all," puffed one of the men.

———

Garret couldn't bear to look at Jorge's lifeless body. Still shaken, she reached out to touch a trembling, tearful Scorpio on the shoulder. "I shall get us blankets," she said. She headed to Jorge's quarters, where she'd earlier taken her own blanket. By the time she returned, Musa and Caber were already standing at the fallen Viceroy's side. They looked shocked. Scorpio, now whimpering, had buried her face in Caber's body. His arms were wrapped around her. Garret turned to Musa. "Please, cover him."

Musa nodded and turned away to retrieve a suitable piece of canvas sail.

Scorpio reached out, sobbing. Garret knelt. The girl was shaking as though cold, despite the night's warmth. Garret draped a blanket around her and sat, pulling her close.

"Why?" moaned Scorpio. "Why did they want to kill us?"

Garret wiped away the last remnants of her own tears. "It is the nature of these men," she sniffed. "They are the most vile serpents of the sea. They seek to have all things their way. Anyone who might choose a different path is their enemy."

"But why us?"

Garret felt a drying stickiness on her face. '*Blood*', she thought. She tried wiping it away but was only partially successful. "Pirates answer to no one, dearest. They simply take what they please. Sometimes they seek revenge for actions taken against them." She immediately thought of the revenge she herself took on the villagers of Santiago del Príncipe, wondering whether that was somehow any different.

"But why?" repeated Scorpio.

Garret wiped the girl's tears. "Perhaps we threatened the order of things in their world."

"I do not understand," the girl cried in frustration.

"You will in time, Scorpi. And you must steel yourself for things of this nature—because others will surely attempt to impose their will on you. But you must never let them. You must always be true to the things you believe in. Be true to who you are, not as others would define you.”

Scorpio sniffed deeply. She gave Garret a heart-filled hug. “I want to go back to London.”

“Were it only that easy, dearest.” She stroked the girl’s hair. “Many challenges lay ahead. You and I shall be defined by how we deal with them. We must take them on willingly, and learn from them; be stronger *because* of them. That shall be our path to a good life.”

The two sat in silence, the warmth beginning to return to their bodies. “I shall miss the Viceroy,” Scorpio sniffed. “He was my friend.”

“We shall both miss him.” Garret stroked the girl’s hair. She thought for a moment. “Admiral Drake once told me, when he was facing death from his illness, ‘*All you take with you is the memory of those you loved. And all you leave behind is their memory of you.*’ He tried his best to leave good memories. And he did.” She pulled up Scorpio’s chin and looked her in the eyes, “Has Jorge left *you* any good memories?”

“He has, yes. He was kind to you.”

“So he was.” Garret began tearing up again.

“He was the first Spaniard I ever met,” Scorpio remarked. “Are they all like him?”

“In some ways, I suppose,” replied Garret, thinking more of his humanity than his talents. “But it matters not where a man is from. Jorge had a large heart. Others looked up to him. *That* is what defined him; not his country of origin.”

Caber felt he'd given Garret enough time with the girl. He knelt beside her. "I am sorry, Cap'n. I know this is a great loss for you."

"A loss for all of us, I am afraid," replied the Viceroy's assassin.

END

Enjoyed Pyrate Assassin? Leave a review on my Amazon book page. You can also follow me on Amazon or at: PyratePubs.com

Be sure to catch a preview of the third novel in my Pyrate Series— 'Pyrate Crossover' at the end of this book.

Like Pyrate Rising (2021) and Pyrate Assassin (2021), Pyrate Crossover was named a Writing Award Finalist by Page Turner Awards, in 2022.

NOTES

A few of the characters in Pyrate Assassin are people who actually lived in the period of interest:

- 'Drake' aka 'Admiral Drake' aka 'the Admiral', are references to the legendary Sir Francis Drake. None of the words/quotes attributed to him herein were things he actually ever said, as far as I know. I simply made them up.

- Thomas Drake was a real brother of the Admiral, though all of the events he's involved in here are fictitious.

- Queen Elizabeth, of course is Queen Elizabeth I. Again, all of the events she's involved in here are fictitious, as are the words attributed to her.

- King Philip, of course, is King Philip II of Spain. Here again, only fictitious events and words.

- Sir William Cecil was the real Lord High Treasurer of England at the time

Every other character in the book is purely fictitious.

The Inagua Islands and Isla Tortuga are real islands in the Caribbean.

Santiago del Príncipe was a real village at the time.

Santo Pedro is purely fictitious.

CHARACTERS

<u>Principal Characters</u>

Garret Connachan: Captain of the flagship Pandora

William Tovery: Captain of Athena and later Orion

Jorge Valdez de Barragan: Maestre de Campo and Spanish Viceroy for Military Affairs in the Southern Seas, based in the Inaguas

Harker: Captain of the ships Red Knight and later Death's Head

De Graaf, Yaugaan: Captain of the ship Cutthroat and partner of Harker

Scrapper/Scorpio/Scorpi: London street urchin rescued by Garret

<u>Secondary Characters</u>

King Philip II: King of Spain

Queen Elizabeth I: Queen of England

Blair, Henry: Garret's Master's Mate

Caber: Member of Garret's crew

Catherine/Cath: Server at the Gente de Mar and niece of its owner, Prince

Drake/'El Draque': Admiral; Garret's former captain/mentor

<u>**Secondary Characters (continued)**</u>

Grant: Ship's Doctor, *Pandora*

Halim: Indonesian Ambassador to England

Le Pen, Alain: French pirate captain

McBride, James: English Naval Captain, transporting Halim on the *Royal Adventure*

Musa: Member of Garret's crew

Ortega: Felipe de Heredia y Ortega aka 'The Phantom'; wealthy Cartageñian

Pantas: Deceased Indonesian Ambassador; Garret's first love

Rivera: Don Francisco Rivera de Mendoza, Viceroy Valdez' First Lieutenant

Prince: Owner of the Gente de Mar tavern

Stevens: Harker's Master's mate

Thomas: Drake's brother; Garret's and William's former fellow midshipman

Tyndale, George: Owner of Orion's Tavern

Webber, David: Garret's Master-at-Arms

Wenman, James: Captain of the warship *Mercilus*, sent to Isla Tortuga to deliver Thomas' message to Garret

Incidental Characters

Bremmer: A Lieutenant who delivered a note from Queen Elizabeth to Thomas Drake

Clutterbuck, James: Constable of the guard at the Tower of London

Kilburn: Harker's Master-at-Arms

Langton: Garret's interpreter

Louis Rodriguez: Spanish Merchant Captain and nephew of King Philip II

Manuel: A Christian seaman captured by De Graaf on his first assault as a pirate captain

Nightengale: The Lieutenant arresting Garret and Valdez upon their return to England

Pereira: Portuguese Captain of a ship assaulted by Harker

Sir William Cecil: England's Lord High Treasurer

Spriggs: A member of De Graaf's crew who dispenses with a mate who accuses him of stealing a dagger

PRONUNCIATIONS

For what it's worth, here are my interpretations of the pronunciations of various names and places:

Caber:	Kay´-bur
Connachan:	Kawn´-a-han
De Graaf:	De Grawf˝
Drake:	Drayk
Elizabeth:	E-liz´-a-beth
Halim:	Ha-leem´
Jorge:	Hor´-hay
Musa:	Moo´-sa
Pantas:	Pawn´-tus
Philip:	Fill´-ip
Tovery:	To´-ver-ee
Cardiff:	Kar´-diff
Cartageña:	Kar-tuh-hay´-nya
Inagua:	In-aw´-gwa
Santo Pedro:	San´-to Pay´-dro
Santiago del Principe:	San-ti-a´-go dell Prin´-cip
Tortuga:	Tor-too´-guh
Gente de Mar:	Zhawnt-de Mawr

SHIPS

Athena
Captain: William Tovery
One of Garret's private fleet of three ships, later commandeered by Captain McBride

Cutthroat
Captain: Yaugaan De Graaf
Originally a Spanish warship, it was captured by Harker & De Graaf in their assault of Nombre de Dios

Death's Head
Captain: Harker
His second ship, originally the Spanish Merchant—*Espíritu de los Santos*

Espíritu de los Santos
Captain: Luis Rodriguez
A Spanish merchant vessel captured by Harker and later renamed *Death's Head*

Oportunidad
A Spanish merchant vessel, captured by Harker, De Graaf & Le Pen

Orion
Captain: William Tovery
One of Garret's private fleet of three ships. William took it on after *Athena* was commandeered by Captain McBride

Pandora
Captain: Garret Connachan
The flagship of Garret's private fleet of three ships

Red Knight
Captain: Harker
Harker's first ship. As a member of its crew, he acquired it after killing its captain. Harker later gave it up in favor of *Death's Head*

Royal Adventure
Captain McBride's ship, on which he was transporting Ambassador
Halim to England from Ternate, Indonesia when it was captured

LOCATIONS

Cardiff:	England
Cartageña:	Columbia
Hispaniola:	West Indies island split politically into Haiti & the Dominican Republic
Inaguas:	South Sea islands (One big, one Small)
Isla Tortuga:	Tortuga Island, north of Haiti
London:	England
Nombre de Dios:	Panamanian settlement titled by Drake as 'The Treasurehouse of the World'
Porto Bello:	Panamanian settlement emerging as Spain's favored location for storing their treasure.
Santo Pedro:	Fictitious village not far from Cartagena
Santiago del Principe:	Home of those who massacred Garret's men
Spanish Main:	The eastern coast of Central & South America

PLACES

Orion's Tavern:	In London
The Seafarer's Inn:	In Cardiff
Gente de Mar:	A tavern on Isla Tortuga

ACKNOWLEDGMENTS

I am extremely grateful for the contributions of those listed below…

Don Drucker, my decades-long consigliere, provided his typical unvarnished feedback. I love him for that. RIP.

Natalia de Oliveira Dal' Evedove, of One Demi-Goddess Books, provided perspectives I would never have seen. I am so grateful for her guidance.

Inspiration for the series comes from my pirate-loving friends on Facebook. Adam Morrow (Shipwrecked with Captain Marrow); Mark Forget (Festival Des Pirates); Dave Carroll, co-author of <u>Thatcher: The Unauthorized Biography of Blackbeard the Pirate</u>. I also have to recognize several Facebook Groups, including Pirates; Pirate Nation; Hoist the Colors, Pirate Enthusiasts; The Republic of Pirates; World Pirate Party; World Wide Pirate Community; Cutthroats, Pirates, Thieves and Fun Lovers; The group administrators and members are valued for sharing their insight, research, context and humor.

 A special shout-out to Edgar Barragan, aka Commodore Crimson, and his Crimson Pyrates & Privateers (also on Facebook). This nonprofit organization's quest is to rebalance the lines of plunder by drawing on those who have so much, to assist those who've suffered without.

A portion of the proceeds from this Series supports Edgar's foundation.

My thanks to Page Turner Awards, whose support and guidance led to this novel's selection as a Finalist for their 2021 Writing Award.

Thanks in memoriam to Roger C. Ambrose, who did the original design for the first four novels in my Pyrate Series. And thanks to James R. Whirlow, who made publishing the novel possible by picking up the torch and lighting the design cannon following Roger's passing.

Finally, a special thanks to JerichoWriters.com. Their website, and the aspiring writers who participate in their forums, have helped immensely, schooling me on writing and pointing me to needed resources.

I feel blessed to have all of you in my life.

Pyrate Crossover

Buckland Abbey

Devon, England

1600

He rubbed his hand softly on the seal. Garret's seal. This was as close as he'd been to her in more than a year. Though his trepidation over the letter's contents ran deep, it was at least confirmation that his beloved friend was still alive—at the time of its writing.

He placed the letter on his desk, rose from his seat, and walked softly across the thick Persian rug toward the cabinet. Opening its glass doors, he pondered his choices. '*Brandy*', he thought. He poured a glass. Returning to his desk, he sat, sipped the brandy, and set the glass on the desk. He picked up Garret's letter, unsealed it, and began reading.

Isla Tortuga

29 October 1599

Dearest Thomas,

I am afraid I may no longer be the woman you hopefully remember so fondly. Nor may William be the same man. All that has transpired since we last met in Cardiff could well have stained our souls. It now seems unclear whether we shall ever again be permitted to enter England freely.

I shall attempt to explain. I hope that by the time you have finished reading this letter, you will understand how it is that life can take you to places you never imagined, and shape you in ways you might once have thought impossible…

I

Being infamous was both good and bad for Harker, thought Yauggan De Graaf. The good part was that Harker's legendary reputation as the most feared of all pirates was now secure. The bad part—he was dead.

As he neared the normally quiet, dingy tavern in Santo Pedro, De Graaf recalled having been here twice with Harker. So he was now surprised at the mass of people pressed beyond the entryway and onto the dusty street. It caused him to wonder what could possibly have drawn so many here to this tiny place in this decrepit little village.

Some who saw the large man coming made way. He pushed through the rest, ignoring their grunts of annoyance. Entering the tavern, the image of his deceased partner flashed through his mind. Though he missed Harker, he recognized this was a new era. It presented an opportunity to claim his partner's throne.

Watts and Dodd shared a small wooden table near the door of the heavily congested tavern. They came to Santo Pedro only when they had no choice, since it always offered the lowest price for their fish. Still, it generally purchased whatever they had left to sell.

"Bloody crowd," complained Watts. "Not a damn server in sight." His warm, watered-down beer was near gone.

Dodd nodded in agreement, "The chatter suggests the locals were drawn here by news of that bloody pirate's death—the one named Harker." He spat on the floor as though Harker himself lay there.

"That news be a week old," smirked Watts. "These blockheads are just now finding out?"

"So it seems. One claims he once saw Harker here in this very tavern."

"Your table," growled De Graaf, interrupting the two.

Watts looked up and down at the dark-skinned man, judging him to be over six feet tall. Broad-shouldered and heavily muscled, he was dressed entirely in black from his bandana to his new calf-covering boots. '*This beast seems born of the damn shadows of the night,*' he thought. The long, greasy hair and full, black beard only served to darken the beast's hardened face. The scars on it evidenced a history of savage combat. His piercing eyes threatened violence.

Watts rose. Dodd followed. They left both table and tankards. Watts watched as the beast sat, downed the contents of a tankard, and began scanning the room.

The crowd flowed as bodies moved and pressed. Some of that was intentional, as women known to oblige patrons with certain physical favors made openly delightful contact. One inebriated sailor stumbled backward, landing hard against the beast's shoulder. The man's beer showered the table. The beast rose instantly, grabbing the offender by the hair and whipping his dagger to the base of the drunk's neck. "Lose your head again," he snarled, "and you shall find it searching for the rest of your worthless body." He shoved the man away, planting a heavy boot firmly on his buttocks. The drunk lurched forward, slamming into the two rugged-looking sailors he was with, both of whom were muscled and leather-skinned. Watts could see they didn't take kindly to the beast's treatment of their friend, nor to the spillage of their beer that his collision caused. He watched them approach the beast's table, hands grasping the hilts of their cutlasses. The beast had already retaken his seat.

"Vous paierez pour vos actions, cochon!" said the larger of the two sailors.

Watts was intensely curious to see how the beast would react. Surprisingly, the dark man didn't flinch or even look at the two Frenchmen, let alone respond. Instead, he simply sipped his beer with his right hand. Slowly. Deliberately. Watts noticed him gripping the handle of his dagger with his left hand, beyond view of the sailors.

"Sur tes pieds, cochon noir!" yelled the larger Frenchman. His words generated a bustling shuffle of feet as several patrons pushed back. Voices hushed in a sweeping wave. Watts watched the beast rise, keeping his dagger hidden. *'These two Frenchies are about to pay for calling him a black pig,'* he thought.

The larger Frenchman began drawing his cutlass. The beast thrust his left arm forward with concentrated violence, hurling his dagger at the man's throat. The penetrating blade entered up the full length of its spine, causing the man's blood to bubble onto the front bolster. His accomplice, stunned and frozen, was hammered across the bridge of his nose by the beast's elbow. The crunching sound caused Watts to cringe as the man's head spun to his left, spewing blood. He crumpled to the floor. The beast's boot hammered forcibly onto his temple, altering the shape of his skull. His body went limp. Silence suddenly prevailed.

Watts glanced at the other Frenchman, who'd been impaled by the dagger. He was on his knees, eyes wide, staring into nothingness. The beast withdrew his dagger from the man's throat. Blood coursed through the opening. A back-handed fist to the temple toppled the dying man to the floor. The beast bent to wipe his blade on the Frenchman's shirt—one side, then the other. Rising up, his beady eyes studied the stunned crowd. Watts averted his eyes, feeling himself shake involuntarily. One man who had vomited was pushed away by another, slipping on his own bile.

The beast retook his seat as though nothing of significance had transpired. He dragged the blade of his dagger back and forth along his thigh before raising it and looking it over. It gleamed even in the dim light. He ran his finger carefully along the edge. Watts and others watched in silence until the dagger was sheathed.

Two men moved forward, their hands raised to indicate they were no threat. The beast nodded and watched as they grabbed the fallen Frenchmen by their armpits. Blood smeared the hard, earthen floor as the two were dragged out the door. Slowly, the tavern rediscovered its voice, though the energy had been sucked out of it.

"Damn," whispered Dodd.

"Thank God we gave up the table," replied Watts.

"And our beer!"

Discussions within the crowd shifted, from the demise of the infamous Harker to the event they'd just witnessed. No one seemed to connect the beast with Harker. They were unaware he'd actually been with the dreaded pirate when he was skewered, or that he'd sworn to take revenge on Harker's killer—Captain Garret Connachan.

II

Weeks earlier…

The deep-pink blush spreading slowly across the horizon drove a free-ranging rooster to shatter the sleepy village's calm. A dog barked in response, suddenly alert to the smell and distant voices of a handful of men rowing their longboat toward a ship anchored in the harbor of pirate-infested Isla Tortuga.

"Harder," ordered the young and virile captain, William Tovery. He worried for the safety of his commander, Garret Connachan. She'd sent him to a pre-dawn exchange with a man named Prince, at a secluded location. But while he was there, the distant crack of pistol shots emanating from the harbor drove him to cut the meeting short. He was rushing back to Garret's flagship, *Pandora*, where she was staying. He knew only two others were on the ship with her. One was a former street urchin she'd rescued, named Scorpio. While the rest of the crew resided onshore during construction of their temporary quarters, Garret preferred keeping the girl onboard *Pandora*, beyond reach of the town's poisonous culture.

The other person onboard *Pandora* was Spanish Viceroy Jorge Valdez de Barragan, a lauded military commander and fierce soldier. Originally their prisoner, he'd long since earned Garret and William's friendship. '*Surely he and Garret together would be able to defend themselves*,' thought William. He'd witnessed many times just how highly skilled Garret herself was in military arts.

"Hail, *Pandora*," William yelled as his longboat drew alongside. Dogs barked in response. Pigs snorted. The village's natural alarm clock was now fully engaged. "Is anyone onboard?"

High above, on *Pandora's* deck, an exhausted Captain Connachan was startled awake by William's call. Scorpio, asleep at her side, stirred. Garret moved the girl's head, placing it gently on the blanket she stuffed beneath it. Scorpio shifted her body.

Garret rose slowly, grabbing her arm; it was partially covered in dried blood. She walked past Musa and Caber. They, too, were beginning to rise.

"Hail, *Pandora*. Captain Tovery here. Declare yourselves." William shouted it with authority, now fearing the ship might well be occupied by pirates. He and his men aimed their pistols at the rail in case shots from above were to answer his call.

"I am here, Captain Tovery," Garret called out. "And safe."

The crew secured their longboat and followed Tovery up *Pandora's* side. Their boots clopped along the wooden deck as they avoided the still-slick splatter of drying blood. William saw Garret and the others next to a canvas bag sewn loosely over what could only be a body. Coming near, he decided against reaching out to hold Garret in his arms. She was his commander; it would have been out of place. He looked at her in sorrow. "Are you alright, sir?" he asked, acknowledging Garret as his superior.

"Everything appears to be in working order," she smiled, grimly. "Scorpio is unharmed."

William nodded toward the canvas-bound body, fearing the worst. Garret, on the verge of tears, sniffed and looked away, "The Viceroy," she said.

William looked down in sadness at the heavily bloodied canvas covering the lump representing his departed friend. He silently prayed for God's blessing of the man's soul.

Scorpio was now up. Garret patted the girl's head. William turned to them, "What bloody Hell took place here?"

"Harker and several others assaulted us after you left."

"I am sorry I was not here." William's mind quickly sought to put the pieces together. "Why just kill the Viceroy and leave?"

Caber stepped forward, "Only one bastard left on his own."

William looked around at all the blood. "So it would seem."

"By da time Musa and I come aboard, the Cap'n and the Viceroy had kilt all but one."

"De Graaf," specified Garret.

Caber continued, "Threw seven dead bastards overboard, we did. They be washin' ashore now. It be a proper message to da rest o' Harker's crew."

"What about Harker? Was he involved?"

"I ended his miserable life," interjected Garret.

"Truth be told, Cap'n, he be still hangin' on when we reached him," explained Caber. "We laid chains on 'im and threw 'im overboard. Thought it best he taste the sea's wrath."

Garret had nothing to add. William looked to Caber, trying to complete the puzzle, "You sewed up the Viceroy's body?"

"We did." Caber paused. "Two pieces of it." He shook his head, slowly.

William was aghast. "Damn," he yelled.

"His ear be missin'. 'Twas his arm was in pieces."

"De Graaf," explained Garret. "He took Jorge's ring as well."

"So, he was the one who slew the Viceroy," William uttered in disgust.

"Not exactly," replied Garret, her eyes now watering. "Jorge was barely alive when I found him. He pleaded with me to end his misery."

"My Lord", gasped William.

"It was his dying wish," added Garret.

Thoughts and memories of his fallen friend weighed heavily on William. He could only imagine how Garret must have felt. Originally commissioned by Queen Elizabeth to eliminate the Viceroy, she and Jorge had ultimately become lovers. He marveled at her composure in dealing with it all. He placed his hand softly on her shoulder. "I am so, so, sorry."

Garret turned to Caber. "Let us prepare for the Viceroy's burial. Now. His death must remain a secret. We cannot afford to have King Philip learn his friend was slain onboard an English vessel."

The third novel in the Pyrate Series, 'Pyrate Crossover' is coming soon. Click 'Follow the Author' on my [Pyrate Rising]() or [Pyrate Assassin]() Amazon book page if you'd like to be automatically notified of its release.

You can also visit:
- *My website: pyratepubs.com*
- *My Facebook Page: Pyrate Publishing*

About the Author

Reidr Daniels grew up reading books like 'Treasure Island' and 'Kidnapped' by Robert Louis Stevenson. But it wasn't until his grandson, Drake, was born that he pulled the trigger on writing his 'Pyrate Series' novels. The first three novels in the series have each been named a Writing Award Finalist by Page Turner Awards, sponsor of an international writing competition—'Pyrate Rising' and 'Pyrate Assassin' in 2021, and 'Pyrate Crossover' in 2022.

A graduate of St. John's High School in Winnipeg Canada, Reidr earned an undergraduate honors degree at The University of Manitoba and a Masters degree at The University of California, Berkeley. He currently resides in California.